CHILDREN OF THE TITHE

TRACEY M. CARVILL

First published in Great Britain in 2022 by SMASHBEAR PUBLISHING.

Office 6945, London, W1A 6US, United Kingdom

www.smashbearpublishing.com

This paperback edition published 2022

Copyright © Tracey M. Carvill, 2022

Donated to charity by "So It Goes" October 2023

This is a work of fiction. Names, places, events and incidents are either the product of the author's imagination or used fictionally. Any resemblance to actual persons, living or dead, is purely coincidental.

ISBN: 978-1-915636-11-9

Also available as an ebook.

Dedicated to my mother, Mary - my first Constant Reader.

CHILDREN OF THE TITHE

Contents

CHAPTER 1

THE ICE FIELD

F or years, Heidi had been hearing people say that she was an "old soul", strangely mature for her twelve years. She didn't know if this was true. She'd been an only child before her parents were killed in a car crash, and there had been no other children around when her grandmother took her in. She had switched schools a few times, once when her parents died, and again when her grandmother got sick and went into hospital for a while. She didn't have any close friends, so she generally just kept to herself and quietly got on with things.

So when she opened her eyes and saw that she was lying in a vast field of ice-encrusted grass, her first instinct – unlike many of the children she could hear around her – was not to cry or scream. Instead, she looked around and, once she was certain that she did not recognise the place, she swallowed her panic and took a moment to think. How had she gotten here?

She remembered being woken from her sleep at the boarding school by a cool hand touching her face. She'd been startled to see the slender, shadowy figure leaning over her, and alarmed when she saw that all the girls in the dormitory had similar figures bending over them. But the figure had whispered to her in a gentle voice, and her fear had subsided almost as quickly as it had started.

'Come with me,' the figure had whispered. 'I will take you to an enchanted land, a vast garden in which you can play, with such wonders like you have never seen.'

'Am I dreaming?' she had whispered.

The figure leaned closer, its bright, jewel-like eyes becoming visible in its shadowy face. 'Oh yes. And it is such a glorious dream.' It smiled, a thin, curved line of white in the dark.

It held out its shadowy hand. She'd reached out, the distance seeming strangely long in the gloom, and took it. Its hand had been cool and dry, but strong as it pulled her gently up from the bed. Her sleep-fogged mind had flickered briefly to the stories of Peter Pan, which she read when she was younger, of how his shadow had run away without him. This figure was like Peter's shadow and it was taking her, she hoped, to Neverland. That would be a lovely dream.

'Second star to the right and straight on "til morning",' she had muttered, and the figure had laughed as its slender fingers enclosed her small hand and pulled her gently forward.

'Yes,' it agreed. 'Come, little Wendy-bird.'

She laughed along with it and let the figure lead her away from her bed. She had half-expected it to lead her to the window, but after a few steps, she'd suddenly felt herself being pulled forward, as if caught in a strong wind, and then...

Then things got ... jumbled.

Heidi screwed up her nose, concentrating. She remembered being pulled through darkness, the sensation of flying, and then the air had gotten very cold. The darkness around her had blurred into meaningless colours and shapes, dim at first and then brighter, and then she'd...

Then she heard a baby crying, and opened her eyes.

The baby was still crying now, somewhere close by, and beyond it, other children were crying too, screaming, calling for their mothers. Heidi got to her feet, shivering in her frost-dampened nightdress, and looked around her. The field was vast, the sky above it black except for glittering stars, which seemed bigger and closer than she had ever seen before. They bathed the field in their cold, silver light, bleaching colours, and leaving deep shadows. Only a few feet away, she saw a tiny baby lying in the grass, its round face purple and mottled with the cold and effort of its crying. Its tiny hands and feet were waving, its white romper suit already drenched through with melted frost. Her heart lurched in her chest in dismay for the tiny thing. She hurried over and scooped it up, holding it to her chest to warm it. Its crying eased a little, and it looked up at her with bewildered, blue eyes swimming with tears.

'I know, baby,' she said gently. 'I'm scared too.'

Now that she was on her feet, she could see all of the other children in the field more clearly. Boys and girls of every age, all either lying in the grass, sitting and hugging their knees, or wandering aimlessly. A few of the older children had done as she had and picked up the babies, but Heidi could see right away that there was no way they'd be able to carry them all. She also realised that none of the other girls from her dormitory were here, or at least not in sight. The field seemed to go on forever.

A young boy of about nine staggered over, blowing on his hands to warm them. 'Where are we?' he asked her, his eyes huge and shining with unshed tears.

She shrugged. 'I don't know. I just woke up here.'

'Me too.' The boy's bottom lip quivered for a moment, but he managed to hold back his tears. 'I was in bed, and then someone woke me up, and then I was here.'

Heidi nodded. 'That's what happened to me too.' She paused, then added, 'I thought I was dreaming.'

The boy shook his head, dark curls tumbling about his forehead. 'It's too cold to be a dream.' He stuck out his hand. 'I'm Tim.'

The gesture was oddly charming. Heidi smiled and, whilst juggling the crying baby in the crook of her arm, freed up her other hand to shake his. 'I'm Heidi,' she said. 'I'm twelve.'

Tim smiled. 'I'm ten.' He pointed at the baby. 'Who's that? Your little brother or sister?'

Heidi shook her head. 'I found them in the grass,' she replied. 'I don't even know if it's a boy or a girl.'

'Aw, that sucks.' Tim huddled closer and reached out to tap the baby on the nose. 'Hey you! Hi!'

The baby looked up at him in comical surprise, and its cries tapered off. Then it gave a wobbly smile.

Heidi laughed. 'They like you,' she said.

Tim looked up, opening his mouth to reply, but his eyes drifted away and he froze, his skin draining of colour. Alarmed, Heidi turned her head to follow his gaze, and an involuntary whimper escaped her lips.

On the far side of the field, or as far as they could see, many figures had appeared. They emerged as if walking out of a mist, fading into view from nowhere. They were all humanoid, but very far from human. Heidi saw things with horns and others with wings. She saw squat, hunched creatures with sharp fingers, and tall, lanky giants that moved in enormous strides. All manner of creatures descended upon the icy field, silhouetted against the starry-bright but moonless night sky.

Heidi stared, all the warmth draining from her already-numb body. She felt Tim's cold hand snake into hers, and she clutched it tightly.

As they watched, the first lanky figure bent down and, with one spindly, white hand, plucked a toddler out of the grass and tucked it under its arm. Then, it turned and faded back out of sight, into the non-existent mist. The squat, hunchbacked creature picked up a smaller baby and shovelled it into its wide mouth, carrying it off between large, blunt teeth. From up above, a blueish-grey, winged creature circled an older child - a girl in a long nightdress. It snatched up both of her hands, flexed its wings, and carried her, screaming, up into the sky. One by one, the strange beings roamed through the field, selected a child, and carried them away. The cries of the children changed from panic and confusion to terror.

Tim let out a low moan. 'I don't want to,' he whimpered.

Heidi knew exactly what he meant. An electric shock of fear burst from her chest and was now bristling through her nerves, every instinct in her screaming at her to flee. She tugged on Tim's hand. 'Come on,' she said, and started walking briskly away. She wanted to run screaming, but she would not allow it. If she did, she would fall, and then...

The long grass was painfully cold against Heidi's bare legs and feet, and before long, her teeth were chattering. Tim, who was wearing pyjamas and was also barefoot, didn't seem to be faring much better. At least the baby seemed to be more comfortable; it was curled up quietly in Heidi's arms, looking up at her and Tim with uncomprehending eyes. They began to pass other children. Heidi caught their eyes, one by one, and said the same thing: 'Follow us. Quickly!' Tim caught on right away and began doing the same, only he added: 'Monsters are coming!' The other children - the ones who were old enough to under-stand - got up and hurried after them, some of them scooping up toddlers and newborns, some leading smaller children by the hand. One little girl, who couldn't have been more than five, tottered along behind them, doing her best to carry a chubby toddler almost as big as she was. Eventually, a bigger girl took the toddler off her and they fell into step beside the others.

'Where are we going?' Tim asked Heidi.

'Just away.'

The terrified screams of children behind them started to sound closer, and Heidi risked a look over her shoulder. Sure enough, the creatures were catching up to them. A large mass that didn't even seem to have limbs flicked out a ropy tentacle and snatched up a girl a few hundred yards away. She shrieked as she was dragged backwards toward it, her voice cutting off abruptly as she was folded into the writhing, wormy mass. Heidi quickened her pace, jogging through the grass, careful not to let it snag her feet and make her stumble. The other children kept pace, the smaller ones struggling as they were dragged along by the bigger ones. Heidi tried to ignore the crawling sensation across her skin, anticipating the sting of monstrous claws sinking into her flesh any second.

Then one of them - she didn't see who - let out a horrified scream: *'Oh god it looks like the babadook!'*

Heidi didn't know what a babadook was, but the raw terror in the child's voice was enough to break her nerve, and she broke into a run. The fear spread through the children like wildfire, until they were all running, stumbling, dragging their companions through the grass.

Suddenly, out of nowhere, a treeline was visible ahead. Like the creatures behind them, the trees seemed to just materialise into existence, whereas before it had just been an endless field of ice. Heidi silently willed her legs to run faster, her breath tearing at her throat. The baby in her arms was wailing in fear and she could hear Tim's ragged panting to her side. The trees loomed bigger as they got closer, impossibly large. Finally they broke through the treeline into a dense, green forest.

Almost immediately, the sounds from behind them muffled and faded away. At the same time, Heidi became aware of a sudden warmth to the air. Confused, she hesitated, and her feet tangled beneath her, spilling her forward onto the forest floor. *The baby!* her mind screamed, but she managed to twist to the side just in time, hitting the ground with her shoulder. It hurt, but the baby was safe - frightened and shaken, wailing at the top of its tiny lungs, but safe.

Tim fell to his knees beside her. 'Get up!' he gasped. 'We have to keep going!' He grabbed her free arm and pulled her to her feet. She glanced back and stopped. Tim yanked on her arm again. 'Come on!'

Heidi shook him off and pointed. 'Look.'

Behind them, the ice field was gone. Beyond the trees they had just run through were ... more trees. The children following her were appearing there, fading into view just like the creatures and the trees had. One by one, they noticed her standing still and stopped too, milling in an uncertain group, looking around. A silence, punctuated only by their panting and gasps for breath, fell over the group.

The silence was broken as one of the older kids gave a shout. 'What the *fuck*?'

The taboo word startled them all. Someone gave a nervous laugh, and then it spread. Before long, every child was giggling, almost hysterically. One by one, they all dropped to the ground, exhausted and damp.

Interview No. 306

Investigating Officer (IO):
This is the interview with Lauren Caldwell, a psychic and medium, being conducted at the London office. Miss Caldwell was one of the many people who came forward with reports of "strange energies" on the days preceding and following what is now being called "The Event".
Task Force E is conducting interviews with some of these people to record and investigate the claims. Thank you for talking to us, Miss Caldwell.

Lauren Caldwell:
Please, call me Lauren.

IO:
Alright, Lauren. Can you please tell us, for the record, what you experienced in the time leading up to "The Event"?

Caldwell:
As you said, I'm a psychic by trade, and I also give tarot readings and conduct seances.

I have a … sensitivity, you see, to other planes of existence, to things that vibrate on higher frequencies than our own.

IO:
Uh-huh. Please go on.

Caldwell:
It was maybe a week or so before… what happened, and I was having a very hard time concentrating on any of my readings, and I'm usually able to go into a trance like that.
(Sound of snapping fingers)
But I just had this sense of … strong waves of very intense energy. Every time I tried … it was like … I don't know how to describe it…

IO:
Please try, Lauren.

Caldwell:
It felt like I was all hopped up on energy drinks, you know? Buzzing. Big energy. Couldn't sit still. I had to keep getting up and clapping my hands and stamping my feet to ground myself, or I felt like I might fly out the window or something!
And over the next few days, it got worse.
I started to feel it all the time, not just when I was trying to connect. I was hyped up and super-charged all the time. I thought I was going crazy!

IO:
Lauren, I have to ask, do you have any history of mental illness or episodes of anxiety or depression?

Caldwell:
No. Like I told you before, I'm perfectly sane. Just sensitive.

IO:

Does anyone in your family have a history of...

Caldwell:

Like I told you before, one of my aunts was supposedly crazy,
but I don't know if she was ever actually diagnosed with
anything or if she was just eccentric. You know?
She was kind of like me. A lot of sensitives are told they're crazy,
you know. We get told we're delusional or schizophrenic or –

IO:

I understand. Getting back to the days surrounding "The
Event", how was this ... energy ... on the day itself?

Caldwell:

Oh, very high. Very high. I was tearing my hair out by then.

IO:

And on the days after?

Caldwell:

It started to fade. I didn't know it 'til after, of course, but the
night when ... when "it" happened, that was when it was the
worst. I didn't sleep a wink all night. Then the next morning ...
you know, after ... then it started to go away. And it went fast,
really fast, much faster than it came on. A couple of days and it
was gone.

IO:

When did you suspect that it might have something to do with
"The Event"?

Caldwell:

A few days afterwards, when the news stories really started to come out and we knew that ... that it had happened all over the place, some people in a Facebook group I'm a member of started talking about it, you know, kind of like, 'hey, what if', you know? And I joined in with it - I thought it was interesting but I didn't really think it was true. Kind of like those crazy conspiracy stories you hear sometimes. But the more we talked about it, and the more people there were saying they'd felt it too.

IO:

Did the other people you were talking to report feeling the same sort of sensations you described?

Caldwell:

More or less, yeah. They all said it was very, er, you know, energetic ... energy.
(She laughs)

IO:

And what made you decide to report it to the police?

Caldwell:

Well, after a month or two, when nobody was getting anywhere, I just felt like, you know, what could it hurt? I didn't really think you'd pay any attention to me. But you hear those stories sometimes about how psychics help the police catch murderers... I don't know, I just figured I'd report it and then I'd have done what I could, and I wouldn't have to feel bad about not doing anything.
And honestly, I thought you had ignored me. I mean, I reported this ages ago! It's been nearly a year since "The Event" happened! I was really surprised when you called!

IO:

Yes well, in the absence of any other leads, we're investigating all possible avenues of enquiry. Even the, er...

Caldwell:
Impossible ones?

IO:
(A short pause)
Yes.

Caldwell:
(Laughs)
I guess you must be really stumped then!

IO:
Indeed. But we take missing children very seriously, Miss Caldwell.

Caldwell:
Oh... Yes... sorry.

IO:
So, in your experience, what would you say this sort of energy activity might be?

Caldwell:
Normally energy fluctuations are the sign of a spiritual presence. Normally, I deal with the spirits of the deceased, which usually have a negative energy impact - cold spots, feelings of dread or fear, a draining of your vitality - so the exact opposite of this. This was more like a massive injection of vitality. I've noticed it before on a very small scale, when the planets are aligned in such ways, or the moon is full, but nothing like that. Nothing like that.

IO:

So you have no idea what it might have been?

Caldwell:

I could only guess.

IO:

And what is your guess?

Caldwell:

Something not human.

IO:

Not human? What would they be then?

Caldwell:

I honestly have no idea.

Chapter 2

The Refugees

When the laughter had subsided, the children seemed a little more relaxed, either calmed by their new-found sense of camaraderie, or just too exhausted to be afraid. Heidi took the time to look around at her new companions. They had settled themselves into a rough circle on the forest floor, some sitting cross-legged, others leaning against trees or kneeling. Like her, in her white nightdress and sleep-scuffed plait, they were all in nightclothes and pyjamas, mostly barefoot, though a few wore socks or onesies. They were all damp and shivering from the melted ice that had soaked into their clothes. The baby in her arms was squirming irritably, and she hugged it close, hoping that the slightly warmer air here would dry them all off.

Heidi counted twelve of them, not including herself. They were an odd mix of young and older children, all looking around at each other with the shy openness or reluctant glances of new kids in school. The laughter had brought them together a little, washing away the panic, but they were still strangers.

Not knowing what else to do, Heidi spoke up. 'My name is Heidi,' she said, her voice sounding very loud in the quiet forest.

Her free hand tried to stray up to the red plait hanging over one shoulder - a nervous habit - but she lowered it with a conscious effort. 'I'm twelve. I was asleep in bed at my boarding school in London when something brought me here.' Looking down at the baby in her arms, she added, 'I don't know who this is. I guess they're just Baby for now.'

There was a long pause as the other children regarded her solemnly. Then, Tim cleared his throat next to her. 'I'm Tim,' he said, tugging nervously at his Avengers pyjamas. 'I'm ten. Um, I was in bed at home ... in, er, Redruth, which is in Cornwall.' He sat down, smiling up at Heidi. She smiled back and sat down next to him, bouncing Baby in her arms, who let out a pleased gurgle.

A small girl with very dark skin and long, plaited, black hair stepped forward, crossing her arms over her thin chest protectively. She was wearing an oversized, grey hooded top over blue, cotton pyjama shorts. 'I'm Monifa,' she said in a heavily accented voice. 'I'm eight. I was asleep at home too ... in Nigeria though.'

There was a small murmur at that. Had children been taken from everywhere?

As Monifa sat down, the next child stood up. It was as if they had fallen into a kind of classroom instinct. The next child was a tall girl with pale skin dusted with freckles, curly hair even redder than Heidi's, and her blue eyes were bright even in the forest's gloom. 'My name is Carla Callahan,' she said in a practised manner. 'I'm eleven years old and I live at number 26 Crescent Road, County Derry. In Ireland.' She paused, her practised recitation over. 'And ... I was in bed at home too.' Her pale cheeks flamed red, and she sat down quickly, her pretty purple nightdress billowing around her legs.

The next child – as it seemed that this had been accepted as the thing to do – was a plump, blonde boy wearing a baseball shirt and checked pyjama bottoms. 'I'm Ricky,' he said in an

American accent, shoving his hands into his pyjama pockets. 'I'm seven. I'm from Newark in Ohio.' He hesitated, then said, 'Am I dreaming?'

No one answered.

As Ricky sat down, a girl of about the same age stood up from where she had been sitting with two smaller children. 'I'm Meghan,' she said. 'I'm from America too. Mountain View, Missouri.' She gave Ricky a friendly smile, which he hesitantly returned. 'I'm seven too.' But the similarities ended there; this girl was skinny, with tanned skin and long, brown hair that hung loose over the shoulders of threadbare Mickey Mouse pyjamas.

Meghan sat down, and a tiny blonde girl clambered to her feet, looking round at everyone with nervous blue eyes. 'My name is Amy I am three years old,' she said in a rush, and sat back down. Meghan reached out and took hold of her hand, giving it a reassuring squeeze.

The next child to speak up was a long-haired Chinese girl in a white cotton nightdress. 'My name is Siu Yi,' she said in lightly accented English. 'You can call me Sue. I'm from Hong Kong. I'm nine.'

As Sue finished, the boy next to her got up. He was also Chinese, and his hair stood up on his head in messy, dark spikes. He had on dark blue boxers and an Overwatch t-shirt. 'I'm Yuen,' he said, but unlike Sue he spoke with no trace of an accent. 'I'm twelve. I'm from Hong Kong too, but my parents brought us to England when I was six, so ... that's where I was taken from.'

There was a long pause before the next child spoke up. He was an older boy with cropped, blonde hair and dark, sullen eyes, and he wore a Chelsea football shirt over boxer shorts. He was sitting a little apart from the others. 'I'm Tyler,' he said gruffly, then dropped his gaze.

A small, dark-skinned boy with close-cropped, curly hair jumped up next, smiling broadly. 'Alright,' he said in a jovial tone. 'My name's Tariq Hall, I'm eight, I'm from Essex, which is in England, south of London, and when the spooky guy appeared, I was taking a piss!'

Laughter erupted around the group, making Tariq's grin widen even more. He sat down, reaching over to mock-punch Tyler, who looked startled, but gave him a small smile in return.

The last child to speak was a small girl with long, blonde hair, wearing a lacy white nightdress. 'Er ... Sylvie Poirier,' she said, in a heavy French accent. 'Er ... no English, sorry.' She smiled sadly.

Silence fell, and after a moment or two, Heidi noticed that everyone was looking at her. With a sinking feeling, she realised that by speaking up first, she had made herself the leader of this group. Reluctantly, she settled Baby into the cradle of her crossed legs and took a deep breath.

'So...' she said. 'Was everybody taken while they were sleeping?'

Tariq shot his hand up. 'Not me!'

Everybody laughed again, and Heidi smiled. 'Right. Anyone else?'

Tyler lifted his hand briefly. 'I was playing *Call of Duty* on my Xbox.'

Heidi nodded. 'Well, I guess that means that we're not dreaming. Which means we're really here. So I suppose we have to figure out where *here* is.' She looked around the group. 'Does anyone have any ideas?'

Nobody spoke. Heidi tried not to look as afraid as she felt. 'No one recognises anything?'

After a long pause, Yuen said timidly, 'I saw something out in the field that kind of looked like this thing I saw in a horror movie a while back. My dad said I wasn't old enough to watch it, but I did anyway. It gave me nightmares for a week. It was called *The Babadook*.'

Heidi smiled. 'So that was you yelling.'

Yuen flushed red. 'Yeeeeaaaahhh...'

'But that's just a movie,' Heidi said gently.

'I know, and it didn't look *exactly* like the Babadook,' Yuen replied, a little defensively. 'It just ... reminded me of it. It had the same pointy fingers and big eyes and ... teeth.' He shuddered.

Ricky looked around. 'I saw one out there that looked a bit like Slenderman. Have you seen Slenderman on the internet?' A few of the older kids nodded. 'It was really tall and thin.'

Meghan was staring at him, aghast. 'Slenderman isn't real!' she protested.

'I know that!' Ricky retorted.

'What's Slenderman?' Tim asked, but at a dark glare from Meghan, he fell quiet.

Tyler snorted. 'Anyone see Pennywise out there too?' he sneered.

The group fell silent, each child pondering their own thoughts. Then Carla spoke up.

'My mam used to tell me faery stories,' she said hesitantly. 'Not like pretty little winged people. They're all sizes and some of them are scary. They live under the hills and sometimes when people go missing, it's because the faeries took them away.'

A few children laughed. Carla looked round at them, scowling. 'What? Isn't that what happened to us? We got taken away?'

'Are we missing kids?' Meghan muttered, horrified. 'Like on the posters and TV?'

Heidi barely heard her. She remembered something she had said that had amused the figure that had taken her.

'Second star to the right and straight on 'til morning,' she murmured.

Tim looked over at her. 'What?'

She raised her voice, and the group turned back to her. 'Second star to the right and straight on 'til morning. The thing said it was taking me to an enchanted place, and that's what popped into my head, and when I said it, it laughed and called me Wendy-bird.'

Sue lifted her hand as if she was in school. 'That's from *Peter Pan*.'

Amy gave a delighted smile and echoed: '*Peter Pan?*'

'Mate, if this is Neverland,' Tariq said, 'I want my money back.'

The children laughed uneasily, looking around them. The forest was dimly lit and the light coming through the trees had no defined source, so the shadows were soft and everywhere. The smooth tree trunks reached high above their heads before they split into branches, and the floor was soft with moss and fallen leaves. They could see a fair distance around them, because there was very little undergrowth. Only the slightest breeze got through to them, smelling of tree sap and damp earth. But most unnerving of all was the quiet. When they weren't talking, the forest was silent. No birdsong, no snapping twigs or small animals rummaging in the grass ... silence.

Heidi tore her gaze from the trees and looked back to the others. 'This isn't Neverland,' she said, 'because Neverland isn't real. It's just a story.' Amy looked crestfallen. Heidi tried to ignore it. 'This might be kind of like it, though. Like another place we've been taken to ... by things like from your stories,' she added, nodding to Carla.

Carla blinked. 'The faeries?'

Heidi shrugged. 'I don't know what they're called. But if they are faeries, it would make sense why they'd think what I said about Neverland was funny. Because that's where faeries live. Tinkerbell and all the others. It would explain why it called me Wendy-bird. Wouldn't it?'

The younger kids looked confused; the older ones sceptical.

Sue shrugged. 'It makes sense to me,' she replied. 'But not really. I mean, it can't be true. Faeries brought us to ... what, Faeryland? That's stupid! It's not real!'

Heidi spread her hands. 'Look around and you tell me what's real.'

Sue subsided, looking around anxiously. Amy crawled into her lap and started to cry quietly, and Sue hugged her close. Her sobs spread to the others like a cold, and soon the air was filled with the soft sound of children crying.

Interview No. 379

Investigating Officer (IO):
This is the interview with Mrs Willow Deane, author of numerous spiritualist books, being conducted in the London office. Mrs Deane approached us some time ago with–

Willow Deane:
Nearly a year ago.

IO:
With a theory about the night of "The Event" that she believes may have some bearing on what occurred. It is a theory that has been suggested by several people in similar professions. Task Force E is now looking into all theories regarding "The Event", and Mrs Deane has kindly agreed to talk to us about what she believes might have happened. Mrs Deane, could you briefly explain your theory, please?

Deane:
I've explained it to you twenty times or so now.

IO:

For the recording, Mrs Deane, please.

Deane:

A lot of my work – my books – deals with the changing of the seasons, the solstices and equinoxes, from a spiritual – a pagan – point of view. The sabbats, the festivals, the significances ... you know? And –

IO:

Pagan, as in...?

Deane:

As in pre-Christian beliefs, nature-based religions, druids, Wiccans and so on.

IO:

I see.

Deane:

(After a short pause)

And, as I was saying, it is a widely accepted belief – in these circles – that the different times of the year have different correspondences, with different effects on us and the world around us. It's like people believing that a full moon heightens their energy or empowers their spellcraft, only on a larger scale.

IO:

Spellcraft?

Deane: Yes. Spells. Magic. Prayers, if you like. Can I continue?

IO:

Of course.

Deane:

So, the different sabbats – festivals – are aligned with different energies and represent different aspects of the Wheel of the Year, the Cycle - whatever you want to call it.

The most well known one is Samhain, or Hallowe'en. Everybody knows some version of the story about ghosts coming out at Hallowe'en – in pagan belief, it's because the veil between this world and the next is supposed to be thinner at this time of year. In some traditions, it signifies the end of the year, after the last harvest is taken in, so it is the point of the year when everything symbolically ends. So, ancient people would harvest their last crops, take in or slaughter their cattle, and get ready for winter. And they'd remember their ancestors and give offerings for protection over the "dead" winter months.

IO:

How does this relate to "The Event"? It happened in June.

Deane:

I'm getting to that. Another festival, Bealtaine or Beltane, you would know it as May Day, has connections with fertility and new life. It's the height of spring, summer is almost here, and there is new life everywhere – lambs, calves, you get the idea. And another one, Midsummer, or Litha, occurs around mid-June.

IO:

Mid-June?

Deane:

Yes.

IO:

What does this festival represent?

Deane:

It's the summer solstice. The longest day of the year, when the world is on the turning point between the rise and the fall of the sun. If you're looking at the sun as a deity, this is when he is at his strongest.

It is also another of the times when the veil between this world and another is said to be very thin.

IO:

"This world and another"?

Deane:

Yes.

IO:

You mean the ...
(Sound of shuffling papers)
... the next world, like at Hallowe'en? The afterlife?

Deane:

No.

IO:

Then, what do you mean, Mrs Deane?

Deane:

(Sighs)

See, here's where I expect you not to believe me. Here's where I expect you to call me crazy and throw me out on my ear.

IO:

We're a little bit past calling anyone crazy at this point. Please, share with us your theory.

Deane:

Alright, if you say so.
(Another sigh)
At Midsummer, the veil is supposed to be thinnest between this
world and the world of the fae.

IO:

Fae? Please elaborate.

Deane:

Faeries, dear. Faeries.

IO:

Faeries?

Deane:

Yes, faeries. And not your Tinkerbell, Cottingley Fairies - pretty
little Victorian ladies with wings. These are elemental spirits,
spirits of nature. Ancient beings of magic that have been around
much longer than we have.
(A long pause)
I told all this to your colleague –

IO:

Yes, I'm sorry, it's just a little hard to get my head around,
that's all.
(Clears his throat)
So, you think "The Event" might have been caused by faeries?

Deane:

It happened at Midsummer when the veil is thin. There have
been all these reports about strange energies – which I felt
myself, as it happens. Plus, it all happened at 3am, right? All over
the world?

IO:
That is correct, yes.

Deane:
They say the veil is thinnest at 3am.

IO:
Who does?

Deane:
Spiritualists, paranormal investigators, anyone involved in this sort of life. There's lots of stories about weird stuff happening at the same time in the early hours of the morning, and a lot of them seem to be at 3am.
I'm not saying I'm right. I'm just saying maybe you should look into it.

IO:
Look into faeries.

Deane:
Yes.

Chapter 3

The Silent Forest

Heidi listened to the others crying for a while, feeling the sting of tears behind her own eyes, but she was determined not to cry. She rocked Baby in her arms, trying to quiet their whimpering, and looked around her, searching for some sign of which direction they should go. Anything slightly different, anything familiar. But there was nothing. For as far as she could see in all directions, it was just endless tree trunks and shadows in the gloom.

Soft green moss and leaves lay beneath them, and above them a canopy of tangled, skeletal branches cut out the light. The situation seemed hopeless, but she fought back the despair trying to rise in her throat. Sitting around crying and waiting for someone to find them would get them nowhere. She would give them a moment, then they would have to pull themselves together and just pick a direction and walk. There was nothing else for it. She sighed and looked down at Baby, who was staring up at her with watery, blue eyes.

It was so quiet that they almost didn't hear it at all beneath the sound of their own sobs, but some stroke of fortune or instinct made Tariq look up as he was fighting back his own tears. He froze, his eyes narrowing as they struggled to pierce the gloom, then widening.

'Uh ... guys?' he squeaked. He reached out blindly; his grasping hand found Sylvie and yanked roughly on her night-dress. She turned to him, scowling, then saw where he was looking and followed his gaze. She screamed.

Her shrill, terrified shriek instantly caught everyone's attention, and in the silence that followed, they all heard the low, papery, slithering sound from above their heads. The group looked up to where Tariq's trembling hand pointed to see what appeared to be a mass of branches unfurling slowly above their heads, as if the trees were reaching down for them. Then, with Sylvie's second scream, the faces appeared.

Sharp-boned oval faces with eyes as bright as shiny pennies, white hair floating around them like newly-spun cobwebs. The unfurling boughs arranged themselves into multiple skeletal arms, ending in hands with too many irregularly jointed fingers, twisted and jutting out like twigs. Emaciated bodies that curled like serpents tapered into tails that wrapped around branches, holding them in place. Tails that now unwound, with that same dry, papery sound, to let the creatures drop.

The children bolted in all directions, their screams rico-cheting between the trees. Heidi jumped up, clutching Baby to her chest, and ran. The heavy thuds on the ground behind her sounded unnervingly close. She dared a glance back over her shoulder. What she saw brought her to an abrupt stop.

Sylvie and Meghan had Amy in an awkward, under-arm hold as they fled from the three ... monsters - there was no other word - that had landed in the spot where they had all been sitting. One of them reached out with numerous arms that seemed to stretch and elongate, and snagged Sylvie's nightdress. Its spindly twig-fingers punched through the fabric and dragged her away from the other girls and onto the ground. She shrieked as she was pulled back across the mossy floor, digging her nails into the ground and leaving thin, bloody grooves behind her as her fingernails tore in the earth.

The thing tangled yet more fingers into her blonde hair and pulled her upright, drawing her into its torso in a spidery embrace. As she struggled, its hair flowed down around her face and started to wrap around her. In just a few seconds, her screaming grew muffled and her entire body seemed to be enveloped in the silvery strands. There was a muffled, cracking sound, and Sylvie's struggling abruptly stopped. The creature looped its tail around a nearby tree trunk and began to climb backwards, its fingers digging into the bark. Sylvie's still form was pulled up after it, dangling from its hair. Her bare feet hung limply. Heidi could see the soft pink nail polish on her toes.

Beyond them, she could see Yuen on the ground, struggling with a second one. He was kicking and punching at it, but in moments the thing had caught both his arms and legs in its crooked hands, and had bowed its face towards his. Its hair slithered down over him, hiding him from Heidi's view, and his screams of terror were abruptly muffled, then stopped as there was another hideous *crack*.

'*No!*' Heidi screamed, and Baby jumped in her arms and started to wail.

The third creature's head jerked around to face her. In the half-second before it lifted itself on its arms and started to dart toward her, she saw that its face had no mouth and no nose, just those bright metallic eyes.

Clutching Baby tightly, she turned and fled. She could hear the thuds of its many hands hitting the earth behind her, making it sound like there were five of them pursuing her, instead of just one. She ran, trying not to think about how tired her legs were starting to feel, or how her breath was starting to tear at her throat, or what would happen if she...

The thuds behind her fell away, and she shot a glance back over her shoulder. The thing had stopped, letting its serpentlike body rest on the ground between its many bent arms. Then, the earth fell away under her feet. Snapping her head back, she saw that she had run off the edge of a small drop and was falling into a ditch. She lifted her arms, thrusting Baby up over her head to avoid crushing them as she landed face down on the mossy earth below. Her stomach smacked into a tree root, winding her. Her lips mashed against the earth and she tasted blood and dirt. Baby tumbled from her fingers and rolled away from her, their shrieks momentarily stopping.

Gasping for air, Heidi scrambled to her knees, dragged Baby toward her by one tiny foot, and backed up against the drop she had just fallen down. She pushed her back into the earth as if she could meld into it. Her breath came back to her in a rush and she gulped down air gratefully, trying not to make a sound. Gathering Baby into her arms, she looked the infant over. They seemed unharmed, but were gazing up at her blankly, taking large, shaky breaths. She hugged them close and put her mouth close to its tiny ear.

'Sssssh,' she breathed. 'Please don't cry, Baby. I don't think I can run much more.'

As she said that, she heard something move above her. Looking up, she saw long, many-jointed fingers curl over the edge of the drop above her head. Holding her breath, she cringed against the earth as the creature's face peered over, its bright, metallic eyes piercing in the gloom. Dry soil dislodged by those cruel-looking fingers trickled down, settling on her cheeks and on Baby's head. She didn't dare move to wipe it away. It couldn't have been more than a couple of feet above her. She froze, watching as it moved its head back and forth, swaying on its thin neck like a snake smelling the air. But it couldn't smell anything, because it didn't have a nose. Nor did it have a mouth; apart from those brilliant eyes, its face was completely featureless and smooth.

The eyes seemed to lock with hers for a moment, then

moved on, roaming back and forth as if searching. Heidi was stunned. It couldn't have failed to see her. She was right there! Craning her head forward, she studied the creature as well as she could. Its eyes, she now saw, were clouded and blank beneath their penny-bright shine. Blind eyes, reflecting what little light there was down here. It couldn't see her, it couldn't smell her. Then how...?

Someone yelled a short distance away. 'Heidi? Sylvie? Tariq? Where are you?' It sounded like Meghan. Instantly, the creature's head snapped around and it slithered away, its body making that awful papery-dry sound on the earth. Heidi clapped a hand over her mouth reflexively as she realised. Sound! The forest was so quiet, and they'd been making so much noise; Meghan was going to bring them right to her!

Gently, she laid Baby down on the mossy ground, putting her finger to her lips. Baby looked back up at her and gave a tiny whimper, then put their fingers to their mouth and stayed quiet. It was an endearingly similar gesture to the one Heidi had made, and for a moment she wondered how much Baby understood.

'I'll be right back,' she mouthed, then stood and crept, as quietly as she could, out of the ditch.

The monster was several feet away, pulling itself along the ground, leaving a faint groove in the moss as it went. It was heading directly toward the sound of Meghan's shouting. Someone else, a boy, was shouting with her now. Heidi tiptoed away from the creature, to its right, making sure she didn't lose sight of the ditch where she had left Baby. When she felt that she was far enough away, she took a deep breath, tried to swallow the fear in her belly, and shouted as loud as she could: 'BE QUIET! THEY FIND YOU BY SOUND!'

The other children's shouting immediately stopped and the monster spun its head around, looking once more in Heidi's direction. Her gut clenched in panic. She darted back toward the ditch as quickly and quietly as she could as the creature lifted itself up on its long, spidery arms and skittered towards her. When she reached the ditch's edge, she stopped and looked back. It had stopped almost exactly where she had been standing when she shouted, and was turning its head from side to side, searching. She stood completely still, watching it. She was in plain sight and not that far away. If it could see, it would be darting toward her any second now, and she tensed, ready to run. But it made no move toward her. Crouching slowly, she picked up a rock from the ground and threw it to one side. The creature's head followed the low thud it made as it hit a tree trunk. It slithered slowly off in that direction, its belly on the ground once more.

Heidi felt pretty confident now that she was right. The only thing bothering her was that she hadn't seen any ears on the creature. Maybe they were hidden under its hair. Still, if it could hear without ears, then the rest of her observations might be wrong, and she didn't like that thought. She was more than ready to get as far away from this thing as she could. Moving as stealthily as she could manage, she climbed back down into the ditch and lifted Baby up, who smiled when they saw her and raised their little arms. Heidi smiled back and hugged them close.

'Sssh,' she whispered again.

With Baby cradled in one arm, she tried to climb out of the ditch again. She quickly realised that this was not going to be possible to do quietly with only one arm; the sides were just too steep. Praying that the baby wouldn't make a sound, she shifted them into her hands and lifted them up as high as she could, leaning forward into the slope of the earth, and half-pushed, half-lifted them out of the ditch. Baby rolled awkwardly away from the lip of the drop with a soft gurgle, coming to rest on their stomach. Heidi winced and started climbing out as quickly and quietly as she could. If Baby started to cry...

Once they were both out, Heidi scooped Baby up again and looked back at the monster. It didn't seem to have heard them; it had the rock she had thrown in one of its hands and was looking around, the tip of its tail flicking back and forth like an angry cat. Heidi shivered as she put her back to it and started walking, very slowly, away from it toward the other children. She scoured the ground with her eyes before taking each step, seeking out and avoiding twigs, rocks, anything that might make a sound and give her away. Even so, when the first unseen twig snapped under her heel, she froze in fear and glanced behind her. The monster was already slithering slowly in her direction. Cursing silently, she turned and carried on at a diagonal from her previous course.

If that thing picks itself up and rushes, she thought, *we're both done for.*

Each time she snapped a twig or kicked a rock, Heidi altered her direction, putting her on an uneven zigzag toward the other children. The creature followed slowly, pausing at each spot where she had made a noise. It was incredibly good at pinpointing where the sound had come from. It was also slowing down. Was it tired? Giving up? Or was it just taking more care about tracking her?

Eventually she found the others. They were huddled together beside a tree and looked up at her miserably as she approached. She put her finger to her lips and pointed behind her. The fear that flickered in each of their eyes told her that they understood.

Meghan stood up and crept over to her, standing close so she could whisper. 'We can't find Yuen or Sylvie.'

Heidi looked at her and shook her head. Meghan's eyes widened with horror and filled with tears. Afraid that she would start to cry and draw the creature's attention, Heidi grabbed her shoulder and shook her, then put her finger to her lips once more. Meghan gave a stifled sigh and nodded.

They crept back to the others. Heidi pointed in the direction of the creature again, then gestured for them to follow her, finishing by putting her finger to her lips one more time. The children stirred themselves and formed a shaky line, Monifa carrying Amy. Everyone was following Heidi away from the beast. Aware that she was now looking for good places for everyone to put their feet, Heidi took even longer searching the ground, exaggerating her movements so that they would see and copy what she was doing. The progress was slow.

Eventually, she felt Meghan tap her arm. She looked round, and Meghan whispered, 'Monifa just saw it go up a tree. Maybe it gave up?'

Heidi smiled in a way that she hoped was encouraging. 'Maybe. Keep quiet though.'

Meghan nodded and turned to pass the instruction back to the children behind her.

They walked in this fashion for what seemed like an eternity. The light around them stayed the same, with no sense of the sun getting higher or lower in the sky. Meghan, Monifa, Tariq, and Sue all took turns carrying Amy as their arms started to tire. At some point, Heidi started to smell an unpleasant odour from Baby, who had fallen asleep on her shoulder, and realised that she was going to have to do something about their nappy. She stifled a groan and tried to ignore the smell. She wasn't about to try and change a nappy here, with those things above their heads, and she didn't have anything to change it with anyway. That was a problem that would have to wait. *Sorry, Baby.*

The more immediate problems were that her feet hurt, her arms ached from carrying the baby, her stomach was starting to growl, and she was incredibly thirsty and tired. She imagined that the other children were suffering as well. Having to keep quiet was also taking its toll on her nerves. She felt jittery and anxious, and if they didn't get out of this forest soon...

Almost as though her thoughts had made it happen, before her eyes, the endless trees ahead of her started to fade away. Through them she could see a bright, grassy plain, sloping downwards into a valley. It was odd, like coming close enough to a sheer curtain to be able to see what was on the other side, except the curtain was the world ahead and once you got close enough, the curtain just wasn't there any more. She would have expected to feel dizzy or sick, now that she was paying attention and really seeing the transition, but there was nothing like that. The world ahead simply changed, like a page had been turned in a book.

The other children saw it only moments after she did, and someone, forgetting themselves, shouted with joy. The sound broke their solemn march and spurred them into running. They all rushed forward, past the fading trees, and out into the bright sunlight and fragrant breezes of a beautiful green hillside.

They ran and stumbled, rolling down the hill, tumbling into the long, soft grass, laughing and shouting in relief. Behind them, the forest faded and disappeared, revealing more rolling hills of lush, green grass. The younger children came to a stop partway down the hill, coming to rest in a tangled heap of grass-stained nightclothes and dirty feet. Heidi and Monifa followed, carrying the smaller children.

'We're out!' Tariq cried, punching the air with his fists. 'We made it!'

Abruptly, Meghan burst into tears. Tariq fell silent, his hands dropping to his sides. The group sat quietly as Meghan sobbed. Carla and Amy began to cry too. After a few minutes, their tears subsided and they settled down.

Leaving Amy sat next to Meghan, Monifa got up and moved over to sit next to Heidi. Speaking low so the others wouldn't hear, she said, 'Okay, we're out of the forest. But where are we now?'

It was a very good question.

Chapter 4

An Awakening

Heidi opened her eyes to see a tiny, green face staring at her. She had been dreaming of Sylvie and Yuen and the spidery things that had taken them, and for a second, her half-awake mind interpreted the face before her as one of them. She jerked back, startled, and the little face did the same, disappearing into the blades of long grass in front of her. It vanished so completely that, for a moment, she wasn't sure that she'd really seen it at all. Perhaps it was just a fragment of a dream?

But then, a single blade of grass moved slightly to one side, and she saw a pair of tiny, bright black eyes looking up at her. She looked behind her at the other children, to see if they could see it too, but nearly all of them appeared to have fallen asleep, like her. Tariq was awake, but he was sitting with his back to the others, the side of his face visible to her uncharacteristically glum. She decided not to bother him.

Looking back, the face was still there. Heidi rolled onto her front, moving slowly to avoid startling the tiny thing, and propped herself up on her elbows. It watched her solemnly. She blinked several times, in case it was some dream face that she could shake from her vision. It didn't go away. 'Hello?' she said softly.

It tilted its head at that, a single very long, very thin, pointed ear drooping forward into view. It gave no sign of understanding her, so she raised one hand and wiggled her fingers in a wave. It watched, then one slender arm emerged, and a tiny, three-fingered hand waved back, mimicking her. She smiled, and it smiled back, showing tiny pointed teeth. Its black eyes – like a bird's – blinked rapidly. She lowered her hand back to the ground, and it stepped out of hiding.

It was truly tiny, no taller than her index finger, and balancing on a single, curled-over blade of grass. It was green-skinned, humanoid, slightly fuzzy, and very slight of frame - except for its head, which was almost perfectly round and just a bit too big for the rest of its body. It had pointed ears as long as its arms, drooping slightly at the top, and a long, thin tail which broadened out at the bottom like a leaf. The hair on its head was a longer version of the fuzz on its skin, the same shade of green, but bushy, and it looked as soft as thistledown. Its nose was a barely visible nub in the centre of its round face, and it had no eyebrows that she could see. But the most curious part – to her, at least – was that it seemed to be wearing tiny, pointed boots made of what appeared to be compacted moss, and a loincloth constructed from part of a leaf.

Heidi had no idea what she should do. Without really think-ing, she lifted her hand again and very slowly held it out, palm up, close to the creature. It flinched back at first, then regarded the outstretched hand curiously, crouching down on the blade of grass it stood on to examine it. She tried not to laugh as it poked at her with its tiny finger, then bent low to sniff at her skin. Eventually, seemingly satisfied, it straightened up and hopped onto her finger, walking along it onto her palm.

Now Heidi laughed, as softly as she could so she wouldn't scare it away.

'Hi there,' she said. 'What's your name?'

The creature – which Heidi guessed must be male since it was bare-chested – looked up at her with a curious tilt of his head. Then he lifted his face to the sky and gave out a shrill whistle.

Heidi smiled. 'Whistle? That's a nice name.'

The creature grinned, his smile stretching widely across his face. From the corner of her eye, Heidi saw movement in the grass, and turned her head to see two more of these strange things emerging from it. One appeared to be identical to Whistle, except his hair was longer and wrapped up in a strange twisting fashion, tied in place with what looked like a blade of grass. The other had longer hair still that it flicked back over its tiny, narrow shoulders as it looked up at her, and seemed to be wearing a very short dress made from several very small leaves. That one, she thought, must be a girl.

'These must be your friends,' she said. 'Er ... Twist and Flick?'

The two newcomers looked up at her and, in unison, gave their own toothy grins.

'It's very nice to meet you,' Heidi said to them. 'Um ... I don't have any food ...'

'Who are you talking to?' Meghan's voice called out softly from behind her.

Heidi looked around. 'Come and see,' she replied. 'But slowly. Don't scare them away!'

Frowning, Meghan got to her feet and wandered over. As soon as she caught sight of the three tiny creatures, her eyes widened, and she dropped slowly to her knees, crawling the rest of the way.

'Oh my god,' she exclaimed. 'This is... What are they?'

Heidi shrugged. 'They were in the grass. I don't know what they are.'

The two others had followed Whistle up onto Heidi's hand,

and when she lifted it, they all put their little arms out to balance themselves, but made no move to jump. Carefully, she rolled over and sat up, taking care to keep her hand level. Then, she laid her hand on her lap. Twist and Flick hopped onto her knees, but Whistle ran up her arm and sat down on her shoulder, pulling at strands of her hair and appearing to smell and lick it.

The two girls laughed with delight. 'They're so sweet!' Meghan exclaimed. 'I wonder if they have names?'

'I call them Whistle, Twist and Flick,' Heidi replied, pointing each one out. 'I think Flick's a girl.'

'How do you know?'

'I don't, really.' Heidi looked down at Flick. 'Flick, are you a girl?'

Flick looked up at her, stuck out a tiny dark green tongue, and blew a barely audible raspberry.

Meghan giggled. 'What does that mean?'

Heidi shook her head. 'I don't even know if they know what I'm saying.'

One by one, the other children were awoken by the girls' laughter, and came to see what was going on. The tiny beings, far from showing any fear of them, instead seemed to get bolder with each new child that gathered around. Soon, they were all circled around Meghan and Heidi, who were being climbed on, prodded and poked by the creatures. Tariq, seemingly cheered up by them, was trying to initiate a very awkward game of patty-cake with Twist. Baby, tucked into Monifa's lap, gurgled and reached for them with chubby, little hands that were still bigger than their heads. Amy insisted on calling them 'Tinkerbells' and kept asking 'Where are their wings?'

Carla, the last to wake up, grew wide-eyed and oddly reverent when she saw them. 'I was right,' she gasped. 'The stories were right! They're real life faeries!'

'Pixies, actually,' a gruff, nasally voice said from outside the group. The children fell quiet and looked around wildly, searching for the source of the voice.

Another small figure emerged from the grass on the far side of the little clearing they'd made, walking over the tramped-down grass as if it weighed nothing. It was small, but still several times larger than the creatures on Heidi's lap. It walked on its hind legs, but its body looked like that of a lizard, brown and scaly, with clawed hands and feet, and a curling tail. Its head was large, with pointed ears and a sharp nose, and coarse hair that stood up like spikes. In fact there were spikes emerging from the hair and running down its back like the spines of a hedgehog. It blinked up at them with large, cat-like, yellow eyes. It stopped while it was still out of easy reach and looked the group over.

'Well, aren't you a find for the ages,' it said.

Amy was the first to find her voice. 'What's that one?' she asked.

It grinned, showing yellowed teeth sharp as the spikes on its back. 'I'm a spriggan,' it replied. 'You can call me Sprickleback.'

'Sprick ... Sprig...' Amy made a face, and one or two of the children giggled.

The spriggan scowled. 'Sprick will do.'

Heidi looked down at the pixies, and noticed with mild concern that they had stopped playing and were standing very still. Was it her imagination, or did Whistle's hair look like it was standing up more? She lowered her voice. 'What's wrong?' she said to him.

In response, he bared his teeth and growled, not looking away from the spriggan.

'Are you a girl Sprick or a boy Sprick?' Amy was asking.

Sprickleback looked at the little girl somewhat scornfully. 'Those things don't matter that much around here, sweetling,' it replied. 'Why don't you decide for me?'

Amy beamed. 'I think you're a boy Sprick!'

He bowed, sweeping one gangly arm before him in an oddly graceful gesture. 'Then, a boy Sprick I am.'

Amy laughed and clapped her hands. 'I like him!'

Heidi looked down at the pixies, who were now visibly bristling. *They don't*, she thought.

Sprickleback straightened up and looked at them all again. 'Now, forgive me if I am mistaken, dear children,' he said, 'But you look mighty lost to me.' The smaller children's faces fell at this, and he gave a sage nod. 'Aha. I was not mistaken, then.'

Heidi opened her mouth to try and come up with something, but she was too slow. Ricky spoke up instead, so she stayed silent.

'We woke up in a freezing cold field, and monsters chased us into a forest,' he said. Heidi didn't like the way the pixies were reacting to Sprick. It was making her uneasy.

But the spriggan was nodding his spiky head sympathetically. 'The Ice Fields,' he said. 'Yes. That's where all the tithes come in.'

'Tithes?' Meghan asked.

'Yes, yes,' Sprick replied. 'The ones we take from the mortal lands.'

'Mortal lands,' Carla repeated, looking over at Heidi with a knowing glance.

'That's right,' Sprick nodded again. 'You do know where you are? At least, broadly speaking?' He spread his long-fingered hands before him, the gesture very broad indeed. When no one answered, he clicked his tongue and shook his head. 'Oh dear, oh dear, what do they teach you young ones out there these days? You're in Faerieland, my pretty ones. The Otherlands. Arcadia. The Land of Promise. Elfhame. Tír na nÓg. Shall I go on? There are so many names.'

The stunned silence this news was greeted with seemed to please the little, brown creature, for he chuckled and gave a curious little stamp of his feet. Then he said, 'If you don't even know that, you're in even more need of a guide than I thought.'

'What do you mean?' Heidi asked.

'Well, you shan't get anywhere without a guide,' Sprickleback scoffed. 'Goodness, no! You'll be eaten up by the dragons, or the boggarts, or the bunyips, or the huldras, or the –'

Heidi held up her hands, causing Whistle to totter precariously on her shoulder for a moment. 'Okay, okay, I get it.' She looked round at the others, hoping they would side with her. 'Look, thank you for the offer –'

Sprickleback hissed and shook roughly, his spines rattling. 'Ugh!' he spat. 'Empty words!'

Heidi was taken aback by this and didn't know how to respond, so she pressed on. '...But I think we can find our own way.'

The other children turned to stare at her, several of them muttering in protest. She looked back at them defiantly. None of them spoke up to argue.

Sprickleback chuckled and straightened his back. 'As you wish, missy,' he said loftily. 'No skin off my scales. I was just trying to be friendly to a bunch of newcomers.' He turned and sauntered back across the flattened grass. 'But if you change your mind, you know who to call.' With that, he disappeared into the long grass with a rustle and a flick of his tail.

The three pixies immediately relaxed, but the other children did the opposite, turning on Heidi in panic and anger.

'Why did you say that?' Monifa snapped, her sharp tone making Baby whimper and squirm in her lap. 'We don't know where to go!'

'We're going to get eaten by ... by hoggarts, or whatever he said!' Ricky cried, actually tearing up a little.

Heidi held up her hands. 'I don't trust him,' she said. 'Did you see how the pixies reacted?'

'At least that one can talk!' Monifa protested. 'They're not going to guide us anywhere!'

'We'll be alright,' Heidi insisted. 'Trust me!'

'Oh yeah?' Tyler interjected. 'Then where do we go next, genius? Go on, tell us!'

They all looked at her, some angrily, others with faint, desperate hope. Heidi sighed and got to her feet, Whistle clinging to her hair and Flick and Twist leaping from her knees to the ground. 'Fine!'

She looked around them. The grass came up to her waist, so she could see over it well enough. They seemed to be near the top of a tall hill, just one hill in what looked like an ocean of soft green waves. The ground rose and fell for miles around them. In one direction, she could see a deep, green forest, far away from where they were now, the trees thick with leaves and stretching as far as she could see. In another, the ground seemed to flatten and grow dull. In yet another, she thought she could see some kind of town, but it was so far away she could barely make out the shapes of the buildings. And in the very, very far distance, barely visible even though the sky was clear and blue, she thought she could see a tall, slender tower. But all of it was so far away; she thought they would be walking across the hills for days, maybe even weeks, before they would reach any of it. They had no food, no water, and two very small children with them. They didn't even have a single pair of shoes between them. And if they should come across something dangerous, how would they defend themselves?

Her pride stung, but Heidi was too sensible to give in to it. She was the leader, and she had to think about what was best for all of them, not just her. She allowed herself a groan of frustration before she raised her voice. 'Sprickleback!' she called.

Instantly, his spiky, brown head popped out of the grass. 'You called?' he said with a grin.

Heidi glared at him. 'You didn't even go anywhere!'

He shrugged as he stepped back into the clearing. 'I was confident you'd change your mind,' he replied smugly.

Heidi gave a heavy sigh. She didn't even look at the other children, who she had no doubt were all looking just as smug.

'Will you please be our guide?' she asked.

Sprickleback's smile grew wider. 'What's in it for me?' he said mischievously.

Heidi glared at him; she was trusting him less and less as time went on. 'What do you mean?'

'Well, I can't be doing things for nothing,' Sprickleback replied. 'I'll get a reputation. So, what'll you give me?'

Now Heidi looked around at the others, who all looked as perplexed as she felt. 'We ... look at us! We're all in our pyjamas! We don't have anything!'

'Oh, I'm sure you do.' Sprickleback stepped past her and wandered around the group, looking them each up and down. He pulled at Ricky's baseball shirt and grimaced at the fabric. Eventually, he came to Tyler and Carla, who were sitting next to each other.

'What's your name?' he said.

Tyler spoke up first. 'Tyler Wade.'

Sprickleback frowned and shook his head. 'No, no, no,' he said disapprovingly. 'What about you, girly?'

Carla looked around nervously. 'Carla Callahan,' she replied.

'Carla Callahan,' Sprickleback repeated, rolling the name around on his tongue. 'Carla Callahan. Yes! That's good. Tastes old. I'll take that!'

Carla blinked. 'Excuse me?'

Sprickleback grinned. 'That's my name now. Pick another.'

Carla hesitated, then laughed. 'Don't be silly!'

'Silly, is it?' Sprickleback scoffed. 'Then tell me your name.'

'My name is C...' She began, then stopped. 'C- C-...'

It was as if the name stuck in her throat and refused to come out. She struggled for a minute or two. 'I can't say it!' she cried eventually.

'That's because it's not your name any more,' Sprickleback said. 'It belongs to me.'

Meghan piped up. 'You can't just take C-...' she started, then came to a stop, just as the other girl had. 'I can't say it either!' she exclaimed.

Sprickleback stood and smiled smugly.

Heidi turned on the spriggan. 'Why did you take her name?' she demanded.

'Payment,' he replied.

'What good is it to you?'

'That just shows what you don't know,' Sprickleback smirked. 'Words have power, girly. And a name - the words you use to define *you* - well, if someone with the right magicks were to get a hold of it, they could do all sorts of things.'

Heidi resisted the urge to grab the spriggan and shake him. 'What are you going to do to her?'

'Me? Oh, dear me, no!' he chuckled. 'I don't have that kind of power! But it's always handy to have a spare name or two in case I should upset someone who does.' He winked.

The girl who used to be Carla let out a wail and started to shake, her eyes filling with tears. 'He took my name!' she cried. 'What do I do without a name?'

Tyler shifted uncomfortably as she started to cry, putting out a hand in an awkward attempt to comfort her. But Meghan jumped forward before he could and swept her up in a big hug. 'It's okay,' she said. 'Just pick a new one. Is there something else we can call you? Like a nickname?'

The girl gulped back her tears. 'My friends at school call me CeeCee sometimes,' she replied. 'Because my initials are ... were ... C.C.'

Meghan smiled and gave her a kiss on the cheek. 'I like it. Hi, CeeCee.'

'CeeCee it is!' Sprickleback declared, spreading his arms wide like a circus announcer. 'Well then, sweetlings, shall we be off?'

Heidi glowered at him. 'Where are we going?'

'Away from here, to start with,' Sprickleback replied. 'It's a wonder you've not yet been picked off by the dragons. We need to get you off of these hills! I think going under would be the best route.' He set off into the long grass.

Heidi hurried after him, glancing nervously up into the sky, almost expecting to see a dragon hovering over them right now. The other children quickly fell in line behind her. Monifa carried Baby this time, and Amy trotted along next to Sue, holding her hand.

'Going under what?' Heidi asked the spriggan.

'Under the hills,' was the curt reply. 'It's the safest way to get to the Shining City, which is where you want to be if you're to find out how to get home.'

'You don't know how we can get home?'

'Me? Course not! I'm just a wee spriggan, how would I know magick like that?'

'You said you could guide us home!' Heidi cried.

Sprickleback stopped, turned, and fixed her with a stern, yellow-eyed glare. 'I did not. I simply agreed to guide you. And since I don't know how to get you home, I'll guide you to those who do.' He spread his hands. 'Can I be any fairer?'

Defeated, Heidi sighed. 'I suppose not.'

'Glad we agree.' The spriggan turned and started walking again. Heidi and the children followed, the three pixies riding along in their hair or on their clothes, clinging to them like goosegrass.

One Year On – More Children Gone

Article from The Daily Mail.

One year on from "The Event", the unthinkable has happened again. Children born in the year since the worldwide abduction have vanished, just like the ones that disappeared before them last June, despite all government and scientific advice assuring us that it could not happen again.

In the 24 hours since the anniversary, reports have been flooding in from the distraught parents of multiple babies less than a year old, all of whom have apparently vanished in the same inexplicable circumstances as a year ago. Parents all across the UK – and all over the world – woke up to empty cots and cribs yesterday morning. Once again, police have no clues, no leads, and no idea where the children have gone.

Already there have been hundreds of angry protesters descending on Downing Street, demanding to know what is being done, and why these children were not better protected. So far the Prime Minister has not issued a statement, not even to offer his condolences to the bereaved families.

So what is being done? Here is what we know – which is very little:

The children all disappeared without leaving any signs of struggle.

No blood was found at any of the sites.

No credible witnesses were able to give a report of any intruders or abductors.

No trace of the children were found with any known paedophile rings, people smuggling operations or any other criminal groups.

No terrorist organisations have claimed credit for the abductions.

No bodies have ever been found.

Scientists have been so far unable to formulate a credible theory as to any natural incident that could have caused the disappearances.

Recent updates have included the names of previously unheard of "experts", who, our sources claim, are in fact folklorists and new age spiritualists. Is our government so inept that it is now turning to charlatans and witch doctors for answers? Can we still put our trust in our leaders? Can the Prime Minister really expect the nation to continue to support him with such a staggering list of failures to his government's name?

We think not. Polls calling for a vote of no confidence in the Prime Minister were already numbering in the thousands before this second tragedy; soon it could be in the millions. The country is on the brink of a revolution.

CHAPTER 5

ON THE SUBJECT OF DRAGONS

Tim looked up at the sky and sighed.

'I'm tired,' he complained. 'How long have we been walking?'

Heidi had no idea. She didn't even know how long they had been here – in Faerieland, or whatever it was called. Time was difficult to tell. In the Ice Fields it had been night-time; in the forest, maybe early morning – or maybe it was just that the trees cut out so much light. Out on the hills, the sun was blazing directly above their heads and had been the entire time, despite it feeling like they'd been there for hours. Some of them were even starting to get red shoulders and cheeks.

'Sprickleback!' she called to the spriggan at the front of the group. 'Can we take a break?'

The little creature looked around, his yellow eyes narrowing. 'What for?' he said impatiently.

'We're tired,' she replied. 'And the baby needs to be changed.'

Ricky screwed up his nose. 'Yeah, it's stinky.'

Sprickleback gave a snort. 'Oh, very well,' he relented. 'But not for long!'

The children all immediately sat down in the long grass,

several of them sighing with relief. Sprickleback stood where he was, glaring at them all. Heidi laid Baby down in the grass and looked at it doubtfully. 'I've never done this before,' Heidi said.

'I have,' Meghan replied, joining her. 'But we don't have any diapers.'

Heidi looked around at the others and saw Monifa shrugging off her hoodie, revealing a blue cotton camisole that matched her shorts. Monifa seized one of the arms and, with some difficulty, tore it away from the body along the seam. 'Here,' she said, holding it out. 'For the baby.'

Heidi took it gratefully. 'Thanks,' she replied, 'But what about your top?'

Monifa shrugged. 'It's too warm for it, really,' she said. 'And the baby stinks.' She smiled.

Heidi smiled back and turned to Meghan and Baby. Meghan had unfastened and pushed up Baby's romper suit and was pulling away a very dirty, smelly nappy. She tossed the dirty nappy a short distance away, hesitated, then grabbed handfuls of the long grass and tore it up, using it to wipe the infant clean.

'This ... is ... disgusting!' she declared loudly, and several of the children laughed. Still, she thought she did a fairly good job, and was soon holding out her hand to Heidi for the arm of the hoodie. Heidi gave it to her and watched as she laid it underneath Baby's raised bottom.

'Huh,' Heidi said. 'Baby's a boy.'

'Yup,' Meghan replied, lifting the ends of the grey fabric and frowning. 'Not sure how well this is gonna stay on..."

Heidi leaned forward. 'It's okay,' she said. 'His onesie thingy will hold it on once it's buttoned up.'

Together they managed to wrap the fabric around Baby's bottom in a way that roughly approximated a nappy. With his romper refastened, he looked weirdly lumpy, but they were reasonably confident it would do the job. Heidi looked at the dirty nappy, which was already starting to attract flies. 'What do we do with that?' she wondered aloud.

Meghan started to answer, but then the three pixies emerged from their hiding places. They converged on a spot on the ground, tearing away the grass, and then started to dig with their tiny claws. In an amazingly short amount of time, they had dug a round hole about the size and depth of a football. The children all watched, fascinated, as the pixies worked. Then, Twist disappeared into the grass and returned with a long stick. He ran up to the dirty nappy, brandishing the stick - which was at least twice as tall as he was - then used it to poke and push the nappy toward the hole.

'Oh, I get it!' Meghan cried. 'Bury it!'

She jumped up and, careful not to step on any of the pixies, picked up the nappy, and dropped it into the hole. Twist threw the stick aside and grinned up at her. Grinning back, Meghan dropped to her knees beside the hole and scooped the loose soil back in, covering the nappy. Flick and Whistle jumped onto the little mound and started trampling the soil down. Twist turned to the other children, who were all still watching, and began to gesture up at the sky, then pointed down at the mound and waved one hand in front of his nose, chattering like a bird.

'What's he saying?' Tim asked.

Sprickleback answered. 'He's telling you to bury your spoors if you don't want the dragons to smell it and come looking,' he replied.

Tim frowned. 'What's a spoors?'

'Spoor – shit, poop, crap,' Sprickleback said with an impatient wave of his arms. The children started giggling. 'What's funny? You don't want to attract predators, you bury your leavings!'

'Predators?' CeeCee exclaimed. 'You mean those lovely butterfly creatures?'

They'd caught sight of several of them as they'd walked: creatures with the bodies of lizards, about the size of house cats, but with huge butterfly wings of many different colours. They flew in long, swooping arcs over the grasslands, occasionally darting down to grab something, but they'd not come close enough to the group yet for them to get a good look. Still, they didn't look anything like the fierce, fiery dragons Heidi had seen in books and movies, and she'd started to relax a little, thinking the spriggan had been exaggerating.

'Oh sure, they're pretty,' Sprickleback muttered. 'And most of you are probably big enough that they wouldn't bother you. But me... Them...' He pointed at the pixies. 'And that...' He pointed at Baby. 'I bet they'd be happy to carry off.'

Heidi quickly gathered Baby into her arms and looked up at the sky nervously. The pixies, done with burying the nappy, all climbed up onto Meghan's shoulders, tangling themselves in her hair.

'Can we carry on now?' Sprickleback snapped.

Ricky spoke up. 'I'm hungry,' he complained. 'Like, really hungry. I don't think I can keep going much longer if I don't get some food.'

Several other children echoed their agreement. Sprickleback stamped his pointed foot in frustration. 'Well, there's no food here, unless you eat grass! If you're that hungry, might I suggest you get up off your arses and come along! The sooner we get under the hills, the sooner you might get some food!'

'There's food under the hills?' Ricky said, perking up.

'Perhaps,' Sprickleback replied cryptically. 'Now, can we go before I end up food for a dragon?'

One by one, the children got up and prepared to continue the walk. Heidi carried Baby. Amy toddled along after Monifa but quickly tired, so she picked her up. Sprickleback led the way, trotting along at a fast pace, barely visible in the long grass.

Tim looked up at Heidi and said, 'I thought dragons were great, big things that breathed fire.'

'Maybe there's different kinds of dragons,' Heidi replied. 'You know, like there's different kinds of dogs, big ones and small ones.'

'Oh,' Tim said, and glanced around as if he expected to see a big, scaly dragon sitting on a pile of gold and jewels. 'I wonder if we'll see a big one?'

Heidi thought about what Sprickleback had said about the ones they had seen. 'I hope not.'

They walked for another long stretch of time, their exposed shoulders and arms getting even redder under the hot sun. Once or twice, they were approached by small groups of the bright-winged dragons, who hovered a safe distance away in twos and threes, watching them. Once, one flew to the back of the line, where Tariq was now carrying Amy to give Monifa's arms a rest, and got almost close enough for him to touch.

'Pretty!' Amy cried, reaching out her hand toward it. Tariq snatched her hand back, and just in time, as the dragon's jaws snapped shut with an audible click where her fingers had been just a second before. Amy let out a little shriek.

'Get out of here,' Tariq cried, waving his arm at it. The dragon gave a low, burbling growl and swerved out of reach. It followed them for a while, then seemed to get bored and flew away.

The children walked a little closer together after that.

Eventually, Sprickleback led them down into a shallow valley between two large, gently sloping hills. For the first time since they'd been out of the forest, they saw something other than grass: a large, broad rock, set into the side of the hill. It had strange, swirling symbols painted on it in blue and green. Sprickleback squinted up at the stone and nodded. 'Here we are,' he said, and raised his knuckles to the stone. He tapped a quick little rhythm on the hard surface – *tap, ta-tap, tap, tap, ta-tap* – then took a step back and waited.

There was a short silence. Nothing happened.

'What was tha-' Monifa began, but her words were cut off by a low rumble, felt more in their feet than heard in their ears.

The ground before them seemed to crumble and fall away, leaving a large, roughly circular hole next to the stone. Rather than being a straight drop down, the hole went into the hill at an angle, like a tunnel, and to the children's amazement, there was light inside. Soft, warm yellow light that flickered like candles.

Sprickleback looked at them and grinned. 'Follow me,' he said. 'And mind your manners.'

CHAPTER 6

THE HOLLOW HILLS

Once they got past the fallen soil and rubble at the entrance, it turned into a uniform tunnel, the packed earth worn smooth by time and use. Sprickleback led the children along in single file, since the way wasn't wide enough for them to comfortably walk alongside each other.

The path sloped gently downward, taking them deeper beneath the hill. At regular intervals, wall sconces made of twisted roots held flickering ivory candles that dripped sweet-smelling wax. Heidi wondered briefly why a dead-end tunnel would be so well-used and kept so well lit, but she soon decided that it must be because it wasn't always a dead-end. After all, hadn't they just come through from outside? Though she didn't understand how it could be, her child's mind interpreted the collapsed hillside as a "door" and accepted it.

Further down, the tunnel began to widen, opening up in all directions until it was three or four times as wide. The further they went, the cooler the air became. The children's line shortened and bunched as they huddled into a nervous group. Only Sprickleback – and the pixies, still hidden in Meghan's hair – seemed at ease.

Eventually, the air started to grow warmer, and a faint breeze reached them, blowing in from ahead of the group. The breeze brought the scent of damp earth and growing things.

Sprickleback looked back at them, huddled together as they were, and seemed to soften a little. 'Not much further,' he said, 'and we can take a rest. Once we get out of the tunnel.'

Nobody answered him; the children were all frightened, exhausted and hungry. They trudged on obediently, heads lowered and hands clasped together. The babies grumbled softly in arms that carried them just a little too tightly. None of them really believed the unpleasant little creature.

But, true to his word, before much longer the tunnel opened up even more, becoming a large cavern complete with stalagmites and stalactites, dirty-looking mosses growing in the crevices of the walls, and the sound of dripping water. The candles in their sconces gave way to a soft, cool light that emanated from a point ahead of them, and the breeze grew stronger. At last, the children found themselves standing in the mouth of a cave, looking out over a lush green valley. The ground sloped gently away from the cave entrance, a grassy, rock-lined path heading down toward a tree-lined basin, where the branches swayed in the wind and let through the occasional glint of water. It was all bathed in the silvery glow of a full moon in a cloudless, star-littered purple sky.

'Children of Mil,' Sprickleback said grandly, with a sweep of his arm at the scene before them, 'Welcome to the Hollow Hill.'

The children gaped, and Sprickleback let them for a moment, preening his spines smugly while he perched on a low rock. Eventually he hopped off and beckoned to them. 'Come on,' he said. 'We'll rest at the lake's edge. I know a good spot.'

The children exchanged excited glances, thoughts of swimming and soaking their sore feet blooming in their tired minds. They followed quickly as the spriggan trotted off down the slope. But something made Heidi look back at the cave entrance.

She had expected to see it jutting out of the side of another hill, an underground tunnel from one place to another. But her eyes followed the shape of the earth the cavern mouth was set into, and she found her gaze going up, up, up, and over her head, tracking the rock wall as it disappeared into the purple haze that, now that she really looked at it, wasn't the sky after all.

Someone tugged on her hand and, tearing her eyes away, she followed her companions down the hill, weaving through them until she reached Sprickleback at the front. 'Sprickle,' she said. 'Are we ... are we still under the hill?'

Sprickleback chuckled. 'You're a sharp one,' he replied.

Heidi looked around them at the trees, the grass, the stars and moon in astonishment. 'How is this possible?' she exclaimed.

'How is anything possible?' Sprickleback replied with a shrug. 'It was dreamed of, and then it was.'

Heidi frowned. 'What does that mean? And what does "Children of Mil" mean?'

'Why don't you save your questions 'til we're sat down?' Sprickleback responded curtly. 'It's about to get steep, and I wouldn't want you to fall and break your neck because you were too busy chattering.'

Slightly affronted, Heidi fell silent.

He was right though – it did get steep. The group's progress slowed as they carefully picked their way down the side of the valley, around the rocks and the uppermost trees, until the ground started to level out and they found themselves heading into the woodland that carpeted the valley floor. The undergrowth became thicker, earth and roots coated with soft green moss, ferns and cat grass swaying as they brushed past, until the trees parted to reveal a large lake, the water a sparkling indigo under the night-time sky.

The children shrieked and whooped in excitement, rushing forward towards the water's edge. Sprickleback watched them go indulgently, then perched on a tree root that had raised itself up out of the earth near the shore. 'Wait!' he shouted, his voice surprisingly loud.

They froze, looking back at him over their shoulders as they hovered at the edge of the lake.

Sprickleback smirked and pointed up. 'You said you were hungry?'

Following the direction of his finger, the children looked up to see that the tree he was sitting beneath had large, low-hanging branches from which hung masses of silvery-green leaves, and dozens of smooth, shiny, circular red objects about the size of...

'Apples!' Tariq cried. 'There's apples!'

The lake was temporarily forgotten as the children flocked to the tree, jumping and grabbing for the shiny fruit, the bigger children snagging the branches and bending them down, plucking the apples, and handing them down to the smaller ones. Soon they each had an armful of apples, and sat themselves down on the ground around the tree to eat. Heidi and Meghan bit small pieces out of theirs to give to the pixies, who settled themselves in a soft patch of moss. A peaceful silence fell upon them as they ate. The apples were sweet, juicy and delicious.

Heidi turned to Meghan. 'I don't know if Baby's big enough to eat this,' she said, sitting the boy on her knee. He was reaching out for the shiny red fruit and gurgling.

Meghan shrugged. 'We don't have anything else to give him,' she replied. 'I guess just make sure it's soft and mushy.' She made a face. 'Chew it up for him like he's a baby bird. Ew.'

Heidi wrinkled her nose. 'Ugh.' Nonetheless, she chewed up a piece of apple and spat it back into her palm, then tried giving some of it to Baby. He looked dubious at first, but was soon sucking the white pulp off her fingers.

'Keep him sat up,' Meghan said helpfully. 'Or he might choke.'

Heidi made sure Baby was propped up straight against her arm. She didn't know what she'd do if he choked.

The peace was broken after a while by Ricky letting loose an enormous burp. The other children erupted into giggles as he grinned shamelessly.

'I don't even like apples,' he said, licking the juice from his fingers, 'But those were great!'

The others murmured their agreement, and Tyler gave a wide yawn. 'God, I can't remember when I walked this much,' he said. 'I'm knackered.'

A few children nodded. Sue said, 'Sprickle, can we stay here a while? Just for a bit, you know, so we can have a swim or a nap or something?'

Sprickleback gave her a thoughtful look. 'I wasn't planning on staying put for so long, but...' He smiled and bowed his head. 'Throw me another apple, child, and you have a deal.'

Sue beamed, jumping to her feet to pluck another apple from the tree. She tossed it gently to the spriggan, who caught it in both of his small hands and sat down to nibble at it. 'Do as you will, then,' he said. 'But don't swim out too far, because I'll not be able to help you if you get in trouble.'

Heidi thought that sounded rather ominous, but the others didn't seem to notice, as everyone except Tyler, Baby and herself immediately jumped up, and ran for the water's edge.

For a short time, it was peaceful. Beneath the sound of the playful shrieks and laughter of the children as they splashed around at the edge of the lake, birds were singing and the trees whispered softly to each other in the breeze. Heidi didn't know how that could be, if they were in a huge underground cavern, but it was. Baby gurgled happily, pulling her fingers into his mouth, searching for more apples. She snuck a look at Sprickleback, who was still crouched on the tree root, nibbling tiny bites out of the apple as he turned it slowly round in his hands, like a squirrel working on a nut. She felt tired – more tired than she could ever remember being – but somehow at peace. She leaned back against the trunk of the tree, watching the others playing in the water.

One by one, their damp clothes clinging to them, the children drifted back up to the tree and sat themselves down on the mossy ground, propping themselves up against rocks or tree roots, or making themselves comfortable on the mossy earth. Only Ricky stayed in the water, floating around on his back in little circles. Occasionally, he would squirt water up out of his mouth like a whale.

Baby made a sharp coughing noise, then started to grumble. Heidi looked down at him in alarm. 'What's the matter, little one?'

Meghan looked over. 'Maybe he needs burping,' she suggested, shuffling closer. 'Hold him so he's sitting up straight – hold his head up, like this – then rub his back.' She demonstrated, then let Heidi take over.

Heidi smiled. 'You've done this before?'

Meghan shrugged. 'I had a little brother ... but he died.'

Heidi's smile vanished. 'Oh no. What happened?'

Meghan gave another shrug, her eyes on Baby. 'Don't know. He just didn't wake up one day. Mom said sometimes that happens, when God needs new angels. I didn't think they had angels that small. He was even smaller than Baby when he died.'

Heidi searched for something to say. 'Your mum sounds nice,' she said at last.

Meghan gave a deep sigh. 'She is ... but she drinks too much,' she replied. 'I miss her though. I wish I was home.'

'Me too,' Heidi agreed, thinking of her grandmother's cosy little home, and the dormitory at school. Either one would be fine right about now, instead of this weird place where nothing made sense. She missed it, even the rubbish bits like having to do P.E., and the thin look her grandmother would get in her face when Heidi had done something wrong. Thinking about it made it seem far away and unreal, like her old life was the dream and this was reality and always had been.

Baby gave a loud burp, then without warning ejected a long line of pale vomit over Heidi's hand and down the front of his romper. Heidi gave a yell of surprise and disgust, struggling not to drop him.

Meghan wrinkled her nose. 'Uh oh, grumpy tummy,' she said. 'Probably the apple. Here...' She held out her hands for him. 'I'll see if I can clean him up a bit.'

Heidi handed him over happily and wiped her hand in the grass. Meghan lifted Baby up to her shoulder and trotted down to the lake with him. Heidi watched as she squatted down and lowered Baby down between her knees until his feet were in the water. He squealed and kicked, splashing water everywhere, and Meghan laughed.

Heidi supposed she should go down to join them so she could wash her hands, but she suddenly felt very tired. Looking around, she could see that nearly all the others had dozed off under the tree. Even Ricky was floating in place on the water. Had he fallen asleep out there?

'Ricky,' she muttered, trying to shout, but she couldn't quite get any power behind her voice. 'Ricky.' Her eyelids drooped. She thought she could hear singing, somewhere far away. It was beautiful, lulling her gently to sleep. She fought against it, blinking her eyes, trying to focus.

Ricky was floating on his back, his eyes closed, his t-shirt sticking to the gentle curve of his belly. The water around him was clear and calm, just a few shadows moving across it. Or were they under it? Heidi struggled to sit up. From her slightly elevated position under the tree, she thought she could see something swimming close beneath Ricky. A fish? If it was, it was a really big fish. Or...

Just behind Ricky, the water rippled gently as something broke the surface. A head, with long, green hair floating around it, slowly emerged. The face, female and fine-boned with skin that seemed to have a silver shimmer, fixed pale eyes on the dozing boy. She smiled, her colourless lips parting to reveal sharp teeth. Two hands rose from the water to reach out for him, fingers splaying to reveal webbed skin between them, and sharp, claw-like nails.

Panic shot through Heidi, waking her in a rush. She sat up and yelled: 'RICKY!'

There was a loud splash and a scream, but not from Ricky. Heidi jerked her head around to see Meghan fall forward into the water, struggling to hold onto something. She screamed again: *'HELP ME! IT'S GOT BABY!'*

The other children were only starting to stir as Heidi leaped to her feet and raced down to the water's edge as fast as she could. She still felt very far away when Meghan was dragged forward again. This time she got up with empty hands. *'Baby!'* she shrieked, and lunged forward into the water. A large silvery tail flicked up in front of her, splashed once, and was gone.

Heidi reached Meghan's side a moment later. She was already waist-deep in the lake. The distraught girl grabbed her arm. 'It took Baby!' she sobbed. 'Help me, we have to...'

The water next to them erupted with a sound like a gunshot as another green-haired figure reared up, grabbing at Meghan with slender but muscular arms. Heidi grabbed Meghan's shoulders and yanked her back, sending both of them tumbling backward and beneath the water. For a moment, the world was obscured by the blue-green waters. Then Heidi got a brief but clear look at the thing that was attacking them. A woman with the tail of a fish, silvery grey skin, sharp quills along her spine and shoulder blades, webbed hands, gills, and pale, cloudy eyes.

That's a mermaid, she thought in disbelief. *That's an actual, real-life mermaid.*

The creature reached out and curled her fingers around Meghan's ankle. Heidi felt her friend being pulled from her grasp and she tightened her grip, praying she could hold on. Her feet scrabbled for purchase as they were both pulled deeper into the lake.

I'm going to get killed by a mermaid, she thought as her lungs started to burn from lack of air. *I thought they were supposed to be sweet.*

'*They'll sweetly kill you if you get too close,*' a voice in her head replied - the voice of a little boy, from a movie about pirates and children and fairytale creatures. With colourful flowers and pink clouds, it was *nothing* like this horrible place!

She heard more splashing from behind and above her. The mermaid released Meghan's ankle and retreated into the depths with a silent snarl. Then, hands were grabbing them both and pulling them up. Heidi's head broke the surface and she gasped in a breath. Next to her, Meghan was coughing and struggling. 'Let me go,' she was shouting. 'I have to get Baby!'

Baby...

Ricky!

Heidi grabbed the nearest person, who happened to be Tyler. 'Where's Ricky?' she cried.

Tyler looked at her blankly. She looked around to where Ricky had been floating. All she could see was a large circular set of ripples, slowly spreading and disappearing.

'No,' she moaned, then shouted, '*RICKY!*'

There was no answer.

Tyler, Tariq, and Monifa dragged Heidi and Meghan out of the water, back toward the apple tree, where Sprickleback was hopping from one foot to another, yellow eyes flashing angrily.

'I told you!' he was shouting in his scratchy voice. 'I told you not to swim out far! Stupid, fat little boy, look what happened!'

Anger flared in Heidi's chest. She shook Tyler off her and strode forward. 'Did you know they were in there?' she demanded.

Sprickleback stopped hopping and gave her a baleful look. 'I expected something was in there,' he replied. 'And I warned you. Didn't I warn you? And now we're a child down.'

'We're down two!' Heidi retorted. 'Baby's gone too!'

Sprickleback paused. 'The baby's gone? Oak and ash, you need to be more careful!'

'You're our guide!' Heidi yelled.

He yelled right back: 'I warned you!'

Meghan was sobbing, repeating 'Baby, Baby' over and over as Monifa and Tariq tried to stop her from rushing back into the water. Eventually, she collapsed to the ground and let them hold her. Tyler was standing to one side, looking dazed. Amy huddled next to Sue, who was doing her best to comfort her. CeeCee and Tim were still sitting beneath the tree, watching Heidi and Sprickleback with wide, frightened eyes.

Heidi glared at the spriggan. 'You should have told us what was in there.'

Sprickleback met her gaze. 'I didn't know it would be merfolk. It could have been a lot of things. Could have been a kelpie. Could have been selkies. Could have been darrigs.' At this last one he gave a shudder and looked around, up and down the shoreline. 'Still could be, with all this noise you're making, so I think it's time we moved on. If that's alright with you?'

Heidi opened her mouth to reply, but she didn't know what to say. They needed a guide – they had no idea where they were going – and he had warned them. They just hadn't listened. Abruptly, her anger drained away, replaced with a grief and exhaustion that felt too big for her small frame.

She was tired. She was so tired.

Eventually she nodded. 'Just... Next time tell us if something might come and get us.'

Sprickleback gave a humourless laugh. 'I'd be saying it every second, lassie. There's always something that might come and get you. Your kind are rare in these parts. If it doesn't want to eat you, then it'll want you for...' He trailed off with a shake of his head and hopped off the tree root. 'Come on.'

Heidi tried to grab him, but he dodged to one side. 'For what?' she asked. 'What do you mean?'

But Sprickleback wouldn't say any more. 'Come *on*,' he repeated forcefully, his spines bristling like the fur of a cornered cat. 'We need to get going.' Saying nothing more, he started trotting off along the shoreline.

With many fearful glances at the lake, the children trailed after him, fearing to be left behind. Heidi went to Meghan's side and helped her to her feet. 'Come on, Meghan.'

Meghan looked up at her, her dark eyes swimming with tears. 'Baby,' she sobbed. 'We lost Baby.'

'I know,' Heidi replied. 'We lost Ricky too.' Then, abruptly, her weariness lifted, and she burst into frightened tears.

Interview No. 408

Investigating Officer (IO):
This is the interview with Ms Elaine Lowry, folklorist and author of several books on Irish, Scottish, Welsh, and English folklore, being conducted in the London office.
Ms Lowry was contacted in response to several suggestions from members of the public of spiritualist and pagan faiths, who all suggested that "The Event" might be the work of otherworldly spirits, also known as faeries.

Lowry:
You're still struggling with that, aren't you?

IO:
A little less every day, but you must admit it's a bizarre theory.

Lowry:
I completely agree. Even I'm used to thinking of faeries as myths, allegories for events of the time. Not literal beings.

IO:

Precisely.
(Sound of shuffling papers)
Ms Lowry, you've written several books on the subject of faeries,
is that correct?

Lowry:

Three that specifically deal with faeries, yes. One on how they
emerged from Celtic myth, one collecting and analysing the
traditional faery tales of the British Isles, and one children's book
– essentially the faery tales without the analysis – and without
the bloodshed.

IO:

Bloodshed?

Lowry:

The original forms of folk tales are often quite grim. They
were designed to teach moral lessons or dissuade dangerous
or undesirable behaviour, after all. Take "The Little
Mermaid".
In the original tale, she suffers agony whenever she walks on her
human feet, has her tongue cut out so she cannot speak, and at
the end, effectively kills herself because she cannot win her love's
heart. All to warn young girls against promiscuous behaviour
and disobeying their parents.

IO:

I see. And you've not written any books on the idea of faeries
being real?

Lowry:

I never thought of them as real. Even now, I'm still doubtful.

IO:

Do any of your books deal with the habit of faeries stealing
children away?

Lowry:

Oh yes. That's quite a common trope.

IO:

Can you tell us a little about that?

Lowry:

There are several reasons given in folklore as to why the faeries
do it. One is that they want their children to be nursed by
human mothers, so they switch them with mortal children, who
they steal away.
But that wouldn't work in this case, as the children were stolen
and their beds left empty. They also simply enjoy stealing away
the most beautiful children – and adults, that occurs in many
other stories. But that doesn't quite fit either, because the
children who vanished were not just the most beautiful – there
was no selection at all; they were all taken.

IO:

You've been giving this some thought, I take it?

Lowry:

When I received the phone call asking me to come in, they told
me a little about why, of course I gave it thought.

IO:

Of course. Please go on.

Lowry:

Some stories claim they take the children out of sheer whimsy or
malice, which is a possibility in this case but doesn't give you

much to work with. Some say it's as a result of a bargain or pact made with the parents.

IO:
What kind of pact?

Lowry:
Oh, you know, as a penalty for breaking rules or for breaking the heart of a faery bride, in exchange for riches or success, or sometimes as a ransom to keep the rest of the family safe or to punish a transgression. But this last one is the one I think you should consider most carefully.

IO:
What's that?

Lowry:
A tithe.

IO:
A tithe?

Lowry:
A tithe, for example in the case of a church tithe, is when followers give a sum of their goods or wealth as an offering. Alternatively, it can be demanded by a ruling power as payment for their protection or for living on their land, like a tax. The word "tithe" comes from the Old English word for tenth and, traditionally, a tithe amounts to one tenth of a person's wealth. But there are plenty of stories – and not just faery stories, either – where the tithe demanded is children, or virginal maidens, or strong youths.

IO:

I see.

Lowry:

The only problem is, the stories that tell of tithes are rather late in the folklore, and usually refer to it being a tithe the faeries have to pay to Hell. This paints the faeries as somehow demonic or in league with the Devil – which points to it being a Church rewrite of older beliefs, where the faeries are demonised in order to encourage their followers to turn to Christianity instead.

So either the tithe stories were fabricated for this purpose, or twisted and the word "tithe" was simply not used in earlier tales. However, it is a very popular concept in faery lore, so I'm inclined to believe it was there originally in some form, with the part about it being a tithe to Hell added later.

IO:

So if the tithe is not to be paid to Hell, what would it be for? Why would they steal away children en masse?

Lowry:

I'd go back to thinking of it as a sort of tax. A payment made to the faeries for some agreement or transgression.

IO:

What on Earth kind of agreement could have been made that would cost the entire world's children?

Lowry:

Ah, now, to answer that question we have to go back to the *really* old tales. And that is where it gets really interesting.

Chapter 7

Misgivings and Meetings

I t was dark, and she was cold; drifting.

She stretched out with her arms and legs, trying to find something solid to orient herself. There was nothing. She blinked furiously, trying to clear the darkness from her eyes, and slowly, colour came back into the world.

Blues and greens and greys and murky browns. Blurred and indistinct. Sound filtered in now as well, all muffled and faraway, as if she was listening through thick fabric.

Or water.

With that realisation came another: she couldn't breathe. She kicked out desperately, trying to propel herself upwards, to the surface. It was close; she could see ripples and sunlight. Her lungs burned. Her limbs felt like lead.

She glanced down and saw lithe humanoid shapes circling below, large, wide-finned tails flicking lazily as they drifted, waiting. When she lost consciousness she would sink, right into their eager arms...

Her head broke the surface and she gulped down air greedily. The sunlight blazed into her eyes, dazzling her, and she threw up her arms to shield them. Her feet touched land; she was standing, waist-deep, in the water. Blinking water and hazy afterimages out of her eyes, she looked around. Not far away, on the shore, Meghan was holding Baby upright in the water, cleaning the vomit from his romper. They were both laughing, Baby kicking at the water with his tiny feet and giggling at the resulting splashes.

Relief flooded through her at the sight of them, and she smiled. Then her smile faded, relief replaced by panic, as she saw those lithe shapes again, just under the water. They were a few feet from Meghan and moving fast, arms outstretched.

She tried to shout a warning, but when she opened her mouth nothing but water came out. She tried to run to them, but the water felt thick and syrupy, holding her back. She watched as the first pair of grey, clawed hands shot out of the water and pulled Baby under. She saw Meghan's eyes widen, her mouth falling open in shock. She saw the second pair of grey hands break the surface and seize her forearms, dragging her forward. She heard her scream.

She could see all of them now, beneath the apple tree. They were all asleep, including herself. Even the pixies. Only Sprickleback was awake, and he watched them with unblinking, emotionless yellow eyes. From the trees behind them, pale spider-things dropped silently down and began to slither toward them, bright eyes gleaming.

'*Wake up!*' she tried to scream, but her voice drowned in the water that spilled from her lips. Helpless, she watched as Meghan was dragged beneath the surface, saw the inky shapes darting away beneath the water, their prey clutched tightly to them. She watched Meghan's legs kick uselessly. She tried to dive after them, but was stopped as another shape rose before her. It shot up from the depths with deadly speed, breaking the surface with a huge splash. Water struck her face, momentarily blinding her. She rubbed at her eyes, cringing away from the cold, grey hands she expected to seize hold of her any second.

When her vision cleared, she was looking at the grey, bloated corpse of Ricky. He rolled in the water and turned a face to her that had no eyes and a gaping, loose-jawed mouth.

'*Why?*' he rasped in a watery burble, from slack lips that did not move.

She screamed.

Heidi woke up with a start, shooting upright, and barely containing the scream that was trying to burst from her throat. She looked around wildly, half expecting to see Ricky's grey, dead face in the shadows.

Nothing, except the other children asleep nearby, and Sprickleback watching them from atop a nearby rock. He cocked his head at her inquiringly, but she shook her head and lay back down.

They had fled the lake and made their way through the valley, following a faint grassy path which snaked through the trees. When the rain started to fall they had pressed on at first, but it soon became a downpour, forcing them to retreat into the thicker woodland on the valley slopes. They had struggled on until they found a spot that was relatively sheltered by the branches above them. At Sprickleback's suggestion, they settled down to wait out the rain (rain that was falling *inside a cave - from a sky that has stars and a moon - inside a cave*, Heidi's mind kept shrieking incredulously). One by one, they had fallen asleep. Unlike the calm, restful dozing on the lake's edge, this sleep came from exhaustion, lulled by the sound of the rain. Nearly every one of the remaining children was twitching and murmuring unhappily as they slept.

The remaining children... Heidi winced. They had lost four of their number so far. Yuen, Baby, Ricky, and the French girl whose name she couldn't quite remember... Her mind strove for it, grasping for it, sensing it just out of reach. It felt vitally important somehow that she remember the girl's name. Isobel? Marie? Madeline? Suzie? Suzie... That was almost right...

She saw again how the blonde girl had been dragged along the ground by the spider-thing that had caught her, saw the grooves her fingers had made in the earth. She saw Yuen struggling with the creature's snake-like body poised above him, held up by thin, many-jointed legs, as the white hair had wrapped itself around him. She heard the muffled *cracks* of their bones breaking. She saw Ricky floating in the lake, and the ripples that had spread out from the spot where he had been. She saw Baby laughing in Meghan's arms as she lowered his tiny feet into the water.

She saw Baby sucking the apple from her fingers.

She saw Baby looking up at her as she lifted him from the icy grass, immediate trust in his blue eyes.

Stifling a groan, Heidi buried her face in her hands and tried not to cry.

I should have been looking after him, she thought miserably. *I'm the oldest. I'm in charge. I shouldn't have given him to Meghan.*

She glanced over at Meghan, who was whimpering softly as she slept. Already thin, her face now looked sallow and drawn. She hadn't said a word since they'd fled the lake. She acted so grown-up, like Heidi, but she was nearly half Heidi's age.

I should have been the one taking care of the baby. I'm the oldest. I'm responsible. It's my fault.

Heidi closed her eyes and listened to the sound of the rain, hoping she would fall back asleep. It sounded lighter now. Sprickleback would want to move on soon. Sprickleback. With his cold yellow eyes and vague warnings, his reaction to losing two of them to the mermaids had been more annoyance than dismay. He had huffed and sulked all the way from the lake, barking curt orders at them, which they had obeyed out of fear.

I told you, he'd said. *Look what happened. Didn't I warn you?*

No attempt to help them, to get them back. No attempt to comfort the others. Just stamping his feet and yelling.

Maybe she was being too hard on him. He was very small, after all. Smaller even than Baby.

But he was their guide. He was supposed to keep them away from danger. Wasn't he? She groaned quietly and turned her face against the mossy ground. She didn't know. She didn't know what to think, what was best. *It's not fair*, she thought. *I'm just a little girl.*

The spriggan's nasally voice cut into her confused thoughts. 'You. Heidi-girl.'

She lifted her head to look at him. 'Yes?'

'I'm going to look around. Keep watch.' He hopped off of his perch, his clawed feet rasping against the stone.

'Look around for what?' Heidi asked, sitting up. 'And it's just "Heidi", by the way.'

He shrugged off her remark. 'I think we're close. I want to make sure we're going the right way.'

She watched as he disappeared into the trees, then looked around at the others. To her surprise, she saw that CeeCee was watching her, her blue eyes clouded with concern. She tried to smile reassuringly.

'You don't trust him, do you?' CeeCee said softly.

Heidi glanced back to make sure the spriggan was gone, then shuffled closer to CeeCee.

'No,' she whispered. 'He's so...' She searched for the word, but couldn't quite find it. 'Not nice,' she finished eventually.

CeeCee nodded. 'He took my name,' she said sadly. 'I didn't think names were things you could take.' After a pause, she said, 'The stories say that faeries take their agreements very seriously, though, so I think we can trust him to do what he said he'd do. Especially since he got my name in return.'

'I'm sorry he took your name,' Heidi replied.

CeeCee shrugged. 'It's just a name. My uncle Frank changed his name and he's auntie Francesca now. Fran for short.' She gave a heavy sigh. 'I wonder if I'll ever see her again. She's nice. She always brings me presents when she visits, even though Dad calls her rude names when she's gone.'

'I'm sure you will,' Heidi assured her. Something she'd said was bothering her, though. She sat quietly for a moment, thinking. 'What did Spricklcback say he'd do?' she said at last.

CeeCee, who appeared to be drifting back to sleep, blinked and looked up. 'Hm?'

'What did he say he'd do when he took your name?'

CeeCee thought. 'I don't really remember,' she replied.

'Nor do I,' Heidi said. 'I asked him to be our guide, and he asked what he'd get for it, and then...'

'Then he started asking names,' CeeCee continued. 'Then he took mine and I got upset, and when I was feeling better he just said "let's go" or something like that.'

'So he didn't actually say that he would do anything,' Heidi said slowly. She looked at CeeCee, who was sitting up now, and frowning. 'Is ... is that bad? It is, isn't it?'

CeeCee took a deep breath. Before she could reply, however, the spriggan suddenly bounded back through the trees. 'Wake up!' he shouted, clapping his small hands together. 'I found it! I found it!'

The children stirred and slowly sat up. Heidi got to her feet. 'What did you find?' she asked.

'The village!' Sprickleback replied triumphantly. 'It's been a long time, but I knew I hadn't forgotten the way! Come along, sweetlings, let's go!'

'You didn't say you were taking us to a village,' Heidi said. 'You said you were taking us to a city.'

He looked at her like she was stupid. 'The village is on the way to the city,' he replied, then clapped his hands again. 'Come along, I said! It isn't far!'

Hearing them mention a village, the children perked up, thinking of houses with roofs, plates of food, and beds to sleep in. Wiping the sleep from their eyes and picking leaves from their hair, they got to their feet, ready to go on.

Heidi shot a glance at CeeCee, who shrugged and got to her feet. 'What choice do we have?' she said quietly.

Heidi shook her head and fell in line with the others as the spriggan led them out of the trees and back to the path.

They were only walking for a short time before the first lights became visible ahead of them, shining warm and yellow in the twilight. As they drew closer, the lights spread out until they were scattered throughout the woodland ahead; most at ground level, but some much higher up in the trees. Eventually, they saw what appeared to be a tall, thick hedge of brambles, weaving in and out of the trees and twisting around the trunks. The brambles were huge; they had stems as thick as a grown man's arm, and thorns like daggers.

The path they were following widened and ran up to a wooden gate set into this hedge, currently standing open. In front of it was a strange humanoid creature, standing to attention and holding a spear in one hand. He stood bare-chested, with what appeared to be furry trousers over his long legs, and had large horns curling back behind large, deer-like ears. His skin was a dusky bronze with swirling patterns drawn on it in what looked like blue paint, and long, thick hair fell in heavy locks around his shoulders. As they got closer, the children could see that the fur on his legs was not clothing; it grew, thick and dark, from just below his navel. Below his knees, his legs bent backwards in an odd fashion, and peeking out from the fur at his ankles they saw not feet, but hooves.

The children fell silent as they looked at this fierce-looking creature, and he looked back at them with large black eyes. His face was narrow and flat, giving him an oddly horse-like appearance, his nose wide at the bridge, but blunt, adding to the flatness. He looked at them all calmly, then his gaze fell on Sprickleback and he frowned.

'I thought we'd made it clear that you are not welcome here, spriggan,' he said in a deep, velvety voice.

Sprickleback blinked, then cringed. 'I cry your pardon for past deeds,' he said fawningly. 'I just need to pass through. Normally I would go around, but...'

'There will be no pardon,' the guard replied. 'Our Lord has made that clear. Your kind are no longer welcome under the hill.'

Heidi watched this exchange anxiously. When Sprickleback faltered, she stepped forward. 'Um, excuse me?'

The guard turned to look at her and smiled. Still addressing Sprickleback, he said, 'Why have you brought these Children of Mil to us?'

'I was just getting to that...' Sprickleback started, but Heidi interrupted him.

'He's our guide,' she said. 'We're kind of lost.'

'That I can see,' the guard chuckled. 'But where are you going with a spriggan as a guide?'

'He said he's taking us to a city,' Heidi replied. 'But it's been a very long walk and we don't have any food or drink. And it's been very dangerous so far. We'd really like to come in and rest for a bit.'

Sprickleback was glowering at her, but stopped when he saw the thoughtful expression on the guard's face. He stepped forward, smiling obsequiously. 'This one speaks truly, friend. I found them on the hills, and took it upon myself to guide them to safety.'

'Out of the goodness of your heart, I am sure,' the guard said to Sprickleback. 'And I am not your friend, spriggan.' Looking back to Heidi, he said, 'We have not seen Children of Mil under the hill for a very long time. I think my Lord would be interested to meet you. And he would be disappointed if we were not hospitable. Come in.' He pointed his spear at

Sprickleback, who flinched away. 'But keep that one close with you.'

'Thank you,' Heidi replied. 'We will.'

For just a moment, the guard's face contorted into a snarl. Startled, Heidi took a step back. Then he seemed to recover himself, and the snarl disappeared. He eyed her carefully, then gave a soft shake of his head, making his locks swing. Small beads and copper rings glinted in the torchlight. 'Follow me,' he said.

As they started walking, Sprickleback trotted up alongside Heidi. 'Quick thinking,' he said approvingly.

Heidi looked down at him and frowned. 'It was just the truth.'

Sprickleback smiled. 'Of course, of course!'

The group followed the guard through the gate into the small, bustling village. It was like no village they had ever seen before. Circular, wooden houses were built around the trunks of large trees, which emerged from their thatched roofs like chimneys. They had no doors, the entrances instead covered with curtains of various colours and patterns. There were no windows. Spiralling up the trunks of the trees were staircases leading to platforms built into the branches. All around them, more of these horned humanoids wandered, going about their tasks in a leisurely, relaxed manner. They walked the streets – which seemed to be formed only where the trees left room for them – in pairs, ducked in and out of the houses with baskets and buckets, and gathered in small groups on the platforms and on grassy areas. All of them had the same slightly luminous bronze skin, flat faces, and black eyes. Some of them were dark-haired (and furred), and others had hair and fur with a deep red tint. Some wore their hair in long locks or plaits, with beads, feathers and pieces of metal in them as decorations. Most were nude, men and women alike, occasionally wearing colourful shawls or scraps of cloth, and many of them had green or blue patterns drawn on their torsos and faces with some kind of paint, like the guard at the gate. Every one of them stopped to look at the children as they passed by.

The guard led them to a building that was larger than the others and ushered them in through the wide doorway. The interior was open, although somewhat dark, and surprisingly airy, with several doorways to the outside letting in the breeze, and cushions and blankets scattered around.

'This is our meeting area,' he said. 'Please make yourselves comfortable while you wait.' Then he looked at Sprickleback. 'You,' he said sternly. 'Come with me.'

Sprickleback shrunk back. 'I should stay with the children,' he protested.

With surprising speed, the guard lunged forward and grabbed the spriggan by his tail, lifting him up with a grimace of distaste. 'No,' he replied. 'You should come with me.'

Sprickleback squawked in dismay. 'I'll walk, I'll walk!' he cried as he was carried outside.

The children exchanged worried glances. 'What do we do now?' Sue said quietly.

They looked to Heidi, waiting for an answer. She hated it. 'What are you all looking at me for?' she blurted, frustrated. 'I don't know!'

Several of them flinched or looked away, and Heidi instantly regretted her outburst. She was the oldest; of course they looked to her. She had to be responsible. Softening her tone, she said,

'Why don't we wait and see what this "Lord" says? They seem... Well, they're a bit scary, but they let us in, and it seems nice here, and they're the first grown-ups we've seen.' She paused. 'I mean, Sprickleback's probably a grown-up, but...'

'He doesn't act like it,' Tim said morosely. Some of them giggled. He smiled and carried on. 'He's bossy, but he's more like the big kid who orders you around all the time.'

'I don't like him,' Monifa chimed in. 'I know we all wanted

to come with him, but that was only because there was no one else around to help us, you know?'

Several voices chimed in their agreement. Heidi felt as if a weight had lessened on her shoulders. 'I thought I was the only one who didn't like him!' she exclaimed, dropping down into a nearby nest of cushions.

The other children settled down around her. 'Nah, he sucks,' Tariq said, wrinkling his nose and puffing out his cheeks in imitation of the spriggan. The smaller children laughed. 'He's a bully.'

'Maybe someone else will help us?' Tim suggested. 'One of these ... er...'

'They're fauns,' CeeCee said, then when everyone turned to look at her, she blushed and looked away. 'I think.'

'How do you know?' Monifa asked.

CeeCee shrugged. 'I'm from Ireland,' she replied. 'My mam is always telling me faery stories. She called them *puca*, though. Fauns are from Greece ... the stories, I mean...' Squirming under the attention of the others, she added quietly, 'They look like fauns, is all I mean.'

Heidi smiled at her. 'Well maybe we can ask them and find out who was right,' she said. CeeCee smiled.

Sue spoke up. 'Um, maybe you can ask right now,' she said, and pointed at the doorway.

They looked round to see several of the creatures crowded into the doorway, staring in at them with wide eyes. There were more of them squeezed together at each door, looking in. All of them had the same expression of silent wonder.

The children moved closer together, staring back nervously. Sue put her arms around Amy protectively. 'What do they want?' she whispered to Heidi.

Heidi had no answer.

CHAPTER 8

THE TITHE

Huddled close together on the dry, earthen floor, the children watched as the crowds of fauns looked in at them from the doorways. For a long time, no one moved on either side. Then, in one of the doorways there was a gentle scuffle, and a female faun was pushed into the hall. She was wearing her hair tied back with a piece of bright, red fabric, and a woven shawl of red and yellow wool covered her torso. She looked back at her companions with uncertainty, then started to walk over slowly, her hooves making muted thuds on the ground. As she grew near, the children shrank away. She paused, cocked her head thoughtfully, then squatted down until her rear was resting on her hind legs.

'You don't have to be afraid,' she said in a low murmur. 'No one here will harm you. We just haven't seen your kind for a long time.'

The children exchanged glances, then looked at Heidi. She swallowed nervously and sat upright. 'We've never seen anything like you before,' she said. 'Except in cartoons and movies.'

The faun cocked her head again. 'What are these things?'

'Err ... like pictures,' Heidi replied. 'What are you?'

'We are Firobolga,' the faun stated. 'I am called Gilla. What do they call you?'

'Heidi.'

Gilla smiled. 'It is an honour to meet you, Heidi,' she said. 'And your kin.'

She reached out with one hand, palm held forward. Heidi hesitated, then lifted her hand in the same way. Gilla leaned forward until their palms touched, then intertwined her fingers with the girl's. The faun's hand was soft and warm. They stayed that way for a moment, then Gilla opened her fingers and released Heidi's hand, dropping her own back to her knee.

The other fauns in the doorways murmured approvingly. Heidi dropped her hand and glanced around.

'The guard told us to wait,' she said. 'What are we waiting for?'

'For the Lord of the Green,' Gilla replied. 'He will want to see you.' She noticed Heidi's alarmed expression and added, 'Don't worry. He is wise and kind. He will be able to help you find whatever it is that you came here for.' She paused, her black eyes flickering to the other children behind her. 'Do you know,' she said softly, 'that one of your friends is crawling with pixies?'

Heidi looked back to see the three pixies all peering out of Meghan's hair. She nodded. 'They're friendly,' she said. 'I think.'

Gilla gave a slow shrug. 'If you say so. They are pests here. They nibble our food, tangle our fur, and put holes in our sheets.'

One of the pixies bared its teeth at Gilla and growled. She ignored it.

'Why did the guard take away our ... our guide?' Heidi asked her. 'Is he a pest too?'

'Your guide?' Gilla shook her head. 'I didn't see him.'

'He's a little, brown, spiky thing with yellow eyes,' Heidi said.

Gilla frowned. 'A spriggan,' she said grimly. 'Those things

are worse than pests. They steal and sabotage to get what they want. At least the pixies only take what they need. Spriggans are greedy and sly and take as much as they can get. And they will always try to get more. They are not tolerated here.'

'The guard said they did something and now they're not welcome,' Heidi said. 'What did they do?'

Gilla sighed. 'It is not my story to tell, little one,' she replied. 'If you stay a while, perhaps you will hear it.'

From the middle of the group, Amy spoke up hesitantly. 'I like stories.'

Gilla laughed, and some of the other children giggled quietly with her. 'Then you will like it here, Child of Mil,' she said, raising her voice a little. 'Stories are our tradition and our trade. We live by them.'

Amy peeked out from behind Sue, smiling. Gilla gave a gasp. 'Oh, she is so small! How did you poor creatures come to be here?'

Heidi opened her mouth to reply, but at that moment a commotion started at one of the doors. The fauns began to mutter and move away, stepping back outside of the hall. They fell to either side, leaving a gap to let someone through.

Gilla looked that way and smiled. 'Our Lord is here,' she said. 'Be polite, and do not fear him.' Then she hopped up and hurried away back to her companions in the opposite doorway. A dark shadow fell across the empty doorway, and all the fauns still visible dropped to one knee, bowing their heads.

The figure that walked in looked like a faun, except it was easily twice their height. It entered stooped almost double, and moved stiffly toward the centre of the hall, where the roof was higher. Even then it had to keep its head lowered. It had the same huge, curling horns as the other fauns, deer-like ears and black almond eyes peering from the same flat face, and legs ending in blunt hooves. But it had no fur or hair; its legs were covered in a thick growth of what appeared to be tree bark. Its arms and torso, while still the same glowing bronze, had a cracked, oak-like texture, and here and there on its body grew patches of fungus and moss. The thick mane that tumbled over its shoulders was made up of tendrils of vines and leaves, which mingled with the leaves that seemed to be growing from its shoulders, like a mantle, and from its face, like a beard. Following it were four fauns with spears, including the guard from the gate, who was carrying a wicker cage in his free hand. Inside it was Sprickle-back, looking as though he couldn't decide if he was angry or afraid.

When the figure reached the centre of the hall, it turned to look at the children. They stared back in a mixture of amazement and terror. Heidi caught Gilla waving at her from the corner of her eye. She was gesturing at herself as she knelt, then back at them. *What did she...? – oh! They should kneel!* Heidi elbowed Tim who was next to her, and he gave a quiet squeak of surprise. She got to her feet, then went to one knee, like the fauns. After a moment's hesitation, Tim did the same, and then one by one, so did the others.

The creature before them smiled, and then a voice like the creak of trees in a high wind came from his mouth. 'You do me an honour, Children of Mil. Be at ease, all of you.'

The fauns in the doorways got to their feet and began to file in, sitting themselves in the same curious squat that Gilla had taken around the edges of the hall. The giant squatted down too, bending its massive legs and leaning against the wide tree trunk rising through the centre of the building. Now that it was able to lift its head, they could see its face clearly, and Heidi had an immediate sense that she'd seen it somewhere before. It was a wide, flat male face, with leaves forming a goatee-like beard, thick sideburns and a pair of eyebrows that all flowed into the greenery of his hair. His black eyes crinkled at the corners in a way that reminded her of her grandfather.

The Lord of the Green waited until the children had made

themselves comfortable again before he spoke. 'It has been a long time, indeed, since we were visited by the Children of Mil,' he rumbled, 'and never in such numbers. Nine of you are here today, and the imp tells me that there were more of you, lost on the way.'

'I'm not an imp!' Sprickleback squawked.

The guard holding his cage gave it a sharp shake. 'Quiet, beast,' he hissed.

The Lord of the Green ignored the interruption. 'I have many questions,' he continued. 'But I am sure you have questions of your own. It is our way to exchange questions. If I ask one, you may ask one in return, and so on. Is this acceptable to you?'

The children looked to Heidi, who got to her feet and nodded. 'Yes, sir.'

He paused briefly, then said, 'What brought you from your world to ours?'

Heidi sighed. 'We don't really know,' she replied. 'Shadowy … things woke us up in our beds and told us to follow them, and then … then it all got confused, and we woke up in a field where it was really cold and icy, and things like monsters came out of the mist to get us, so we ran away.' She paused. 'I know it's not a very good answer. I'm sorry.'

'It is answer enough,' The Lord of the Green said. 'It is as I suspected. It is the Tithe.'

A quiet murmur ran around the room at this, and then faded away. Heidi looked around to see that all eyes were on her.

'May I ask my question now?' she asked.

The Lord of the Green bowed his head to her and gestured with one huge, long-fingered hand. 'Of course.'

'What is the Tithe? Sprickleback mentioned it but he never told us what it was.'

The Lord of the Green lifted his head, looking up at the roof briefly. 'That is an old story from the earliest days of this world,' he replied slowly. 'It is a story that belongs to all of Faerie, so as leader here, it is my place to tell it.'

There was another murmur, and Heidi saw the fauns' attention shift to him, smiles and looks of eager anticipation on their faces.

'The Tithe,' the Lord of the Green began, 'Was put in place when the Tuatha, those who "rule" Faerie, first came to this world. They fled here from your world after the Sons of Mil, your people, drove them away. Long ago, your world belonged to the Tuatha, and to us, the Firobolga, and to the Formori, who if you are lucky, you will never meet. The Tuatha fought many wars against the Formori, who are warlike and savage. Eventually, the Tuatha drove them to a small island, where they imprisoned them beneath the hills. Then they turned their attention to the Firobolga, who had much in common with the Formori, as they came from a common ancestor. We do not share their warlike nature, however, and would have lived peacefully alongside the beautiful Tuatha. But they did not give us the chance. They drove us to the same hills and banished us alongside our cousins. And there, we lived in the darkness and cold, for a long, long time.

'The Tuatha are beautiful, and they make wherever they dwell beautiful too. While they lived in your world, it was lush and vibrant, and many wonderful creatures thrived there. The very first "men" were among them. The Tuatha saw no threat in men, and allowed them to flourish. They saw them as little more than animals. But they were wrong. The men watched them and learned from them and envied them, and before long, had grown in such strength and number that they were able to drive the Tuatha away and take land from them. For the Tuatha - though beautiful and gifted and very clever - were not strong, and eventually, they were driven to the very island they had sent us to – a small island hidden in the misty, cold seas. Recognising that they could not regain the lost land, they made the island their home, and it became as beautiful as they, while the rest of the world dimmed in comparison. Many wonderful creatures died away, as well as many great forests, majestic mountains, and shining lakes.'

The Lord paused, glancing for a moment at the rapt faces of the children before him. Then he continued.

'The men were unable to find this hidden island, and in time forgot about it. But Tuatha seers had foretold that eventually they would come, and they began to lay plans for that day. They worked their magic and made the mists thick around the island; they made the seas stormy and freezing cold. And they made sure they had somewhere to run.

'When the men finally did rediscover the island, it was by chance. A young man lost at sea found his ship washed up on the shore, and was aided by its inhabitants, who gave him food and shelter, helped him to repair his boat, and sent him off home. He went back and reported that this island was the most wonderful land he had ever seen, the people the most beautiful, the food the most delicious. Unfortunately for the Tuatha, however, this boy was the son of a king, and he immediately desired this land for his own. This king's name was Mil.

'With his son as a guide, Mil's armies found the island and waged war against the Tuatha. The Tuatha won, but barely, and as was their way, they sent the wounded soldiers of the enemy home without harassment. For the Tuatha value honour and vows above almost all else, and once their word is given, they will keep it. This is true of all fae, of course, but the Tuatha hold it more sacred than most. Sadly, the same could not be said of the Sons of Mil. They shot burning arrows from their ships as they left, causing much harm before they were gone, and vowed to return. The Tuatha knew that they would not survive a second battle, and so their king declared to the retreating Sons of Mil that if they could ever find the island again, they could take it without a battle. He did not want his people to be slaughtered, you see.

'When the Sons of Mil were gone, the Tuatha strengthened their defences, thickened the mist around the island, and caused great storms to rage in the seas. They hoped they would not be found a second time. But of course they were. When the Sons of Mil returned, this time their king, Mil, was with them. He demanded the Tuatha surrender the island as they had promised, but he clearly did not believe they would keep their word, for he had brought an army with him. The Tuatha king, Lugh, informed Mil that as promised, there would be no battle, so he would not need his army. Instead, he challenged Mil to single combat, with the winner to take the island.

'Mil was very strong, and also very vain, and he accepted this immediately. But Lugh was also strong, and he had magick on his side. Nonetheless, the combat raged for hours, until both sides were equally exhausted. They agreed to rest and tend their minor wounds, and to carry on the next day. This went on for many days. Finally, it was agreed that both kings were equally matched, and there would be no winner. But who, then, would take the island?

'It was here that Lugh made a suggestion, one that the Tuatha had thought of in advance. He suggested that they split the land in two, and each king would rule one half. He suggested this because the Tuatha had prepared hidden gateways in the hills all over the island – gateways to this land – for when the Sons of Mil would eventually drive them back. He remembered the prophecy, you see, but he did not wish to surrender. He hoped that they would be able to defeat the Sons of Mil with cunning, using these gateways, or at the very least be able to flee when the Sons of Mil inevitably went back on their word.

'Mil agreed to the solution, and asked if the Tuatha king would be gracious enough to give him the first pick of the two halves.

Lugh felt he could not refuse, and in any case, he felt it did not matter, for his gateways were everywhere. But Mil was cunning as well as strong. He chose the half of the island that lay above the ground, and told the Tuatha that they could have the half that lay under the ground. He believed this impossible, of course, and expected the Tuatha to argue, and for there to be the battle he had brought his army for. When he said that they could rule beneath the ground, he meant that their bodies would be buried there.

'But to his surprise, Lugh agreed. He bade his people pack their things and go beneath the hills, to the same place they banished the Formori and Firobolga to so long ago. And so they did. The Sons of Mil were left with the island, and the Tuatha came to this world – a world, as I understand it, that exists just beneath the world they left behind. They then sealed the gates behind them, for they did not trust the Sons of Mil.

'What the Tuatha found here was a dark, formless world of potential. A place of vast untapped magic – quite possibly the very place their limited magic in the world above had come from. And just as their very presence made the world above bloom, so it did here – only much, much faster. They quickly realised the potential of this world and began to utilise it, with their magic becoming stronger than ever. One of the first things they did was to find the Formori and the Firobolga and banish us again, beneath new hills they created for that very purpose. This,' the Lord of the Green said, waving a hand, indicating everything around them, 'Is our prison.

'To pay Mil his due, he did not go back on his word and no army was sent beneath the hills after the Tuatha. But his son, Amergin, did, when he became king. But by this time, the Tuatha were much stronger, having tapped the magic of this world and learned how to use it. The new king's army was utterly destroyed almost as soon as they found their way through the gates. Only a few survivors were sent back, and they took a message with them for King Amergin. They described horrifying deeds, immense magical power, and a slaughter unlike anything the Sons of Mil had ever seen. Then the pact was offered, and to save his people, King Amergin accepted it.'

The Lord of the Green lifted his head and closed his eyes as he recited:

> *'The Sons of Mil will ever be*
> *The rulers of the lands above.*
> *The Tuatha de will ever be*
> *The rulers of the lands below.*
> *Oaths were made and set in stone,*
> *That this would ever be so.*
> *For oaths now broken, Tuatha de*
> *Demand their rightful recompense.*
> *In a year and a day*
> *Our shining armies come to Mil,*
> *And this time we will not retreat*
> *To lands beneath the silent hills.*
> *Or else to keep the promised peace*
> *And mend the broken oaths of old,*
> *The Sons of Mil will tithe this day*
> *One tenth of all their daughters and sons.*
> *And for any insult made henceforth,*
> *The Sons of Mil will tithe anon.*
> *And if ever the Sons of Mil*
> *Open the gates to faerie halls,*
> *The Tithe will then be claimed in full,*
> *And we will take your children all.*
> *And while the Tuatha grow in strength*
> *The Sons of Mil shall wither and fall.'*

The Lord of the Green lowered his head and looked at Heidi. 'That is the Tithe. If it has been enacted, then your people have broken the pact and opened a gate.'

Heidi was dumbfounded. For a while, all she could do was shake her head. Eventually, she managed to blurt out: 'But that's... Why would... That's impossible. No one even believes in faeries any more!'

The Lord of the Green gave a slow nod. 'We know. We have been forgotten, and for the most part we are thankful. We are safer forgotten. But it seems someone in your world has remembered.' His face seemed to darken as he added, 'Or has been meddling with things best left alone.'

THE GATE

Article from NBC News Online.

CERN Scientists Ready to Open Portal to Another World

"Dimensional Gateway" to attempt to access Broussard's "Mirror Universe".

In June 2019, physicist Leah Broussard carried out an experiment at Oak Ridge National Laboratory in Tennessee, to see if it was possible to send neutrons into a parallel universe. It was a simple enough experiment, conducted with equipment that was already on hand, with a "wacky" goal that nobody, even Broussard herself, really expected to achieve. But they did – and the implications for physics, and the universe as we know it, were huge.

Broussard's experiment involved shooting subatomic particles through powerful, magnetic fields at an impenetrable wall. The magnetic fields would cause the particles to oscillate at such a frequency that they would become what Broussard calls "mirror matter" – essentially passing into a different level of existence – allowing them to pass through the wall and reappear on the other side.

Running the test only took a day, but analysing the data collected took much longer. Eventually, Broussard was able to confirm that nearly all of the neutrons sent through the magnetic field disappeared, and only one or two were detected by the equipment set up on the other side of the wall. This raised two questions: one – had the neutrons that made it through the wall really become "mirror matter", slipping into a different plane of existence to get through? And two: if they had, where were all the missing neutrons?

After this amazing discovery, plans were immediately started to try to delve further into this "mirror universe" to try and see what lies beyond the confines of our own. The project was moved to the CERN laboratories in Geneva, with scientists anticipating the need for vast amounts of energy to fuel any potential gateway. Using technology inspired by the recently upgraded Large Hadron Collider, scientists have been working hard over the intervening years to build an apparatus capable of creating a large, sustained magnetic field that will allow them to attempt to send magnetically shielded probes through and recall them, hopefully bringing back information on the parallel universe beyond.

It is only now, many years later, that they are ready to make their first attempt.

Lead physicist Genevieve Powell told us, 'This is an extremely exciting time for physics. We have no idea if our probe will be able to get through the incredibly strong magnetic fields without damage, or safely cross over into the mirror world, or if it will even be capable of picking up any data if it does. This is only the first in what is likely to be a long succession of experiments while we ascertain exactly what can and cannot be sent through. Working with magnetic fields makes things extremely tricky; everything, including ourselves, has a magnetic field, and disrupting those can be disastrous. But, if we can get it right, we'll be able to find out where Leah Broussard's neutrons went in 2019.'

When asked if they would be sending any people through, Powell laughed. 'That would be the dream, wouldn't it? While we'd love to, it is a long way off, if it would ever be possible at all. We just don't know how to do it yet. But we're working on it!'

The "magnetic gateway" has undergone several trial runs, and the first probe is due to be sent through in a week's time.

Investigating Officer's Note: The initial gateway experiment was conducted approximately four months before "The Event". The results following this experiment were not made available to the public.

CHAPTER 9

THE FIROBOLGA

I t is my turn to ask a question,' the Lord of the Green said. 'If you are ready?'

The children had been sitting in thoughtful silence for some time following the end of the Lord's story. His low voice interrupted Heidi's reverie, and she blinked, confused, before nodding.

'Why did you come to us?' he asked.

'Sprickleback brought us here,' Heidi replied. 'He said he would be our guide.'

The tall faun's leafy head turned to look at the spriggan, sitting unhappily in his wicker cage. Sprickleback cringed and averted his gaze.

'Did he?' the Lord of the Green rumbled. 'I wonder, spriggan, if these children know what we spoke of when you were brought before me.'

Sprickleback gave a nervous chuckle. 'There's no need...' he began, but, with a scowl and a shake from the guard holding his cage, he fell silent.

The Lord of the Green gestured toward Heidi with one large hand. 'Your next question?'

Heidi stared hard at Sprickleback as she spoke. 'What did Sprickleback say to you about why he brought us here?'

The Lord of the Green smiled. As he replied, the smile turned into a disdainful sneer. 'He wished to trade some of you to us in return for permission to once again live here, beneath the hill.'

A collective gasp came from the children. Out of the corner of her eye, Heidi saw Sue pull Amy closer. One of the group started to cry.

Heidi took a step closer to the spriggan in his cage. 'You were going to *sell* us?' she said slowly. She could feel herself shaking. Her blood felt like ice in her veins.

Sprickleback looked up at her and shrank back against the bars. 'Not ... not *all* of you,' he muttered. 'It's nice here! You'd like it here after a while!'

'You said you'd be our guide!' Heidi shouted. She could feel her nails digging into her palms, her fists clenched in rage. 'You nasty little liar! How could you?!'

A low mutter started amongst the fauns. Sprickleback jumped forward, his tiny fists grabbing the bars in front of him. 'I did not lie!' he yelled above the muttering. 'I did not lie! I said I'd guide you, and I did, and I will! But I never said I'd guide all of you!'

Heidi uttered a cry of disgust and turned away. To think they'd had no choice but to trust this nasty little monster! She could feel angry tears burning behind her eyes, and she had to squeeze her eyelids shut and bite down on her lower lip to hold them back.

The Lord of the Green turned to the guard holding the cage and waved a hand toward the exit. 'Take that thing out of our sight.'

The guard gave a quick bow before turning on his hoof and swiftly marching out. The fauns in his way quickly parted to let him through, shaking their heads as they watched him leave.

Sprickleback bounced to and fro in the cage, shouting in protest. 'But we had a bargain!'

Once the guard had left, the Lord of the Green raised his hands for silence. Slowly, the fauns stopped their muttering. When it was quiet, the Lord said, 'What, to your understanding, was the spriggan to be guiding you toward?'

Heidi paused before answering. His phrasing sounded strange to her, and she had to take a moment to decipher it. Finally she said, 'We thought he was going to take us to someone who could help us get home.'

'Little shit,' Tyler muttered from behind her. There was a faint titter of laughter from a couple of the other children.

Heidi winced, but none of the fauns reacted to Tyler's swearing, so she carried on. 'He said something about going to a city. He said people there would be able to help us.'

'The Tuatha,' The Lord of the Green said with a grave nod. 'In the Shining City. I have no doubt they will know a way to get you home.'

The other children looked up happily at this, but something bothered Heidi about the way he said it. 'But aren't the Tuatha the bad guys?' she asked.

The Lord of the Green chuckled, a deep, bassy sound that reverberated around the room. Some of the other fauns laughed with him. 'From our point of view, perhaps,' he replied. 'They did imprison us in the hills ... twice. But they are not without reason. It is by reasoning with them that we at least have a habitable prison this time around. We agreed to never seek to live anywhere else if they would make it as beautiful as the lands above. And so they did, and by that agreement we are permitted to leave the hill ... as long as we return to it. Other fey creatures have even sought to live here with us ... as your "guide" would attest.'

Heidi was thinking of the mermaids. She stayed silent as he went on.

'Even so, you would likely not call the Tuatha "good". Good and evil are mortal concepts, not ours. We do not concern ourselves with them. But each group of fae have their own rules and will abide by them. We Firobolga, for example, do not take that which we do not need, and we share what we have with those who need it. But we do not abide those who are greedy, and we do not suffer liars and thieves.'

Something in the way he said this made Heidi shiver. She wanted him to go on. But instead the Lord asked, 'With that in mind, what do you need?'

Taken aback, she looked at the other children. Sue shrugged, and Monifa waved her hands at her in a "go on" gesture. Turning back to the Lord of the Green, she replied, 'Um, well... We need to go home. So... I guess we need a new guide to take us to the Shining City.' She paused, then added, 'And some food would be nice. We've only had a few apples since we've been here.'

The Lord of the Green looked her up and down. 'I would say that you also need some new attire.'

Heidi looked down at her bare feet and dirty, ripped night-dress and gave an embarrassed laugh. 'Yeah, some shoes would be nice,' she admitted.

'Shoes, regrettably, we do not have,' the Lord replied, indicating his large, blunt hooves. A ripple of laughter ran through the gathered crowd, and some of the fauns hammered their hooves on the ground. 'But we can find you something, I am sure.' He paused, thinking. 'A good meal, a good rest, and some more suitable clothes, and when you are rested we will find you a guide. The route to the Shining City is not a safe one.'

'Thank you so much,' Heidi exclaimed, smiling.

To her surprise, the Lord of the Green reacted by recoiling, his lips turning back in a snarl. The other fauns hissed and spat, some of them pawing at the ground with their hooves and shaking their heads as if they were bulls ready to charge. Heidi looked around, panicked. 'What did I do wrong?' she cried.

The Lord of the Green composed himself, and lifted his hands for silence. When the fauns had settled down, he turned to Heidi.

'A few words of advice to you, Child of Mil,' he said coldly. 'Those two words are not well received by our kind, nor by any fae folk. We have long learned that those words are nothing but meaningless sounds, used to express a gratitude that does not truly exist. Your kind says them without thinking and with no mind to what they have been given. Here, words have power, so much so that words that have no meaning are a poison. If you wish to express your gratitude, do it with any words but those. And think on the worth of what you are grateful for.'

There was a long, icy silence in the large room. Heidi stared up at the big faun, trying to make sense of what he had said. Eventually, she said, 'I'm very sorry. I didn't know. I really am grateful for your help. I don't know what we would do without it.'

The tension in the room noticeably lessened as the Lord of the Green gave a gentle nod, and the fauns relaxed. 'I accept your apology,' he said.

'It's okay to say sorry, isn't it?' Heidi blurted, and a chorus of laughter rippled around the room.

'Sorry is tolerable,' the Lord of the Green replied with a smile, 'Though it means little on its own. Do you have any more questions, child?'

Heidi thought for a moment. 'Yes,' she said at last. 'Do you think the Tuatha will help us?'

The Lord of the Green regarded her silently for a moment. 'I think they know how to help you,' he finally replied, 'And I think that if you can strike a bargain with them that they find pleasing, they may. But I do not know if they will. For remember it was the Tuatha who created the Tithe, and I do not know entirely why. If they have a reason for wanting you here beyond mere vengeance, they may refuse to help you.'

At Heidi's crestfallen expression, the giant leaned forward. 'If that should happen,' he said softly. 'You can always return to us. We do not turn away those in need. In fact, if you wished to abandon your quest to go to the Tuatha, you would be welcome to call this place your home.'

'Is that what you think we should do?' Heidi asked in a small voice.

'I cannot advise you on that,' he replied sadly. 'All I can tell you is that I do not trust the Tuatha. They keep their promises, yes, but they will twist their words to trick you if they can. If you do go to them, be careful.'

His large black eyes looked deep into hers, and she saw herself reflected in them. She looked very small and lost.

Then he sat back. 'But you have time to think on that,' he said. 'Tonight, you stay with us. You will eat and rest, and we will see what we can do about those poor clothes you are wearing. When you wake, we will find you a guide to the Shining City.' He clapped his large hands together. 'First, a feast!'

THE THIRD EVENT

Article from BBC News Online.

Global Child Tragedy Strikes for Third Year

For the third year in a row - and despite millions spent on protective measures by governments in multiple countries - inexplicable tragedy has struck families across the globe as "The Event" has repeated itself once more.

Children in every country mysteriously vanished again last night, on the third anniversary of what is known as "The Event" – the night when all children under the age of thirteen disappeared without a trace.

Children born in the years since "The Event" have all vanished in the same way on the night of the anniversary, despite counter-measures put in place to prevent it from happening again.

'Last year, we didn't really expect it to happen again,' said John Gallagher, head of operations for the government's special task force investigating "The Event". 'The first "Event" was so unexpected, so unprecedented, that it seemed a million to one chance that it would repeat. When it did, we immediately got to planning counter-measures for the following year.'

These counter-measures included – at least in the UK – the construction of special "protective custody" facilities outside London, Birmingham, Leeds, and Cardiff, where parents and their babies were taken to wait out the anniversary night. Attendance at the facility was mandatory, and the army was deployed to carry out escort operations throughout the country in the 24 hours leading up to the night. Similar facilities were constructed near Glasgow and Dublin. Many other countries followed suit, including the US, who built 47 such facilities across the country.

We take a look inside London's "baby cage" – exclusive pictures

But these measures proved to be ineffective when early this morning alarms were raised. Reports from the UK suggest the mass disappearance happened around 3am – just like previous years. US reports echo this, with their disappearances happening at 3am locally in each location. Witness reports are currently being gathered, but those collected so far are practically identical – parents report waking up to find cots empty, or children gone from their arms. Some report being aware of a shadowy presence in the room, and of trying to stay awake but finding themselves unable to at the crucial time.

The UK Prime Minister has scheduled an emergency press conference this evening. He can expect to face many tough questions, in particular about the cost of this immense national and global failure, and about the implications of the loss of our future generations for the country. With his tenure already on shaky ground, the reaction to this press conference could be disastrous for his government.

More on this story.

"The Event": Three Years On

The "Child Riots" reach Spain, Mexico and Russia

CHAPTER 10

THE DEAD BOY'S CLOTHES

Gilla took Heidi to a small hut not too far from the meeting hall. Inside was cosy and warm, with a log fire already burning in a stone fireplace. There was a hammock suspended from one corner, draped with woollen blankets, and the floor was thickly coated in dry leaves. Other than that, and several pots and jugs made of what looked like hand-turned clay, there wasn't much else inside.

Heidi looked around curiously. 'You don't have a lot in here,' she said, then wondered if that seemed rude.

Gilla smiled. 'We don't need much,' she replied. 'Most of what we value is outside. The trees, the sun... We don't need much in the way of possessions, besides what we need to hunt and weave and cook.'

The faun crossed over to the hammock and rummaged around in the blankets and furs. She pulled out what looked to Heidi like a costume from a pantomime or an old movie; a long blue tunic with a lace-up collar. Gilla held it out to her. 'This might fit you,' she said.

Heidi took it and held it up against herself. It did seem to be about the right size. 'Th – I mean, um...' she faltered, and fell silent.

Gilla smiled and shook her head. 'It's alright,' she said. 'Try it on.'

Heidi looked around, but there were no other rooms to the hut, and Gilla showed no signs of leaving. Feeling a little self-conscious, she put the tunic on the ground and stripped off the dirty, torn nightdress she was wearing. As quick as she could, she pulled on the tunic. It reached down to just above her knees, and the sleeves almost reached her elbows. She pulled at it experimentally. The fabric was thin and a little coarse, but it felt much better than the cheap material of her nightdress.

'Did you make this?' she asked.

Gilla shook her head. 'Not that one. We make blankets and some clothes for ourselves, but mostly we don't need them. That was found.' She pulled a brown leather belt out of one of the pots. 'We found this too. Perhaps it will help? That looks a little big on you.'

Heidi took the belt and wrapped it around her waist; it went around twice. The buckle looked familiar to her – modern. 'Where did you find them?'

'They came from the Children of Mil who have been here before,' Gilla replied, still rooting around in the pots.

Heidi looked up sharply. 'What children?'

The faun looked a little surprised at her sharp tone. 'The ones taken in previous Tithes, I imagine,' she said. 'Mostly they are claimed by the Tuatha and their servants right away, but occasionally some escape. Just as you did. They leave things behind.'

Heidi looked down at the tunic she was wearing and frowned. She had a sick feeling beginning in the pit of her stomach. 'They leave their clothes?'

Gilla shrugged and picked up her discarded nightdress. 'Sometimes. Sometimes they leave them.' She lifted the nightdress and began to fold it. 'Sometimes they don't survive, and so they no longer need them.'

The sick feeling grew stronger. 'Am I wearing a dead boy's clothes?' Heidi whimpered. Suddenly the cloth of the tunic itched and prickled against her skin.

Gilla looked at her with her big, black eyes and shrugged again. 'He doesn't need it any more.'

Tears pricked the back of Heidi's eyelids, and for just a moment, she was sure she was going to cry, scream or throw up. She wondered if one day they'd be giving Ricky's baseball shirt or Sylvie's nightdress to some other lost children - scavenged from the wilderness like lost trash. Somehow she held it back. Instead she took a deep breath, held it for a moment, and then simply said, 'I suppose he doesn't.'

Gilla regarded her carefully. 'Do you not see much death where you come from?' she said softly. Heidi shook her head, and the faun came to her and crouched down on her haunches, resting her hands on her dark-furred knees. 'May I give you some advice?'

Heidi sniffed back tears and nodded. 'Yes, please.'

'Our home is beautiful, and we love it,' Gilla said, 'But there is much death here. We are used to it. We mourn our dead, but we also are grateful for what they gave to us, and for what they leave behind.' She placed one hand on Heidi's shoulder, stroking the blue fabric. 'The boy who wore this came here a long, long time ago. He was brave, like you. But he grew sick, and he died. That is sad. But now he provides you with something that will help you, and that is good.'

'It just seems mean to be happy that he died just because I get to have his stuff,' Heidi said weakly.

'I didn't say you should be happy that he is dead,' Gilla replied. 'Just be grateful for what he has left behind for you.'

Heidi thought about it. It was a strange way to think, but

she had to admit it made some sense. She nodded reluctantly. 'I am grateful,' she said.

Gilla smiled and stood up. 'I'm glad,' she said. 'Now, shall we go get you some food? I can smell the meat cooking already.'

Heidi sniffed the air; she couldn't smell anything. Tugging at the tunic one last time, she followed Gilla to the door of the hut. The faun swept aside the curtain and ushered her out.

The moment she was outside, Heidi became aware that the main clearing was much, much brighter than it had been before. As they headed toward it she could see that a massive bonfire had been built there and was already blazing, the flames licking at the branches of the trees above with such ferocity that she was amazed they weren't catching fire too. Around the fire she could see about a dozen fauns rushing around, silhouetted against the firelight. She couldn't make out the details of them, but she could see that some were carrying bundles of sticks, and others large bulky objects that she couldn't identify. She watched as two of them fixed one of these bundles onto a long, sharp stick and then propped that stick onto two upright poles, suspending it over a smaller fire to one side.

Her jaw dropped. 'That's the meat?' she exclaimed. She'd never seen joints of meat so large in her life!

Gilla smiled. 'We eat well,' she said simply. 'Come.'

Now Heidi could smell the cooking meat, it made her mouth water and her stomach twist. She hurried ahead of Gilla as they made their way into the central clearing. Looking around, she saw Sue sitting on a log that served as a bench a few feet away, dressed in what looked like animal skins that had been stitched together. She was clutching something on her lap.

'I'm going to go and sit with my friend,' Heidi said to Gilla, who nodded and gestured for her to go.

Heidi ran over and sat down next to Sue. 'What are you wearing?' she asked.

Sue shrugged. 'They said it's sort of like deerskin,' she

replied, looking uneasy. 'It's not bad. It's softer than I thought it would be.'

'That's good,' Heidi said. 'I'm in a ... boy's tunic.' She stopped herself from saying "dead boy"; she didn't want to upset Sue. Besides, the young girl already looked unhappy.

Sue looked her over and forced a smile. 'Blue suits you,' she said.

'Thanks.' Heidi paused, then said, 'Are you okay?'

'Um...' Sue looked around furtively. 'Promise you won't tell?'

'Of course, if you don't want me to,' Heidi replied.

Sue looked around again, then held out what she was holding in her lap. It was a pair of green leggings, the stretchy fabric torn in a couple of places but otherwise in good condition. Heidi turned them over in her hands. 'What's wrong with them?' she asked.

'There's nothing wrong with *them*,' Sue replied in a low voice. 'It's ... me. I can't wear them.'

Heidi blinked, confused. 'Why not?'

'I...' Sue swallowed, her dark eyes suddenly brimming with tears. 'I have a tail.'

Heidi gaped at her. 'You ... what?' she gasped. She must have heard wrong.

But Sue said it again. 'I have a tail! It's just grown, like, since we've been here, and I can't put these on, and I don't know what to do...' Her breath started to hitch in her throat. 'Heidi, what am I going to do?'

Alarmed, Heidi leaned over and hugged her. 'It's okay, I won't tell anyone,' she said. 'Can I see?'

Hesitantly, Sue shifted her weight onto one thigh and lifted the hide tunic at the back. Peeking beneath it, Heidi saw the pale skin of her hip, then, at the very base of her spine, about as long as her hand and twitching slightly as if in agitation, a smooth, hairless tail. She jumped back, stifling a squeak of surprise.

'Oh my God, you really do have a tail,' she exclaimed. Sue just looked at her miserably and jammed the tunic down over it, tucking it underneath her legs. 'Why do you have a tail?'

'I don't know!' Sue wailed. 'I didn't before we came here!'

'Okay, it's okay,' Heidi assured her. 'Look, you can still wear these. Nobody needs to know!' Seizing the seat of the leggings, she forced her fingers through the fabric, tearing a large hole. 'See? You just put the tail through the hole and these will be fine! And your tunic covers it up so no one will see.'

Sue sniffed and gave her a watery smile. 'I didn't think of doing that,' she said. 'You're so smart, Heidi.'

Heidi shrugged and opened her mouth to reply, but it was at that moment that Tim and Meghan came running over. Tim was wearing a pair of brown cloth shorts that had been torn off just below his knees and patched in multiple places with different fabrics. Meghan had a strip of red fabric tied around her waist for a skirt, and a strip of the same material bound around her skinny chest. Tim looked panicked, and Meghan was running with a strange, limping gait. Sue shot Heidi a warning glance, and Heidi nodded.

'Heidi!' Tim shouted when they were close. 'Look at Meghan's feet!'

The girls both looked down as Meghan and Tim reached them, and saw that Meghan's feet were bare, dusty with the dry earth from the clearing - and where her toenails should have been, there were curved, black talons, short but wickedly sharp.

'Oh my God,' Sue muttered. 'What happened?'

Meghan shrugged. 'My feet hurt,' she replied, 'And I was rubbing them, and...' She swallowed hard. 'And my toenails just ... just...' She stopped, pressing one hand to her mouth as if she might throw up.

Tim gleefully picked up the story. 'Her toenails fell off!' he cried. 'And these little black claws were just underneath, poking up! It was gross!'

Heidi tried to control her expression as Meghan blushed a deep red and looked away. Sue reached out a hand to her and beckoned for her to sit with them. 'It's okay, Meghan,' she said, and gave Heidi another warning glance.

Heidi turned to Tim. 'Has anything happened to you?' she asked.

'No,' Tim replied. 'Why, do you think it will? Oh, I hope I grow wings and can fly! That'd be cool!'

Heidi frowned. 'Yeah ... cool,' she muttered. 'Where are the others?'

She wondered who else had changed since they had been here. She wondered if CeeCee had any stories that would explain it.

The fauns were gathering in groups now, talking and laughing and passing around bone and clay tankards and bowls filled with sweet-smelling amber liquid. One of them approached the group and gave a bowl to Tim. He took it with a shy smile, then took a sip and his eyes widened. 'This is *beer!*' he exclaimed, and lifted it to his lips again.

Quickly, Heidi stepped forward and snatched it away. 'Oh, no you don't, you're too little,' she said. Giving it a sniff, she shook her head. 'And it's not beer.' Ignoring his complaints, she took a sip. It tasted like honey and flowers, and it was quite strong.

'Aw, come on Heidi,' Tim was whining. 'You're too little, too! We all are! And there's no grown-ups here!'

'The fauns are grown-ups,' Heidi pointed out.

'They gave it to us!' Tim retorted. 'Please, Heidi!'

She looked around at the others, who shrugged. Sue said, 'Why not? It's not like anything's normal here.'

Heidi sighed and handed the bowl back to Tim. 'Fine. But don't make yourself sick.'

Tim grinned and took a large mouthful, then passed the bowl to Meghan. They each took a sip in turn. It was nice, but it made Heidi's head feel swimmy, so she declined the second time it reached her. She was grateful when she saw the other children heading their way.

Before long, all the children were together again, all of them dressed in assorted scraps of fabric and scavenged clothes, and most of them had some strange new feature to show. Monifa's eyes were glowing bright yellow in the dark. Tyler kept rubbing his jaw, and pulled down his bottom lip to reveal a pair of sharp bonelike tusks emerging from his gums beneath his teeth. Tariq turned up wearing a ridiculously orange, wool bobble hat, and eventually took it off to reveal pointed tips to his ears.

'When did this happen?' Heidi asked everyone. All she got in response was a chorus of shrugs.

CeeCee twisted the hem of the white shirt she wore anxiously. It was big enough to be a dress on her, tied at the waist with a bit of leather cord, with the pointed collar flapping loosely around her neck. She kept her hands balled up to hide the thin skin that had grown between her fingers. 'My hands were itching when I woke up from our nap in the woods,' she said. 'I only noticed after we came out of the big hall here that something was different.'

Tariq nodded. 'I didn't notice my ears until I was getting changed just now,' he replied.

'My teeth have been hurting all day,' Tyler added, then looked up at the unchanging night sky and said, 'Well... I guess since the woods, like CeeCee.'

'So ... since we woke up?' Heidi frowned. 'I wonder why we haven't all changed?'

Gilla came over with another faun. 'Children of Mil,' she said. 'This is my mate, Tuan.'

Tuan bowed low in front of them. 'It is an honour,' he said in a deep, gruff voice. His hair fell in thick locks around his angular face.

The children looked up at him awkwardly. 'Hello,' Tim said quietly.

'If there is anything I can do for you,' Tuan continued, 'please, let me know.'

'I'm pretty hungry,' Tariq said, and several other children echoed their agreement.

'Ah! That I can easily resolve!' Tuan gave a wolfish grin and trotted off toward the fire. A few minutes later he returned with a large wooden plate holding a huge joint of roasted meat, still steaming slightly. He set it down in the midst of the children. 'Please, eat.'

There was a momentary pause before Tariq shrugged and tore a strip of meat off with his fingers. The others all followed suit, falling on the meat like starving beasts. Within a few minutes the joint had been ravaged. Gilla and Tuan waited until the children were all eating before they took some meat for themselves.

'How are you enjoying the evening so far?' Gilla asked them.

Heidi looked around at the others before answering. 'Well, some of us are ... um ... a bit different now,' she replied.

'How so?' Gilla asked.

Heidi pointed to Monifa. 'Look at her eyes,' she said. 'And Meghan's got claws on her feet!'

'And look at my damn ears!' Tariq cried around a mouthful of meat.

Gilla gave Tuan a knowing look. 'Ah. Yes. That happens.'

Heidi stared at her. 'This is normal?'

'For your kind, yes,' Gilla replied. 'The longer you're here, the more you'll change. That's why you haven't seen more of your kind here. Eventually, you'll become more like us.'

'How long does it take?' Heidi asked.

'It's different for each of you,' Gilla replied. 'And it's hard to say. Here, time is different from your world. I don't think it passes in the same way. All I know is that the change happens faster if you eat the food here, or so I've been told.'

The children all froze, their mouths full of meat or their hands lifting pieces to their lips. Mouthfuls of half-chewed meat were swallowed reluctantly or discreetly spat into hands. Heidi placed the piece she had been eating back onto the plate, trying not to show her alarm to the fauns who were still watching them with interest.

'The apples,' Tariq muttered. 'It must have started after we ate the apples.'

Meghan looked around anxiously. 'How long have we been here?' she asked the group.

They all looked at Heidi. She considered, then said slowly, 'I think we've been here for maybe a couple of days...'

Gilla looked solemn. 'It's likely been much longer in your world,' she replied gently.

From the other side of the bonfire, music began to play.

EXCERPT FROM AN ESSAY ON OTHER WORLDS

From the book "New Science and Old Gods" by Professor Kuma Bowman.

Now we get to the most recent scientific discovery: that there are other worlds than this one.

The idea of worlds other than our own existing may be considered somewhat outlandish and far-fetched in scientific circles, but in religious and spiritual circles, it has long been considered not only conceivable, but widely accepted as a core part of many belief systems across the world.

In science, we find it in quantum physics, where string theory suggests that there are parallel realities running alongside our own. This idea has great similarities with ancient teachings from India.

Hinduism teaches that our universe has multiple realms existing simultaneously, and in some cases connecting, alongside our own. One of these, the Deva Realm, is home to beings who control the laws of existence. They are not viewed as gods, as you might expect, but rather as beings like ourselves, only of a higher level of consciousness, with tasks that they must fulfil in order for our universe to behave as it should. In fact, the word "deva" means "beings who work in the light", denoting them as workers, below Brahman (the Supreme Being) in the grand hierarchy, but above humanity, enforcing the laws of existence that keep the universe spinning. Vishnu and Shiva are devas, whose job it is to preside over the functioning of the cosmos and the evolution of creation. Lesser devas control the forces of nature, such as Vayu, the Lord of the wind, Varuna, the Lord of water, and Agni, the Lord of fire.

In addition to these material levels of existence, there is also what is thought to be a transcendental realm which, from time to time, connects with the material realms, including our own. Beings from this realm are known as "avatars" and are thought to occasionally visit us.

But this belief is not just found in Hinduism. Buddhism also refers to devas. In Buddhist texts, "deva" refers to both a type of being and one of the six paths of the incarnation cycle. Devas as beings include different types, ranked in a hierarchy according to what they have achieved over many lifetimes, the lowest class being closer in nature to humans than to the higher classes of their own kind.

Japanese Shinto venerates "kami". Kami are spirits or holy beings who can be elements of the landscape, forces of nature, or the spirits of revered ancestors. They are an essential part of nature, possessing both positive and negative characteristics. Kami are manifestations of the energy of the universe, and are considered to be the pinnacle of what humans should strive to be. Often believed to be hidden from this world in an existence that mirrors our own, only those who are in harmony with nature are able to perceive them.

In the Abrahamic religions, we find the concept of angels, also considered to be higher beings who are separated into hierarchies. Descriptions of the hierarchies vary between Judaism, Christianity and Islam, but the fundamental premise is the same: there are angels, they are better than us, and they exist on a different plane of existence (Heaven).

In esoteric cosmology, there are seven planes of existence, which merge at the centre with our own physical world, the solar systems, and all the known physical structures of the universe. It is thought that the planes came into being when the universe was created, and they are acknowledged by esoteric religions such as Shamanism and Kabbalah.

Pre-Christian Western mythologies and folklore also include ideas of multiple levels of existence. For example, the World Tree, Yggdrasil, links multiple worlds in its branches; the Great Chain of Being links the divine all the way down to inanimate matter; or the Celtic idea of the Tuatha de Danann and their retreat to an Otherworld once they were displaced by our warlike ancestors.

That is by no means an exhaustive list of belief systems which include the concept of multiple worlds, inhabited by beings much more spiritually advanced and enlightened than ourselves. In fact, with so many religions and spiritual paths agreeing on this, the most incredible part of this new scientific "revelation" is that we find it incredible at all.

CHAPTER 11

THE FEAST

They had never heard music like it. It was wild and primal, consisting mainly of wood flutes and drums. The fauns capered and spun to it around the massive central bonfire, their shadows contorting like demons.

The children shrank together, mesmerised. Gilla and her mate looked down at them with amusement, the skin around their unreadable black eyes crinkling.

'You don't like to dance?' Tuan asked them.

The children looked at each other nervously. Some shrugged, some shook their heads; only one or two nodded. The youngest just stared.

Tuan took Gilla's hand. 'We love it,' he said. 'It is sacred to us. We dance to show we are free, even though we are imprisoned. We dance to show our freedom in our chains.' He turned to Gilla. 'Come dance, my love.'

Gilla smiled and bowed her head, and a moment later the two fauns bounded off to be lost among the dancing, shifting shadows and flames, leaving the children alone.

Meghan looked at Heidi. 'Should we dance?' she asked.

Heidi thought about it, then shrugged. 'I don't know,' she replied. 'I mean, they might think it's rude if we don't.'

Monifa grabbed Amy from where she was sitting on the ground and balanced her on one knee. 'Some of us need to stay and look after the little ones,' she said, giving Heidi a pleading look with her new yellow eyes.

'That's fine,' Heidi replied. 'You don't have to dance if you don't want to.'

'Are you going to?' Tim asked her.

She considered, then nodded. 'For a bit. I don't want to be rude.'

'Then, I will too,' Tim replied.

She gave him a grateful smile. The two of them got to their feet and stepped forward, out of the safety of their little circle, and as they did a few more got up: Meghan, CeeCee, Tariq and Sue. Tyler shifted himself so he was leaning against the fallen trunk and folded his arms, scowling. Monifa clasped Amy tighter, who wriggled a little as she watched the flickering flames, eyes large and a little frightened.

It was strange, but as Heidi stepped into the invisible ring around the fire, where the fauns were all dancing and spinning, she could have sworn that the music became a little clearer, a little louder. The fire became a little brighter, the air a little sweeter, and she felt a sudden swell of energy flood through her body. She turned to look at Tim and saw that energy, that excitement, reflected in his eyes. He grinned at her, and she grinned back. Dancing had been the right choice, she thought. She wanted to dance. No – she *needed* to dance. She raised her arms and gave a little spin, and then her mind emptied, her feet ran away and she was lost.

The world around her became at once distant and magnified. Her aches and pains, the grief and fear balled up in her chest all dissolved away. Nothing could touch her, yet at the same time it all seemed impossibly close; the flickering flames of the bonfire, the stamping hooves of the fauns, the laughing faces of the other children. Her limbs felt light as air, but strong as oak. She was flying; she was burning. She looked up and the stars were glittering just beyond her fingertips. She looked down and her feet were skimming the earth. The melody snaked around her, twisting her, spinning her, lifting her fingers and slamming down her feet. A strange and primal joy flickered into life inside her, filling her belly and rising up into her throat, and she heard herself hooting and shrieking along with the fauns; she had to, it had to be let out or it would burn her up. She had to keep dancing, keep dancing or she would … she would…

When the music stopped, it felt to Heidi like someone had ripped a hole in her chest. She stumbled and dropped to her knees, a horrible empty feeling inside her stealing away her breath. Then, it passed. She gasped in a big lungful of air and looked around. All around her the fauns and the other children were doing the same, some fallen to the ground, others staggering or leaning against each other to stay standing. The fire, much smaller than it had seemed a moment ago, crackled noisily in the silence. Heidi realised she was breathing hard, and sweating, and her muscles ached. How long had she been dancing? It had only felt like minutes.

The silence stretched on for a long, aching moment. Then, one of the drummers pounded once, hard, on their drum. The fauns all pricked up their ears and looked around expectantly at the meeting hall. As if on cue, the curtain parted and out unfurled the tall, treelike figure of the Lord of the Green. He straightened up and looked around, and Heidi was amazed to see he towered almost twice as tall as the meeting hall.

'Kindred,' he boomed, his voice carrying across the clearing like a rumble of thunder. 'We have among us a transgressor!'

The fauns gasped and muttered darkly among themselves. Heidi didn't know what that word meant, but she judged from the reaction that it was nothing good. She looked at the other children, scattered among the fauns, and they returned her blank stare. A childish instinct to hide struck her and she slowly crept back to the tree trunk where Monifa, Amy and Tyler still sat. She wasn't surprised to see the other children doing the same. Someone had done something wrong, her instinct was telling her, and she didn't know if it was one of them.

The Lord of the Green took a few steps forward, clearing the distance between the hall and the edge of the clearing where the fire burned. He lifted one hand, and two guards stepped forward from the shadows of the meeting hall, escorting between them a female faun with hair cascading down over her shoulders that glittered with buttons and baubles of all kinds. She stood between the guards calmly, holding her head high, her black eyes narrowed.

The Lord of the Green raised his other hand and two more guards stepped forward. These two, however, walked with their spears pointed at the back of another faun who they pushed ahead of them. This faun was another female, with wildly curly hair that shone red in the firelight. She was glancing from side to side nervously, and her hands were clenching and unclenching in the fur at her thighs.

The Lord of the Green lowered both of his hands, and the low chatter among the fauns ceased.

'One of these two is an oathbreaker,' he boomed. 'Either a thief ... or a liar.' He spat the words with disgust, as if they burned his tongue. 'You will judge them.'

He looked to the first faun, the woman with the beads in her hair. 'Accuser,' he said. 'Speak your name and tell your tale.'

The first faun took a step forward. 'I am Nemed,' she said in a strong voice. 'I accuse Rudraige of taking that which was right-fully gifted to me.' She lifted a hand and pointed at the faun across from her, who recoiled, taking a step back that brought her against the points of the spears at her back. She flinched and stayed where she was.

'I was kindly given a gift by one of the Children of Mil,' Nemed went on. 'The gift was a beautiful berry-coloured garment she wore, in return for the sturdier clothing I gave her. I tucked it safely away in my hut so that I would not lose it before I walked with her to the fire for the feast. But when I returned to my hut for my cup, I saw Rudraige coming out ... and she had the gifted garment in her hands!'

The gathered fauns hissed and hooted savagely. The Lord of the Green held up a hand to quiet them, and then turned to Rudraige. 'You,' he said. 'State your name and tell your tale.'

The other faun took a small step forward, her eyes wide.

'I am Rudraige,' she said, her voice much weaker. 'I did go into Nemed's hut ... but ... I did not know the garment had been gifted to her ... I thought she had thrown it away! It was on the floor, I only took it because I thought it was free!'

Nemed bared her teeth at Rudraige and hissed. 'Liar! Thief *and* liar!' she cried. 'I tucked it away safely! It was not on the floor! You would have had to search to find it!'

The gathered fauns hooted and stomped their feet angrily. It was pretty clear to Heidi who they were going to side with. She watched as the Lord of the Green raised his hand again.

'Which child gifted it to you?' he asked Nemed when the noise had died down.

Nemed turned to where the children huddled. 'The red-haired one,' she replied. 'Called CeeCee.'

'CeeCee,' the Lord of the Green said. 'Step forward.'

Reluctantly, CeeCee got to her feet and crept out to the front of the group. As she brushed past, Heidi could feel the girl trembling. The Lord of the Green looked sternly down at CeeCee, then his expression softened a little. He could see that she was scared too.

'Child,' he said in a gentler tone. 'Tell us. Is it true that you gifted your garment to Nemed?'

CeeCee swallowed and nodded. 'Yes, sir,' she replied.

'And did you see where she put it?'

CeeCee nodded again and cast a look at Rudraige that was almost apologetic.

'She ... she tucked it into a wooden chest,' she replied. 'She put it under some other things. She said she wanted to keep it ... "for special".'

Nemed gave a satisfied smile, and Rudraige seemed to visibly shrink. The other fauns began to stamp and hoot again. The Lord of the Green held up his hand once more.

'One last question,' he said to CeeCee, and from somewhere within the greenery that covered his chest pulled out a piece of cloth. Heidi squinted and could make out the pretty purple fabric of CeeCee's nightdress. 'Was this the garment you gifted to Nemed?'

CeeCee nodded again. 'Yes, sir.'

The Lord of the Green nodded once, solemnly.

'You may sit down,' he said. As CeeCee shrunk back into the group, he turned to Nemed. 'Your words ring true,' he said, and held out the nightdress to her. She took it from him with a small bow. Then he turned to face Rudraige.

'Rudraige,' he boomed, raising his voice so it carried above the crackling of the fire. 'Your words ring false. I name you Liar.'

The fauns hissed and stamped angrily. Rudraige cowered away, and the Lord of the Green raised his voice again.

'I name you Thief!'

The stamping of the fauns began to merge into a steady rhythm, making the ground tremble underfoot. The guards behind Rudraige jabbed forward with their spears, forcing her forward as she tried to shy away.

'I name you *Oathbreaker*!'

The fauns shrieked and howled like beasts, fists punching at the sky. Heidi heard the drummers take up the beat, making the pounding of dozens of hoofbeats seem even louder. The Lord of the Green swung his arm up, pointing toward the fire.

'Kindred,' he roared. 'Give to this one the Oathbreaker's reward!'

Even over the howling of the crowd, Heidi could hear Rudraige screaming as they surged forward to seize her. She was lifted hand over hand above their heads, passed back over the crowd toward the fire. As she reached the back of the crowd, strong hands reached up and clamped onto her arms and legs, forcing them down and out until she made a star-shape above them. Her screams changed, the shrill shrieks of fright becoming lower, longer sounds of pain, and with horror Heidi realised they were *pulling*. A bright flash of firelight on metal dazzled her for a moment. When her vision cleared she saw that blades – short-swords, hatchets, butchering knives – were being raised all around the condemned faun. She gasped and turned away, but not before she saw the first blade bite into Rudraige's armpit. Blood sprayed through the air, and the faun screamed even louder.

Heidi stretched out her arms to the other children. 'Don't look!' she cried. 'Close your eyes!'

Some of them did - Amy, Tim, CeeCee. The others kept watching with wide, stunned eyes. Heidi grabbed Amy and hugged her close, pressing her face against her belly, and tried not to look. She could hear it, though: the howling of the crowd, the agonised shrieks of Rudraige, and a horrible, wet tearing sound. She couldn't stop herself from taking another look. She turned her head in time to see one of the faun's arms cut and torn away from her body with a sickening crunch of severed cartilage and bone. The crowd surged to one side as the limb came free, like a ripple when a stone is dropped into still water. Then one of her legs was torn free, and they surged again, an angry sea keeping the unfortunate faun afloat.

Heidi found her eyes following the severed arm, which was carried away from the body by two fauns who kept it held above their heads. They took it to the edge of the fire, to another faun who was clearing a spit of roasted meat. This one lifted the spike from the spit with hands wrapped in rags, and Heidi watched the three of them work the spike into the meat of Rudraige's severed arm. Her mind went back to the meat they had eaten earlier that night, the impossibly large joint of meat.

What had they eaten?

Her stomach churned. Suddenly she felt dizzy and sick. Turning her head away again, she hugged Amy closer and closed her eyes.

After what seemed like both a very short and very long time, Rudraige's screams stopped. The crowd grew quieter and spread out around the clearing. Looking back, Heidi saw them carrying the separated parts of the dead faun to different spits and cooking pots around the fire. Some were crouched around a pile of her belongings, handing out the bangles and beads and pieces of cloth between them. Other than a large bloodstain quickly seeping into the dirt, there was nothing of Rudraige left. And the Lord of the Green had disappeared.

The children were still stood in place, looking at the fauns around them in terror. Heidi tried to think of what to say to them, how to comfort them, but no words came. She couldn't think of what she should say.

A warm hand fell onto her shoulder, and she looked up to see Gilla staring down at her with those unreadable eyes.

'Why don't we get you children inside,' she said kindly. 'You can all rest in my hut together.'

Not knowing what else to do, Heidi nodded. She turned back to the children and cleared her throat. 'Come on.'

Gilla took Heidi's hand and reached out her free hand to Amy, who took it with a dazed expression that Heidi didn't like much. The other children clustered around and allowed Gilla to lead them back to her hut. For just a moment, Heidi felt a fierce relief to have a grown-up to tell her what to do. But then she remembered what had happened to Rudraige. Tuan and Gilla had remained at the edge of the crowd, far from the slaughter, but they had been howling and cheering like all of the others. Her relief evaporated quickly.

At the hut, Gilla swept aside the curtain at the door and ushered them all in, nodding to each child as they passed by her. When they were all inside, she stood in the doorway and looked at them for a long moment.

Eventually, she said, 'I think perhaps you would like to be left alone for a while. I can tell you are disturbed by what you have seen tonight.' She paused, taking in the dazed and terrified children looking back at her. 'I know it is strange and frightening to you, but it is how we live,' she went on. 'We do not tolerate those who go against our laws. Rudraige knew this. It was just.'

CeeCee spoke up, her voice small and choked with tears. 'It was just a dirty old nightdress,' she said.

Gilla hesitated, her eyes closing for a moment. She frowned and shook her head, her horns swaying heavily to and fro. 'I will speak to the Lord of the Green about finding you a guide,' she said finally. 'I think perhaps you will want to be leaving soon.'

None of the children responded. Without another word, Gilla let the curtain drop between them, and they heard the soft thud of her hooves as she slowly walked away.

There was silence in the hut for a long time. Heidi stared at the gently swaying curtain, somehow afraid to look at the others. She didn't want to see the fear in their eyes; it was too much like her own.

Eventually, though, someone said, 'What do we do now?'

With a weary sigh, Heidi turned around. They were once again all looking at her - except for Amy, who was staring at nothing with that same dazed expression.

'I think we should try to get some sleep,' she replied. 'Then, in the morning – I mean, when we wake up - we'll be ready to go.'

'Are we really going to try and find the Shining City?'

Monifa asked, her yellow eyes round and solemn. At Heidi's nod, she went on: 'But the Green Lord said they're bad.'

'This lot ain't exactly good though, are they?' Tyler muttered.

Monifa scowled at him, but some of the other children were nodding.

'My head hurts,' Tim said quietly.

Heidi sighed. 'He also said that the Tuatha are the only ones who will know how we can get home,' she replied. 'They're the only ones who can help us.'

'But will they help us?' Monifa pressed.

'I don't know,' Heidi snapped. She was tired – so tired, and just as scared as everybody else. 'But if nobody else *can*, it doesn't really matter, does it? We have to try them.'

Monifa was quiet at that. Heidi glanced at her and saw the abashed look on her face. She was sorry she'd snapped at her. She was opening her mouth to apologise when Tim spoke again. 'Heidi, I have a headache.'

Heidi gritted her teeth and turned to him. 'Not now, Tim – '

Her words died on her lips as she caught sight of the boy. His forehead looked angry and red, and two large lumps were raised on either side, just above his temples. The skin on them looked stretched tight, and even as she watched it began to crack and bleed. Tim groaned and lifted his hands to his head.

'Don't touch!' Heidi cried, hurrying to his side. Very aware that everyone was staring, she took his hands in hers and pushed them down, taking a closer look.

It was dark in the hut, the only light coming from the flickering lantern that was suspended from the centre of the roof and the firelight glowing through the curtains at the door and windows, but there was enough light to see the points of the two horns that were forcing their way through the skin. Tim moaned in pain as they emerged with a slight cracking sound. They grew to only a couple of inches long, then seemed to stop. They were small, pointed, and curved slightly upwards.

Apart from Tim's pained noises, the hut was silent again. Heidi looked around for something to clean away the blood with before it could drip into Tim's eyes. Finally, she got up to pull her old nightdress from the hammock and used that. When she was done, she smiled at him. 'Feeling better?' she asked.

'Yeah,' Tim replied with a weak smile. 'Yeah, it's not so bad any more.' He glanced around and saw that everyone was looking at him. 'What?'

Tyler pointed at him. 'You've got horns,' he said.

Tim's hands flew to his head before Heidi could stop him, and he ran his fingers over the new horns. His jaw dropped.

'I've got horns!' he cried. 'Why have I got horns?'

'We've all got -' Heidi began, but he interrupted her.

'You don't! And no one else has got horns! Why have I got horns? I don't want horns! Why can't I have cool eyes like Monifa, or ... or...'

Monifa looked surprised, then smiled. But then Tim burst into tears and her smile faded. She came over and sat beside him, wrapping her arms around his skinny shoulders.

'It's okay,' she said. 'I think your horns are cooler than my stupid eyes anyway.' She gave Heidi a strange look and shook her head. It was a look that said "You wouldn't understand".

Stung, Heidi moved aside and watched as the other children - who had all changed in some way - gathered around Tim to comfort him. CeeCee spread her fingers wide to show Tim the webbed skin between them. Tariq pulled off his bobble hat and wiggled his pointed ears, making Tim laugh. Meghan lay on her back and waved her clawed feet in the air. Even Sue joined in, lifting up her leather tunic to display the tail poking out of her leggings. After the fuss she'd made about keeping it hidden earlier, Heidi found that particularly annoying. She stood by the door and looked at them all. Through the blonde curtain of Amy's hair, she could see pointed tips to her little pink ears.

They were all changing, then. All except her, it seemed. Why wasn't she changing? She felt absurdly left out. *It's not a good thing*, she scolded herself. What if they kept changing, like Gilla said? What if they changed too much and couldn't go home? And if they did get home, would they change back? They had to get home as soon as they could. *She* had to...

Suddenly overwhelmed, she slipped unnoticed out of the door and sat outside, her back against the side of the hut. It wasn't much better out there. She could see the fauns in the clearing, dancing to the music that had started up again, cooking and eating their meat. Where before it had seemed a merry scene, it had now turned sinister and obscene. Even the music didn't appeal to her any more.

There's a word for it, she thought glumly. She'd read it in a history book.

'Cannibals,' she whispered to herself.

Suddenly, she felt the sting of tears behind her eyes. Burying her face in her arms, she let them come. She was impossibly far from home, surrounded by danger with no clue who to trust, and now she wasn't even part of the group any more. She felt more alone and helpless in this moment than she ever had in her life. Even after her parents had died, she hadn't felt this alone. She'd had Grandma to turn to, even if she had always been half-aware of the old woman's resentment at having to take care of her. Who did she have now? *She* was the one everyone was turning to.

A gentle tap on her shoulder startled her, and she glanced up fearfully. It was Tim, looking down at her, his horns already looking oddly a part of him.

He gave her a sad smile. 'You okay?'

She wiped away her tears hurriedly and smiled back. 'I'm fine,' she replied. 'Just ... homesick, I guess.'

'Me too.' Tim sat down next to her and snuggled close; she had to turn her head to avoid one of his horns poking her in the eye. 'But I was worried that I hurt your feelings when I said you didn't have any ... you know.'

She knew. She shrugged. 'It's not your fault,' she replied. 'You were upset. But I do feel a bit...'

'Left out?'

'...Yeah.'

Tim wrapped his arms around her waist and gave her a fierce hug. 'Well, I think you're the coolest whether you're changed or not changed,' he said firmly. 'You're the bravest one, and you look after us all. You're the best.'

Heidi smiled and hugged him back, the hollow feeling in her chest receding a little. 'Thanks, Tim.'

'Will you come back inside?'

Heidi pretended to consider. 'Depends. Has Sue stopped waving her butt around?'

Tim giggled. 'Yeah.'

'Alright then.' She got to her feet, pulling Tim up with her, and let him lead her back inside.

What Do We Do Without Our Children?

An article from The Daily Mail.

Six months after the catastrophic failure of the government's plan to protect our newborns from abduction by an unknown force, and three and a half years after "The Event" first happened, its legacy of misery is wreaking destruction upon our society.

Primary schools and nurseries across the country are all but extinct, and the recent surge in unemployment continues to rise. Secondary schools and colleges – now running on borrowed time without a constant influx of younger children - are becoming fortified institutions akin to prisons, with heavy security outside and government mandated lunch rotas and health plans inside ensuring that our youngest members of society are kept as healthy as possible. Teenagers from various schools have referred to the scheme as "controlling", "demeaning", and "draconian", with the latest proposal by the government to make all schools function as boarding schools being hotly protested from multiple camps, including some of the Prime Minister's own party.

Life inside a secondary school – "We've committed no crime"

Contraceptives of all kinds and abortions were made illegal immediately after the "Third Event", with government-run organisations offering to buy babies from women who will willingly give them up. These babies are to be brought up in secret locations with the thin hope that they will not be located on the fourth anniversary in six months' time. New parents who want to keep their babies are reportedly being "strongly encouraged" to give up their children to the scheme, though the Prime Minister has hotly denied this.

But the Prime Minister has enough to worry about, with outrage at the passing of emergency measures without parliamentary approval, some comparing it to a dictatorship. Protests are occurring regularly outside the Houses of Parliament and throughout London – and throughout the UK – against what is seen as an overthrow of democracy. Parliament itself is up in arms, with the Leader of the Opposition accusing the Prime Minister of being an "opportunistic narcissist", and of using a time of national tragedy to push for ultimate power. And, with the rate at which his own MPs are deserting him, the Prime Minister may soon have no choice but to become the dictator he is accused of trying to be.

The Prime Minister's private emails – leaked!

In between the protests about the demise of democracy, parents across the UK are revolting about the right to liberty being denied to our children. In addition to the fortification of schools, strict curfews are still in place for anyone under the age of 18, and have been since two weeks before the "Third Event". Government officials still loyal to the Prime Minister have not responded to complaints that the curfew should be limited to the days leading up to the anniversary, stating that the safety of the young people of the UK continues to be their number one priority.

And that's just here in the UK. Similar things are happening in the US, with schools employing armed guards and installing high walls, whilst presidential debates turn into screaming matches about what to do with the children. There are signs from news leaks online that US relations with Russia, China, North Korea, and the EU are all at breaking point as they look for someone to blame.

There are disturbing reports from other countries as well, though they are hard to verify with so many smaller countries closing their borders and cutting off communication with the outside world in attempts to protect themselves from what some are calling a "terrible act of God". Reports include stories of newborns being forcibly taken from distraught parents, women being recruited into baby factories, and a steep increase in cases of rape and sexual assault. Terrorist groups are rumoured to be gathering their forces, claiming The Event to be a divine condemnation of Western values, of the corruption of youth by modern society, or simply a condemnation of humanity itself. The UK, the US, and all countries in the EU are on a high level terror alert, and sources state that there is no plan to lower the alert anytime soon.

The shocking story of the asylum seekers stopped at Dover last week

So what do we have to look forward to? Riots? Dictatorships? Terrorist attacks? Outright war? With still no answer to what happened to our children, nearly four years on, hope for their return is all but gone. And hope for our future is fading just as fast.

CHAPTER 12

MOVING ON

They awoke sometime later, huddled together in furs and blankets from Gilla's hut. The music had stopped, and when they peered out past the curtain in the doorway they saw that the feast was over. Fauns were going to and fro, doing normal, everyday things – or what normal things there must have been. They were carrying baskets of fruit, repairing damaged huts, sweeping away the embers of the massive bonfire, and piling up branches and logs for the next one.

Gilla and her mate Tuan were waiting outside the hut, and they turned to greet the children as they slowly filed out. Gilla knelt down to address Heidi. 'Your guide has been decided,' she said, with a trace of apprehension. 'Tuan will go with you.'

Heidi looked up at Tuan, who was standing nearby, a soft smile on his face. 'It's very kind of you,' she said, careful not to say the T-word.

Tuan chuckled. 'It's very foolish, if you believe her,' he replied, nodding toward Gilla. 'She thinks I'll never come home.'

Gilla shot him a narrow-eyed glare. 'Hush!'

Winking at her, Tuan continued. 'It's not without risk for me, I cannot deny. But I'm not about to let Children of Mil head to the Shining City without a guide. And I'm not about to let the honour of being your guide go to someone else.' He grinned.

'Is it an honour?' Heidi asked.

'Oh yes,' Tuan replied. 'There's all sorts of stories about the Children of Mil returning to Arcadia. I'd like to be in one.'

'What sort of stories?' Tim asked from behind Heidi.

Tuan looked at him and shrugged. 'I'll tell you a few on the journey, perhaps,' he replied. 'But we really should be off. It's a long way, you know.'

Another faun approached. Heidi recognised him as the stern guard from the gate – the one who had taken the spriggan away. Suddenly, she gasped. 'Where's Sprickleback?' she cried. She had completely forgotten about him.

The guard grimaced. 'That little pest you brought in with you? He was thrown out of the village.' He noticed the relief that spread across her features and chuckled. 'Don't worry, we didn't kill your pet. Though he was lucky we didn't. I was all for it, but the Lord of the Green said he deserved clemency for bringing you here. He should be long gone by now.' Turning to Tuan, he said, 'Are you ready to go?'

'Almost.' Tuan turned to the children. 'Irgoll will be joining us on the journey. With there being so many of you, we thought two guides would be best. Consider yourselves blessed indeed – he's one of the finest warriors we have.'

Irgoll snorted, an oddly horse-like sound. 'Flattery,' he said gruffly. 'I'll wait for you at the gate.'

As he turned away, Heidi noticed that he carried a large leather bag on his back, hanging from one shoulder. One hand held the strap steady while the other held his spear. Now she noticed that Tuan had an axe on each hip, hanging from a belt around his furry waist.

'Is this going to be dangerous?' she asked.

'Oh, certainly,' Tuan replied, and grinned again. 'That's why you have us. Are you ready?'

With some fuss, the children gathered up what scant belongings they had and lined up before Tuan. Gilla busied herself pressing small parcels of food into their hands, pieces of cloth wrapped around fruits and chunks of fresh bread, before grabbing Tuan by his shoulders and giving him an oddly affectionate headbutt. Their horns collided with a loud, dull thunk.

'Stay safe,' she said to him, her voice strained.

'I'll be back before you have time to miss me,' Tuan replied, lifting a hand to caress her cheek. As he turned away, he whispered to the children, 'That gives us plenty of time – she'll be glad of the peace!'

The older children gave a half-hearted chuckle, and he grinned and trotted on ahead of them, leading the way to the gate.

Following near the front of the group, Heidi wondered where Sprickleback would have gotten to. She felt a little bad for him. Alright, so he had been pretty unpleasant, and had done nothing to keep them safe. But he'd been hoping for a reward for getting them where they were going, and the only reward he'd had was not being killed.

Then, her thoughts turned to Baby and Ricky, lost in the lake, and she didn't feel so bad for him any more.

A small crowd of fauns was waiting at the gate to see them off. The Lord of the Green was not among them. As they filed through to where Irgoll was waiting, the fauns draped over them garlands of flowers, woven blankets, and strange charms made of wood and string. More bags and parcels of food were thrust into their hands, and by the time they got to the gate, their arms were full.

Irgoll surveyed them with a disapproving eye. 'It's a good thing I didn't fill my bag,' he said, and swung it off of his shoulder. 'Put as much of that in here as will fit. If it won't fit in a bag, eat it now or leave it behind.'

Most of it fit, although a few apples and handfuls of bread and nuts ended up in pockets or shoved into mouths. Tim was already crunching merrily at an apple as Irgoll shouldered the bag again and they set off down the path. He offered some to Heidi, who shook her head, thinking of Sue's tail and Meghan's feet. 'I'm not hungry,' she said.

Tim shrugged. 'Suit yourself,' he replied, taking another large bite. 'I'm eating it before we run out again.'

They retraced the path they had taken with the spriggan, and when they got to the shore of the lake the children huddled close, giving the water's edge a wide berth. Noticing this, Tuan launched into a merry story about a group of mortal children who had come to Faerieland through a hidden doorway, and had ended up tricking and defeating a cruel witch. Heidi thought it sounded vaguely familiar.

'Can I ask you a question?' she asked him, when he was done. By this point the lake was behind them, and the children had relaxed a little.

Tuan smiled down at her. 'If I can ask you one in return.'

Heidi smiled back. 'Alright. I've noticed that you've called this land by a couple of different names. Why do you do that? What's its real name?'

Tuan chuckled. 'That's two questions,' he replied, 'But they have the same answer, so I'll give it to you. No one knows the real name of these lands. We use the names it's been given, by us and by outsiders. Some prefer one name or the other, but it makes no real difference.'

'No one knows what this land is called?' Heidi repeated.

Tuan bent low to her as they walked. 'Some say the only one who knows the true name of Faerieland is its rightful king or queen,' he said in a mock whisper. 'And when the day comes that they utter its true name, they will be crowned, and all the fae creatures will be united.'

'A pretty story,' Irgoll said from ahead of them. 'But I doubt it will ever come to pass.'

Tuan snorted derisively. 'That's no way to think.'

'It's a perfectly fine way to think,' Irgoll retorted. 'It keeps me focused on now, not on some hopeful future.' Falling silent, he quickened his step. The children struggled to keep up.

Tuan looked at Heidi and shrugged. 'I guess he didn't like my stories,' he said.

Heidi giggled. 'Guess not. What's your question?'

'Hm? Oh...' Tuan shrugged again. 'I'll keep it and think of something later.'

With the fauns leading them, and cutting out some of the ambling paths the spriggan had taken them on, the group reached the entrance to the Hollow Hill in good time. As the mouth of the cave came into sight, the children grew excited and ran ahead, eager to see the sun again. Irgoll roughly reminded them to stay close, his eyes on the trees around them, but they made it to the tunnel without incident. Before long, they were out of the hillside again, blinking in the bright light of a summer sun in a cloudless blue sky.

Heidi turned her face up to the sun, basking in its warmth. 'Ah, that's nice,' she sighed, and took a deep breath. The air up here seemed sweeter, free of a faint muskiness that she hadn't noticed inside the hill until she was out of it.

Tuan stood beside her, his head tilted up, too. 'It is,' he replied. 'I always like being sent out here.'

Even Irgoll seemed happy to pause for a moment, and suggested they stop to eat. The group spread themselves out on the hillside, passing out food between them. Soon they had made a strange little picnic, camped out in the long grass.

They'd only been sat for a few minutes when Meghan gave a small shriek of surprise. The fauns turned to face her, their hands flying to their weapons, but then they relaxed as they saw the smile on her face. Three tiny figures were climbing up the woollen weave of the cloth around her chest as if it was a ladder.

Heidi grinned as she recognised Twist, Whistle, and Flick. 'Where have they been?' she exclaimed.

Meghan shrugged, helping one of them up onto her shoulder with her fingertip. 'I don't know,' she replied. 'I lost track of them after we got to the village. I thought they'd run away!'

Irgoll grunted. 'More pests.'

Tuan shook his head at him. 'Pixies aren't that bad,' he replied. 'They do make me itch though, so kindly keep them to yourselves if you can.'

One of the pixies stuck out their tiny tongue at the faun. However, they seemed quite happy to remain with Meghan, disappearing into her hair as they had before.

'You'll never get the knots out,' Tuan warned her with a sad sigh.

Meghan giggled. 'I don't mind.'

They all munched in contented silence for a while. Then Tuan spoke up.

'I've thought of my question,' he said to Heidi.

Everyone looked at her. She nodded. 'What is it?'

'What was it like for you, in your world?' Tuan asked. Behind him, Irgoll leaned forward, interested.

Heidi hesitated, then sighed. 'Well,' she said, 'it was ... safe. Boring, I suppose. But I felt safe. I lived at a boarding school, so there were always grown-ups around to keep an eye on me.'

'You lived at a boarding school?' CeeCee repeated. 'Were you rich?'

Heidi hesitated again. 'My grandmother was,' she replied eventually. 'I had to live with her after my parents died.' She frowned. 'I don't think she really wanted me around.'

CeeCee blushed. 'Sorry,' she said softly. 'I didn't mean...'

Heidi shook her head. 'It's okay.'

'It's just that my parents were quite poor,' CeeCee blurted. 'And the rich kids went to the boarding school and the poor ones went to the normal school and had to go home each day.'

Meghan spoke up. 'My family was poor too. But I always felt like they wanted me.' She looked at Heidi. 'That sucks that your grandma didn't want you. And I'm sorry about your parents.'

'I miss my parents,' Tim said sadly. 'We were going to go to Disneyworld for the summer holidays.'

Heidi looked around the group as everyone started talking about their homes and their families, as if a floodgate had been opened. Sue described the busy streets and street food vendors of Hong Kong; Tariq told them about the gang of friends he'd hung around with; Tyler spoke about how his dad really wanted him to play football, but he hated it; Monifa said how she wanted to be a nurse, like her mother. Amy started to cry a little, until Monifa pulled her close and hugged her tightly, whispering in her ear.

Throughout it, the two fauns listened intently. As the conversation died down, Tuan gave a deep sigh. 'I asked for one answer, and I got many,' he said. 'You Children of Mil are generous.'

'Maybe you can repay us with another story,' Heidi suggested.

Irgoll spoke up. 'Repay them when we next stop. We've rested enough for now.'

Tuan gave an exaggerated groan, making the smaller children laugh. 'You are a hard master, Irgoll!'

Irgoll frowned and nodded his head upward, toward the sky. Tuan looked up, and then he frowned as well. 'Ah. You're quite right. Time to move on.'

None of the other children seemed to catch this exchange. Heidi looked up as they all got to their feet and started putting any uneaten food into pockets and bags. In the sky far above them she could make out a few dark shapes, wheeling in lazy circles. As they started to walk, she caught up to Tuan and tapped his arm.

'Are those dragons?' she asked.

Tuan looked down at her and nodded. 'Don't tell the others,' he said. 'Hopefully they'll decide there's too many of us and won't bother us.'

'But Sprickleback said they only go after small prey,' Heidi replied.

'Did he?' Tuan gave a wry smile. 'Well, he was half-right. The faery dragons only go for small game. The bigger types, though...' He trailed off ominously.

Heidi looked up again. She couldn't tell how big the shapes in the sky really were from this distance. 'How do we tell if they're not faery dragons?'

'It's their wings,' Tuan replied, 'and their movement. Faery dragons have thin, iridescent wings, like a dragonfly. They have to keep them moving fast to stay in the air, and they tend to move quickly and stop suddenly. They're also not very smart. True dragons have leathery wings that move more slowly, and they can float on the winds like birds. They can move as fast or as slow as they like. And they hunt in packs.'

Heidi glanced up again. She counted three shapes, still moving in slow circles. Shading her eyes from the sun, she could make out the shapes of wings. She looked back to Tuan, who regarded her solemnly. 'What do we do?' she asked.

His response was grave. 'We keep moving, we stick close together, and we hope they don't have friends.'

It was a couple of hours later when Tariq hurried up to Heidi and pulled on her sleeve. 'Something's following us,' he hissed in her ear.

Heidi looked back, then up at Tuan, who nodded with a grim smile. 'I know. I spotted him almost as soon as we got out of the hill. It's your pesky little spriggan friend.'

'Sprickleback?' Heidi looked back again, past the children walking behind them. She couldn't see anything except for the long grass, swaying slightly in the light breeze.

Tuan saw her looking and snorted. 'Trust me, he's there. Your friend has sharp eyes; spriggans are very good at hiding when they don't want to be seen.'

Tariq beamed proudly. 'I've got sharp eyes,' he repeated, mimicking the faun's admiring tone.

Heidi suppressed a giggle. 'Why do you think he's following us?' she asked Tuan.

He shrugged. 'Probably hoping to still get his reward for you somehow. Whatever the reason, it'll be for no one's good but his. I'd advise leaving him to skulk behind us. If he tries to do any of you harm, it will be the last thing he ever does.'

The threat in his voice was not lost on Heidi, and she tried not to shudder. Just when she was starting to see these creatures as friends, they said or did something that reminded her of just how dangerous they could be. She turned to Tariq and smiled.

'Thanks for telling me,' she said to him in a low voice. 'Do you think you could keep an eye on him? You know, with your *sharp eyes?*

He grinned back at her and gave a playful salute. 'Aye aye, captain,' he cried, and bounded back to the rear of the group. The other children looked at him curiously, some of them falling into step with him and shouting piratical phrases. Suddenly the group of children hiking across the grassy plains had become a pirate ship, sailing through a green sea.

It was a few hours later, when the game had worn off and the children were starting to slow and tire, that Tuan gave a soft curse. Heidi saw him exchange a glance with Irgoll, and one hand fell to the handle of one of his axes. Irgoll shifted the strap of his bag from across his body so that it hung from only one shoulder. At about the same time, Tariq – who had taken Heidi's request seriously – called out, 'Hey, look at all the dragons up there!'

In unison, the children all looked up. Above their heads, much lower than before, were five large, leathery-winged dragons. They were all varying shades of a dusty green colour, and they floated on the breeze above them, their heads dipped down. The children, all except for Heidi, shouted and laughed and pointed, but before long the mood of the two fauns filtered through their delight, and the laughter stopped.

'Tuan?' CeeCee said timidly. 'Are we in trouble?'

Tuan looked up at the dragons, no longer trying to hide it, and frowned. 'Depends how hungry they are,' he replied. 'Dragons are smart, and strong, but they're also lazy. If we can give them enough trouble, they may decide that we're not worth the effort. Are you children able to run?'

The children exchanged frightened looks. Some of them nodded. Sue took Amy from Meghan, who was starting to struggle under the toddler's weight.

'I'll lead,' Irgoll said.

'I'll follow,' Tuan responded. 'Children, you need to follow Irgoll. Run as fast as you can, and stay together. I'll be behind you. Ready?'

The children all nodded.

'Good.' Tuan glanced up once more, then gave a single clap of his hands. 'Go!'

Irgoll instantly leaped forward, his powerful legs carrying him swiftly ahead. As the children raced after him, he slowed his pace to match theirs, staying just an arm's reach or so ahead. Behind him the children ran, and behind them came Tuan, with both axes now in his hands and his eyes on the sky. Heidi dropped to the rear of the group and ran near him. When she heard him curse again, she looked up to see the dragons break their lazy circle and follow after them. They were getting bigger. No – they were getting closer.

'Where are we going?' she cried. The land here was a seemingly endless plain of grass; there was nowhere to hide.

Tuan glanced up again. 'Nowhere,' he replied, then raised his voice. 'Irgoll! We're not shaking them!'

Irgoll stopped and turned to meet the children as they stumbled to a halt before him. He looked up, then over their heads at Tuan. 'What's the plan?'

Tuan watched the dragons as they resumed their circling, but this time much lower and faster. 'Can we lead them off? Send the children on?'

'They'll go for the ones without weapons,' Irgoll replied.

'Stick together then?'

Irgoll nodded and dropped the bag to the ground, hefting his spear in both hands. 'Maybe we can fend them off. Children, lie down and keep as low as you can.'

The breathless and terrified children obediently dropped to the ground, some flat on their stomachs, some curled into balls, some holding onto another's hands or with an arm around a neighbour. Heidi found herself lying next to Sue, who was curled protectively around Amy. The toddler was crying quietly into Sue's tunic as she rubbed her back comfortingly. On the other side of her was Tariq, who was lying on his stomach with his arms wrapped around his head. Heidi put out a hand and grabbed one of his, and he squeezed it hard. She could feel him trembling.

The two fauns put their backs to the huddled children and faced the dragons, who were now swooping almost close enough to be in range of Irgoll's spear. They were about the size of large horses, and yet somehow Heidi managed to feel relieved that they were not the massive creatures from the fairytales she had read. Then she remembered that they were still dragons – five of them – and her relief vanished. She wondered if they breathed fire. God, she hoped they didn't breathe fire.

One of the dragons swooped in even closer, and Irgoll stabbed out at it with his spear. It recoiled and spiralled upward with an angry hiss, its wings buffeting the air above their heads. Another dived down toward Tuan, who gave a fierce roar and aimed a swing at it with an axe. Again, the beast dodged and curved away.

'What's happening?' Tariq said softly, his voice muffled in the grass. 'I can't look.'

'They're testing them out, I think,' Heidi replied.

A couple more dragons took turns swooping in to snap at the fauns. They could have been the same two; Heidi couldn't tell. The fauns responded fiercely, keeping them at bay with their weapons. The dragons seemed to retreat for a moment, gathering together briefly in the sky, then they separated and two of them closed their wings and dropped like stones toward Tuan. He swung at one, his axe slicing into the scales on the creature's foreleg, and it shrieked angrily and flew up out of reach; but the other dragon kept on course, forcing the faun to dodge aside. The children screamed in terror as they felt the rush of the air inches above them as the dragon passed over. Heidi saw sharp claws reaching, grasping for them, but Irgoll spun around and thrust his spear at the reaching talons, forcing the creature upwards.

Tuan jumped up and swiped at a third dragon that was bearing down on him. 'Get away!' he screamed at it. It turned to the side before his axe could connect and circled back up to the others. Irgoll managed to fend off two more who dove at him with a nimble stab and sweep of his spear. The dragons flew upwards, regrouping again. Then, they separated once more.

This time, they all dove at once. Irgoll repeated his attack with his spear. The first dragon redirected away, and the second was pierced through its wing as it tried to get past him. It shrieked, trying to pull up and away, but Irgoll hung onto his spear and brought it crashing to the ground. Tuan buried one axe in the shoulder of the third dragon, but the fourth hit him headfirst, barrelling him out of the way. And the fifth dragon was able to dive in while the fauns were occupied.

Heidi pulled her hand from Tariq's and covered her head as the dragon's rear feet hit the ground on either side of her with a deafening thud. Then, an ear-splitting scream made her look up again. The scream was coming from Sue as those long, sharp claws sank into her back and dragged her into the air. Heidi screamed with her, reaching out a hand to try and grab her. The most she could do was briefly brush her fingertips as she was swept away. Something warm and wet splattered across her face and outstretched hand. Her stomach clenched as she saw the bright crimson of Sue's blood on her pale skin. Panicked, she swiped at it with her palms, leaving long red smears.

Amy tumbled from Sue's grasp, wailing hysterically. Heidi grabbed the tiny girl by her nightdress and dragged her close, leaving red handprints on the white cloth. The air around them was filled with flying grass and dirt, and she tucked Amy under her arm, trying to shelter her with her body. The dragon's wings thundered over their heads as it took flight again, Sue clutched in its claws. Her pained screams faded as she was carried away.

Four dragons remained.

Irgoll wrestled his spear free from the dragon on the ground, and it immediately struggled to its feet, kicking and snapping at him and lashing its tail to and fro to drive him back. Then, it beat its wings and took flight awkwardly in a dipping, half-falling fashion, keeping close to the ground, retreating from the attack. But while Irgoll struggled with it, the first dragon swooped in behind his turned back. The children were lying as flat as they could, shaking and sobbing with fear. Only a few of them dared to look. Meghan was looking, and when she saw the dragon swooping down on them her nerve broke and she scrambled to all fours and tried to run. Irgoll turned too late, swiping at the dragon as it passed, and saw her.

'No!' he cried.

Meghan was still trying to get up to her feet when the dragon's talons wrapped around her middle and she was hoisted, screaming and kicking, into the sky. A jet of dark blood was forced from her mouth as the claws sank into her belly as easily as a knife slicing into butter. Heidi saw her eyes widen in pain and surprise before the dragon soared away.

Two dragons left.

Tuan had managed to hang onto the dragon that had head-butted him and was half-wrapped around its neck, holding on with one arm while he hacked at the beast's head with his axe. The dragon bucked and shook, trying to throw him off, and snapped at his legs as he kicked and fought to stay away from its jaws. The other was bearing down on the huddled children, all four clawed feet stretched out, ready to land and snatch one of them up. Heidi looked up to see it getting closer and bigger, and felt the rushing wind from its beating wings pushing her down. She closed her eyes and buried her head in the grass, sheltering Amy as best she could. She didn't want to see any more. She didn't want Amy to see any more. She could hear her heart thundering and her panicked breathing echoing in her ears. The skin on her back crawled, feeling horribly exposed. Any second now, the claws would come. Any second...

Then, she heard two loud footfalls and an agonised shriek. Opening her eyes, she saw Irgoll standing above her, his spear raised in both hands and thrust into the creature's chest. It reared back in the air, pulling itself free, and tried to fly away. Irgoll let it, running to help Tuan. Heidi recoiled at the warm splash of blood from the dragon's wound - much more than Sue's - as the beast flew low over their heads. Looking up, she saw it falter and dip in the air not far away before it crashed into the grass, wings flailing.

Another pained shriek made her turn her head, where she saw Irgoll pushing his spear through the side of the dragon struggling with Tuan. It threw back its head and howled, and Tuan let go and dropped to the ground. He rolled, then came up and brought his axe down between its snakelike eyes with a loud, wet crunch. It shrieked again, gave a shudder, and fell limp.

A hush fell over the plain, softly punctuated by the sobs of the children that still huddled on the floor. Tuan and Irgoll were panting heavily as they untangled themselves from the dead dragon. Tuan winced and limped over to the children. 'Blasted dragon took my axe,' he muttered.

'Which one?' Irgoll asked as he wrenched his spear free.

'The one with it stuck in its shoulder,' Tuan replied.

Irgoll crossed over to him. 'Are you hurt?'

'Just a nip. My leg.'

'Let me see.'

From her position on the ground, Heidi watched as Irgoll helped Tuan sit down and start inspecting his injured leg. Amy squirmed in her arms, still crying, and she shushed her gently, stroking the little girl's hair with shaking hands. The effort seemed to calm her as well as Amy, and she was thankful for it.

Gradually, the children started to sit up. Monifa and Tim were with CeeCee. Tyler was sitting on his own, hugging his knees to his chest, rocking back and forth. Tariq had rolled onto his back next to Heidi and had an arm over his eyes. She could see the tears streaming down his dark cheeks. She sat up, pulling Amy into her lap, and looked with dismay at the red stains on her nightdress. Tim, CeeCee and Tyler were speckled with red too; the dragon's blood. It was drying on Tim's bare back, and soaking into CeeCee's white shirt in widening crimson stains. A diagonal streak showed vividly on Tyler's pale face as he rocked back and forth. The rough linen weave of the green blanket he wore like a poncho was splattered with red.

A shudder of revulsion ripped through her, and she swiped

at the blood on her skin and clothes frantically, wanting it gone. How much of it was Sue's blood, or Meghan's? She could feel her breathing starting to speed up again as a dull panic set in. Amy tumbled from her lap and started to cry again. She barely noticed. Only when Monifa and Tariq approached, Monifa scooping up the crying toddler and Tariq wrapping his arms around her, did she stop scrubbing at the bloodstains.

'Heidi,' Tariq said quietly, through tears. 'They're gone. They're gone.'

Who was he talking about - the dragons or their friends? Heidi wanted to ask, but she couldn't seem to form the words. Instead she let him hug her, clutching her bloodstained hands to her chest to keep them still. Gradually, her breathing slowed and the panic that had threatened to overcome her receded.

A small movement on the ground nearby caught her eye, and she looked over to see one of the pixies stumbling toward her in an unsteady line. She thought it was Twist. As the pixie approached, she could see that he was pointing up into the air with one hand, the other tugging at his tangled hair. Gently pushing Tariq away, she put out a hand for Twist to climb on, and he did, dropping down to sit in the centre of her palm. In an almost identical manner to Tyler, he pulled his knees up to his tiny chest and started to rock back and forth, crying in small, shrill wails.

'What's wrong?' Heidi asked him, lifting him up so she could see him better. He pointed upward again and let out a loud wail. Heidi looked up - and then it dawned on her. 'Were your friends ... with Meghan?' He nodded, and with another loud, miserable cry, buried his face in his arms.

Heidi watched the tiny figure weeping in her hand and felt her heart ache for him. They'd been treating these creatures like pets, but really they were tiny people, just like them. And just like them, Twist had lost friends. She looked up again, but there was no sign of the monsters that had attacked them. Meghan and Sue were long gone. She felt hot tears running down her cheeks and lowered her head, curling the hand holding Twist to her chest protectively. She wanted to hug him, but he was too small. Instead she hugged Tariq even more tightly with her other arm. Briefly, she wondered where Sprickleback was, and if he had managed to hide from the dragons. He was probably too small for them to bother with, she thought. She was angry for a moment that he hadn't tried to help them, but then pushed it aside. He was so small; what could he have done?

Tuan gave a muffled yelp as Irgoll started wrapping a piece of cloth around his leg. He looked away, and his eyes fell on the children. He dropped his gaze and sighed. 'I'm sorry,' he said, raising his voice a little to address them all. 'We tried.'

There was a short, miserable silence. Eventually Monifa spoke up. 'Probably would have taken us all if you weren't here,' she mumbled.

Tuan paused, then nodded. 'Almost certainly.'

Irgoll finished wrapping his leg. 'It's just a glancing wound. Not very deep. It'll hurt for a while, but as long as it heals well it shouldn't cause you any lasting harm.'

'Good,' Tuan replied, 'because we need to get off of these hills as soon as we can.'

Some of the children glanced nervously at the sky.

'Will they come back?' Tim asked.

'They may,' Tuan replied, climbing carefully to his feet. He tested his injured leg and winced, then nodded. 'I'll manage. Are you children ready to move?'

None of them looked ready. But nobody protested as they all got slowly to their feet, brushed away the dirt and grass on their clothes, and gathered their things. Heidi lifted Twist to her shoulder, where he disappeared, sniffling miserably, into her hair, and then she hefted Amy in one arm. She saw Tim go to CeeCee and take hold of her hand.

Irgoll took up his spear and swung his bag back onto his

shoulder. 'We walk until we have to stop,' he said, and pointed with his spear. 'This way.'

He set off across the grassy plains, Tuan limping along beside him. Falling into a bedraggled line, the children followed silently after them.

Interview No. 561

Interviewing Officer:

This is the interview of Professor Genevieve Powell, lead physicist on what has become known as "The Gateway Project". Professor, were you present for the initial experiment in 2019?

Powell:

No, I was not. I only became involved once the project was moved to CERN, following its ... unexpected success.

IO: For the recording, "CERN" refers to the European Organisation for Nuclear Research. And once it was moved to CERN, what exactly were you doing?

Powell:

We were duplicating the original experiment, only with much more powerful equipment. The original experiment only sent neutrons through the magnetic gateway it created; we aimed to send through cameras, probes – things which could send back information on what was on the other side.

IO:

Were you successful?

Powell:

Yes – at least partially. We were able to send a camera through, but it was destroyed in the process.

IO:

Why was that?

Powell:

The magnetic fields used to create the "gateway" aren't really opening a gate – what they do is cause the particles of whatever passes through the fields to behave differently. They cause them to oscillate at a different frequency, which is what allows them to pass through whatever it is that separates our world from this other world. Unfortunately, the camera was not able to withstand this change in the behaviour of its particles, and cut out shortly after going through the field. But we had designed the camera to withstand the process at least temporarily, so we did get a small amount of footage from it before it died.

IO:

Were you able to retrieve the camera?

Powell:

No. But we were never expecting to, not at that stage in the experiments.

IO:

The results of your experiments were never made public, were they?

Powell:

No.

IO:
Why not?

Powell:
Certain scientific discoveries are often withheld if it is believed that they may cause dissent or panic among the public, or if they might somehow be a threat to national security.
Though the experiment was carried out in Geneva, it was done by an American team, and so the Swiss and US governments were consulted. There was concern that the technology might have military interest, so it was kept quiet until the CIA could determine if it should be announced.
I imagine they were thinking of being able to open portals or some such thing, to allow them to move soldiers around secretly.

IO:
That's conjecture?

Powell:
Oh of course, just my thoughts on it. I've no idea what they thought they might do with it, really.

IO:
We'll make a note of that. Please continue.

Powell:
Not long after that, The Event happened, and the CIA was rather too busy to come to a conclusion on our experiment. So nothing was announced.

IO:
But you kept on experimenting?

Powell:

Of course.

IO:

Tell us about the footage you managed to obtain from the cameras you sent through.

Powell:

It was incredible and confusing. We received images of seemingly different places on the other side of the gateway, yet the location of our experiments was always exactly the same, implying that the location of the other side of the gateway was changing, presumably at random.

We had no idea where the camera would emerge each time we sent it through. The images it sent back were actually rather familiar.

IO:

How so?

Powell:

The first was of a forest of what appeared to be pine trees, though they were incredibly tall. Another was a grassy plain that went on as far as could be seen.

We saw another plain, much flatter, wintry and dark, whereas the first was in bright sunshine. Uh, what else? There was a sort of marshland or something. Another forest, but much more tangled. I'm sorry, I'm not an expert on this stuff.

IO:

Not a problem, go ahead.

Powell:

One appeared to show a very distant city.

IO:

A city? So the land is populated?

Powell:

We can only assume so. We never saw anyone or anything that appeared sentient. But as I said, the city was distant.

IO:

And it definitely wasn't a natural structure?

Powell:

Absolutely not. It was definitely deliberately designed and constructed. It was ... uh...

IO:

Professor Powell?

Powell:

I'm sorry, it sounds stupid, but... It was... It was beautiful. Like something out of the "Lord of the Rings" movies.
(*She laughs*)
Not very scientific of me, I know.

IO:

Have you been able to get a closer look at this city?

Powell:

No. As I said, we don't have any control over where our camera comes out. It seems to be random.

IO:

(*After a short pause*)
You said that you were unable to retrieve the camera. Why?

Powell:

We've only perfected a one-way route through the magnetic field. To be able to bring something back again would require us figuring out how to keep its particles stable through the change in their behaviour, and the subsequent cessation of that change. That's what we're working on next.

IO:

Do you have plans to send anything living through the gateway?

Powell:

Not as yet, but I suppose that would be the logical next step, once we figure out how to stabilise inanimate objects. But... I have to be honest, I don't know how much success we're going to have.

IO:

Why is that?

Powell:

We might be able to figure out how to stop our cameras being destroyed by the process, but living things... Nothing in nature can change its own electromagnetic field. We can withstand small changes in the fields around us, but the strength of the magnetic fields we have had to use for this would be almost instantly lethal to anything living we might try to send through. I don't know how we could compensate for it... I imagine we would have to have some kind of ... suit, like a space suit or something. But as of yet, we've no idea how to go about making it.

IO:

So humans can't go through.

Powell:

Absolutely not.

IO:

What would happen to them if they tried?

Powell:

The strong magnetic fields would literally change the shape and behaviour of their atoms. It would be catastrophic. The person would be... we're not entirely sure, possibly burned alive from the inside out in a matter of seconds, or disintegrated entirely.

IO:

And nothing could come through to our world?

Powell:

Unless the beings over there can change their magnetic fields at whim – which is incredibly unlikely because, as I said, nothing in nature can do that – then no.

IO:

Professor Powell, your initial camera experiment was conducted roughly four months before the first occurrence of what we now call "The Event". Correct?

Powell:

Yes, I believe so.

IO:

Do you believe there could be any link between your experiment and "The Event"?

Powell:

(*After a long silence*)

I know the timing is incredibly suggestive. And I know that, with the children just vanishing and never being found, it is very attractive to wonder. But it just doesn't make any scientific sense.

IO:

Professor Powell, are you familiar with these?
(*Sound of books being put on the table*)

Powell:

Old folk tales? I'm sorry, I've not read them.

IO:

The stories speak of an "otherworld" where old gods and heroes went centuries before the societies we know of inhabited the lands. These stories are from the United Kingdom. Lots of other countries have similar stories.

Powell:

What are you suggesting?

IO:

Based on what you saw in your camera footage...

Powell:

These – these are make believe! Fantasy!

IO:

Based on what you saw, do you think...

Powell:

No! Absolutely not! This is absurd! I can't believe you're even asking me this! You think we saw some ... some fairytale land?
(*After a long silence*)

Is that really what you think?

IO:
At this stage, it's all we have left.

Powell:
You can't be serious.

IO:
Millions of missing children, millions of grieving families, millions in government funding in multiple countries, civil unrest worldwide. Professor Powell, we are very, very serious.

Powell:
(*After a long pause*)
My God.
(*Another long pause*)
But nothing could get through alive ... in either direction... I don't understand...

IO:
We need you to understand. At the risk of sounding overly dramatic, the world needs you to understand.
(*The sound of papers being moved*)
You're to continue your research into the gateway. Report your findings to us as well as your usual channels. We'll make sure you have all the funding you need.

Powell:
But it could cost *millions* of...

IO:
All the funding you need.

CHAPTER 13

THE QUESTION GAME

They seemed to walk across those hills forever. However, it was hard to tell under a sun that never moved, a sky that never grew dark, on terrain that barely changed, and when their shadows never grew longer. There were hardly any trees to offer them shade, and before long nearly all of them were sunburned. CeeCee and Heidi in particular, who were both fair skinned, had their noses, foreheads and cheeks glowing red and tingling with warmth. They did their best to shield Amy from the sun by holding her close or covering her head with their clothes. Tariq gave his woollen hat to her so she could wear it while she walked. It was much too big and kept sliding down over her eyes, but she wore it with a smile.

Eventually, they came across a tree that stood not too far from their path. It was a skinny thing with high branches and large leaves to soak up the sun. At a nod from the fauns, they all clustered beneath it, grateful for the rest and the shade. Heidi thought that she had never been so glad to see a tree.

Many of the children dozed there for a time while the fauns kept watch. Tuan sat with them, Amy snuggled against his furry legs, and Irgoll strolled a short distance away, looking at the route ahead. At the top of the gentle hill they were climbing, he paused. Lying at the base of the tree, it looked to Heidi like he stood at the edge of the world; beyond him, the grass fell away and all she could see was the sky. He looked like a character on a book cover for some fantastical story.

'We're almost out of the hills,' he said when he came back, a small smile on his face. There were exclamations of relief from the children who were awake. Irgoll continued, 'We should reach the river crossing in an hour or two.'

'There's a river?' Heidi asked, intrigued.

Irgoll nodded his head toward the crest of the hill. 'Come and see.'

Suppressing a tired groan, Heidi climbed slowly to her feet and followed Irgoll back to where he had been standing. Tariq and CeeCee got up and followed. Standing on the crest of the hill, they saw that from there the land rolled gently downwards toward a wide, glittering river. It curved gently at the base of the grassy hills, splitting into two with one fork veering away. On the opposite side was a large, dense forest, the trees crowding up to the riverbanks. Tucked into the fork of the river was a large, ramshackle city, with roofs of different sizes, shapes and colours. Here and there a trail of white smoke drifted up from chimneys that - from this distance - looked tiny. Further downriver, beyond where the city's buildings trailed off, a wide, flat expanse of greyish grassland spanned the space between the two forks of gushing water.

'Is that the Shining City?' Tariq asked, sounding disappointed.

Irgoll laughed. 'Goodness, no. The Shining City is far beyond the Great Forest. Look.'

He pointed beyond the ramshackle roofs, over the forest. Straining their eyes, the children could just make out the shapes of tall spires, almost invisible against the blue sky.

'That is the Shining City,' Irgoll told them, a hint of foreboding in his voice.

Heidi looked at the forest that separated them from it. She couldn't see an end to it in either direction; it was like a huge green wall.

'Do we have to go through the forest to get to it?' She didn't like the idea of that. The forest looked dark and spooky. It reminded her of the forest they'd come through after escaping the Ice Fields. Suddenly something occurred to her.

'Wait – how come we can see all this? We didn't see the other forest from the Ice Fields. And we didn't see the hills from the forest. We just sort of ... popped out.'

Irgoll smiled at her phrase. 'The Ice Fields and the Silent Forest are this land's borders,' he replied, 'And they are our first protection against those who would enter. The Tuatha wove powerful magicks to make it difficult for anyone to find their way beyond them, and to know when anyone appears there, so that they can send their soldiers to collect them. You did well to break through.'

'Soldiers?' Heidi thought of the vague, frightening shapes she had seen scooping up children in the freezing mists and shuddered.

'Does that mean that the ones who got taken there aren't dead?' Tariq asked.

Irgoll considered. 'If they were taken in the Fields, perhaps,' he replied. 'They are taken to the Tuatha.'

'Why?' he blurted.

Irgoll shrugged. 'We do not know.'

Heidi said slowly, 'And what about the ones taken in the Silent Forest?'

For a moment she felt hopeful. Maybe Yuen and the French girl – she felt a stab of shame when she realised she still couldn't remember her name – were still alive. Maybe they could find them in the Shining City.

Irgoll met her gaze briefly, then his black eyes slid away. 'The creatures in the Silent Forest hunt to feed,' he said.

Heidi's heart dropped. 'Oh.'

There was a short, uncomfortable silence. Irgoll made a noise that was somewhere between clearing his throat and a horse-like whinny, then said, 'To answer your earlier question, we're hoping we won't have to go through the Great Forest. There are many things there that are dangerous. We're going there.' He pointed to a bridge that spanned the river's nearest fork, connecting the hills to the ramshackle city. 'The goblins of Goblin Town have tunnels that run beneath the forest, giving them access to the Shining City. We're going to try to barter with them for use of the tunnels.'

'Goblin Town?' Tariq said with a grin. 'Like in that movie with David Bowie?'

Irgoll frowned, confused. 'I don't know what those are,' he replied.

CeeCee was also frowning. Heidi nudged her. 'What's wrong? Are goblins bad in the stories?' From all the ones she could think of, goblins were nasty, ugly creatures, usually the bad guys. But CeeCee was the expert on stories.

CeeCee shrugged. 'It depends on who's telling the story,' she replied.

Twist made a rude noise from beside Heidi's ear, making her jump. She'd forgotten the little pixie was still in her hair.

Irgoll gave a shrug. 'They're not like us,' he said. 'They steal, they lie, they cheat and trick. They're a mercenary race who will take anything they can get. We usually try not to deal with them too much. But they're our main source of information from the Shining City.'

Heidi didn't know what "mercenary" meant, but she understood the rest and didn't like it. 'What do we have that they'll want?' she asked.

Irgoll shrugged. 'There's no telling with goblins. We took

some scales from the dragon we killed. Maybe those. Dragon scales are useful for all sorts of things.'

'Like what?' Tariq asked curiously.

Heidi tuned them out as Irgoll began talking about making armour, potions, weapons and so on. It all sounded like fantasy movie nonsense to her. She stared down at the bridge and the town beyond it, then out at the forest. She followed the progress of the river with her eyes until it disappeared into the hazy distance. The greyish plains beyond Goblin Town went on as far as she could see, and behind them, across the other fork of the river, the Great Forest did the same.

She pointed at the plains. 'What's that?'

Irgoll looked. 'The Grey Moors,' he replied.

'Are they dangerous too?' Heidi asked.

He shrugged. 'They're not safe.'

'Is anywhere safe here?' Tariq asked, suddenly sounding gloomy.

Irgoll gave him a blank look. 'Not for you, Son of Mil.'

Something about his tone made Heidi's flesh crawl. She rubbed her arms with her hands. 'Let's get back to the others,' she said.

They returned to the tree and sat a little longer in the shade. Heidi tried to nap a little, but she couldn't doze off. She couldn't shake the feeling of being surrounded by predators; even the fauns didn't strike her as entirely safe. Her teachers had called it "stranger danger" and had told her to always trust her instincts, but here they didn't seem to have much of a choice about who they trusted. Tariq and CeeCee didn't seem to sleep either. She wondered if they had the same feeling she did.

She sat up with a sigh, and Tuan looked over at her. 'Something on your mind?' he asked.

'Only a million things,' she replied.

'Well, why don't you pick one and go from there,' he said with a cheeky grin.

Heidi's mind went back to the conversation they'd had with Irgoll. 'The Ice Fields,' she said. 'People who turn up there get taken by the soldiers to the Tuatha. Right?'

'Right,' Tuan replied.

'How do people get there in the first place?' she asked. 'How did we get there? I mean, I know we were taken...'

Tuan shrugged. 'That's the only way I know,' he replied. 'The soldiers know how to open the way and bring mortals through. It's why they serve the Tuatha.' At Heidi's questioning look, he sighed and shook his head. 'This is going to use up all of your questions,' he said.

'Irgoll didn't charge us any questions,' Heidi retorted.

Tuan chuckled. 'Yes he did.' He lifted his hands, displaying eight fingers.

Heidi scowled. 'Fine, all my questions,' she replied. 'How many do I have left, anyway?'

'Do you really want to ask me that?' Tuan said, grinning.

Heidi opened her mouth to reply, then paused. 'You're teasing me.'

Tuan's grin widened. Heidi felt the corners of her mouth tug up into a smile, and she tried to repress it. Eventually, she gave in and grinned. 'Okay, fine, never mind.'

Tuan chuckled. 'You're learning,' he said. 'Alright, so, the soldiers. A long time ago, when the Tuatha had not long been here and the Tithe was still quite new, the boundaries weren't so strictly enforced. Fae used to bring mortals through all the time, for all sorts of reasons. Some even left paths open so they could go back and forth easily, and sometimes mortals found the paths and came through. You might have noticed that we're all rather interested in your kind.'

'Yeah,' Heidi replied, thinking of the reactions of Sprickle-back and the fauns when they had first seen them. 'Why is that?'

'For the most part, it's because the Tuatha are interested in you,' Tuan replied. 'They're the ones with all the magick, so what they say is what happens. So if they say you're interesting, well ... we're interested. But I suppose the bounty helps.'

'Bounty?'

'There's a standing bounty for any Child of Mil found in our lands. Just in case you make it past the Forest. Anyone who finds your kind is supposed to send word to the Tuatha and they send soldiers to pick you up.' He gave her a pointed look. 'That's why Sprickleback thought he could bargain with you. Unfortunately for him, we Firobolga swore off taking anything from the Tuatha after they imprisoned us in the hills.'

Heidi frowned. 'Okay.'

'Anyway, after some time the Tuatha decided to close the boundaries right up, and declared that none could pass into or out of Arcadia without their sanction. They declared that the Children of Mil were dangerous and could not be trusted. Then they stated that they were raising an army, and those who served would be able to go back and forth. When we heard about this, we thought they were planning an invasion of your world. But this was a very long time ago, and the invasion never happened... They just keep recruiting soldiers and sending them out to your world to collect your kind.'

'For the Tithe,' Heidi said.

Tuan nodded. 'Every time the Tithe is broken, even if it's just a little.' He shook his head ruefully. 'Mil should have paid more attention to the words.'

'What do you mean?'

'Don't you remember what the Lord of the Green said of the Tithe? "When any insult is made henceforth, the Sons of Mil will tithe anew" ... or something like that.' He snorted. 'The Tuatha have always been tricksy.'

'But how do they even know what we're doing, if the boundaries are closed?'

'Good question. Afraid I don't know the answer.' Tuan plucked a blade of grass from the ground and started chewing on it thoughtfully. 'But they must have their ways. Like I said, they've always been tricksy. And every so often we get word through the goblins that the soldiers have brought more of you back, so they must be watching you somehow.'

The other children started to stir, and Irgoll suggested they move on. When he mentioned Goblin Town, they reacted with a mixture of excitement and fear. Tuan turned to Heidi and smiled. 'Looks like you're out of questions,' he said.

Heidi got to her feet and scowled. 'That doesn't feel very fair,' she complained.

Tuan shrugged. 'When does anything in life feel fair?' he retorted.

Heidi stuck her tongue out at his back as he stood up.

The walk downhill was almost pleasant; the glittering river below them served as a marker of distance that they hadn't had before, and seemed to make their journey go faster. In no time at all, the ground was levelling out beneath their feet and they could hear the water splashing over stones and lapping at the riverbanks.

Irgoll stopped them before they got too close to the bridge. 'Listen carefully,' he said to the children. 'Don't accept anything from the goblins without paying for it, keep a close eye on your possessions, don't answer any questions unless we tell you to, and absolutely do not wander off on your own. You stay close to us at all times, no matter what you see, no matter what you hear, no matter what they tell you. Understood?'

The children nodded, their expressions suitably alarmed and apprehensive. Irgoll studied them all carefully for a moment, then nodded. 'Good.'

He started walking again, and the children huddled close together as they followed behind. Heidi looked around; Monifa was behind her, CeeCee was holding hands with Amy, and Tim was walking with Tariq. Tyler was shuffling along at the back, absently scratching at his new tusks with his fingernail. Heidi thought they might have gotten longer.

As they got closer to the bridge, the buildings on the other side started to become clearer. Heidi realised as they walked that there was a kind of smog floating around and between the buildings, making them indistinct. It was like a kind of greyish heat haze. The thought of walking into it made her feel vaguely itchy.

On either side of the bridge on the far side of the river, two towers appeared. Towers might have been a bit generous; they were rectangular buildings made of planks of wood roughly nailed and tied in place. Gaps near the top served as windows, and a pair of small red eyes gleamed in each, staring out at them. Moments later, the eyes disappeared, and the group could all hear a bell ringing. The path beyond the bridge erupted into movement as dozens of small, long-limbed shapes scurried about frantically, then bunched together and raced across the bridge toward them.

They were short – none taller than Tyler, who was the biggest of the children – with rounded bodies and long arms and legs that ended in spindly, clawed hands and feet. Their skin was mottled greyish blue and green and their eyes were large, round and gleaming red. They had flat, almost non-existent noses above wide mouths filled with thin, sharp teeth, and their ears were pointed and long enough to droop down. They wore armour made of scraps of stiff leather and bits of metal that had been beaten roughly into shape, and they wielded spears resembling knives tied to the ends of sticks. Wings of varying sizes protruded from between their shoulder blades, all similar shades of blue and green, thin and powdery like a moth's wings. They moved fast, and within seconds the children were surrounded.

'Are these goblins?' Heidi whispered to Tuan. He nodded silently.

Tuan and Irgoll hefted their spears defensively, but didn't move. Between them, the children crowded together, shying away from the fierce creatures who were snarling and poking at them with their makeshift weapons. One, wearing what looked like a Roman legionnaire's helmet, stepped forward and banged the shaft of his spear on the wooden planks of the bridge. The goblins fell silent.

'What's your purpose in Lagamoora, Firobolga?' it said in a strange, squawking voice. 'And what do you bring us?'

Irgoll lifted his spear. 'We come for passage to the Shining City,' he replied. 'We are guiding these ... strangers there.'

''Zat so?' The helmeted goblin leered, craning its neck to peer around him. 'Are those human children?' A blackish tongue snaked out of its mouth and licked its lips menacingly.

Irgoll's shoulders slumped a little. 'Yes,' he replied shortly. 'We seek to bargain for passage through your tunnels.'

'Do you now?' the goblin chuckled. 'A'right. You'd best come with us. Old Mother Korrigan will want a word with you, I'll wager.'

'There's really no need to bother her,' Irgoll argued.

'I disagree, faun,' the goblin replied. 'Where Children of Mil are concerned, she'll want to be bothered. I'm not going to be the one to tell her that I let them through our town without telling her, oh no!'

It gestured, and the surrounding goblins clustered closer, jabbing at them with their spears and pressing them forward, onto the bridge. Tuan fended off a few jabs, but none of the blows came close enough to land. Irgoll looked around and shook his head. 'Come on,' he said wearily. 'It looks like we're going to be here a while.'

With the helmeted goblin leading the way, and the other goblins flanking and following behind, the group shuffled across the bridge and into the grey smoke and fog of Goblin Town.

CHAPTER 14

GOBLIN TOWN

They walked into a chaotic hubbub of energy and life, shockingly loud and cramped after the quiet, open emptiness of the grassy plains. Buildings crowded the path they followed, seemingly constructed of scavenged planks of wood, pieces of stone and lengths of canvas and rotting fabric. Shacks, sheds, teepees and tents crushed against each other, on top of each other in places, creating precarious towers that leaned in over their heads.

Lanterns were hung from every available nail, hook or anything jutting out, and candles and burning torches were stuck into the ground in a feeble attempt to burn away the grey fog. Goblins scurried to and fro, sometimes on two legs, sometimes on all fours, sometimes half-hovering above the ground as their dusty wings flapped frantically. They wore clothes in all styles and colours, but like everything around them, the colours were muted and faded, almost lost in the murk.

As they walked, the children stared at everything around them with wide eyes. Heidi thought she saw a familiar object plugging a hole in one wall. She blinked and looked again. Yes - that was a bicycle tyre, serving as a window! Elsewhere she spotted what looked like a rusty spoon that had been bent and repurposed as a door handle, and hanging from an awning like a decoration she saw a pair of old-fashioned headphones, the wire frayed and tattered.

Here and there, pieces of surprisingly elegant craftsmanship were jammed in with the strange jumble that made up these homes. The corner of one tumbledown shack was propped up with a wooden pole that was beautifully carved with an intricate, flowing pattern. Another had a stunning tapestry, torn and stained, serving as a curtain in a doorway.

Tuan saw Heidi looking and snorted scornfully. 'Scavengers,' he said to her in a low voice. 'That tapestry probably came from the Shining City.'

'There are things here from my world,' Heidi said.

'Probably from others who were brought over,' Tuan replied.

Heidi fell silent, wishing she hadn't said anything, and they continued to walk. Beyond the goblin guards flanking them more creatures crowded in, dipping and craning their heads to catch glimpses of the children. Most of them were goblins, but among them were small, squat creatures with rough, almost rocky brown skin, and leathery-looking humanoids with patchy beards and dull red cloth caps covering their heads. Some were long-necked, cat-like creatures with hairless bodies and tufts of mottled hair on their faces; one or two figures looked almost human. She saw one girlish figure weaving through the crowd alongside them, her porcelain white skin and thick mane of red hair flashing brightly amid the muted greens, browns and blues.

The guards stopped them in front of a large set of metal double gates, set awkwardly into the side of a wooden building. More guards stood in front of them, who stepped aside reluctantly as the ... captain? ... waved them away and pulled one of the gates open.

As they were ushered through the gate, CeeCee frowned and

tapped the metal with one finger. It was a dark reddish-black and rough in texture, and some of it flaked off at her touch. She looked confused. Heidi opened her mouth to ask her what was wrong, but the guards were hurrying them through, spears held threateningly low, so she closed her mouth again and kept moving.

The group were marched through the wide open room beyond, and into a small, cramped side room which appeared to be made up purely from the walls of the buildings around it. It was irregularly shaped, and boxes were shoved into corners. Hanging from the ceiling close by the door they came in through was a large brass bell. The captain grabbed one of the guards and muttered something into its ear, and it filed in after them, looking resentful.

The captain paused at the door and grinned. 'You stay here,' he said. 'Until the Mother wants to see you. Don't cause trouble – we hear that bell, you'll have half the city on you.' With that, he closed the door, and they could hear the sound of numerous creatures scurrying away.

The guard left with them sat itself on a box next to the bell. There was a rope cord hanging down behind it, and the goblin made sure it was within reach, eyeing them all balefully. Tuan and Irgoll leaned themselves against the walls, leaving the other boxes for the children, and they all made themselves comfortable on the boxes and the floor.

After a long, uncomfortable silence, Tariq cleared his throat. 'Hey, man,' he said to the goblin.

In response, its arm shot up, hand poised to yank the bell cord. Tariq held up his hands.

'No trouble,' he said hastily. 'Just talking.'

The goblin eyed him suspiciously but didn't reply. Irgoll let out a scornful snort. 'This is a better reception than I expected, to be honest,' he muttered. 'I was expecting them to try and rob you and steal you at every step.'

The goblin gave Irgoll a frosty glare, which he ignored. Tariq subsided into a defeated silence, letting his hands drop into his lap.

Heidi shuffled over to CeeCee. 'What was that about at the gate?' she asked.

CeeCee looked confused for a moment, then shrugged.

'Probably nothing,' she replied. 'It's just, I think the gate was iron. It was all dark and rusty like our old garden gate, and my grandma used to joke that it kept the faeries out of our garden. Faeries don't like iron; it burns them. In the stories, at least.'

Heidi looked over at the goblin. 'It didn't burn them when they opened it,' she said.

CeeCee nodded and shrugged. Heidi thought about asking Tuan about it, but decided she didn't feel like owing him another question right now. In this place, the last thing she wanted to do was think about home.

Tariq was leaning forward, trying to engage the goblin again. 'Hey. Is it against the rules for you to talk to us?'

Irgoll frowned disapprovingly. The goblin shot him another glare, then looked at Tariq. 'No,' it croaked eventually.

Tariq smiled. 'Great! So let's talk.' He got to his feet, and the goblin's hand shot toward the bell cord again. Tariq instantly sat back down. 'Okay, I can stay here if you're more comfortable with that.'

The goblin lowered its hand again, and Heidi watched the exchange with fascination. The other children were watching too.

'What's your name?' Tariq asked the goblin.

The goblin scowled and spat. 'Not telling you that,' it rasped. 'Names have power.'

'Ooo-kaaayy,' Tariq sighed slowly. 'What shall I call you, then? How about ... Joe? Can I call you Joe?'

The goblin shrugged.

'You kinda look like a Joe to me,' Tariq went on. 'It's a good name. Good for girls and boys. And you're a ... boy?'

"Joe" paused, then nodded.

'Cool, okay,' Tariq nodded. 'Someone told us it doesn't always matter, but goblins have girls and boys, is that right, Joe?'

Joe hesitated, then nodded again. 'Ain't no bloody pixies or hobs, springin' up from the ground,' he muttered.

Tariq blinked. 'Cool,' he replied. 'I'll be honest with you, Joe, I don't really know what that means, but okay. Where we come from, it's kind of important. Boys don't like being called girls and girls don't like being called boys, and some people don't like being called either... It's a whole thing. I didn't want to offend you.'

Joe looked puzzled. His yellow eyes flitted to the others in the group, who were all watching the exchange with interest. Even the fauns looked taken aback. 'You talk a lot,' he said to Tariq.

Tariq smiled. 'Yeah, I do that when I'm nervous,' he replied. 'And I've got to be honest with you, Joe, I am very nervous right now. All of you with your spears and your armour, and us in...' He gestured down to the woollen blanket that was tied around him like a toga and fastened at his waist with a faded leather belt. 'I feel like ... you ever had that dream where you go to school and you realise you're naked?'

A few of the children tittered at that. Joe's eyes darted over them, and he gave a weak smile.

'I'm guessing you don't have school here,' Tariq said, and the goblin shrugged. 'It's a place where the parents send the kids so other grown-ups can teach them stuff?'

Joe shook his head slowly, never taking his eyes from the group. 'No children here,' he replied. 'Just you.'

Tariq paused. 'Wow, okay,' he said eventually. He trailed off for a moment, uncertain, then cleared his throat. 'So, who's this Mother we're going to see, Joe?'

'Old Mother Korrigan,' Joe replied. 'She takes care of the city. She likes to know who comes in and who goes out.'

'So, she's like your leader?' Tariq asked.

Joe shrugged. 'Don't really have a leader,' he sniffed. 'But everybody listens to her.'

Heidi wondered briefly if goblins considered questions in the same way fauns did; if so, Tariq was racking up a big debt for himself. Tuan didn't seem too concerned about it, though.

'Cool, cool,' Tariq was saying. 'So what do you think she'll do with us?'

Joe grinned. 'Mother is fond of humans,' he replied through his sharp, jagged teeth.

Tariq gave a nervous laugh. 'Oh Joe, I don't like the way you said that. Sounds like she's fond of humans like I'm fond of burgers.'

Tyler giggled at that, but it sounded strained.

Joe was still wearing that unsettlingly sharp grin. 'She keeps them,' he went on. 'She treats them well. She likes to see them change. Then when they are done changing...' He shrugged.

'Changing? You mean like this?' Tariq pointed to his elongated ears, and Joe nodded. 'You know about this? How long does it take?'

Joe gave him a crafty look. 'What will you give me if I tell you?' he asked.

Irgoll gave a weary sigh. 'There it is,' he muttered.

Tariq spread his hands. 'Look at me, man. I've got nothing to give. Can't we just have a friendly conversation?'

'I've told you enough,' Joe sneered. 'Information is not free. And I'm not your friend.'

Tariq recoiled as if he'd been slapped. 'Ouch,' he remarked. 'I thought we were getting on, Joe. I thought we had a connection.'

'You want information,' Joe went on, 'I want something in return.' He looked him over carefully. 'A lock of your hair.'

Tariq's hand flew up to his hair. It curled tightly against his head, doing nothing to hide his newly pointed ears. 'My hair?' he repeated incredulously.

Irgoll's voice rang out, sharp and final. 'No.'

Joe snarled up at him, his hand slowly rising toward the bell cord. 'Not your bargain to make, Firobolga.'

Irgoll glared at him darkly and repeated, 'No.'

Tariq looked from one to the other. 'Think I'm gonna keep my hair, Joe,' he said with forced lightness.

Joe turned his snarl on him. 'Fine,' he snapped. 'Then shut up.'

Tariq glanced at Tim, who was sitting beside him. 'Guess that told me,' he murmured. Tim giggled.

'Why does he want Tariq's hair?' Heidi whispered to Tuan, her debt of questions momentarily forgotten.

Tuan shrugged. 'Could be he just wants it for a good luck charm, or for bragging rights. Children of Mil are rare here. But it could be that he knows a little magick. Or knows someone who does. If you want to cast a spell on someone, I'd expect a lock of their hair is very useful. And hair from a Child of Mil would be a very rare ingredient for any spell.'

Heidi stared hard at the goblin. 'He doesn't look very magical to me,' she said.

'Nor I,' Tuan agreed. 'But I wouldn't take the risk.'

They lapsed into silence. Joe's hand gradually drifted back down into his lap, and he glowered at them from across the room.

Thankfully, not much more time passed before the door opened and another goblin guard waved them out of the room. They emerged to see a smaller group of guards waiting for them. Whether they were the same goblins or not, Heidi couldn't tell. As she glanced around, she saw the pale girl again, staring at them from the street through the bars of the metal gate. She was dressed in what looked like a white silk dress, but the hands clasping the bars were clad in heavy gloves. Heidi didn't get much more of a look, however, as they were swiftly shoved and herded toward a wide, rickety looking staircase on the other side of the room.

Unstable as it looked, the staircase held the weight of them all with only a little creaking and swaying, and they emerged into a wide open space that was brighter than the previous room. They found themselves on a large, roughly circular platform, with poles and ropes holding up awnings high above them like a ramshackle circus tent. The platform had views on all sides of the city below, and of the greyish smog hovering above the roofs and platforms of the jumbled, mismatched buildings. It was almost as though they were floating on a sea of grey cloud, catching glimpses of a city that seemed both ruined and bustling at the same time. Beyond the city, the hills and the forest could be seen, but hazily, as if the distance had faded their colours.

Scattered around the circular platform, more creatures were gathered in small groups, seated at low tables filled with food and jugs of drink, or lounging on cushions and soft rugs. There were no goblins here. Every creature, to some degree or other, was – or might once have been – human. They turned to look at the group as they stumbled gracelessly onto the platform. Human eyes looked at them from scaled or oddly hued faces; eyes that were glowing, black, or almost reptilian looked at them from the faces of cherubic children. One boy was clutching what looked like bunches of oversized grapes in his four slender arms. Another shrugged his shoulders, and leathery wings unfolded from his back and flexed. A girl of about six had long, pointed horns curling back from her forehead, sweeping over a mane of frizzy blonde hair. And a tiny, golden-skinned child grinned at them, perfect except for the wickedly sharp teeth in her mouth.

In the very centre of the platform, nestled comfortably on a huge pile of cushions and blankets, was a large, almost elephantine figure. The stout body was naked and female, but the coarse greyish skin was scaly and armoured, making clothes seem unnecessary. The scales made spiralling patterns across her shoulders, back and breasts. Her arms and legs were long and thin, so thin they looked like they wouldn't support her weight if she stood. She was sitting amongst the cushions with her legs bent up, her bony knees sticking up near her long, drooping, doglike ears. Her face was elongated like a rat's, ending in a small pointed nose above a wide mouth. Small black eyes peered out from deep sockets set beneath a shelf of a brow, above which hair the same grey as her skin hung lankly to either side of her face. When she saw the children, her wide mouth stretched into a cheerful smile, revealing large blunt teeth the shape of tombstones.

'Ahhh, our new guests!' she said in a voice that was surprisingly melodic. She spread her long arms wide in an inviting gesture. 'Welcome to Lagamoora, friends! Come, come! Sit a while and take refreshments!'

The goblin guards prodded them forward with their spears, reminding them that they didn't really have a choice. As one, the group shuffled shyly forward, the two fauns flanking them and looking around warily. As they reached the vast creature that beckoned them, Irgoll stepped forward and gave a short, grudging bow.

'Old Mother Korrigan,' he said stiffly. 'We are honoured by your hospitality. We came with no mind to disturb you, but to barter for travel through your tunnels to the Shining City.'

The Korrigan's small eyes widened in what appeared to be genuine surprise. 'The Shining City?' she exclaimed, 'And why would you want to take these dear little ones all that way? They would be much happier staying here than they would ever be in among the pomp and ritual of the Tuatha!'

Irgoll straightened from his bow. 'That's as may be,' he replied, 'But they wish to return to their home.'

She snorted derisively. 'Not possible.'

Some of the children whimpered at that. Irgoll ignored them. 'You may be right,' he responded mildly, 'but if there is a way, it is the Tuatha who will know of it.'

She paused. 'Well, that may be true,' she admitted. 'But what makes you think they'll help these poor wee mites, even if they do know a way? How do you know they won't just take these little ones and keep them for pets and playthings, and twist them to their own ends? That is what they do, after all.'

'With respect, Mother,' Irgoll said, 'That's what you do as well.'

The huge creature recoiled as if she had been slapped. 'Not so!' she cried. 'I treat my little ones well!' She swept a long arm around, gesturing to the food and drink, the cushions. 'They are treated like princes here, and I do no twisting. You know well enough, Firobolga, that only the Tuatha hold magicks like that.'

Tuan stepped forward and whispered something in Irgoll's ear. Irgoll scowled in response, but nodded, and then gave a low bow. 'I meant no offence, Old Mother. But the children have stated their wishes, and we have agreed to escort them to the Shining City.'

'That was before they came here,' Old Mother replied. She looked over the group of children and gave them a wide smile. 'Honoured Children of Mil, you must stay a while and enjoy my hospitality. I have a soft heart for poor lost souls like yourselves, and I will happily give a home to any of you who wish to remain here. Just stay a while and enjoy yourselves. Eat, drink. Talk to your kin. Dance! Be merry!' She looked back at Irgoll and said in a blunt voice, 'I insist.'

The children looked up at the faun, who was still scowling. 'And for those who wish to leave?' Irgoll asked. 'May we use the tunnels?'

'Pssh!' She flapped a hand at him irritably. 'We shall discuss that when the time comes. Perhaps none of them will wish to leave! It is a dangerous journey to the Shining City. They'd be much safer here.'

'It's less dangerous if we can use the tunnels,' Irgoll retorted, but she waved him off again.

'Where are my pipers?' she demanded loudly.

Two of the childlike creatures stood up from the cushions they were sitting on and produced thin wooden pipes. The Korrigan smiled. 'Play for us, darlings,' she crooned. 'Something merry and bright.'

The pipers bobbed their heads obediently, and putting the pipes to their lips began to play. The music they made was intricate and lilting, and almost immediately, the children began to relax. The creatures around them smiled and laughed, and some began to dance while others sat and clapped or nodded along. Despite her misgivings, Heidi felt her apprehension melting away, replaced with a feeling of strange elation. Her mouth twitched upward into a smile and before she knew it, she was bouncing on the balls of her feet, eager to dance. Tuan was grinning widely, and even Irgoll had lost his scowl. He sighed wearily and gestured for the children to go ahead.

'Remember what I told you,' he said to them as they scattered.

Heidi tried to remember what Irgoll had told them as her feet carried her away to dance with two girls of about her height whose legs bent backward and ended in hooves like horses, but she couldn't quite grasp it. It had been something that they shouldn't do... But what, she could not recall. She thought she should probably be worried about that, but it was hard to be worried when such sweet music was playing, and when she was surrounded by such beautiful creatures and pretty things! The colours of the cushions and throws, and the awnings above their heads, were so bright and vibrant... The air smelled of wonderful perfumes... The laughter of the girls she danced with was like sweet tinkling bells ... and as she spun by a table laden with food, she caught just a whiff of the most wonderful, enticing smells- of fresh bread and honey, sweet fruits and rich meats.

Her stomach growled angrily, and she realised just how hungry she was, though they'd stopped to eat twice on the plains. She came to a stop in front of the table and dropped to her knees in front of it. It all looked so wonderful.Her eyes roamed greedily over a plate of sweetbreads, piled high; a dish laden with cuts of some juicy, pinkish meat; a bowl of golden honey; sprigs of grapes as big as her fist, and the reddest, shiniest apples she had ever seen. Some dimly-recalled instinct made her avoid the apples, but she plucked one of the grapes and bit into it eagerly. Cool juice spilled down her chin as she bit through the skin and into its sweet, tender flesh. It tasted like sunshine and strawberries and the pink wine her mother had given her at Christmas dinner that she hadn't realised she remembered. She wolfed it down, sucking the juice from her fingers, and grabbed one of the sweetbreads. It looked like an iced bun, but instead of icing the bread itself had a gentle sheen and smelled like sugar. She tore a piece off and popped it into her mouth, sighing happily. It was still warm, and tasted light and syrupy.

As she took big mouthfuls of the bread, she realised that Tyler had come up beside her and was happily helping himself to the slices of meat, dipping them into the honey before dropping them into his mouth whole. He gave her a full-mouthed grin, honey oozing from between his lips where his tusks stopped them closing fully.

'This is great,' he said after he'd swallowed.

Heidi nodded in agreement. 'What meat is it?' she asked, vaguely remembering the Firobolga's bonfire.

Tyler shrugged. 'Tastes kind of like pork,' he replied, 'But it's the best pork you ever had!' He grabbed another slice as if to illustrate, and bit into it greedily. When he had finished his mouthful, he asked her, 'Do you think she meant it about letting us stay here?'

Heidi looked at him, surprised. 'Why? Do you want to stay?'

Tyler hesitated, his enthusiasm dimming a little. 'I don't know...' he said defensively. 'I just ... you know ... maybe. I'm thinking about it.' He paused, then added, 'I mean, what if we get all the way to the Shining City and they won't help us? What do we do then?'

Heidi frowned. 'Don't you want to go home and see your parents?'

'I ... I guess,' Tyler muttered abashedly.

'Then it's worth a try, right?' Heidi nudged him with her elbow. 'Hey, cheer up. If we get there and the Tuatha can't help, and we can't get home, we can always come back, right?'

Tyler considered it, then nodded slowly. 'I guess so.' He picked up one of the sweetbreads and nibbled at it thoughtfully, then his eyes widened. 'Man, this is good!'

Heidi giggled as he stuffed nearly the entire roll into his mouth, hampered only slightly by the tusks. Looking around, she saw Amy being spun around by a tall, willowy girl with hair that was green and seemed to be sprouting leaves. She was laughing delightedly as the girl lifted her up above her head and then pulled her in close to kiss her cheeks. Heidi couldn't see any of the others. Had there been so many of these half-human children on the platform when they'd arrived?

A shock of red hair caught her eye, and she saw the same girl who had been watching them in the crowd. She stood out from all the others because she was the only one not smiling. She stood quietly near the stairs, just watching, her eyes darting to and fro from creature to creature. She looked like a lonely kid at a birthday party. Instinctively, Heidi trotted over to her.

'Hi,' she said.

The girl looked at her and blinked as if she was just waking up out of a dream. Now that she saw her up close, Heidi could see that her eyes were large, slanting slightly upward, and were a very bright shade of green. Other than her eyes and her red hair, everything else about her seemed colourless; her skin was milky pale, and the dress she wore was thin white silk. The tips of very long, pointed white ears stuck out from her thick red curls. She wore no shoes, and there was a pale grey knitted shoulder bag on the floor by her feet.

'Hello,' she said softly, her voice laced with uncertainty.

'You followed us here, didn't you?' Heidi asked.

The girl shrugged. 'I saw you come over the bridge,' she replied. 'Your kind don't come here often.'

'My kind?' Heidi looked her over again, then glanced over her shoulder at the other children cavorting behind her. 'Aren't you ... one of us?'

The girl gave a sad smile. 'Once I was. Don't know what I am now.'

'What do you mean?' Heidi asked.

The girl shrugged again. 'They call us changelings,' she said. 'The stories got it wrong, you see. It's not just the ones left in the cribs and cradles at home that are the changelings. It's the ones who are taken out of them too. We're brought here and we change, you see. Some faster than others.'

'What do you change into?' Heidi asked, feeling a twinge of fear before the music whisked it away.

The girl gave another shrug. 'Everyone is different,' she replied. Abruptly, she reached out and grabbed Heidi's arm. 'Come and sit with me,' she said in a half-whisper, and pulled her over to an empty pile of cushions nearby.

Heidi let the girl lead her down onto the cushions. The girl sat so close that their shoulders pressed together, putting their backs to the rest of the gathering. Her red hair tickled her cheek. 'I need you to listen to me,' she said urgently.

Heidi looked at her with wide eyes and nodded. 'What is it?'

'The Korrigan is only interested in us while we're changing,' she said. 'Afterwards, she sends us away. I don't know where to... I think it depends on what we become. I've been here a while, and I've been watching. I think we're turning into ... into *them*.'

She swept her arm out toward the city. Heidi gaped. 'Into goblins?'

'Not just goblins,' the girl replied. 'All of them. There was a boy whose skin went grey and he got skinny and eventually you couldn't tell him from the goblins. But I saw a girl who turned into something like the Korrigan, but smaller. And me...' She hesitated, then said fearfully, 'She calls me a "Shining Girl"... I think I'm going to the Shining City when I'm done changing.'

'You sound scared,' Heidi said. She found herself reaching out to hold the girl's slender hand.

The girl nodded. 'I am. Mother says the worst things about the Tuatha. Sometimes she says they eat children. Sometimes she says they use children up. I don't know what she means. She also says they're thieves and that they stole Faerie's magic. And sometimes she says things about some plan they have, and I don't know what it means but it sounds bad.'

'What kind of plan?'

'I don't know!' The girl squeezed her fingers almost painfully. 'But from what I can gather, it's something to do with you.'

'Me?' Heidi squeaked incredulously.

'No. *You*. The Children of Mil!' the girl hissed. 'They want Children of Mil and I don't know why, and I don't know why the Korrigan doesn't want them to have us. Anyway, that's not what – I'm trying to warn you not to stay!' The girl looked around anxiously. 'She only keeps us while we're changing, and then she sends us away.'

'What happens to you?'

'I'm not sure. I think...' The girl shuffled even closer. 'I think it's like, the ones that turn into goblins go to the goblins, and the ones that turn into fauns go to the fauns. I've been into the city to look around and I think I recognise some of them from when they were up here... It's hard to tell. But it's horrible down there – the goblins fight and kill each other all the time – and I just...' Her bright green eyes filled up with tears, and her lips trembled.

Heidi grabbed her and gave her a tight hug. 'It's okay,' she said into the mane of red hair. 'I'm sure your goblin friend is okay. And ... well, maybe the Tuatha aren't that bad?'

The girl stiffened and pulled away awkwardly. 'I just don't want you to think you can stay here forever and be happy because you won't,' she said, sniffing back the tears. 'That's all.' She looked around and frowned. 'I'd better go before I get in trouble.'

'Why would you...' Heidi began, but before she could finish the thought, the girl had jumped up and disappeared into the jovial throng.

Heidi tried to follow her, but the crowd jostled and bumped her, and the girl slipped smoothly away to the stairs and out of sight before she could take more than a few steps. She ran down the stairs after the girl, but there was no sign of her when she reached the bottom. The room below was deserted, the great metal gates slightly ajar. Figures hurried to and fro beyond them, the earlier crowd no longer there. Peering through the bars was only one small, dejected looking goblin, who started visibly as he caught sight of her.

Heidi gave him a small wave. 'Did you see a girl with red hair come by here?' she asked.

The goblin looked at her shrewdly. 'What's it worth?' he asked in a gruff voice.

Heidi sighed in frustration. 'Oh, never mind.'

She turned and started to head back upstairs, but the voice stopped her. 'Wait a moment!'

She turned back. 'What?'

The goblin blinked nervously. 'Maybe we can bargain?'

One of the things Irgoll had told them came back to her,

now that she was clear of that music. She shook her head. 'I'm not supposed to bargain with you.'

'Wait!' the goblin cried as she started up the stairs again. 'Come on, don't be a spoilsport! I never spoke to a Child of Mil before, and...'

Heidi eyed the small creature cautiously. 'And what?'

He shrugged, a slow roll of his bony shoulders. 'Well, I'm bored,' he said finally, then added in a surly tone, 'No one here can be bothered with me.'

The first stirrings of sympathy tickled in Heidi's chest. 'Why not?'

'Too small,' the goblin replied. 'Can't stick up for meself. That's what they think, anyhow.' He sniggered viciously, then looked up at her with wide, muddy-green eyes. 'So what do ya say?'

'What do I say to what?' Heidi asked. 'You haven't made me an offer yet.'

The goblin sniggered again. 'You're getting the hang of it,' he remarked. 'Alright. You tell me why you're here and I'll tell you where your girl went.'

Heidi considered briefly. She didn't see the harm in it, so she nodded. 'Alright.' She paused, then wandered over to the gate. 'I'm Heidi,' she said, putting out her hand. The goblin regarded it curiously, and she pulled it back, feeling foolish. 'Never mind.'

The goblin shrugged and gave her a jagged-toothed grin. 'Nishkyn's what they call me,' he said. 'Well, that's not entirely accurate. They call me Snot or Squeak or Piece of Piss. But Nishkyn is what I'm called otherwise.'

'You goblins don't sound very nice,' Heidi remarked.

Nishkyn's grin widened. 'We can be,' he replied. 'When it's worth our time. So ... why are you here, with those two lanky goat-legged bumpkins?'

Heidi frowned. 'They're fauns,' she said sharply, 'and they're very nice. I think. To us, anyway.' Nishkyn sniggered again.

'They're taking us to the Shining City,' she went on, 'and they want to use the tunnels to get there.'

Nishkyn's eyes widened. 'Oho, really?' he exclaimed. 'And what are ye paying to the Old Mother to get a boon like that?'

Heidi wasn't sure what a boon was, but she answered anyway. 'We haven't figured that out yet,' she said.

Nishkyn gave another ugly snigger. 'Good luck with that then,' he said, smirking. 'Hope you've got another way of getting there when she says no.'

'Why would she say no?'

'Those tunnels are our best bargaining chip,' Nishkyn replied. 'Old Mother ain't going to barter cheap for the use of them. What sort of message would that send to everyone else who wants use of them? Be smart, now.'

Heidi sighed. The goblin had a point. 'But we don't have anything to give,' she said miserably.

'Ooohh, I'm sure you do.' Nishkyn leered at her in a way she really didn't like. 'But if you don't strike a bargain, the only way to the Shining City is through the Forest.' He shook his small head ruefully. 'And you don't want to be going that way. Least-ways, not without a guide.'

'We have the fauns,' Heidi retorted.

The goblin snorted scornfully. 'A pair of blundering goat-legs? Spare me. I'm talking about a real guide, one who knows the forest, knows its dangers.'

'Like who?' Heidi demanded.

The goblin puffed out his chest and stood a little taller. 'Like me, child,' he replied.

Heidi looked at him, aware that she'd played right into his trap. Maybe she could play him at his own game? She forced out a short laugh. 'You? But you're so small!'

Nishkyn's face fell, and he deflated a little. 'Don't mean I can't keep you safe!' he protested. 'In fact, since you're small too, a small guide is just what you need!'

Heidi shook her head. 'I appreciate the ... suggestion,' she said carefully. 'But we have the fauns.'

Nishkyn shrugged, leaning against the gate like it was of no importance to him. 'Fine,' he said. 'It's your hides the Witch'll be hanging up to dry, not mine.'

Heidi paused. She didn't want to ask – she knew what the response would be – but she couldn't help herself. 'What witch?'

'Oh, deary me,' Nishkyn scoffed. 'You don't know about the Witch of the Woods, and you're planning to go walking right through her forest?' He shook his head, chuckling. 'Fine guides you've got there if they don't even know about the Witch!'

'I'm sure they do,' Heidi said uncertainly. 'They just haven't told us yet.'

'Course,' Nishkyn replied flatly. 'I'm sure a pair of hill-rats know all about it.'

He fell silent, suddenly fascinated with the dirt under his sharp fingernails. Heidi waited for a moment, then sighed. 'How much for you to tell me about the witch?'

Nishkyn grinned. 'I'm feeling charitable,' he replied. 'You just give me your word that if you need a guide through the Great Forest, you'll call on me.'

'Really?' Heidi hesitated, not liking the way the goblin was grinning. 'Alright,' she said reluctantly.

'Alright, what?' Nishkyn pressed her.

Heidi took a deep breath. 'I give you my word.' At his prompting nod, she continued, 'That if we need a guide through the Great Forest, I'll call on you.'

Nishkyn grinned. 'Excellent.' He dug into the pocket of the tattered grey coat he was wearing and pulled out what looked like an unused match. He held it out to her through the bars of the gate. 'You just speak my name as you strike it,' he told her. 'Don't lose it – they're hard to get out here.'

Heidi turned it over in her hands. 'It's just a match,' she said.

'Shows what you know.' Nishkyn smirked again. 'Now, let me deliver my side of the bargain.'

He gestured for her to sit down, and with some misgivings, Heidi lowered herself to the ground, propping her back against the cold metal of the gate. On the other side of the bars, like one prisoner whispering secrets to another, Nishkyn began to tell his tale.

CHAPTER 15

A GOBLIN'S TALE

Nishkyn shifted about, making himself comfortable before beginning his story. Heidi waited in silence.

'So, the Witch of the Woods,' he began. 'This happened to a friend of mine – well, not really a friend, but someone I nested with for a bit not long ago. He came back in a real state, you see, and his clan took one look at him and kicked him out on his ear.' At Heidi's reproachful glance he shrugged. 'Weakness,' he said. 'Brings the whole clan down. That's why I'm on my own. Too small.'

He gave a scornful sniff, and went on. 'So my "friend" – let's call him "Kit" - he got sent out into the Great Forest by his clan on a dare; there was a disagreement about who should be in charge, as he told it, and he wanted it to be him. So the dare was that whoever went into the Great Forest and faced the most dangerous opponent, and brought back proof, would win and be in charge. It was between Kit, a big bullying bugger we'll call "Spit", and a wily old fella we'll call "Nip", who had been in charge for ages and was bloody smart for a goblin, but getting old and slow. So Kit was all "No problem!" and Spit was the same, so of course Nip had to agree. So Kit got his stuff together, a knife and some food, a blanket and some rope, and off they all went into the Forest, one after the other.

'So Kit's walking deeper and deeper into the Forest for what seems like forever ... and the trees are so big and so close together that not much light gets through, so it's dark and damp and weirdly quiet – not a lot of wind gets in – and all you can really hear in there is animal noises and your own feet crunching through the undergrowth. And Kit knows better than to tire himself out trying to fly over it all, so he walks. Which is tiring enough, mind, and eventually he stops to rest. He finds a good-looking tree, climbs up and lashes himself to the branch with his blanket around him, and he goes to sleep. Some time later, he wakes up and there's a furry thing with big eyes perched on the branch with him, poking at him like it's trying to figure out what he is. He pretends to be asleep for a bit, and then when it's close enough, he grabs it and gives it his fiercest goblin snarl...' Nishkyn bared his jagged teeth to demonstrate. 'And the thing shrieks and runs off, but not without leaving Kit with a handful of its fur. He tucks this away in his pocket, but he doesn't think that's going to be the most dangerous thing he'll face, by far. So he unties himself and climbs down, and keeps walking.

'He stops to rest a few more times. Sometimes nothing happens. One time, he has to fight off a pack of bramble pixies trying to steal his food, but they're little more than pests so he doesn't bother to take a trophy from them. While he's walking he sees a few other forest creatures, but nothing much – some deer, an old woman wandering about, and a horse or two drinking by the streams that run through the Forest. He ignores these and keeps looking.

'Then finally, he comes across what looks like a little garden, with a low fence made of twigs and what looks like herbs and stuff, planted in rows and well taken care of. He sniffs around a bit and spots a big old tree to one side of the garden with a door cut into the trunk. It's disguised, but Kit's eyes are sharp and he spots it anyway. He thinks maybe it's where the old woman lives, and he's content to just swipe some of the tastier plants and move on, but then he hears voices from the other side of the tree. So he hunkers down and sneaks around to where he can see who's talking.

'He sees a woman, clad in scraps of fur and leather, with moss green skin and long greenish hair so dark it's nearly black. She's talking to two other women - one who's got skin as brown and craggy as tree bark, and another who's dark-skinned wearing this big black wolfskin cloak. The green one seems to be giving the other two instructions, but Kit can't make out the words. When she's done, the brown one hands over a burlap sack she'd had lying between her feet and then she and the other one head off, deeper into the Forest. The green-skinned woman opens the sack and looks inside, and whatever's in there strikes her as funny, because she starts laughing. And it's this husky, deep laugh that gives Kit the tingles. Then she bundles up the sack and heads to the tree. Kit hunkers down in the bush he's hiding in, and she passes by close enough that the sack brushes the branches of the bush, and he hears something squirming and squealing inside it. He looks up at the woman and sees the charms hanging from her wrists and neck and belt, and sees the marks on her arms – like ritual scars – and sees the twinkle in her bright green eyes, and the sharpness of her teeth as she's smiling, and suddenly he realises who she is. He's looking at the Witch of the Woods!

'At first, Kit is terrified! He thinks that if she catches him, he's dead for sure. But then he thinks to himself, what foe in the Great Forest is more dangerous than the Witch of the Woods? He stays in the bush for a bit, thinking, and watches her go to the tree and open the door and go inside. He reasons that he doesn't actually have to fight her, or even face her, if he's clever – he can just find a trophy to take back, something that's obviously hers, and say that he did. He can even knock himself about a bit on the way back to make it convincing. And what's more, he's really, really curious to see what was in that sack!

'His mind made up, he sneaks over to the door, which swung shut behind the Witch, and looks it over. His keen eyes find the knothole that serves as a handle easily enough, and he pulls it open just enough for him to squeeze inside. He noticed that when she opened it that it didn't make a sound, so he's grateful he doesn't have to worry about that. Inside, he finds that he's standing in the hollowed out tree trunk, at the top of a tunnel of earth that's dug in between the roots of the tree. It's steep at first and the mud is damp, so he takes care going down. Before long, it flattens a bit, but keeps going down, real deep. As he reaches the bottom, he gets a whiff of something sweet burning and he ducks down to peer around the corner as the tunnel curves.

'He sees a wide open space dug into the soil, with tree roots dangling down from the roof all over. It's done up like a living space, and it's actually quite cosy. It's lit up with greasy looking candles that are just stuck everywhere. The mud has dried out here, and there's reed mats on the floor and charms and bells hanging like ornaments from the tree roots in the ceiling. There's a bed in one corner made up of loose reeds and grasses and lots of blankets, and there's a table and a couple of chairs fashioned out of rough branches. There's a firepit in the middle of the room where herbs are burning, making the room warm and sweet-smelling. The smoke is gathering near the roof as it's got nowhere to go, but the roof's high enough that it's not too bothersome. To one side there's a kitchen space where a large cooking pot is sat, along with smaller pots and bowls and a collection of wicked looking knives that are all hung on the wall from wooden pegs. The table is littered with what looks like more half-made charms and talismans, and Kit thinks to himself that one of those would make a good trophy. He could say he snatched it from the Witch's very wrist!

'Speaking of, the Witch is crouched down near the centre of the room untying the sack. She pulls down the edges of the sack and sitting there, with a gag in his mouth and his hands and feet tied up, was none other than Nip! When Nip sees who has him, his grey face goes even greyer. The Witch gives another laugh and grabs him by his hair, then lifts him up and throws him into a cage hanging from the roof by a big iron chain. She locks him in with a key that's hanging around her neck on a thong. "You'll come in handy for a rite I'm preparing," she says to him, "But I'm not quite ready to do it yet. So get comfortable."

'Nip shouts something at her, but he's still gagged so Kit can't understand him. The Witch ignores him and goes back to her table, sitting with her back to the cage. Kit sits and thinks. This could work out better than he'd expected! Not only could he face the Witch of the Woods, but he could bring back Nip, prove that Nip was too weak to lead the clan, and that he was strong enough to have rescued him! The only problem is, he has to bring Nip back alive and get him to tell the others that's what he's done – if he brings Nip back dead they'll probably accuse him of killing him to take him out of the game. Which would have been a smart tactic, if they hadn't already agreed when the dare was set not to do it.

'So Kit looks around for a place to hide where he can watch the Witch and wait for a chance to make his move. He spies a low table covered by a cloth off to the left of the entrance to the room with all sorts of bowls of herbs and dried flowers and a bunch of the lit candles on it. He creeps over and peeks under the cloth, and there's plenty of room for him under there. So he goes in, hunches down close to the floor so he can peer out from under the cloth without having to move it, and he watches.

'The Witch works on her charms for a while, muttering to herself, and every now and then she gets up to stir the fire so the herbs keep burning and making that sweet smelling smoke. Eventually the fire burns low, and she gets up again, but this time she goes over to the bed and curls up on top of the blankets, and before long, Kit can tell from her breathing that she's asleep. He creeps out from under the table and over to Nip, who is sat in the cage in as comfortable a position as his bindings will allow. Nip sees him right away and sits up and starts trying to speak through the gag, but Kit puts a finger to his lips and gestures for him to shut up. Nip does, and waits as Kit creeps around the side of the room - keeping as far away from the bed as possible - and heads toward the cage. But Kit goes right past the cage, and Nip starts trying to yell again! The gag keeps him quiet enough, though, and the Witch doesn't wake. Kit goes to the table and climbs up onto one of the chairs. He selects a couple of charms – small things made of bones and twine, hanging from leather cords – and pockets them. Then he turns and glares at Nip, who falls silent again.

'Kit sneaks over to the cage and this time he stops. "I'll let you out," he whispers, "But you need to make me a deal first. And I want your solemn oath on it." Nip gives him a nod, so he goes on. "When we get back to Lagamoora, I'm going to tell the clan how I rescued you from the Witch of the Woods, and how it was a fierce fight, and how I snatched these charms from her wrist as we fought. And you're going to back me up, and tell them that if it weren't for me, you'd be dead. Understand?"

'Nip pauses for a long time, his eyes wide and full of rage, but he evidently decides he's got no real choice, so eventually he nods. "Do I have your solemn oath?" Kit asks. Nip hesitates, then nods again. Kit grins at him and looks over the cage. The lock is above his reach, so he climbs up and pulls a thin tool out of his pocket and starts trying to pick it. The rough iron bars instantly make his hands and feet itch faintly. The cage swings on its chain, but mercifully it doesn't creak. Kit thanks his luck for his, then curses his luck once he realises that he can't pick the lock.

'He looks over to the sleeping Witch, and thinks. She sounds like she's fast asleep, and she hasn't stirred once, so he figures he might be able to sneak up and steal the key around her neck. It's a lot closer to facing her than he really wanted to do, and he's tempted to just leave Nip to his fate and go back with the charms, but the idea of coming back as the old leader's rescuer is just too good, so he climbs down again and starts creeping over to her. Nip's shaking his head like it's a terrible idea, but Kit ignores him. He creeps closer and closer to the sleeping Witch. Up close, he can see that everything about her is green – her skin, her hair, her sharp teeth, her long pointed nails – all different shades of green. She smells like damp moss and stagnant water. The scars on her arms and legs make him feel sort of dizzy, so he stops looking at them and concentrates on the cords around her throat. He quietly pulls his knife from his belt.

'Her hair has fallen around her face and neck, so he has to push it very carefully aside with the tip of his knife. He does this so slowly he barely feels like he is moving. The Witch doesn't stir. Eventually he sees the key he is looking for, and ever so slowly he reaches in and plucks it up with trembling fingers. Again, ever so slowly, he cuts through the cord with his knife, thanking his luck that he'd sharpened it before he left. He gently slips the key from the cord and tiptoes away from the Witch and back to the cage. When he gets there, he begins to feel dizzy again, and realises that he's been holding his breath. He lets it out carefully, taking care not to make a sound, and breaths in a big gulp of smoky air.

'The key is made of wrought iron, like the cage, and the skin on his palm is itching and crawling where he's been clutching it so tight. He switches the key to his other hand and wipes his palm on his tunic to try and get rid of the itch. Then he climbs back up on the cage and slides the key slowly into the lock, and turns it even more slowly, trying not to make a sound. The click as the lock opens sounds deafening, and he turns to see if it has disturbed the Witch.

'The bed is empty.

'"Oh shit," Kit says, and then he feels sharp nails stab through the back of his tunic and he's plucked off the side of the cage and lifted up into the air, the key still in his fingers. Now, Kit's not a big goblin, but he's not a small one either, and the Witch lifts him up above her head like he's a tiny little kitten, weighing nothing at all.

'She looks at him with a grin, showing off all her sharp green teeth, and she says, "Even if you weren't as loud as a bear, you disturbed at least a dozen warding runes while you scurried about, little thief."

'Kit looks down and sees now that there are runes scratched into the mud floor all over the room, and where he'd been walking some of them were glowing slightly with a dull green light. "Oh shit," he says again, and not knowing what else to do, he throws the key at her face. Through pure luck, it hits her squarely in her right eye. She lets out a horrible shriek and drops him, her hands going to her face. Kit jumps to his feet in time to see Nip hop to the open door of the cage and tumble out onto the floor. He gets his knife out and cuts Nip's legs free, and then they run for the tunnel.

'The Witch looks up, and her right eye is red and weeping, and the look on her face is pure hate. She waves her hand and the walls of the tunnel start to crumble as tree roots sprout out all around them, weaving like snakes to try and knock them down or block their way. But goblins are fast and nimble, and though Nip lags behind a bit, they dodge and hop and twist and get through to the door at the top of the tunnel. Kit barges it open with his shoulder, ignoring the pain that runs down his arm, and they flee out into the forest.

'The Witch doesn't seem to be following, so after a while they stop to rest, and Kit cuts Nip's hands free and pulls away the gag. Nip looks at him and says "Looks like I owe you a drink."

'"You owe me more than a drink, old man," Kit replies. "How'd you end up in that sack anyhow?"

'Nip tells him how he found one of the sisters washing at the stream and tried to steal her sack because he was hungry and thought she might have some food. But he wasn't quick enough to get away and she caught him. He'd tried to talk his way out of it, which stopped her killing him herself, but then she'd said "My sister will like you," and then tied him up and stuffed him in the sack.

'Kit whistles. "The Witch has sisters?" he says, and he tells Nip about the third woman. Nip's about to say something, but then he stops and points up. Kit looks to where he's pointing and he sees that the tree branches are moving. Not like the wind's blowing them – the wind doesn't get through much in there – but just moving, slowly, on their own, bending and turning so that they're all pointing in the same direction. He looks around and sees that it's not just the trees – it's the bushes, the ferns, even the damned grass – all bending and pointing in the same direction – at them.

'Kit says "We should go," and Nip nods, and they take off in the direction of Lagamoora. As they run, the trees, the grass, the bushes all twist round to point them out. And that isn't all. Tree roots pop up out of the ground to snag their feet, patches of brambles spring up from the undergrowth to tangle them up, and crows start cawing loudly in the trees above them, and swooping down to peck at them. They struggle on through all this as fast as they can, but soon enough they hear the Witch's voice behind them. Kit looks back and she's just strolling through the Forest, and the undergrowth that's popping up to trip them is actually parting to make a clear path for her!

'The Witch calls out to them, "You can't escape me, little thief. I am the Forest, and the Forest is me. Your little friend was caught fairly and gifted to me by my sister. He belongs to me. Give him back and I'll consider letting you go."

'Kit glances at Nip, considering it, but Nip says "Don't you bloody dare." They keep running. But then the Witch whistles, and they hear the sound of running feet ahead of them. Big feet, getting closer. And suddenly a huge black wolf with burning red eyes is standing in front of them, snarling and bristling, and they have to stop. They turn around and the Witch is walking up behind them and smiling. All the trees and bushes are pointing at them in a big circle.

Kit gets his knife out and starts waving it at the wolf and Nip turns to the Witch and puts his hands up. "Surely we can come to some kind of arrangement," he stammers.

'"You can't," the Witch replies. "You already belong to me. But the little thief here ... he's younger, stronger – he'd make a much better sacrifice. Maybe he'd like to take your place?" Quick as a snake, she reaches down and snatches Kit up again, batting his knife away with one hand. "Or maybe I'll just make use of you both," she says, and then she holds Kit's face up to hers and takes a deep breath in. And suddenly Kit feels all of his energy, his life, draining out of him, and he can see something like smoke passing from his mouth into hers, and his whole body shudders and aches and he can feel his skin drawing tight against his bones...

'And then the Witch shrieks in pain and drops him, and a whole bunch of things happen at once. The trees and bushes all suddenly spring back into their normal positions, the wolf yelps and flinches back, and Kit sees that Nip has driven his knife deep into the Witch's bare foot, and is now running as fast as he can past the wolf. Kit of course runs straight after him, but then the Witch yells, "Get them!" and they hear the wolf snarling and pounding through the undergrowth after them.

'There's no way they can outrun it. The wolf pounces on them, knocking them both off their feet at once, and Kit feels strong jaws clamp onto his shoulder and he's flung about like a ragdoll before he's tossed into the air and crashes to the ground in a bloody heap. He hears Nip screaming off to his left, and can only assume he's getting a similar mauling. Then, the sharp teeth bite into him again and he is tossed about once more, and he thinks: *This is it. I'm dead.*

'At that moment, there's a sharp whistle from behind them, and the mauling stops. The wolf pricks up its ears, then lopes off in the direction of the whistle. Kit and Nip are left there on the ground, with bleeding wounds and broken bones, wondering what just happened.

'They get themselves up and limp on through the Forest, deciding not to think about why the Witch decided to call off her dogs, only counting themselves lucky that she did. They keep on going until they see the misty shape of Lagamoora through the trees, and then Nip, who had been leaning heavily on Kit, straightens up, says "Sorry about this, mate" and punches him right in the face! Kit goes sprawling, and Nip sticks his hand in Kit's pocket and pulls out the charms. Then he hauls Kit to his feet and starts carrying him to the treeline. "It's a good idea you had," he says. "Be a shame to waste it." Then he starts hollering for the guards to come help him.

'Kit spits out blood and says, "You gave me your solemn oath, you sneaky shit!"

'Nip just shrugs and says "Don't see how I could do that with a gag in me mouth." And he keeps hollering.'

Beside Heidi, Nishkyn shifted uncomfortably against the gate and shrugged, shaking himself out of his storytelling reverie.

'Long story short, Nip tells the clan that it was him who rescued Kit from the Witch, and the other goblins take one look at Kit and decide to side with Nip. You see, Nip might have been older, but whatever the Witch had done to Kit had shrivelled and shrunk him, making him smaller and weaker, and he looked haggard and ill. So no matter how much Kit argues, they side with the stronger goblin, and Kit gets booted out. Nip's declared to be clan leader again, and Spit never returns from the Forest to challenge him.'

'That's horrible,' Heidi exclaimed. 'It's so unfair!'

Nishkyn shrugged. 'That's just the way things are.'

Heidi fell silent and studied the small goblin carefully. His green skin looked strangely fitted to his bones, as if it was too loose in places, and too tight in others. His limbs were even thinner than seemed to be normal with the other goblins, and his wings lay shrivelled and curled in on his back.

Heidi pursed her lips and said, 'Well, it's probably for the best. It sounds like Kit would have been a terrible clan leader.'

Nishkyn looked around at her sharply. 'What do you know?' he spat. 'I would have - I mean...'

Heidi grinned. He regarded her warily, then smiled back. 'Clever,' he said. 'Not that it matters. Knowing it won't get you anything.'

Heidi shrugged. 'It might come in handy at some point,' she replied. 'Now, you owe me an answer.'

He looked at her blankly. 'Do I?'

Heidi gave him a non-nonsense glare. 'The redheaded girl. Where did she go?'

Nishkyn blinked. 'Oh!' He pointed down the street. 'Thataway.'

Heidi looked down the street, then back at him. 'Yes, but where?'

'How should I know?' Nishkyn shrugged. 'I've been sat right here talking to you.'

'You ... little cheat!' Heidi cried, exasperated. She smacked the gate with her hand, making it rattle loudly, and climbed to her feet. 'You're horrible,' she said fiercely. 'All you goblins are horrible!'

'Boo hoo,' Nishkyn replied mockingly.

Heidi opened her mouth to say something else, but in that moment she heard the sound of running feet behind her, and she turned to see Tim hurrying across from the stairs. He looked panicked. 'Heidi!' he cried. 'Come back up, we need you!'

'Why?' Heidi asked, already on her way to the stairs. 'What's happened?'

Tim shook his head helplessly. 'It's the Old Mother,' he replied. 'She's made her decision.'

CHAPTER 16

FAREWELLS

Heidi headed up onto the top level to hear a huge argument in progress. The music had stopped, and all the strange fae-child creatures were standing at the edges of the platform, listening in silence as the fauns and the children shouted and gestured angrily. Old Mother Korrigan towered over them, her long arms folded resolutely across her ample chest. Heidi rushed over to find out what was going on, Tim close on her heels.

'This is completely unreasonable!' Irgoll was saying to the Mother. 'The whole point of this expedition is to get these children home!'

'You're not taking them home, foolish faun,' the Korrigan replied. 'You're taking them to the Tuatha. You really think the Tuatha will let them out of their clutches after you've handed them over? Of course not. With the trouble they go through to get them here, they're not going to just let them go back. They are always collecting them. They want every single one they can get.'

'And you're not?' Irgoll countered.

The Mother snorted. 'How I treat the Children and how the Tuatha treat the Children is very different, believe me.'

Meanwhile, Tuan was furiously addressing the children. 'You don't have to do this,' he was saying earnestly. 'We will get you to the Shining City with or without the use of the tunnel. Don't let her fool you that this is our only option!' He seemed to be focusing in particular on Tyler.

Heidi slipped in beside Monifa. 'What's happening?' she asked, absently scratching at her ear.

Monifa's reply was glum. 'Old Mother Korrigan wants half of us to stay here as the price for using the tunnel,' she replied.

Heidi frowned. 'That's ridiculous,' she scoffed. 'We're not going to do that.'

Monifa shrugged. 'You think? Tyler's already said he's going to stay.'

'What?' It came out shrilly, and the argument lulled for a moment as all eyes turned to her. She looked at Tyler. 'Tyler, you don't have to do this,' she said.

Tyler gave her an exasperated look. 'I know,' he replied. 'This lot have told me that about a million times. What no one seems to be listening to is that I want to.'

Heidi hesitated. 'Well ... why?'

He gestured to his face. His tusks seemed to have grown even longer in the time that Heidi had been downstairs. 'This is why! Look at me! I'm a freak now! I can't go home like this!'

There was an uncomfortable silence. Several of the children shuffled uneasily. CeeCee slid her hands behind her back. Tim poked resentfully at the horns curling up out of his head.

'It's not that bad,' Heidi began, but Tyler cut her off sharply.

'Oh, don't give me that! It's alright for you – *you* haven't changed! And you, with your cool glowing eyes!' he gestured at Monifa. 'And you, Tariq, pointy ears, big deal!' But these!' He pointed to his face again. 'They're growing out of my fucking mouth, man! I can't even shut my mouth all the way any more! I look like a fucking pig!'

Some of the children winced at the swearing, but for the most part they just looked embarrassed. 'I'm ... I'm sure we'll change back once we're home,' Heidi said timidly, looking to Tuan for confirmation. He just shrugged.

Tyler saw, and gave a bitter laugh. 'Well, there you go. Nah, mate. I'm not going back like this. I'd rather stay.' He gestured around them, at the food and the soft cushions. 'I mean, it's a pretty sweet deal, I think.'

'If you stay here, you'll keep changing!' Heidi protested.

'But at least here I won't be a freak!' Tyler went on. 'I will be if I go home. That's assuming we even make it home. Look at how many of us are already dead!'

'They're not dead...' Heidi began, but Tyler ignored her.

'I'm bigger and slower than the rest of you. It's just dumb luck I made it this far. If I go into the forest with you, I'll probably end up like Yuen and the rest. I'm not stupid.' He folded his arms across his chest, in a very similar way to the Mother, and looked around at them all defiantly. 'I'm staying.'

Tuan spoke slowly. 'If it's truly what you want...'

Tyler gave a nod. 'It is.'

Tuan looked at the other children. 'Does anyone else want to stay?'

Nobody else moved.

Irgoll turned to the Mother with rage in his eyes. 'You have one,' he snapped. 'Is that not enough?'

Old Mother cast her eyes over the group. 'I asked for half. That's, at the very least, three.'

'That's not fair!' CeeCee cried, then clapped her hands over her mouth as if she had said a rude word. Everyone looked at her, then back as Irgoll addressed Old Mother again.

'Fair or not,' he said, pointing at Tyler, 'This is the one who wishes to stay. This is the only one who is going to stay. If it is not enough, we will make our way without the use of the tunnel.'

The Korrigan gave a toothy smile. 'Then enjoy your stroll through the Great Forest,' she said. 'I think I am through offering my hospitality for now. You may go.' Then her beady eyes turned to Tyler, and she reached out to him with her spindly arms. 'And you, my sweet boy, come to Mother. She will take good care of you!'

Goblin guards appeared as if out of nowhere, and the children – minus Tyler – were herded to the stairs and forced down, once more kept at spearpoint. Heidi glanced back and saw him standing in front of the Korrigan as she bent down low to talk to him, her large hands cupping around him to screen him from view. Heidi watched as he disappeared behind those large, spade-like hands, her last glimpse of him looking eerily as though he was about to be shovelled into the Korrigan's vast mouth. Then she was too far down the stairs to see.

They were marched back through the city and out to a bridge so identical to the one they came in over that Heidi thought they'd been taken back to where they had first arrived, until she looked up and saw the wall of trees on the river's opposite bank. They were tall and broad-trunked, with branches that reached high and hung low, crowding together and creating a thick canopy of dark green leaves. Beyond the first few trees, all that could be seen were shadows. It didn't have the unnerving uniformity of the Silent Forest, but it was frightening in a wholly different way. It was the kind of forest that looked as though it would be home to all sorts of hungry, stealthy predators. The kind of forest that children got lost in, never to be found again.

The goblins left them on the other side of the bridge, huddled together on the grassy banks of the river. Tuan protested, asking if they could at least barter for provisions, but the goblin he spoke to was firm.

'Mother says you go, you're gone,' he hissed. 'Piss off.'

'I thought you goblins loved bargaining!' Tuan yelled at his retreating back. The goblin ignored him. Tuan turned back to the group and shrugged. 'It's fine,' he said. 'We can hunt and scavenge in the forest if we need more food.'

Heidi looked around at the diminished group and thought glumly about how the food would go further now. It was just herself, CeeCee, Monifa, Tim, Amy, and Tariq now. Her ear itched, and she scratched at it without thinking.

Tim watched her curiously. 'What's with your ears?' he asked. 'You've been scratching at them like that a few times now.'

Heidi paused, then felt her ear with her fingers. It made them itch even more, but the small, pointed tip she found took her mind off of that. She felt the other ear and it was the same.

'I guess I'm changing too now,' she said to Tim, tucking her red hair behind her ears.

Tim looked at her solemnly. 'I think it suits you,' he said with a shrug. 'Not like these.' He pointed at his forehead, frowning. The horns had definitely gotten longer.

CeeCee smiled over at her. 'Guess you really are one of us now,' she said. 'Not that you ever weren't.' She regarded her hand solemnly, spreading her fingers. The webbed skin between them had turned a silvery grey colour, which was spreading across the skin of her hand.

Irgoll gave them a stony look and shrugged. 'I told you not to eat the food.'

The children looked up at him anxiously. CeeCee gave a low groan. 'Oh, I just remembered,' she said miserably. 'The stories say if you eat faery food, you can't ever leave.'

At their panicked looks, Irgoll sighed and said, 'I don't know about that. But it certainly quickens the change.' He turned to look at the trees. 'We might as well get going.'

'Um...' Heidi held up her hand. 'Do you ... do you know the way?'

Irgoll looked back at her. 'I know which direction we need to walk in,' he replied.

'Okay. It's just...' Heidi's fingers fiddled with the match in her pocket. 'I met someone who might ... might be able to guide us.'

Irgoll gave her a cool look. 'Were they a goblin?' At her nod, his lip lifted in a sneer. 'I don't think it's a good idea to trust a goblin to get us safely anywhere.'

'He said he knew about the Witch,' Heidi added. The other children immediately looked around in alarm. Irgoll paused, then sighed.

'Where is he?' he said wearily. 'I will concede that it might be useful to talk to him, at least.'

'Hang on,' Heidi said. 'I have a thing to summon him with.' She pulled out the match, then looked around. 'Um ... I don't know how to light it.'

Tuan took the match from her and struck it with one nail, then handed it back to her. It sputtered orange, then a yellow flame bloomed, which quickly brightened and turned a blazing, vibrant blue. Sparks, just as blue as the flame, spat out in a fierce halo, reminding her of the sparklers they had once been given at the boarding school on Bonfire Night. Heidi held it between her fingers and looked at it intently. 'Nishkyn,' she said, then hesitated, unsure of what to do next.

'You might want to hold it up,' Tuan suggested with a slight smile.

Heidi lifted it above her head. 'Nishkyn,' she said again.

Almost immediately, a familiar looking goblin popped up from behind a low hut at the edge of the city and came trotting over the bridge toward them. ''Ello,' he said when he reached them. 'Fancy seeing you here.'

'This is Nishkyn,' Heidi said, as the two fauns fixed the goblin with a suspicious stare.

Irgoll looked down at the goblin disapprovingly. 'What did you agree with this human child, exactly?'

Nishkyn smiled. 'She wanted some information from me, which I agreed to give on her promise that she would call for me if she should need a guide through the forest.'

'Ah,' Irgoll nodded. 'Then your agreement is finished.' At Nishkyn's confused look, he went on, 'She thinks we might need a guide, so she signalled you. I disagree, but I am willing to consider it, if your information is good enough.' He squatted down on his haunches, leaning his weight on his spear like a staff. 'Tell me what you told her.'

Nishkyn's expression turned sly. 'What will you give me for it?'

'Nothing, you greedy creature,' Irgoll quickly retorted. 'You already gave it to our friend here, and I'm not paying for something we already have. I'd rather hear it from your lips than hers, is all. In case she forgets, or misunderstands something.'

Heidi frowned, somewhat offended by this, but said nothing. She supposed he had a point. It was a very strange story.

Nishkyn looked around at them all, and shrugged. 'If I tell you, and you want me to guide you, what will I get then?'

Irgoll gave an exasperated sigh. 'Be sure, goblin, we will treat you fairly!' he snapped. 'Unlike your kin, we believe in giving what is owed. Now, tell me the tale.'

Nishkyn grumbled something under his breath, but nodded. 'Alright.'

He sat down in the grass, and eager to listen, the children shuffled closer, forming a rough circle around him. Heidi noticed Tuan positioning himself between Nishkyn and the bridge, and from the way the goblin's long ears twitched in that direction, she was pretty sure he had noticed too.

Nishkyn repeated the story to his new audience, his eyes flitting slyly to Heidi as he mentioned "Kit". Heidi gave him a slight nod, and said nothing.

The group listened without interrupting, the children wearing expressions of bewildered horror, the fauns those of deep concentration. When he was finished, Irgoll leaned back on his haunches and was silent for a moment. Then, he looked back down at Nishkyn.

'You're Kit, aren't you?' he asked.

Nishkyn hopped to his feet and gave a frustrated yell. 'You told him!' he accused Heidi, jabbing a sharp-clawed finger in her direction.

Heidi shook her head, smiling gently. 'Sorry, Nishkyn, it's pretty obvious.'

Nishkyn looked down at his shrivelled hands and sighed. 'Yeah, you might be right. Alright, yes, I am Kit. Kit is me.'

Irgoll gave a small chuckle. 'You know – all the conniving aside – it actually does you credit that it was you. You went into the Great Forest to prove your bravery, you faced the Witch of the Woods, and you rescued your rival when you could have left him to die.'

Nishkyn snorted. 'Yeah right, and I got the strength sucked out of me, and I let a slow old goblin trick me and beat me up. Really makes me look good.'

Irgoll leaned forward. 'Maybe that's how goblins see things, but I see some potential in you, Nishkyn.'

Over the goblin's shoulder, Heidi saw Tuan's eyebrows shoot up in surprise. She suppressed a giggle. Nishkyn, however, looked just as surprised.

'You do?' he exclaimed. 'But... I'm so ... small and weak!'

'These ones are small too,' Irgoll replied, 'but they haven't let it stop them trying to make their way home. They've already faced great dangers getting this far. But they're still going. Being small doesn't mean you can't be brave. And you don't have to be strong to be capable.'

Nishkyn straightened up and puffed out his chest. 'I know that,' he said gruffly. 'I'm capable of plenty. I can get in and out of places without being seen. I can sniff out something interesting a mile off. And my eyes are sharper than any other goblin I know.' Despite the gruffness of his proclamations, his yellow eyes sparkled with pride.

Irgoll smiled. 'Alright, goblin, let's make a deal. We don't need a guide to get us to the Shining City; we already know which way to go. But it would be useful to have with us someone who has traversed the Great Forest before. Someone who knows how to spot and avoid the dangers. We don't have much to offer now, but we promise you a fair share of anything we find worth keeping, and we'll give you our protection there and on the way back. And when we do get back, we'll be sure to sing your praises to your kinfolk before we head home.'

Nishkyn looked around at Tuan, who nodded in agreement, and then to Heidi and the children. 'I don't know,' he replied. 'Seems mighty cheap for such a dangerous job.'

'Do you have anything better to do?' Heidi asked him. 'You said back at the gate that you were bored.'

The goblin shot her a dirty look, then smiled thoughtfully. 'You know,' he said, 'Travelling with Children of Mil ... working alongside the fearsome Firobolga... I bet no other goblin can boast that. Alright, we have a deal.' Then he spat in his hand and held it out to Irgoll. Irgoll grimaced, sighed, and very reluctantly held out his hand. Nishkyn grabbed it and shook it forcefully, giving it a long squeeze before he let go. He cackled at the pained look on Irgoll's face.

Irgoll wiped his hand on the grass and stood up. 'Well, if that's settled,' he said wearily, 'shall we get on? Before the guards start throwing their spears at us?'

There were indeed several goblin guards watching them from the other side of the river, with one or two more joining them as Irgoll spoke.

Nishkyn sneered. 'They'd never get those things across the

river,' he said, but nonetheless he scuttled a little further away from the bank.

Tariq sidled up to Heidi and elbowed her in the side. 'Nice job with that one,' he said, nodding at Nishkyn. 'You did better than I did with that other one earlier.'

Heidi smiled shyly. 'I didn't do much,' she replied. 'I just talked to him.'

'My dad used to tell me that talking is a superpower,' Tariq responded wistfully. 'If you can just get talking to people, you can do anything. He's a counsellor,' he added, as if in explanation.

'What's that?'

'It's someone who talks to people and listens to their problems and then helps them figure out how to fix them,' Tariq replied. 'At least, that's how it sounds to me. Dad says it's more complicated than that, but I don't know.' He shrugged.

'Do you miss him?' Heidi asked.

'Oh man,' Tariq sighed. 'So much.' His eyes welled up with tears. Impulsively, Heidi lifted her arms and hugged him. He hesitated, then hugged her back. 'It's okay,' she said in his ear. 'We're going home.'

Tariq pulled away with a tearful sniff, but he was smiling. 'Yeah we are,' he replied. 'So let's get a move on!'

He hurried away to where Monifa was sitting with Amy. Heidi watched him go, wondering if she'd upset him. She hadn't meant to. But he seemed cheerful enough now.

Irgoll was gesturing for them to follow him, so the children gathered themselves with a strange mixture of excitement and reluctance. Having Nishkyn to guide them was encouraging, but the tale about the Witch had been terrifying; CeeCee held a sniffling Amy in her arms while Tariq and Tim walked side by side, discussing their favourite Marvel characters with a forced brightness. Tim was a big fan of The Hulk, while Tariq preferred Iron Man.

Irgoll led them along the treeline, looking for a good place to enter the thick undergrowth of the close-growing trees. Heidi fell in next to Monifa and Nishkyn wandered up beside her.

'Told ya those two bumpkins would need my help,' he said smugly.

'You did,' Heidi replied.

'You know, I'm putting myself at great risk, joining you on this trip,' he went on.

'You are,' Heidi agreed. 'And we all appreciate your help. You're very brave.'

He leaned in closer. 'Just so you know, there was some creepy little spriggan following you. I saw him in Lagamoora while I was hanging round the gate.'

Heidi looked down at him sharply. 'Sprickleback? He's still behind us?'

Nishkyn grinned. 'Not any more. I took care of him.'

Heidi looked at his sharp-toothed grin and felt a chill run down her spine. She slowed her pace so that they dropped back behind the group. 'What did you do?'

Nishkyn's tongue, which was long, pointed and strangely purple, slid out across the front of his teeth before it disappeared once more behind a conspiratorial grin. He winked. 'He was crunchy,' he said.

Heidi gaped at him. 'You ate Sprickleback?'

'Was he a friend of yours? 'Cause the way he spoke about you, sweetling, I gotta tell you...' The goblin shook his head in feigned disapproval.

Heidi frowned, remembering what Tuan had said about the bounty the Tuatha were offering on children like them. 'No, not really. But that doesn't mean he deserved to be eaten!'

Nishkyn shrugged. 'He was all set to hand you over to the Tuatha so he could get his due from the Firobolga. We had a nice little chat, you see, before I cut his throat. Oh boy, was he mad about the fauns taking you away from him! When they chased him off, he decided to wait around and follow you so he could steal one of you away – the little one, he said – then he could hand it over to the Tuatha himself. He didn't care what they would do with you. For all he knew, they want to eat you.'

Heidi felt sick. A wave of nausea surged through her and she had to swallow it back. 'I can't believe you just ate him, though,' she replied. 'You could have just chased him off!'

'What, like the fauns did? That worked well.' Nishkyn snorted. 'Besides, I have to eat.'

'But Sprickleback was ... like a little person! He talked and –'

'Oho?' Nishkyn gave a wicked grin. 'Is that the rule? You can only eat it if it doesn't talk? Because I haven't heard that little one say a word yet.' He pointed at Amy and cackled.

Heidi glared at him. 'Don't you dare!' she cried. At her shrill tone, Monifa and both of the fauns looked around curiously.

Nishkyn cackled again. 'I'm teasing,' he chuckled. 'I won't hurt her. Why doesn't she speak, though?'

'Because she's just a little baby,' Heidi replied, waiting for her heart to slow down. 'And she does speak, just not that much. She doesn't know that many words.' Now that she thought about it, she thought that Amy might have been speaking much less than she used to. She wondered if that was something she should be worried about.

Nishkyn frowned and shrugged, pulling Heidi's attention back to him. 'Humans are odd.'

'Do goblin babies know how to talk as soon as they're born?'

'Don't have babies,' Nishkyn replied, matter-of-factly.

Heidi vaguely remembered that the goblin guard Tariq had been talking to had said something similar. And what the pale girl had said about her friends changing. 'Then how do you ... you know, get more goblins?'

Nishkyn grinned again. 'Wouldn't you like to know, sweetling?'

Something about the way he said it disturbed her. But then

most of what he said disturbed her. So she fell silent, walking faster to catch up with the other children. Nishkyn didn't seem to mind, choosing to amble along at the back of the group alone. Once or twice Tuan or Irgoll would glance over their shoulder at him, but other than that nobody paid him much mind.

Everyone was much more preoccupied with their walk into the Great Forest.

Joining the Dots

Excerpt from a personal audio recording by one of the Investigating Officers of Task Force E.

So, we have a clear picture now – or as clear as it's going to get, I think. I can hardly believe what I'm about to say, even now. It's beyond ... everything. But we've come to the point where we just don't have anything else it could be. My only concern is that we've come to that point too late.

The whole thing reminds me of one of my daughter's join-the-dots puzzles. You start with one thing and then you link it to another, and then another and another, making logical links as you go until you get a complete picture. But this picture is just insane.

God, I miss Julie. Wherever she is, I hope she's okay.

Anyway, sorry.

After the first "Event", we put all of the eyewitness descriptions together and all anyone ever speaks of is some kind of shadowy figure. This matches eyewitness accounts from the following "Events" as well. They may be few and far between, but they all match. So our suspect is ... a group of shadowy ghosts? Research on the subject has suggested that they're visitors from another plane of existence, or dimension, or whatever you want to call it.

"The Events" always happen at the same time of year, and according to the pagans and witches and New Age hippies out there, it's a specific time of year: midsummer. Apparently, it's a time when spiritual energies are high and when the veil between worlds is supposedly thinner. This creates a possible connection point specifically between this world and - wait for it - fairyland. Our ... "advisors" ... claim that it's common for things to come through from that world, and that sometimes people go back with them. The thing is, we did a bit of digging and in some parts of the country, missing persons cases do tend to spike around that time.

So, to recap, we have visitors from another world popping in at a time when the veil between this world and another is thinnest. And then, all of our kids go missing. And who, according to folklore, likes to steal kids?

Fairies. Yes, you heard that correctly. Fairies.

So, where's the proof, right? Because who the hell is going to swallow a story like this without proof? Well, they dragged in this physicist lady who works on the Gateway Project and she has been feeding us images of the ... world, I guess ... on the other side. The thing is, if I looked at the images without knowing where they came from, I'd think that they were from some Hollywood movie like "*The Lord of the Rings*" or "*The Hobbit*", or that "*Elder Scrolls*" game my kid keeps playing. It looks like ... here, but ... better. Brighter. Greener grass, bigger trees. The few buildings that we've seen are either mud huts with thatched roofs or beautiful palaces like we could never build. There's no in between. And when you look at them in context with what we know ... it fits. And not only that, it ... feels right.

Yeah, I know, that's hardly going to hold up in court. But there's just something in the back of my mind that's telling me "yes". Our folklore advisor and some of the hippy types are suggesting that it's a kind of instinct passed along from our ancestors, the ones who believed in all this stuff. Ancient Celtic lore apparently says that their people used to live along-side the ... beings ... in this world, and that they chased them away, or something.

No one is going to believe this unless we can get proof. The folklorists are going nuts looking through books and papers and websites trying to find anything that would give us a reason why, but we need concrete, physical, hold-it-in-your-hands proof. Because the whole world's going to hell in a handbasket blaming each other for this, and if we pop up and just say, "hey, guess what, it was fairies" ... I mean, can you imagine? The whole Task Force will get fired. And that's the best case scenario. Worst case – our government actually announces that fairies are real and the rest of the world nukes us for either making fun of them or for being the place where fairies come from. I mean, where the stories come from. The Celtic ones – I don't know, I'm not a bloody historian.

The Gateway team think they've managed to build some-thing that can withstand the magnetic effects of the portal. They're turning it into some kind of cage or harness or some-thing. We told them that we need proof, and that the only proof that would be believed would be a creature from this world, captured and brought back here so that people can see it. So far they've only seen figures from afar, and they don't have any control over where the portals seem to open up in that world, so we're relying on blind luck, opening and closing and reopening the Gateway as much as we can until we manage to snatch something.

And this is our plan to avert global world war and nuclear catastrophe, people. We're trying to catch a fairy.

What the hell has happened to my life?

CHAPTER 17

THE GREAT FOREST

Stepping into the Great Forest had the same kind of jarring feeling as they had had when crossing from the Silent Forest into the hills. When Irgoll found a suitable gap in the foliage, they crossed almost immediately from a place of sunlight, breezes and green grass into a dim, damp world of thick-trunked trees, tall undergrowth and still, cool air.

The ground beneath their feet changed from the smooth grassland of the riverbank to mossy, turbulent soil, pushed into mounds and ripples by the twisting roots of the trees.

The canopy seemed to hang low over their heads, and they often had to stoop to avoid the branches. The vines that spiralled up the tree trunks and dripped from the boughs dangled like loose green garlands, occasionally brushing the heads of the taller members of the group.

The further in they walked, the warmer the air seemed to get, and they soon grew acclimatised to the shadowy forest. After the strong sunlight of the open plains, the cool semi-darkness, the quiet insect chirps and the soft bird calls were a welcome change. The children looked around eagerly, but the wildlife of this forest chose to remain unseen, save for the occasional darting light of what may have been a firefly, or something more fey. Now and then they passed over small streams trickling through the undergrowth like silver snakes, hearing the low piping of frogs.

Not far into the forest, Heidi looked over and was surprised to see Twist peering cautiously out of CeeCee's's hair. She wondered when the tiny pixie had jumped from her own locks to CeeCee's. Her friend glanced over and noticed her looking at the pixie, and smiled over Amy's little blonde head.

'I think he's happier now we're out of Goblin Town,' she said quietly.

Heidi returned the smile. 'I don't blame him,' she murmured. She realised that they were all talking quietly; there was something about the forest that made them want to keep their voices down.

Twist stepped out of CeeCee's hair and crouched on her shoulder, looking at the dense foliage around him. He seemed in awe of the trees as they passed by. How big they must look to such a small creature, Heidi mused, a small smile tugging at her lips as she watched him.

Then Nishkyn saw him, and without warning he lunged forward, swiping at the pixie with one clawed hand. Startled, CeeCee stumbled back, struggling not to drop Amy, but Nishkyn's lunge was too quick and his claws ripped through her shirt sleeve, high up on her arm. The pixie, however, was even faster, vanishing back into CeeCee's hair with a tiny shriek. CeeCee yelled in pain and backed away from the goblin. Amy, who had been dozing, looked up and started to whimper.

Instantly, the two fauns were on him, their spears against his narrow chest. Nishkyn threw his hands up. 'I was after the pixie!' he cried. 'I didn't mean to hurt the girl!'

Irgoll looked at CeeCee. 'What pixie?'

'He's talking about Twist,' CeeCee replied, one hand raising protectively to her hair. 'He was on my shoulder. Why would you want to hurt Twist?'

Irgoll rolled his eyes and moved back to the front of the group. 'I thought those pests had left us,' he muttered.

Struggling to suppress a grin, Tuan lifted the point of his spear away from the goblin. 'Don't eat the pixie,' he told him. 'They like it.'

'You eat pixies?' CeeCee squawked, her eyes wide.

Nishkyn looked at her in open confusion. 'What else would I do with it?' he replied.

CeeCee gave a cry of disgust and hurried to the front of the group, rocking Amy in her arms to soothe her.

Perplexed, Nishkyn turned to Heidi. 'You're not actually keeping it as a pet, are you?' he exclaimed. 'You know those little shits will tangle your hair and take bites out of your food? They'll take bites out of you too if they're feeling mean. They're vermin!'

Heidi scowled. 'I think they're sweet,' she replied, but she couldn't deny that her hair was getting very tangled ... but it wasn't Twist's fault she didn't have a hairbrush.

Nishkyn shook his head in disbelief. 'Humans,' he sighed. 'Your faun friend had it right; pixies and imps are pests, nothing more. You'll see. Wait till the twig imps find us.' He gave an exaggerated groan. 'I hate those.'

From up ahead, Tariq's voice floated back, a welcome distraction from the goblin. 'Woah, Monifa, your eyes are glowing!'

Immediately, the children clustered around her to look. They did indeed appear to be glowing in the shadowy gloom of the forest, the golden irises shining with a soft luminescence. Monifa gave a self-conscious smile.

'Yeah, I got these too,' she said, pushing up her top lip to display short, pointed fangs. 'My mouth is killing me.'

'Damn, Monifa,' Tariq said admiringly. 'You're kind of

scary!'

The children laughed, and when Amy lifted her hands to Monifa's face and said 'Neeef!', they laughed again. With their laughter, the oppressive atmosphere of the forest seemed to weigh a little less, and they walked on slightly faster than before.

Some time later, Heidi started to notice movement in the ferns and bushes to either side of the group. It was slight enough at first that she thought it must be a breeze, then she thought it might be a mouse or some other small creature startled by their passing by. But then she saw that the movement seemed to move toward them, not away. Small rustles in the bushes, and a ripple in the long grass. Something small and well hidden, she realised, was running alongside the group and gradually getting closer.

'Nishkyn,' she said quietly, and the goblin's ears pricked up. 'Do you see that?'

Nishkyn followed her pointing finger and nodded. 'That'll be the twig imps I was talking about,' he replied.

'Twig imps?' Heidi smiled. 'Are they like the pixies?'

Nishkyn snorted. 'You wish.'

Heidi's smile faded. 'Are they dangerous?'

'I mean, they're annoying,' Nishkyn responded. 'They're vicious and they'll attack anything. But they're too small to be dangerous.' He considered for a moment, then added, 'Unless you get swarmed by them, I suppose.'

Heidi glanced back nervously at the movement in the undergrowth. 'Should we tell the fauns?'

Nishkyn looked up at the two fauns ahead of them. 'Nah,' he replied. 'Don't spoil the surprise.'

Heidi frowned, and was opening her mouth to argue when Tuan suddenly yelped and danced off to one side. 'Blight and bone!' he swore, hopping on one hoof. 'My ankle!'

Sticking out of the fur at his ankle was a twig, around the size and width of a pencil. He reached down to yank it free. The end was pointed and bloody. He held it up to show Irgoll, who groaned. 'That's all we need,' he remarked.

'What is it?' Tuan asked.

Suddenly, Monifa let out a shrill shriek as something darted out from the undergrowth and jabbed into the top of her bare foot. It was a small brown creature about the size of a pixie. CeeCee let out a yell of surprise and swung her foot at it. The toes of her boot connected squarely with it, but instead of knocking it away, the blow shattered the creature, sending a small cloud of broken wood scattering into the grass.

Nishkyn cackled. 'You've got the right idea!' he said to CeeCee.

Looking stunned, CeeCee clutched Amy tightly and hurried on.

Irgoll called back to the group. 'They're twig imps,' he said. 'Keep moving, and if they attack you, just knock them away. They're nasty but they can't do much harm.' He gave CeeCee an approving nod and started sweeping the butt of his spear through the undergrowth ahead of him. Tuan stopped rubbing his ankle and did the same with his axe, driving the creatures away.

Nishkyn pulled a small, thin knife from his belt and held it, point down, in front of him. Heidi looked at it enviously, wishing she had a weapon. She caught movement from the corner of her eye and looked down to see a tiny person with a misshapen, featureless head, seemingly composed entirely of twigs and dried grass, run out from the undergrowth using a sharpened twig as a spear. She drew her foot back in time to avoid the savage thrust it made at her ankle. Swinging her leg back, she kicked at the thing, the sole of her bare foot connecting with what felt like a bundle of splinters. The creature shattered, just like the first one they had encountered, and the sharp shards dug savagely into her foot. She yelped and hopped about, trying to brush away the splinters with her hand. Her other arm waved about as she tried to keep balance, suddenly coming down on a bare shoulder. She looked up to see Tariq as he slung an arm around her waist and helped her limp on. Up ahead, Monifa was hurrying along behind the fauns and Tim was behind her, hopping from foot to foot like someone walking on a hot floor.

An imp rushed at Nishkyn and he skewered it with his knife. The creature squirmed angrily on the knife's tip, not seeming to feel any pain, still trying to stab its little spear into the goblin's hand. Nishkyn curled his lip in distaste and flicked the knife, sending the imp flying off. It hit a tree trunk and shattered.

'Not gonna eat it?' Tariq remarked.

Nishkyn sneered at him. 'Please. They're just dry twigs and dirt.'

'Ah come on,' Tariq retorted as they hurried along. 'It'd be crunchy. Like Twiglets.'

Nishkyn looked at him as if he were a madman, then spun to kick at another twig imp running up behind him. His grey-green foot shattered it into tiny pieces, but if he had splinters in it after, he didn't seem to notice.

The imps came on relentlessly, and the group hurried along as fast as they could, kicking and lashing out at their tiny tormentors. Heidi thought she must have killed – if it was possible to kill something made of twigs – at least a dozen of them before their numbers started to dwindle. By the time they stopped, all the children, except for Amy in CeeCee's arms, had numerous bleeding scratches and puncture wounds on their legs and splinters in their feet. The fauns had fared a little better, their fur saving them from the worst of the attacks, and Nishkyn didn't seem to be hurt at all.

They trudged on a little further until they reached another small stream. Irgoll lifted his hand and called for them to rest and tend their wounds. The children sank down gratefully, gathering in the widespread roots of a tall tree. One by one, they wandered over to the stream to bathe their injuries. It was barely wide enough to accommodate their aching feet and only just deep enough to submerge their toes, but it was cold and clear, and it soothed the sting of the cuts.

Heidi limped back to the tree. She had pulled five long, jagged splinters out of the ball of her foot and it was still pretty sore.

'Nishkyn,' she said as she sat down. 'Those imps aren't poisonous or anything, are they?'

'Nah, they're just annoying,' Nishkyn replied, pulling what looked like a strip of dried meat from his pocket and chewing on it. 'Good thing that was only a small swarm, though.'

Heidi didn't want to know how many twig imps made a big swarm. She sank down next to Tim, who handed her an apple. Her ears seemed to give a warning tingle, but she was too hungry to worry about it and bit into the fruit happily. The other children were helping themselves to food from the bags as well. Apparently, one of them had had the foresight to add to their supplies from Old Mother Korrigan's feast. Tim, she saw, was eating one of the sweet bread rolls.

'Don't you worry that'll make you change faster?' she asked him.

He paused in his chewing, then shrugged and swallowed his mouthful. 'Got to eat something,' he replied. 'And I guess I'm hoping we'll change back when we get home.' He pointed to his legs. 'But look.'

Heidi glanced down, not entirely sure what she was supposed to be looking at. Below his shorts, his legs were pale beneath the coarse hair, but... *Oh wait. The hair.*

'That was not there before Goblin Town,' Tim said, almost proudly. 'You know what I think?' He jabbed his thumb at the two fauns, who were sitting a little way off from the tree, keeping a lookout. 'I think I'm turning into something like them.'

Heidi pondered it as she munched on her apple. The red-haired fae girl had suggested as much in Goblin Town - that the children who came here turned into the creatures who lived here. She wondered what she would turn into. Hopefully, she wouldn't be here long enough to find out.

Amy started to giggle, pointing at something in the grass beside her. Looking over, Heidi could see a small human-shaped creature standing just out of the toddler's reach. She started to jump up, alarmed it might be another twig imp, but then she saw it had a tiny human-like face, though its skin was muddy brown and its hair appeared to be a mane of sharp green thorns. The thorns extended down its back like the spines of a hedgehog. It was another pixie.

CeeCee threw the pixie a small piece of bread and it jumped up and snatched it out of the air, stuffing the whole morsel into its mouth so fast it was gone before its feet touched the ground. Amy laughed happily and clapped her hands. CeeCee grinned and pulled off another scrap of bread to throw to the pixie, but then Twist suddenly emerged from her hair and ran down her arm, snatching the bread from between her fingers and jabbering angrily. He shook the crumb at the other pixie and yelled. It stuck its tiny tongue out at him before scampering off. Twist turned to CeeCee and stood on the back of her hand, pointing at her and jabbering.

CeeCee laughed and held up her other hand in surrender. 'Alright, sorry!' she cried softly. 'I guess you don't like those guys, huh?'

Nishkyn leaned over to Heidi. 'Can I eat that one?' he whispered.

Heidi gave him an exasperated look. 'Please don't.'

More pixies started to appear, gathering around the group like hungry birds, hopping closer and closer but never quite within reaching distance. The children laughed and fed them scraps while Nishkyn eyed them hungrily and the fauns rolled their eyes and shook their heads in disapproval. Twist stopped shouting when CeeCee shared her bread with him, but he glared furiously at the other pixies from his perch on her shoulder.

Eventually, Irgoll stood up, and the pixies scattered. 'We should get moving,' he announced. The children gathered themselves and stood up. Tariq offered to carry Amy but she clung to CeeCee fiercely, who gave an exasperated smile. 'Thanks though.'

Tariq shrugged and tweaked Amy's nose. She giggled and swatted him away.

Heidi realised Tim was still sitting under the tree, staring off into the distance. She went over and put her hand on his shoulder. 'Tim,' she said. 'You okay?'

Without answering, Tim pointed off into the trees. Following his finger, Heidi saw a dark shape half-obscured by bushes, and a pair of pale luminous eyes watching them. Her heart leaped into her throat. 'Err ... Nishkyn?' she called.

The goblin hopped over. 'What?' His eyes followed Tim's outstretched finger. 'Uh oh.'

'What is it?' Heidi asked.

'Not sure,' Nishkyn replied, 'But the last one I met tried to eat me. I'll, er, I'll go tell the fauns.' He scurried away with a nervous backwards glance.

The thing watching them - apparently noticing it had been seen - stood up and loped toward them through the bushes. It was about the size of a grown man, but it moved in a crouching run, supporting itself with long arms similar to a gorilla. It was slender and covered in coarse black fur, and had long, pointed ears that reminded Heidi of a rabbit. Its face looked more like a fox's, with a short, thin snout and a mouth full of small, sharp teeth. Its tongue lolled out of the side of its mouth as it seemed to grin. With a short, sharp bark from the creature, the trees around them rustled and suddenly there were three more of them, perched on the branches like monkeys, long tails as thick as their arms curled around the limbs to hold them steady. They poured themselves out of the trees, climbing headfirst down the trunks in movements so smooth they seemed almost fluid. It appeared that their feet were as dextrous as their human-like hands, and the claws on their toes as sharp as the ones on their fingers. Heidi pulled Tim to his feet and dragged him backward as the creatures began to advance.

Then, the first one, which was closest, spoke. 'Ooooh, what's this, what's this?' it snickered in a rough, hyena-like voice. 'Two Firobolga in our forest, with human children in tow! What precious cargo, precious cargo!'

'Steal 'em from the Mother, did they?' another added as it slithered on its belly through the grass toward them, studying them with its eerie silvery eyes.

'And so far from home,' the third remarked.

Nishkyn came back with the fauns in tow, and they positioned themselves between the children and the creatures, their weapons levelled and ready. 'Leave us be,' Irgoll shouted. 'We're only passing through.'

The first creature cocked its head to one side impishly. 'Passing through our forest,' it replied, and tutted in a curiously prim fashion. 'Naughty.'

'I hope they brought us something tasty to eat, at least,' another said.

The children huddled together behind the fauns, with Nishkyn working his way behind them, knife in hand. Irgoll answered, 'We have a little food. We will share it if you will leave us to pass through peacefully.'

'Don't want silly faun food,' said the one to their left. 'We want fresh meat.' It grinned widely, displaying many sharp teeth and a long, dangling tongue, and slowly it began to creep forward.

'Keep back, phooka,' Irgoll responded, pointing his spear at him.

'Phooka?' CeeCee murmured, frowning. Heidi glanced at her, but she didn't say any more.

The first phooka was now crouched just beyond the reach of the faun's spear, sitting up on its haunches. It brought its hands up and steepled them just below its chin, like a person in deep thought.

'Children of Mil are very, very tasty,' it said, nodding, 'but rare out here. Think the Witch would like them?'

'Oooh,' said another. 'Good idea, good idea! The Witch will thank us for them!'

'She likes new things to use as sacrifices,' said the third.

The first one nodded again. 'Yes, yes,' it said. 'She will reward us for these.'

'But does she need them all?' the one on its belly whined.

The first one gave a hyena-like grin. 'No, not all. And not the fauns or the goblin, no no.'

At this, the phookas erupted into a chattering, unnerving laughter. Nishkyn spun round and cursed. A fifth phooka had snuck up behind them while the other four were talking. He brandished his knife at it and it paused, frozen in its low crawl, its eyes fixed on the goblin. The fauns glanced round, and in that moment of distraction the other four phookas attacked.

Blood flew as the first phooka leaped high over Irgoll's spear, claws raking at the faun's face. Irgoll stumbled back with a yell, swinging his spear up instinctively, knocking his attacker off balance and sending it tumbling into the undergrowth. But the next was right behind it. Barely managing to get his spear round in time to fend it off, Irgoll crouched low to defend himself. Tuan, meanwhile, was swinging his axe wildly at the other two, who were trying to get past him to the children.

Nishkyn snarled at the fifth phooka as it started creeping forward again, a wide grin on its fox-like face. It swiped at him with one clawed hand and, quick as a flash, the goblin ducked and lashed out with his knife. The grin vanished and the creature yelped like a dog as it pulled back a hand now bereft of two fingers. Nishkyn plucked up the fallen fingers and stuffed them into his mouth, eyes on the phooka. It gave a menacing growl and retreated into the trees. As soon as it was gone, Nishkyn spat the fingers out and grimaced. 'Eurgh.'

Tuan managed to drive his axe into one phooka trying to slip past him, knocking it into the ground with a fierce yell. The creature wailed in pain and writhed terribly. Its companion saw Tuan's exposed back and dived for it, latching on and digging its claws deep into the flesh of his shoulders. Tuan screamed, let go of his axe and jumped in the air, pitching himself backwards so that when he hit the floor, the phooka was beneath him. It let out a 'Whoof!' as the air was crushed out of its lungs, and its grip loosened. Tuan twisted round, yanked his knife from his belt and sank it into the phooka's throat. By this time, the first one was free of the axe, tossing it aside contemptuously. It looked at Tuan, and noticing the bandage around his leg, darted forward, locking its jaws around the wounded limb. Tuan shrieked and tried to shake it off, but it held fast. His face tightened in pain as he forced himself to stop struggling, long enough for him to kick out with the other leg and smash his hoof into the phooka's face. Now it let go and scrambled away, yelping and clutching at its eyes.

Irgoll was still trying to strike the phooka facing him, but it deftly dodged each thrust of his spear, countering with lunges that forced the faun to retreat. Soon he was almost on the children. The two phookas who had disappeared into the undergrowth returned, one cradling a wounded hand, and rushed him from the side, barrelling him to the ground, biting and clawing. Tuan struggled to his feet and began slicing at them with his knife, driving them off. He stood in front of Irgoll as he got back on his feet and lifted his spear. The faun's chest was covered in long bleeding scratches, his arms covered in bite marks, and one of his eyes was lost beneath a curtain of blood from a long, deep claw wound down one side of his face.

The four remaining phookas regrouped. Two were wounded. They barely exchanged glances before they turned back and squared off against the two fauns. The wounded pair sloped off to either side as the others menaced them, keeping their attention. Nishkyn swore from his spot behind the children.

'They're going to circle us,' he cried. 'I can't hold two off by myself! I couldn't hold off one if it really tried!'

Heidi, CeeCee, Tariq and Monifa had pushed Amy into the centre of the group, trying to shield her with their bodies. Suddenly CeeCee looked up, her eyes wide with excitement. 'I have an idea,' she said.

'Whatever it is, do it!' Nishkyn cried.

CeeCee lifted her head and shouted at the top of her voice. 'Phookas!' she cried. 'I have a riddle for you!'

The phookas all froze in place. 'Riddle?' said one, popping its head up from one side of the group. They had indeed been circling round them. It was the one Tuan had kicked in the face, distinguishable by an eye that was beginning to swell shut.

'We do like riddles,' said one of the phookas in front of the fauns.

'It's really hard,' CeeCee shouted. 'I bet you couldn't solve it!'

'Oh, but we are very very good at riddles!' the now one-eyed phooka grinned. 'Tell us it, girl!'

'Only if you promise to stop attacking us,' CeeCee replied.

'While we're at the riddle, we shall of course stop,' the phooka replied.

'But only while we're at it,' another said from behind them, emerging from the bushes.

The fauns slowly lowered their weapons as the two phookas in front of them sat back on their haunches and lifted their hands, peering past them toward CeeCee. Heidi noticed that they paid absolutely no attention to the dead phooka whose throat Tuan had slashed.

'Okay,' CeeCee said, pausing. She glanced nervously at the other children, then cried, 'I'm part of a bird that's not in the sky, I swim in the sea and yet I remain dry. What am I?'

The phookas all froze, only their eyes moving as they thought. Then the two flanking the children bounded back to the others, and the four of them sat, heads together, muttering.

Tuan looked back to CeeCee, astonished. 'What's happening?' he asked.

'The stories my gran told me say they're very smart, and they like to prove it,' CeeCee replied. 'So you can distract them by asking them riddles.' She paused, then added, 'We should probably run because it's not that hard a riddle, and I don't know very many.'

They all began backing away from the huddled phookas. But they only managed a few steps before the phookas all raised their heads and in unison triumphantly cried: 'Shadow! Shadow!'

'Damn,' CeeCee muttered.

The phookas began stalking toward them, their bellies low to the ground, grinning widely. Tariq jumped forward.

'What about this one then?' he yelled. 'What is broken when it is not held?'

'Promise, promise,' one of the phookas growled. 'Heard that one before.'

'Damnit,' Tariq swore, and shot CeeCee an apologetic glance.

CeeCee raised her voice again. 'The shorter I am, the bigger I am. What am I?'

The phookas froze again, and then once more retreated into their huddle. Tuan nodded. 'Okay, now let's really run,' he said.

As one, the group turned and fled as fast as they could

through the forest. A few minutes later they heard a shrill howl from behind them: 'Temper! Temper!'

Irgoll swore. 'They'll be on us soon enough,' he said. 'Someone needs to hold them back.'

Tuan nodded. 'Alright. I'll meet you at the forest's edge if –'

Irgoll was shaking his head. 'I'll do it.' At Tuan's horrified expression, he went on, 'That first one took my eye, Tuan. I'm not much good with one eye. You saw me! I couldn't hit anything with my spear.'

'But...' Tuan stammered. 'No – I'm injured too! My leg...'

'Your leg will heal,' Irgoll retorted. 'Besides, they'd be able to catch you.' He grinned.

Tuan didn't return the grin. 'But Irgoll...'

'No time,' Irgoll interrupted. The phookas were hooting and howling as they gave chase, sounding closer all the time. 'Go. Get them to the City.'

The children started to protest, but Irgoll waved them to silence. 'Go! Now!' he cried. 'Tuan, you know I'm right. We gave our word.'

Tuan sighed and nodded sadly. 'Alright,' he said. 'Don't make it easy on them, friend.'

'You can count on that.' Irgoll smiled, clasping Tuan's shoulder. Then he turned away, hefted his spear, and ran back the way they had come. 'Here I am, you ugly curs!' he yelled. 'You like riddles? I've got one for you you'll never figure out!'

Tuan turned to the children and gestured for them to run. 'Quickly,' he said. 'We've made a lot of noise. We need to get far away from here.'

They didn't argue, but it was with tearful backward glances that the children ran on. Nishkyn ran ahead of them, eyes darting to and fro, and Tuan was at their rear, softly calling out directions. Monifa carried Amy and Tariq had Tim riding on his back. They ran until their legs burned and their breath was tearing at their throats. It wasn't until they were stumbling and falling down that Tuan called for them to stop.

When they finally did, they collapsed onto a mossy slope, gasping for breath, and found themselves close to the bank of a wide, fast-flowing river.

WORLD AT WAR

TRANSCRIPT OF A LOOPED NEWS REPORT FROM THE BBC.

Reporter: War has broken out between multiple countries: China, Korea, Japan, the USA, Russia, Germany, France, Saudi Arabia, Iraq, Libya, Pakistan, and India. All have mobilised their armies and a militarialisation of their borders has begun, with multiple air strikes reported to have been inflicted upon each other. Of these countries, at least seven have - or are believed to have - nuclear weapons, and it is thought to be only a matter of time before they are used. The United Kingdom is so far keeping out of the conflict, but the Prime Minister has announced that any attack on UK soil will be met with "equal and deadly" force.

World leaders are now being moved to top secret military bunkers in order to escape what is thought to be an inevitable nuclear attack. Martial law is in place in nearly every country in the world, as the wave of hysteria and rage over "The Event" and its handling has caused worldwide rioting and destruction. But, increasingly, military forces trying to keep order on the streets are being overpowered by sheer numbers of angry civilians.

Members of the public are being urged to stay in their homes; to lock and barricade all doors and windows; and, if they have access to a cellar, basement or any kind of air raid shelter, to go to these and stay there until further notice is given.

I repeat, the threat of nuclear attack is imminent across the globe as worldwide war has broken out...

CHAPTER 18

THE KELPIE

'Get up,' Tuan panted as he stood, favouring his good leg. 'They'll be after us eventually. We need to keep going.'

Heidi looked around at the other children. They were all exhausted and miserable. 'We can't,' she replied. 'Please.'

Nishkyn looked at them, then the flowing water in front of them. He glanced up and down the river, scowled, then turned to the faun. 'Do we need to cross this river?' he asked. Tuan nodded, and his scowl deepened. 'Thought so. Well, the state these children are in, if we try to cross now, all you're gonna do is watch them drown. I don't see a bridge or a ford nearby, do you?'

Tuan's gaze swept the length of the river visible to them, and he shook his head. 'You're right,' he said reluctantly. 'I apologise.'

'Besides,' Heidi added, 'Don't you need a rest too? Your leg...'

Tuan winced, as if the mention of his leg caused him pain. 'I'm hurting, but I'm alright,' he replied. 'Okay, we need to keep a lookout. Nishkyn, can you climb this tree?'

'Course I can,' Nishkyn replied irritably.

'Well, get up there and keep an eye out – they may come at

us through the treetops. I'll keep watch from down here. Children, keep an eye out along the river. I won't be far away. Shout if you need me.'

The children nodded, and Tuan limped away, looking strangely naked without his spear.

'I'll keep watch,' Heidi said. 'You guys can sleep if you need to.'

Curling up on the moss, the children clutched each other, seeking comfort. Heidi sat with her back to the tree and listened to them sniffing and moaning. She wondered if they felt as tired and hollow as she did.

Tariq shuffled up next to her, sitting back against the trunk until his shoulder touched hers. He looked at her wearily. 'You okay?' he asked.

Heidi did her best to smile. 'I'm fine,' she replied.

Tariq fixed her with a stern look. 'And the truth?'

'What do you mean?'

'My mum always says "I'm fine" when she's not fine at all. So I know that one. Come on, are you okay? Honestly?'

She sighed, her shoulders slumping. 'I don't know,' she admitted. 'It's like ... we've lost so many of us, and I'm almost ... waiting to see who's going to be next. It's horrible.'

Tariq nodded. 'Yeah. And Irgoll, man ... he was protecting us. He's from here. He wasn't supposed to die. It's sort of worse. Scarier.'

'Do you think he's dead, then?' Heidi asked.

Tariq met her gaze, his eyes tired and full of sadness. 'Go ask Tuan what he thinks,' he replied. 'You see his face when he walked away?' Heidi shook her head. 'Well, I did. It was the same look as the one on my dad's face when he got the phone call that Gramps had died.'

Heidi let out a long sigh and rubbed her face with her hands. God, she was tired. She looked at the children around her. Monifa was curled up on her side, quietly crying and trying not to show it. Tim and Amy were snuggled up together, holding hands and fast asleep in that exhausted, motionless sleep that only young kids can fall into. CeeCee was lying next to them, fidgeting and scratching at her neck, muttering thickly in her sleep. Heidi wondered what she was dreaming about. It didn't seem to be good, and her neck was looking pretty red. She thought about waking her, but then she seemed to grow calm, so Heidi decided to leave her alone. They all needed rest.

A soft sound reached her ears from slightly further away. It took her a moment to identify it, but then she realised that she was listening to Tuan sobbing. Her heart sank. She looked at Tariq helplessly. Tuan was about as close to a grown-up as they had here; what do you do when the grown-ups are crying?

'I can keep watch if you want to go check on him,' Tariq said.

'Do you think I should?'

'Hell, I don't know,' he replied with a sad laugh.

Heidi listened for a moment longer. Tuan's sobs were faint, but she didn't think she could sit there for long without at least trying to help. 'Yeah, I'm going to go check on him,' she said. 'Thanks, Tariq.'

'No problem,' he replied, raising one hand to wave her away. As he did she noticed that his fingernails had grown long and pointed.

Climbing to her feet, she picked her way carefully over the sleeping children and crept the short distance to where the sobbing was coming from. She found Tuan crouched on his hindquarters behind a fallen tree trunk, elbows resting on his knees, and his face in his hands. His bronzed shoulders shook with the force of his sobs and the effort of trying to keep them quiet. Heidi hesitated for a moment, feeling unsure.

Tuan froze, sensing that he was being watched and looked up. His black eyes shone even more than usual with the tears that streamed down his cheeks. He looked at Heidi in silence, not knowing how to respond.

Heidi reacted instinctively. She ran over to the faun and threw her arms around his shoulders, hugging him fiercely. He stiffened, then wrapped his strong arms around her and hugged her back, his sobs returning as if torn out of him. His whole body shook. Heidi let her own tears come as she clung to him; tears for Irgoll, yes, but also tears for all the others. She cried for Yuen, Meghan, Sue, Ricky, and Baby. She cried for the French girl whose name was Sylvie, it was Sylvie, she remembered now, and for Tyler who had left them. She even cried for her grandmother who didn't really want her, and for the boarding school she didn't really like. She cried for those of them who were left, and for whoever might be lost next. She cried for Tuan, who had left his home to help them and might never, she realised now, see it again. She cried for Sprickleback, who had been the first to help them even if he hadn't really been helping them at all, and for Whistle and Flick, and for poor Twist who was alone now. She cried for the redheaded fae girl who had seemed so scared, for Nishkyn who had been kicked out of his clan and had to fend for himself, for all the children they'd left in the Ice Fields who were either dead or who knew what by now. And she cried for this place. It was so beautiful, so wonderful, but so savage and frightening too.

Eventually they both seemed to run out of tears, and Tuan released her. 'Some lookout I am,' he sniffed with an embarrassed laugh.

Heidi shrugged. 'It's okay,' she replied. 'Nishkyn's watching too.'

'I sure hope so,' Tuan replied.

'Tuan, I'm really sorry about Irgoll,' she said softly.

He nodded. 'Me too.'

'Maybe he got away?'

'I doubt it. He was wounded. He was staying to hold them

back. He might have given them a chase, or fought them off for a time, but...' Tuan sighed. 'He was very brave, and proud to be a guard. He would have given them a grand fight, held them off us for as long as he could, and he would not have hesitated to give his life to do it.'

'Do you really think the phookas will still be after us?' Heidi asked quietly.

Tuan nodded. 'Either that, or they'll go tell the Witch about us,' he replied. 'Whichever it is, we need to get through the Forest as quickly as we can.' He paused, then asked: 'How much longer will your friends need?'

She shrugged. 'I'll go see,' she replied. 'I'll come get you when we're ready to go.'

He smiled and put a hand on her shoulder. 'Heidi,' he said. 'I appreciate the comfort you gave me.' He hesitated, then licked his lips and took a deep breath. 'Thank you,' he said.

She smiled. 'I thought you didn't like to say that?'

'We don't,' he replied, 'But it means something to you, so...' He shrugged.

Heidi stepped forward and hugged him again. 'It's the best thank you I've ever had,' she said.

He hugged her back, briefly this time, then pushed her away. 'Go see to your friends.'

Heidi nodded and ran back to the tree where the other children were sleeping. She felt better – still tired, but lighter of heart at least. When she reached the side of the tree where they were gathered, she saw that Tariq had dozed off where he was sitting, his chin resting on his chest. Monifa seemed to have stopped crying and fallen asleep too. Heidi glanced up at the tree branches and hoped that Nishkyn hadn't fallen asleep too.

She sat down on the grass, deciding not to disturb Tariq, and looked up and down the river. It was wide and fast flowing, the water churning so much she couldn't tell how deep it was. She wondered how they would cross it, or if they'd have to trek further along to find a better place. The bank by them dipped steeply down to the water's edge, and beneath the river weeds and ferns it looked muddy and slick.

The branches of the trees on either side of the river stretched out and met each other, forming a leafy tunnel through which a few shafts of sunlight broke through, spears of light piercing the gloom. It was a little spooky, but the sound of the water rushing by was soothing and she soon felt herself relaxing, despite the situation they were in. Before long, her eyelids were drooping and she was struggling to stay awake.

She thought she must be dreaming when a beautiful black horse, its coat shining like silk, stepped out from the treeline on the other side of the river and began to graze on the grass there. Its long tail flicked languidly to and fro as it ate, seemingly completely at ease. She held her breath as she watched, not wanting to startle it.

The horse raised its head slowly, its white teeth flashing as it chewed, and looked directly at her. Heidi smiled. 'Hi,' she whispered under her breath.

The horse gave a loud snort and shook its head briefly, sending its long, thick mane flying. It walked slowly toward the water's edge, long legs moving with liquid ease, and started to wade in. To Heidi's amazement, it kept going until the water was up to its flanks, moving across the flow of the water as if it were a still pool. She couldn't tell if it was walking or swimming as it crossed the middle of the river. Then it emerged from the water, climbing up on her side of the river without a single stumble or slip on the steep, muddy banks. It stood perhaps a dozen feet away from her and gave a flick of its wet tail, sending a spray of water flying through the air. It looked at her and gave a low whinny.

Slowly, Heidi got to her feet. 'Hey there,' she said softly. 'You're so pretty. Are you friendly? I'm friendly. I won't hurt you.' Cautiously, with one hand held out in front of her, she started to move closer to it. The horse didn't move, just kept regarding her placidly. Its eyes were so similar to the fauns' eyes, she thought – big, black, and liquid. Beautiful.

She was just a few feet away when the horse dropped its head, seemingly losing interest in her, and began to graze on the grass again. She moved alongside it, her hand still outstretched, admiring the blue-black sheen of its coat and the powerful muscles moving just beneath. It was big; her head didn't quite reach to its shoulders. She vaguely remembered hearing somewhere that horses liked it best when they were petted on the neck, so she reached out her hand to stroke it there. She stretched out her fingers, wondering how soft its coat would be, if the hair would be rough or smooth, warm or cool. The horse's ears flicked back toward her and it snorted softly. She took another step forward...

The cry from behind her was loud and shrill. '*Heidi! Stop!*'

She looked around to see CeeCee running toward her, her white shirt billowing around her. Before she could respond the girl barreled into her, knocking her off her feet. She landed in the grass heavily, dazed, and looked up in time to see CeeCee struggling to regain her balance as the horse's head whipped up and around, and it took two shuffling, dance-like steps toward her. CeeCee's outstretched arm connected with its flank. Then, the horse *changed*.

The shining black coat rippled like water. Suddenly, the short hair was longer, bristling, and wrapping around CeeCee's arm and hand like tiny, hungry tentacles. CeeCee yelped and tried to pull away, but she was held fast. The horse's previously placid black eyes began to glow with a baleful blue light. And before CeeCee could open her mouth to scream, it reared back, twisted, and plunged headfirst into the river, dragging her with it.

Heidi shot to her feet and ran to the water's edge, searching desperately. She saw a faint cloud of red hair sinking rapidly into impossible depths as the water churned and boiled along. Then nothing. She turned to the others and screamed. '*Help!*'

Instantly, Tuan came crashing through the undergrowth, and Nishkyn dropped down from the tree, knife in hand. 'What happened?' Nishkyn cried as the children stirred and sat up.

'CeeCee!' Heidi cried, pointing into the water. 'A horse, it – it took CeeCee!'

Tuan swore and ran to the riverbank, crouching down to peer into the water. Nishkyn hurried to Heidi's side, quickly followed by the other children. 'A kelpie? Really?' Nishkyn remarked, eyeing the river cautiously. 'She didn't really touch it, did she? Everyone knows not to touch a bleedin' kelpie!'

Heidi shook her head. 'I don't... She didn't...' She gulped back tears. 'She ... she was trying to warn me. I was going to ... I – I didn't know!'

Tuan lifted a hand to silence her, still searching the waters with his eyes. He pulled his knife from his belt and ran it across his other palm, drawing blood with a wince, and let it drip into the water.

'What are you doing?' Heidi cried shrilly.

'Trying to call it,' Tuan replied. 'But I don't know if it will come if it already has what it wants.'

The other children gathered around Heidi, who despite herself was starting to cry. 'What's a kelpie?' Monifa asked.

'Water horse,' Nishkyn replied. 'Likes to drown things. Anyone – or thing – that touches it gets stuck to it, and then – whoosh – in they go.' He inclined his head toward the water. 'I thought everyone knew that!'

Tuan opened and closed his hand, squeezing more blood into the water. Nothing happened. Heidi watched with her hands pressed over her mouth. She could almost feel the seconds ticking away. *She can't hold her breath for this long*, she thought frantically. *She's gone, CeeCee's gone and it's my fault...*

Suddenly, Tuan reared back with a shout of surprise. An

instant later CeeCee shot out of the water as if thrown, arms and legs flailing, and landed in a damp heap on the bank a few feet away. Heidi cried out in relief and ran to her, helping her to her feet. Her red hair hung in a sodden curtain on either side of her face, and she was gasping. The others flocked around her, grabbing at her, hugging her, chattering in relief. All except Tuan, who was frowning and watching the river's surface, knife still in hand.

Then, with a mighty splash and spray of water, the horse emerged from the river, leaping gracefully out and landing on the bank just beyond Tuan. The faun shot to his feet and stood facing it, barring its way to the children. The horse gave a furious neigh and pawed at the ground with one strong hoof, tossing its head in agitation.

'What's going on?' Tim cried.

Nishkyn shook his head in bewilderment. 'They don't usually give people back,' he muttered.

CeeCee clutched at Heidi's shoulder frantically. 'It took me to the bottom,' she exclaimed, her eyes wide. 'It shook me off and it stood on me, it was looking me right in my eyes ... but I didn't drown! It couldn't drown me! I could breathe down there!'

Heidi started to reply that that was impossible, but then she looked at her friend's hand, with the webbed skin between her fingers. She glanced at CeeCee's neck, and saw that what she had thought were scratches were now open, bloodless slits.

'Your neck,' she said. 'You've got gills!'

CeeCee's hand flew to her neck, her fingers exploring the small slashes. She gave a shrill laugh. 'I didn't before,' she said.

Meanwhile, Tuan was still trying to fend off the horse, which was dancing back and forth, looking ready to charge. 'Get away, kelpie!' he cried, brandishing his knife in front of him. 'You're not getting one of us!'

In reply, the kelpie gave a low snicker that sounded like a

rumble of thunder, put its head down, and charged. Tuan tensed himself, ready to strike...

And then there were two sharp, loud claps from behind the horse, and a stern shout: 'Ach! Enough!'

The kelpie pulled up sharply, its hooves digging into the grass, and stopped. It turned its head and peered at a small, hunched woman in a tattered brown shawl who was standing there, scowling at it. She waved her hand dismissively.

'Get away, ye beast!' she scolded. 'These aren't for you!'

The kelpie turned to face her and neighed in protest. The woman seemed to understand it, shaking her head.

'No, I said!' she snapped. 'Go on with ye, git!'

The kelpie gave a high-pitched whinny, then abruptly turned and dived back into the river. With a loud splash, it disappeared, and the churning water seemed to calm a little.

The woman turned back to the group and gave them an apologetic smile. 'Awfully sorry about him,' she said cheerily. 'Such a pest, he doesn't care who he bothers.' She chuckled heartily and trotted toward them. 'But what do we have here? Children of Mil, so deep in the forest! And in the company of a Firobolga and a goblin! My my, I never thought I would see such a thing!'

Tuan seemed completely at a loss. He stepped aside as she passed him, but kept his knife raised in one hand. He seemed to have forgotten he was holding it.

The woman crouched down before the group of children and started to look them over carefully. She appeared to be old, with deeply tanned, wrinkled skin and long, dry brown hair. In the crook of one arm hung a wicker basket, its contents covered with a dirty cloth. She reached out bony, long-fingered hands to the children, turning heads this way and that, taking hands and examining the palms, brushing aside hair and plucking clothes. She tutted in approval. 'Good, good,' she said happily. 'You're doing well.'

'What does that mean?' Monifa asked.

'Are you the Witch?' Tim added.

Nishkyn shook his head. 'Nah. Witch was green,' he said.

The woman cocked her head at this and gave a strange smile. 'Oh, don't you worry your heads about her,' she replied, ignoring Monifa's question. Then her eyes fell on CeeCee's arm. 'Oh, precious girl! Did that nasty beast hurt you?'

Everyone turned to look at CeeCee, and she blinked in surprise and looked down at her arm. Where the kelpie's hide had caught her, the skin was beginning to rise in red bumps and welts. She gasped in horror. 'My arm!'

The woman reached out and took hold of her arm, tuning it this way and that, getting a good look at the marks. 'Don't you fret,' she said. 'I can heal it. And I can do something for that wound in your friend's leg,' she added, nodding her head to where Tuan stood behind her, 'if he'd only put that blade away.'

Tuan started, looked guiltily at the knife still raised in his hand, and sheathed it quickly. 'Sorry, who are you?' he asked.

'Folks call me Peg,' the woman replied. 'Those that I see, anyways, which isn't many out here. Which is how I like it, normally, but we don't see Children of Mil all that often, does we? No sir, this is something of a rare treat!'

'Peg,' Tuan said with a small bow of his head. 'We are well met indeed. I am called Tuan, and I am grateful for your help with the kelpie.'

Peg smiled over her shoulder at him. 'No bother,' she replied. 'You can repay me by honouring me with a visit to my home. It's not far, and I can get you patched up in no time. Is anyone else hurt?'

The children checked themselves, but other than a few cuts and scratches left by the twig imps, they were fine. Peg nodded approvingly and got slowly to her feet. 'Come then,' she said. 'It's not far.'

As she trotted off, with the children following, Heidi

glanced behind her and saw Nishkyn and Tuan exchange a worried glance. She fell back to wait for them. 'What?'

Nishkyn shrugged and headed off after the other children. Tuan patted her on the shoulder. 'Just... Be careful,' he advised her. 'This seems ... a little too good to be true.'

Heidi considered, then nodded. Now that she thought about it - now that she was starting to get over the fright of the kelpie and almost losing CeeCee - she had to agree. She hurried along next to him as they caught up with the group. 'Are you sure she's not the Witch?' she whispered to Nishkyn.

Nishkyn shot her an exasperated glance. 'Did you not hear me the two times I told the story? The Witch is *green*. She's *brown*. Are ya blind?'

Heidi scowled back at him. 'Alright, alright,' she muttered sourly. 'You don't have to be so rude.'

THE TITHE, REDISCOVERED

Interviewing Officer:

This is the recording of a requested meeting with Elaine Lowry, our folklore expert.

She has been looking through the known information on the beliefs and practises of our ancestors, and in particular, those regarding...

Elaine Lowry:

Oh for heaven's sake, is this really necessary?

IO:

It's just procedure, Ms Lowry.

Lowry:

Procedure? Even now? We're stuck in a bunker trying to figure this out and you're still clinging to procedure?

IO:

(With a heavy sigh)

What is it you wanted to talk to us about, Ms Lowry?

Lowry:

The gate. I want to talk to you about that goddamn gate!

IO:

You're referring to the dimensional portal created by the CERN
team?

Lowry:

You know I am. Listen, you have to tell them to stop!

IO:

Stop what, Ms Lowry?

Lowry:

All of it! Stop poking it, stop putting things through, stop
opening it and closing it and opening it again! I don't
understand why you haven't figured this out, this is ridiculous!

IO:

Figured what out?

Lowry:

(Taking a deep breath)
When I came to you the first time, and I told you about the fae, I
told you about how they like to make pacts and bargains,
remember?

IO:

I read the paper, yes.

Lowry:

The fae are all about pacts and deals and words. It's a big part of
the old stories. And there's a very specific tithe – it's in my book,
you were given my book, I told you...

IO:
Yes, please, go on.

Lowry:
The tithe – the tithe on the Sons of Mil if they should displease or insult the Tuatha de Danann – the fae – one tenth of their children – and if the Sons of Mil ever attempt to enter the land of the Tuatha, the tithe will be all their children. Remember?

IO:
(A short silence)
Yes, I remember.

Lowry:
That's it, don't you see? We have entered their land – with that bloody gate! We've broken the pact and the tithe is being enforced in full! All of our children! That's why this is happening! They will take all of our children and return to wipe us out!

IO:
You think they're going to come and attack us here?

Lowry:
(Laughing)
Have you looked outside recently? I don't think they're going to need to!

IO:
You can't really expect us to believe that –

Lowry:
(Shouting)
How can you not believe it when it is right here in front of you?

Are you really so dense that you just can't get over the "faery" word? This is real! It is real and it is happening! And you need to shut down that gateway project before we do any more damage! I don't know if it'll make them stop, but...

IO:

How are we supposed to get our children back if we just abandon the project?

Lowry:
(Shouting)

I am telling you that the thing you are doing to try and get them back is the thing that caused them to be taken in the first place! You are making it worse! You have to stop!

IO:

Ms Lowry, please –

Lowry:

We'll have to make reparations somehow – I've no idea how, hardly anyone believes in them and God knows what we have that they'd want, especially now...

IO:

Alright, I'm going to terminate this convers-

Lowry:
(Shouting)

Why won't you just call them and tell them to stop?

IO:
(After a short silence)

Ms Lowry, we can't call them. We haven't had contact with the CERN team for weeks.

CHAPTER 19

THE WITCH

Peg's home turned out to be a ramshackle little wooden hut with a scruffy thatched roof, perched on top of a huge tree stump. The stump, the remnant of a tree fallen long ago, had been hacked at to make a level flooring, worn smooth now from years of use. A short distance away, the body of the fallen tree could be seen, hollowed and splintered.

'I made this home myself - when I was much younger of course,' Peg said conversationally as they approached. 'All from this one tree. It was a mighty thing when it stood, and then when it fell I just hated to see it go to waste.'

She opened the door and ushered them inside. Heidi had severe doubts that they would all fit, but somehow they did, comfortably. Inside it was just as ramshackle, but despite its fragile appearance the hut and everything in it seemed quite sturdy. There were stools around a central table – just the right amount of stools for them all – and a large hearth fire in a chimney breast made of clay bricks. Peg busied herself lighting the fire, and handed lanterns to the children to place around the hut so they were well lit. 'We don't get an awful lot of sunlight in the forest,' she said almost apologetically. Once the fire was burning merrily, she ushered CeeCee to sit in front of it to dry off. Rummaging through a large chest in one corner, she brought out a rather threadbare grey linen dress and presented it to her.

'It's not much, dear,' she said, 'But it's dry.'

CeeCee took it with a grateful smile. 'It's wonderful,' she replied.

'And a better fit than that old shirt, I'd wager – will you trade me it?'

'Of course!' CeeCee said eagerly.

There was no other room in the hut, so everyone turned their backs while CeeCee changed. When they turned back, there was a small murmur of appreciation. The dress seemed to be made for her; it fit so well.

'I don't suppose you want to trade any more clothes?' Monifa asked, enviously plucking at the wool blanket that was tied around her like a toga.

Peg chuckled. 'I might have a few things,' she replied, turning back to the chest. A few minutes later she pulled out another dress for Monifa, two grey tunics for Tariq and Tim, and two grey pairs of lace-up trousers for Tariq and Heidi.

'A fair trade, like for like,' she said, handing them out. 'Keep what you need, I'll take what you don't. I'm sorry they're not prettier, but they'll do you better than the bits and pieces you have now.' She cast a bemused smile at Tuan, who returned the smile apologetically.

The children dressed quickly, no longer minding who was watching. Heidi was amazed at how secure and comfortable the trousers felt on her. They were a remarkably good fit! Tariq and Monifa were posing and preening happily, glad to be out of their makeshift wool togas, and Tim seemed happy to not be bare chested any more, continuously stroking the arms of his tunic wonderingly. 'It's so comfy,' he said. 'It looked like it would be scratchy!'

Peg beamed proudly, gathering up the discarded garments. 'I might not have much,' she said, 'but I do good work with what I have.'

'You made these?' Tim cried.

She nodded. 'Got to do something to pass the time,' she replied. 'Now, who's hungry? I've got some leftover stew that just needs warming up!'

The children exclaimed happily, eager for a warm meal, but Heidi caught another uncertain glance pass between the goblin and the faun. 'Good lady,' Tuan said haltingly. 'We ... we have no means to repay you for all this kindness...'

'Your company is repayment enough,' Peg insisted, already heaving a heavy bronze pot onto a hook over the fire. 'Don't fret! Now, while it warms, tell me, what brings you to the Great Forest?'

The children all looked to Heidi, who in turn glanced at Tuan, who shrugged. She looked back at the old woman, who was standing and stirring the pot while she waited for a reply, a friendly smile on her face. Heidi knew Tuan and Nishkyn had misgivings, but she was so tired and she just wanted to be able to trust someone. Besides, she didn't see a point in lying when everyone they met seemed to know more than they did. 'We're going to the Shining City,' she said. 'We're hoping the Tuatha will help us get home.'

Peg's eyebrows shot up in surprise, disappearing into her unruly mop of hair. 'I see,' she said. 'That's quite a hope. You know the Tuatha are the ones who bring your kind here?'

Heidi nodded. 'Yes, but the fauns say they're the only ones who have any magic and would know how to get us home. So we have to try.'

'They do hold most of the magick in Faerie, yes,' Peg said thoughtfully, watching the stew as she stirred. 'And you're probably right that no one else would know the means. I have to say I don't fancy your chances, but I admire your courage. Just be careful – the Tuatha may try to keep you rather than send you home.' She shot Heidi a sideways glance. 'I would counsel you to stay, but I can sense that your minds are made up.'

'We can't stay,' Heidi replied. 'It's so dangerous here! And we're changing.'

'Dangerous, yes,' Peg agreed. 'But if you're clever, you can adapt. As to the changing... There's not much to be done about that. It's just what happens. But those changes will also help you to adapt.' She looked at CeeCee and winked. 'I suspect you won't need that dress for too long, if you stay. Dresses aren't much good underwater, I imagine.'

CeeCee blinked, then put her hand to her neck and frowned.

The smell of the stew began to waft around the small hut as it heated, and Heidi felt her stomach give a strong lurch of hunger. She suddenly felt as if she hadn't eaten in days. She heard the stomachs of the other children start to growl and grumble as well. Peg sniffed over the steaming pot and smiled. 'That should be warm enough. Would one of you get the bowls? They're in that basket over there.'

Tariq and Tim both jumped up eagerly, and together they dragged the basket over to the fire. Tariq held out the wooden bowls to Peg while she spooned hot, thick brown stew into them, then passed them to Tim, who handed them out to the group. Just like the stools, there were just the right amount of bowls, and enough stew to fill each one. Peg went to a shelf and picked up a roll of cloth, unrolling it to take out a handful of well carved wooden spoons – again, just the right number – and passed them out.

'There you are,' she said fondly. 'Eat, you poor things, you look famished!'

The children tucked in eagerly. Nishkyn watched as Peg started to eat hers, then studied his bowl with narrowed eyes. He sniffed at the stew cautiously, dipped in a claw and tasted it, then shrugged and started shovelling it into his mouth. Finally, Tuan sighed quietly and began to eat his. After the first couple of mouthfuls, even he was eating faster.

Their supper was delicious – a simple meat stew with some vegetables and potatoes, as far as Heidi could tell – but it was warm and thick and full of flavour, and it settled in her stomach with a comfortable heaviness. She wolfed it down eagerly, and scraped at the bottom of the bowl for the last morsels when it was gone. She saw CeeCee trying to help Amy eat hers without spilling it all down her nightdress. Putting aside her empty bowl, she took over so that CeeCee could eat. Her friend gave her a grateful smile and started eating rapidly.

Nobody said a word until all the stew was gone. Peg stood to collect the bowls and spoons and put them back into the basket. 'I'll take them to the river and clean them later,' she said.

The group around the table, bellies full and warm, began to chatter contentedly to each other. Heidi smiled at how much more relaxed they all were, grateful for a moment of real rest. She pondered again how funny it was that the hut had just the right amount of stools, just the right amount of bowls, and just the right amount of leftover stew to accommodate their group. It was almost as if she had known they were coming…

A dull niggle of alarm pricked at the corners of her mind, but it just didn't seem important enough to bother with. She looked around at the others. Tim and Tariq were sitting on the floor and playing with Amy. CeeCee was brushing out her damp hair with her fingers by the fire. Tuan and Monifa were both leaning forward on the table, and Tuan was actually smiling! Nishkyn was watching the old woman, but with his head propped in his hand and his eyes half-closed, his long ears drooping. He had a look of faint confusion on his face.

Heidi nudged him gently. 'What's wrong?'

Nishkyn jumped as if he'd been woken from a doze. 'Oh! Oh … er … nothing,' he replied. 'Just … I could swear I've seen this

Peg somewhere before. I just can't think where. It's probably not worth worrying about though,' he added with a shrug, resting his head in his hand again.

Heidi leaned back with a nod. He was probably right. But now she had two things niggling at her. Like two sharp quills in a feather pillow, they jabbed at her each time she tried to settle down and get comfortable.

She leaned forward again. 'Where have you seen her before?' she whispered. 'Think.'

'I don't know,' Nishkyn muttered irritably. 'Lagamoora, maybe?'

'Why would she go to Lagamoora?'

'How should I know? To trade, maybe?' Nishkyn shooed her away with a wave. 'Stop bothering me!'

Leaning back again, Heidi looked around the hut once more. She didn't see anything in it that might have come from Goblin Town; everything looked homemade. The woman had said herself she made the hut from a fallen tree.

Peg was sitting on one of the stools near Tariq and Amy, cooing over the little girl's pointed ears and blonde hair. Her shawls were as brown as her hair and skin, the clothes beneath barely distinguishable. Heidi found herself chewing on her thumbnail anxiously. Those two quills just kept jabbing at her, no matter how badly she wanted to relax. Something wasn't right...

Nishkyn continued to stare at the woman with that mildly confused look on his face. Then, he sat up straight, his eyes widening.

'I've got it!' he cried, and pointed at her with one sharp claw. 'I saw you talking to the Witch!'

Everyone froze, and all eyes went to Peg. She smiled gently. 'Yes, I know the Witch,' she replied. 'We share the Forest, after all. I can't help but bump into her from time to time.'

'You gave her my clanmate as a sacrifice!' Nishkyn continued, jumping to his feet in anger.

Peg laughed. 'How preposterous! I did no such thing.'

Heidi felt something change in the corner of her vision. Looking round, she saw that the walls of the hut appeared to be damp and rotting. Had they been like that before? She looked back and saw that the fireplace behind CeeCee was gone, replaced with a jagged spike of dead wood that jutted out of the floor. The smell of damp and rot crept around her. Nobody else seemed to notice; they were too busy looking at Peg.

'Er ... guys?' she called.

'You did!' Nishkyn was insisting. 'I had to sneak in and set him free! She had him in a cage! I heard her talking about what she was going to do with him!'

The room seemed to get suddenly darker. Heidi looked up and saw that the lanterns were gone, and so were the windows. They were sitting in a round space in a hollowed-out tree trunk, but now the roof was gone and the damp, mouldering sides reached up around them toward the treetops. The table and stools were replaced with stones and a large lump of dead wood. Of the pot, basket, bowls and other utensils there was no sign.

'Guys!' she cried, louder this time.

Tuan and Monifa glanced at her, the expression on her face enough to make Monifa shake Tariq's shoulder so that he looked round too. At the same moment, Nishkyn's eyes grew even wider and he looked around them in horror. 'What the...'

The other children started to look around now too. One by one, Heidi saw the spell on them break. Tuan shot to his feet, axe in hand. 'What's going on?' he cried. 'Who are you?'

Peg gave a regretful sigh. 'We were having such a nice time,' she said sadly. 'Trust a goblin to spoil it.'

Suddenly, as they looked at her, she no longer seemed to be a kindly old woman. It was hard to say what had changed, but they now realised that her brown, wrinkled skin was rough and scaly like tree bark. Her clothes were ragged and patched with mould. Her bony hands were almost skeletal, with sharp, jagged nails. And her hair was matted and damp, with twigs, dead leaves, and moss tangled in it.

Tariq and Tim leaped over the piece of wood that had been their table, Tariq pushing Amy into Monifa's arms ahead of him. CeeCee, sitting next to the old woman, tried to dart around with them, but the hag's emaciated hand shot out with surprising speed and pulled her in close.

'Now now,' she said, her gentle voice now grating and dry. 'No need to be rude. Let's all just sit down and be nice. You won't have long to wait.'

Heidi spun round, looking for the door. It was gone. She couldn't see any way out of the hollow tree stump – which now seemed much smaller and more cramped than the pleasant little hut had been.

'What are we waiting for?' Tuan asked.

Peg smiled, revealing black, filthy teeth. 'For my sister,' she replied. 'She'll be so pleased with all of you.' She looked at Nishkyn and gave him a nod. 'Well done, bringing these back to us,' she said to him. 'Such a useful little fellow, aren't you?'

Tuan's eyes slid distrustfully toward Nishkyn, and the goblin snarled. 'No you don't, you old bitch,' he spat. 'Don't try to get them thinking I'm on your side.'

Peg cocked her head. 'Are you not? Would you like to be? We can reward you well for these.'

The children were looking at him now. He gave the old woman an ugly sneer. 'You can reward me with your nose after I bite it off your ugly face!' he cried, and vaulted over the dead wood toward her. She lifted her free hand and caught him around his small neck with ease. Now she held the goblin in one hand, and CeeCee in the other. CeeCee was straining away from her, her face twisted in revulsion.

'Your sister,' Tuan repeated. 'Your sister ... is the Witch?'

Peg threw back her head, cackling with laughter. 'It's so funny to me,' she said, 'how everyone assumes that there's only one Witch of the Woods.'

Tuan winced. 'There's two witches?'

Heidi remembered Nishkyn's story. 'No,' she said. 'There's three.'

Peg gave her an approving nod. 'Very good, little one,' she said. 'And my sisters are on their way here now, so why don't you all get comfortable and stop making a fuss?'

With surprising strength, she threw both Nishkyn and CeeCee forward, into the group huddled behind the dead wood table. CeeCee stumbled on the uneven, spongy floor, but managed to keep on her feet. Nishkyn, however, was thrown clear across the table and over the childrens' heads, colliding with the rotting stump walls behind them. He slumped to the floor with a pained moan. In the same second, Tuan sprang at the witch, slicing down at her neck with his axe. She lifted her arm to deflect the blow, and it sank into her forearm with a sound like the crunch of splintering wood. The blade stuck and held. Before Tuan could even try to wrench it free, she dodged to one side, lifted her foot and kicked him, sending him flying into the far wall as if he weighed nothing. He struck the rotting wood, which groaned at his weight, then found himself pinned in place as large jagged splinters sprang up from the floor at the witch's gesture, punching into the walls around him like wooden bars.

Peg examined the axe stuck in her arm, seized the handle and wrenched it free. The blade came out of her arm, leaving a bloodless, wooden cut. She sniffed disdainfully and tossed it aside.

'Be careful, Firobolga,' she rasped. 'You are expendable.'

Tuan tried to force some of the spikes of wood apart, but they were strong and held fast. He glared at the witch, but said nothing.

While she was distracted by this, Tariq and Heidi both ran to Nishkyn and helped him up.

'Should have seen it sooner,' he was muttering. 'Stupid. I'm so stupid!'

Heidi shook her head. 'Not just you,' she reassured him. 'She fooled us all.'

'The rest of you, sit down,' Peg shouted. 'Do not make me ask you again.'

Reluctantly, the children sat down, some back on the stones they had been using for stools, the others huddled around them. Peg caught sight of Nishkyn among them and smiled.

'Goblin,' she said. 'Still want to die for these outlanders? Or have you thought better of it? My sisters and I can make much use of a resourceful little fellow like you.'

Nishkyn hesitated, his eyes sliding slyly toward Heidi, then Tuan, then back to the witch.

'Nishkyn,' Heidi said, her heart sinking. 'No!'

He shot her a dark look, then stepped forward. 'I guess I've thought better of it,' he replied.

Peg nodded as if she'd expected nothing else, and waved him aside. 'Keep an eye on the faun, then,' she said, 'and when my sisters get here we'll make sure you're duly rewarded.'

Avoiding the horrified gazes of the children, Nishkyn sidled off toward Tuan. Heidi glared after him, and saw him glance back. He shot his eyes to the witch, then back to her, raised his eyebrows, and then turned his back.

Heidi didn't know what to make of it. She didn't have much time to think about it, however, before CeeCee was talking. 'Why are you doing this?' she cried, her voice shaking with fright.

'Because you're Children of Mil,' the witch replied. 'It's really as simple as that, dear. You're valuable.'

Heidi glanced back toward Nishkyn one last time, then turned her attention to the witch. 'Are you going to try to trade us to the Tuatha too?' she asked angrily. 'Everybody else in this bloody world seems to want to.'

Peg chuckled. 'I wouldn't give the Tuatha my morning shit,' she responded, the leer as she spoke making the phrase even uglier. 'Not that they've ever shied away from taking what they want. No, I think my sisters and I can put you to better use.'

'How?' Heidi demanded. She glanced over at Nishkyn again and saw that he was no longer next to Tuan. He seemed to have vanished. She thought – she *hoped* – he was up to something useful. 'Are you going to sacrifice us? What will that even do? I thought the Tuatha had all the magic.'

The witch smirked. '*Nearly* all the magick,' she corrected. 'Oh yes, when they were banished from the upper world to here they were very clever and adept at twisting this world to their will. They didn't give a thought to those who were here already, my sisters and I. I believe they weren't even aware of us. But when they came and imposed their "*laws*" upon this world -' She spat the word as if it tasted bad– 'And forced us into physical forms, we were at least able to snatch a little of the magic before they leeched it all away into their Shining City.'

'What were you before?' Heidi asked. Nishkyn was still nowhere to be seen.

Peg sighed wistfully. 'Nothing. Everything!' she replied. 'We were formless ... powerful ... peaceful. Then, the beautiful ones came and gave the nothingness form, and that included us. We snatched what we could and it turned us into what we are.' She put a hand on her chest and gave them a mock bow. 'I have power over that which is dead. My sister Jinny has power over that which grows, and my sister Annis has power over those that hunt. Together, we made this forest, and made it dark enough and dense enough that we can keep the Tuatha out. The forest is ours, and we are the forest.'

'Is that why you want to sacrifice us? To keep the Tuatha out?' Heidi thought she saw a flicker of movement in the shadows behind the witch, but she wasn't sure. She concentrated on not letting her eyes leave the hag's face.

'We can manage that just fine on our own, deary,' Peg replied scornfully. 'Besides, all the Tuatha care about is getting back to where they came from – even while they strip us of our magic and enforce their forms upon what was once formless. They have no care to make a claim on our Forest. No, you will be useful in taking back what was stolen from us, I think. Although...' She paused and gave a curiously girlish giggle. 'From what our spies in the City tell us, we might be well served by just waiting a while.'

Heidi frowned. 'What do you mean by that?'

The witch opened her mouth to answer. Before she could speak, her eyes bulged as a long blade burst from her throat, splattering black blood across the dead wood that had served as her table. The children shrieked in surprise and horror. She made a soundless croak and grasped for the blade, but before she could touch it, it was wrenched violently to one side, tearing through her neck in a burst of black gore and stringy flesh. She clawed weakly at the wound as her strength drained from her, before sinking bonelessly to the floor. Her eyes darkened and seemed to fall into her skull, the sockets becoming hollow knots in her wooden face. She lay motionless before the horrified children, and the longer they looked at her the more she seemed to resemble nothing more than a decayed and mouldering old tree.

Behind her, Nishkyn was clutching to the rotten wall at head height, his long knife, dripping with black blood, hanging from one hand. He grinned down at the witch's lifeless corpse. 'I thought better of it again,' he said, and spat.

The children let out a combined sigh of relief. Tim clapped, and Tariq gave a weak cheer.

'You scared me!' Heidi shouted at Nishkyn.

Nishkyn shrugged and hopped down, sheathing his blade. 'Well done keeping her talking,' he said. 'You made it easy.'

As he spoke, there came a low wooden cracking sound. Suddenly, the walls around them seemed much, much lower. The spikes pinning Tuan in place crumbled and collapsed into dust, and when they looked back at the body of the witch, there was nothing but a rotten tree branch. Heidi glanced behind them and saw that where the hut's door had been, there was a large hole in the side of the tree stump. Somehow, the stump itself seemed to be getting smaller still; they were now pressed up against each other in order to fit inside, where before there had been room to move around.

Nishkyn shook his head in disgust. 'Magic,' he said scornfully. 'Let's get out of here.'

Before anyone could agree, there came an ear-piercing shriek of grief and rage from the forest, loud enough to shake the birds and pixies from the trees and send them fleeing. It was followed by a bone-chilling howl from what sounded like a massive wolf. Then the first voice came again, a female voice, this time screaming out a single word:

'*SISTER!*'

The colour drained from Nishkyn's already grey face. 'Oh no,' he muttered. 'We really, really have to go.'

Tuan retrieved his axe from the floor and nodded. The children grabbed what they could and without another word they followed their two guides as they fled into the forest, back toward the river.

They ran as fast as their legs would allow them. They leaped over tree roots and ducked under branches, weaved in and out of the tree trunks, never slowing down. Tariq was up front with Tuan and Nishkyn. Monifa had Amy tucked under one arm, clinging to her dress, the skirt of which she had pulled up high around her thighs and held bunched in her free hand. CeeCee had her skirt held up in both hands, and Heidi and Tim each had a bag of food slung over their shoulders. They were the only bags they had left; somewhere in the journey, among the attacks and the panic and the running, they'd lost the others.

They'd not been running for long when a loud rustling noise came from all around them, as if a sudden strong wind had blown up, but with no clear direction. Heidi's heart sank like a stone when she saw that the branches on every tree and bush, and even each blade of grass, seemed to be pointing directly at them.

Nishkyn swore. 'It's the Witch!' he cried. 'She's found us!'

'Keep running,' Tuan replied grimly.

Now the tree roots were getting higher and harder to spot, the undergrowth more full of tangling brambles and tripping vines. More than one of the children stumbled and nearly fell in their flight. Tuan ploughed ahead of them, limping only slightly now, chopping at the foliage and hanging vines as he went, trying to clear a path, while Nishkyn hopped and leaped nimbly, avoiding the hazards with relative ease.

Monifa's foot caught on a tree root that seemed to push itself out of the ground to meet her, and she fell heavily, twisting as she fell to avoid crushing Amy. She landed with a cry of pain and pushed herself immediately to her feet, falling to the back of the group but keeping pace. Heidi glanced back and saw that she was no longer holding up her skirt, that her face was twisted in pain, and that the arm that was not holding Amy was bent oddly. She fell back and held out her arms.

'Give me Amy,' she said.

Monifa handed the small child over with a grimace and gathered up her skirt with her good arm. Heidi hefted Amy in both arms and ran on. The little girl wailed in dismay, reaching out for Monifa with her tiny hands.

Ahead of them came the soft roar of the river, and through the trees they could see the shimmer of the fast-flowing water. They reached the water's edge and paused.

'How do we get across?' Nishkyn cried.

As if in response, from the centre of the river there emerged the black ears and glowing eyes of the kelpie. It regarded them hungrily, its submerged nostrils blowing bubbles in the water that were quickly snatched away by the rushing current.

Tuan cursed and turned. 'Upriver, quick!' he said. 'We'll have to find another place to cross.'

The group turned as one and ran along the riverbank, heading against the current. From behind them they could now hear the distant sound of heavy footfalls thundering toward them. They were growing steadily louder. Heidi heard Nishkyn give a miserable wail. Her mind flashed back to his story and her blood ran cold. *The wolf!*

Tuan's voice rang out, bright with relief. 'There's a ford up ahead!'

They reached the ford about the same time the wolf became visible through the trees behind them. It was a huge black mass in the shadows, with only its burning red eyes and sharp white teeth clearly visible. It gained on them steadily, its footfalls like thunder and its breath an endless, rattling snarl.

They stumbled to the edge of the ford. It was a shallower section of the river where large boulders poked up just above the water, their surfaces slick and shiny. Nishkyn darted straight across. Tuan stopped on the riverbank and began ushering the children ahead of him. They ran in a long, straggling line: first Tariq, then CeeCee, then Tim, then Heidi with Amy. Monifa, Heidi realised with horror, had fallen behind, cradling her hurt arm. She reached the opposite shore and turned to see Monifa struggling along the bank toward the ford, Tuan standing with one hand outstretched to her. As she watched, the immense form of the gigantic black wolf burst from the trees. It caught up with Monifa in one bound and brought its front paws down upon her back, claws sinking into her shoulders. She screamed in pain and terror and sprawled onto the grass, blood flying from her back. Tuan yelled and started towards her, axe raised, but before he had taken two steps the wolf had clamped its massive jaws around Monifa's head and bitten down. There was a sickening crunch, and blood spurted from between its teeth. Monifa's screams cut off with a wet gurgle as her skull was crushed. Blood poured from her open mouth in a ghastly torrent. Her hand, stretched out to meet Tuan's, fell limp onto the grass.

Heidi screamed and spun around, trying to shield Amy from the sight. The other children, gathered behind her, screamed too. Tuan wailed in grief and horror, staggering to a halt. Then the wolf dropped Monifa's ruined head into the grass and spoke.

'Yooooouuuuu.....' it said in a low, drawn-out growl, the words thick and awkward coming from behind those teeth. Monifa's blood dripped from its snarling lips. 'Yooooooouuu mmmmmurrrrrrrderrrrred   mmmmmMMMMMYYYYYYYYY SSSSSSSISTERRRRRRRR!'

The children shrieked again in fear, and Nishkyn's eyes went wide. Tuan shot to his feet, standing only a few feet from the wolf, and raised his axe. Heidi could see his arm trembling.

The wolf gave a strange twisting motion with its shoulders and then reared up on its hind legs. The children watched in astonishment as the great creature seemed to shrink in on itself, the fur on its chest parting, and two grimy, blood-streaked hands poking through the rent flesh. The hands parted the fur like a curtain, and the children watched as a woman, naked and coated head to foot in mud and gore, pushed the black pelt back from her shoulders like a cape. She pushed the head of the wolf pelt up so that it sat on her head like a hood, but she still had the burning red eyes. And her mouth was still smeared in Monifa's blood.

The woman regarded them from across the river, standing over Monifa's body, her face twisted in rage. 'You murdered my sister,' she said again, her voice clearer now. 'You will pay!'

Tuan started to back toward the ford. 'Children,' he called. 'Run!'

The woman's gaze shot to him. 'Trust me when I say I can catch you,' she spat. She stepped forward over Monifa, her bare feet squelching in the bloodsoaked grass. 'Children, stay. Stay and hope for the mercy of my now only sister. Or run...' She grinned savagely, and they could see even from across the river that she still had the sharp fangs of the wolf. 'Run ... and I will catch you and I will tear you limb from limb.' She looked back at Tuan. 'Starting with you, Firobolga.'

Tuan stopped, one hoof on the first boulder of the ford. He looked over at the children, and Heidi saw his head lift and his shoulders square. 'Go,' he called. 'I'll hold her off.'

'No!' Heidi wailed. 'Please don't do this, Tuan!'

'Just keep going straight and you'll reach the forest's edge,' Tuan told her. 'Nishkyn can guide you. Once you're out of the forest, you'll see the city.' He paused, then added, 'I hope you get home.'

The woman growled and pulled the wolf head down over her face like a mask. 'Good,' she rumbled. 'More sport for me.' The pelt wrapped around her like a living thing, and as she crouched she disappeared beneath the rapidly filling and growing form of the black wolf.

Nishkyn's shrill cry cut through Heidi's thoughts. 'Run!'

The children spun and ploughed into the trees as Tuan leaped over Monifa's mangled body at the black wolf. It opened its jaws wide and roared as it jumped to meet him. Heidi turned away before she could see what happened. But before she did, she saw the branches and foliage behind them, bending away to clear a path, and down that path she saw someone else appear. A tall, statuesque, green-skinned woman, walking toward them with a murderous look on her face.

WARNING

TRANSCRIPT OF A BBC *RECORDING BROADCAST LOOPED ON REPEAT ON TELEVISION, RADIO AND INTERNET CHANNELS.*

This is the Wartime Broadcasting Service. We have been attacked with nuclear weapons. Communications have been severely disrupted, and the number of casualties and the extent of the damage are not yet known.

CHAPTER 20

THE SHINING CITY

Heidi could feel herself flagging. The children were pulling further ahead of her, and the sinister rustling of branches and bushes bending to trip them was all around. Her breath tore at her throat, her legs were burning, and Amy was getting heavier by the second. Any moment now she expected to hear heavy black paws thundering up behind her. To feel hot, carrion-stinking breath on her neck, or for a green hand to land on her shoulder and yank her off her feet. She wanted to call out to someone to take Amy from her, but she didn't have the breath to shout.

And then Tariq shouted: 'I can see sunlight ahead!' The relief that washed over her was so strong it almost made her legs give out.

Somehow she managed to keep running. Putting her head down, she willed her legs to keep moving, just a little longer... And then suddenly, she was out of the trees and stumbling at high speed down a soft decline, into waist-high grass and wild-flowers. The warm sun hit her face like an old friend, even as it dazzled and blinded her. Her feet finally gave up on her and she stumbled and fell, rolling onto her back as she did to save Amy.

She landed in thick, soft grass and lay there, looking up at the cloudless blue sky.

I'm gone, she thought dreamily. *No one can see me in the grass. They'll never find me.*

Then, she heard the grass rustling, and for a panicked moment thought that the witch was upon her. But it was Tariq and CeeCee, one on each side, hauling her to her feet. CeeCee picked up Amy and they ran on together. Up ahead, Nishkyn and Tim were waiting for them, Nishkyn jumping up and down anxiously.

Heidi risked a glance behind them. The grass was rippling and parting like the Red Sea in the Bible stories, and through the parting strode not Moses, but the Green Witch. She was not the old hag that Heidi had expected; she was smooth-skinned and beautiful, with long, thick, greenish-black hair that shone like oil in the sunlight. She had bright emerald eyes, and long, muscular legs displayed in full by the short, ragged tunic she wore. Heidi could easily imagine her breaking into a sprint and running them down.

She looked back in the direction they were running, and for the first time her eyes fell on what they were running toward. The grass field they were running across sloped down into a slight valley, then up again, and on the top of that uphill slope there was a vast, tall, and truly shining city. Delicate white spires wound up into the sky, windows of coloured glass glittered in the sun, cheerful flags and pennants fluttered in the breeze. A tall, smooth wall of golden-coloured stone encircled the city, and a huge pair of golden gates, embellished with curling and floral designs wound into the bars, were set into it. Guard towers like castle turrets flanked the gate, and she could make out figures moving inside them.

'Heeeeeeeeeere, little chickies,' the witch called out in a voice like warm honey. 'Come to me, my loves.'

For a moment – just the barest fraction of a second – Heidi

actually wanted to, wanted nothing more than to stop and turn around and go to the beautiful green woman and feel her arms around her. From the way the other children stumbled and glanced back wildly, they wanted it too. But Heidi only had to conjure up the memory of that enraged shriek that had cut through the forest to break the spell. She clutched tighter to Tariq's hand and kept running.

As they drew closer to the gate, the figures in the guard towers vanished, and then a smaller entrance cut into the large double gates swung open and they slipped out, slender spears in hand. They wore shining plate armour, complete with plumed helmets that reminded Heidi of the pictures of Roman legionnaires in history books. There were four of them, and in their armour they looked identical. They positioned themselves in front of the gates and brought their spears down, pointing at the rapidly approaching band of children.

'Who goes there?' one of them called.

Tim, who was in front with Nishkyn, put on a desperate burst of speed and raced toward them. He took a deep breath and cried out in one breath: *'Please help, the witch is chasing us, she's gonna eat us!'*

At the sight of the young horned boy, the guards' spears dropped a little, but at the mention of the witch, they lifted again. One of the guards raised a curved horn from his belt and blew a long, clear blast on it. In response, the top of the wall around the city almost instantly came to life with more guards, these ones holding longbows, arrows nocked. The same guard stepped back and pushed open the smaller gate again, and started to beckon the children inside. One by one, they hurried in through the gate, stumbling to the ground beyond it.

The guard snatched Nishkyn up by his collar as he hopped through. 'Not you, goblin,' he said, and once all the children were inside, he tossed him unceremoniously back out before slamming the gate closed. The children uttered breathless cries of protest, but he silenced them with a cold-eyed glare.

Nishkyn picked himself up outside the gate and tried to dart back past the three guards still standing outside with him, but they blocked his path with their spears. He glanced desperately back into the field, where the green-skinned woman was striding forward through the parting grass. He glared at the guards, then cast a last miserable look at the children beyond the gate before he dove into the long grass, vanishing.

The witch came to a halt just outside the range of the guards' spears. 'Give me the children,' she said, her voice dripping with venom.

The guards raised their spears to her throat. 'Begone, witch,' one of them said. 'You know the laws. The Tuatha have claim to all Children of Mil.'

She smiled. 'You didn't even know they were here until they ran up to your gates,' she replied, with a gentleness that screamed danger. 'What difference will it make to you? It makes a great difference to me.'

The guard who spoke didn't move. 'We know they're here now,' he replied. 'Now leave, before we make you.'

At that, the sound of dozens of longbows being drawn taut echoed out from the tops of the walls. The witch looked up almost lazily and eyed the archers, all pointing their arrows at her. 'You think a few arrows scare me?' she said contemptuously.

'The arrows might not,' the guard replied. 'But the enchantments on them should. You know well that our people hold far more powerful magick than the tricks you can conjure up.'

She bared her sharp teeth at him in an ugly snarl. 'How like the Tuatha to be thieves,' she spat. 'Fine. I can be patient.' She looked through the bars of the gate at the children. 'I know you by your smell, little chickies,' she called, 'and no matter how the magick changes you, I will know you still. And I will remember you long after you have forgotten me.'

With one last disdainful glance at the archers on the wall, the Green Witch turned and strode off through the grass, back to the Great Forest.

The children picked themselves up and looked around at their new surroundings. The change was drastic; they'd gone from a world of savage wilderness and primitive settlements to a shining, orderly, beautiful civilisation simply by diving through a gate. Heidi felt small and lost, acutely aware that they had lost all the native creatures who had been guiding them.

Fresh on the back of this thought was the realisation that the last time she had seen Twist, the pixie was hiding in Monifa's hair. It all came flooding back. Monifa... Tuan... She let out a wail of grief and sank to her knees again. The tears came swiftly, followed by wracking sobs, and through a haze of grief and pain she was only dimly aware of Tim helping her to her feet.

The guard looked down at them, confusion evident in his amber eyes. He was – like the other – very tall and very thin, though his plate armour added a little bulk. Long, pointed ears could be seen poking out of small slits in his helmet. The small amount of skin that could be seen was a pale golden colour. A second guard joined them, in his armour looking identical to the first. They conferred for a moment over the heads of the children, then one of them crouched down to their eye level, leaning on his spear in a manner so similar to the fauns that it sent a fresh pang through Heidi's heart. He looked at the four larger children and said, 'You're safe from the Witch here. We're going to take you to an inn, where you can rest and have some refreshments, while we summon the Magister. She'll know what to do with you.'

'Will she be able to help us get home?' Tim asked.

There was a long pause. 'You'll have to ask her that,' the guard eventually replied.

Heidi did not like that pause. But at present, they seemed to have little other choice. She let Tim guide her along as she wiped the tears from her eyes and tried to calm herself. The other children were crying too, she noticed. Amy was cradled in CeeCee's arms, whimpering. CeeCee and Tariq wept silently as they walked, and Tim sniffled softly, wiping away tears with his free hand as he guided Heidi with the other.

They were led through streets so clean and beautiful that they didn't feel real. It was like walking through a movie set, everything was so perfect. The streets were smooth cobblestones, the buildings pale gold or white stone that looked a lot like marble, with doors and shutters of honey-coloured wood. Most dazzling was the golden trim around the doorways, windows, the eaves of the light grey-tiled roofs... It was everywhere. Small areas of manicured lawns and perfectly pruned bushes and trees were located at every corner and outside every home, so that the city seemed almost as green and lush as the lands outside of it. Tall towers spiralled upward everywhere like delicate glass ornaments, gleaming in the bright sunshine. There didn't seem to be any kind of order to where houses and public buildings were situated; cosy little homes were nestled in between tall towers and shops with swinging signs outside. Despite this, it didn't seem disordered, but rather it gave the impression of harmony, of a city grown organically over time. Even the buildings had that organic feel to them, with very few sharp angles and winding, spiralling decorations that mimicked vines and branches and tree roots. It all reminded Heidi somehow of her grandmother's Fabergé eggs – beautiful and obviously manmade, but so smooth and perfect that she could not imagine how it had been done.

The building they were taken to had a sign outside declaring it to be The Snapdragon Inn. Outside, there were a few tables and chairs set out, all in that same mellow amber-brown wood. A couple of patrons were sitting at one of the tables, chatting over delicately crafted clay mugs. They turned their heads to stare as the guards approached with the children, so Heidi didn't feel too bad about staring back. They were tall and thin, like the guards, but their thin frames didn't look bony or gaunt, but rather as if they simply had finer bone structures. Their ears were long too, extending out above the tops of their heads from beneath long, thick, golden hair. One had hair that fell in gentle ringlets with a reddish hue whilst the other's was poker straight and the colour of butter. Both pairs of eyes were large, almond shaped and amber, and their skin pale gold. Each wore pale blue robes that fit snugly around their limbs, but were loose around their bodies, embroidered in great detail with designs that Heidi couldn't quite make out. She honestly couldn't tell if they were women or men.

Inside were even more of these creatures, all with the same varying shades of golden hair and skin, some with eyes of bright green or blue, but mostly of amber. They all wore the same fashion of robes in different light colours, and they all turned to stare as the children were led inside. A person with a small goatee and a pristine white apron over their robes stepped out from behind a long, curving bar to meet the guards, a confused smile on his face. He conferred with them for a moment, then nodded and headed for a staircase at the back of the large room, gesturing for them to follow. The guards wound through the tables of now silent patrons, and the children followed close at their heels. They heard the conversation start up again as they ascended the stairs.

The barkeep showed them to a room, opening the door for them and stepping back to allow them inside.

'I'll have refreshments brought up directly,' he said with a small bow, and departed back the way they had come. One of the guards left with him, while the other ushered the children into the room. 'I'll be right outside the door if you need me,' he said.

Heidi was starting to doubt if the guard really was a "he"; their voice was soft and strong and gave no clues, and she wondered if gender wasn't important to the Tuatha just as it wasn't to the pixies. The guard closed the door gently, leaving them alone.

There was a moment of stunned silence before some of the tension left the air and the children let out a collective sigh. It felt like weariness rather than relief to Heidi. They looked around at the room they had been left in, trying to make themselves comfortable. It was a nice room. There was a double four poster bed with ivy carved into the posts and multiple blankets in a dark green hue that matched the curtains. A round table and upholstered chair stood in the corner, again in that dark green, and a wooden chest was in another corner that, on inspection, was empty. But it was designed for one or two people at most. After a bit of poking around, CeeCee and Tariq settled on the bed with Amy, Tim perched on the chest, and Heidi curled up in the chair.

There was a long silence. Then, finally, one of them said it.

'Monifa.' It was Tim. The word hung heavy between them. Tim started to cry again, then so did Amy. Heidi felt the tears welling up in her own eyes again and didn't fight them. Only CeeCee and Tariq fought back the tears as they tried to comfort Amy.

'And Tuan,' Tim gulped.

'And Twist,' Heidi added.

The children all looked up at that, horrified as it sank in. Twist had been in Monifa's hair. Tim's tears turned to sobs, and CeeCee dropped her head so that her hair would hide her own tears. There was a long moment when the only sound in the room was the sound of weeping.

A gentle knock on the door interrupted them, and they all sat up, wiping their eyes as the door opened and the barkeep reappeared. He was carrying a large golden tray loaded with bowls of some kind of hot soup, crusty bread rolls and a pot of steaming tea. He put it down on the table next to Heidi and exited silently with a polite nod, pretending not to notice their sorrow. Heidi had the impression that they didn't have to deal with children much. In fact, she hadn't seen a single Tuatha child since they got here. She looked over the food without much interest. She wasn't hungry. Turning to the others, she said, 'Does anyone want something to eat?'

No one responded. Then, CeeCee gave a small shriek and flinched away from Amy as something crawled up the inside of her nightdress, onto her shoulder, and then squirmed its way out of the neck and looked up hopefully, tiny nose sniffing at the smell of the soup.

'Twist!' CeeCee cried. 'It's Twist!'

'Twist,' Amy agreed solemnly, and suddenly – miraculously, Heidi thought – they were laughing.

CeeCee scooped the pixie up in her hands and brought him over to the table. He hopped off onto the tray and pointed at the bread, looking at the two girls pleadingly. Smiling, she was so relieved to see him, Heidi tore off a small piece of bread and handed it to him. He gave her a wide grin, dipped the bread into one of the bowls of soup, and started to munch on it so enthusiastically that the children were able to hear him.

The little pixie's reappearance seemed to break the paralysis of grief on the children, and they got up and gathered around the table, reaching out over each other for food. Heidi took another look over what was there. The soup was red and smelled of herbs, with large chunks of vegetables in it. She caught a different, familiar scent coming from the little turquoise teapot – hot chocolate! Maybe they did understand children after all! She announced this to the room, and started pouring it out into the funny little china mugs that came with the teapot – they were more like small round pots with no handles, but when she cradled it in her hands she could feel the warmth radiating into her palms, and decided they were quite clever.

Once the bread and soup were gone and the children all had their hot chocolate, they made themselves comfortable once more. Yet again, everyone looked to Heidi. She suppressed a sigh as she realised that now that they were on their own, she was in charge again. She decided that the best thing to do was to be honest with them. They had all been through so much.

'I don't know how this is going to go,' she said. 'We know now that the Tuatha are the ones bringing children here, but there doesn't seem to be anyone else we can ask to help us get home because nobody else has any magic.'

'Except the witches,' Tim said glumly. 'And they're not going to help us after we killed their sister.'

'Actually, Nishkyn killed their sister,' CeeCee said, a little haughtily.

Tim gave her a scornful glance. 'I don't think they care about that,' he replied.

Heidi glared at both of them, and they fell quiet. 'Anyway,' she continued. 'We're here now, and ... I guess we just have to try our best to convince this Magister person to help us.'

'What if they say no?' Tim asked.

Heidi shrugged. 'Then I guess we stay here and turn into ... whatever it is we're turning into.' Her hands rose to her ears again. It might have been her imagination, but they felt a little longer.

What wasn't her imagination was the sudden weariness that was creeping over her. Her head felt heavy and her eyelids were drooping. She realised she was resting her head on her hand, leaning on the table, and that she was going to fall asleep like that if she didn't move. She got to her feet and started to pace. It helped – but only a little. 'What we need to do is think about what we're going to say,' she said. Talking helped a little too. 'Any ideas?'

She turned to the bed to see that Tariq, CeeCee and Amy had all fallen asleep, and Tim was nodding off as he sat on the chest, looking in real danger of tumbling to the floor. Heidi sighed. 'Tim, get on the bed,' she said. 'Have a nap.'

Tim gave her an apologetic look and climbed slowly up onto the bed with the others. 'Sorry,' he mumbled. 'I'm just so sleepy all of a sudden...'

He'd barely finished speaking before his head hit the pillow and he was snoring lightly. Exasperated, Heidi sat down in the chair again and cast a suspicious glance at the teapot. Was there something in the drink? But they had come here willingly. *Why would they...*

She sank further back into the chair, her chin drooping down to her chest. It was no use, she thought. Just a few minutes. Just a few minutes to rest and then...

She woke up in a different room.

For a blissful moment, she thought she was back in her dormitory at the boarding school, and all this had been a horrible dream. But then she blinked and looked again, and saw that though the room was long and full of small beds, it was definitely not her boarding school. The room was a long series of arches and domes, making it look a bit like a church, except for all the gold filigree climbing the pillars like vines. And the small glowing orbs that floated slowly around the room like massive fireflies were definitely not something they'd had back at home.

A willowy woman with straight golden hair that fell almost to her knees looked up from across the room, where she was sitting at a desk, reading something. Her eyes were pale blue and her skin milky white, with just a hint of golden sheen. She was wearing a plain white dress that somehow still managed to look elegant, with its perfect fit and long, sweeping hem. She smiled and got up, crossing the room to crouch at Heidi's bedside.

'You're awake,' she said softly. Her voice was like bells. 'How are you feeling?'

Heidi frowned. 'Who are you?' she said sharply. 'Where am

I?' Looking round the other beds, she saw her companions sleeping soundly in some of them, and felt a small measure of relief.

The woman's smile didn't falter.

'I'm Enne,' she replied. 'I'm a maidservant. You're in the Magister's guest chambers. The Magister did not want you to be woken, since you seemed to so badly need the sleep.'

'What was in the hot chocolate?' Heidi asked, struggling to sit up. She still felt groggy, and the sheets were tucked in snugly around her.

'Just something to help you sleep,' Enne replied. 'Your head will clear soon, just sit still and give it a moment.'

Reluctantly, Heidi did as she was told, and found that the maidservant was right. Her head did clear, and after a minute or two she was able to get a better look around her. There was a single exit to the room – the arched door at one end, set high in the wall with two stone steps leading up to it. The room had small windows, close to the multi-domed ceiling, making her think that they must be underground, and each window had vertical bars across it set inside the thick, purple-hued glass. Perhaps "guest chambers" might not have been an entirely accurate term, she thought. Her companions, however, were sleeping soundly and in comfort, and appeared to have been taken good care of; their hair had been brushed and their faces and hands cleaned, which was all she could really see above the pristine white covers. She looked herself over and discovered that she was definitely cleaner, and though she was still in the same blue tunic, someone had put her in a pair of slim-fitting white trousers to cover her legs. The idea of a stranger putting clothes on her made her feel strangely uneasy.

She snapped her head up to meet Enne's gaze. 'I want to speak to the Magister,' she said firmly, biting down on the automatic "*please*" that tried to follow.

Enne's smile brightened. 'Wonderful,' she replied. 'She is so looking forward to meeting you. Would you like to go now or wait for your friends to awaken?'

Heidi hesitated. She hadn't expected them to be so willing to grant her request. She didn't relish the idea of going alone, but she didn't want to wait and lose her nerve. And they all seemed to want her to be their leader anyway... 'Now,' she said.

Enne nodded. 'Very well. Follow me.'

The maidservant led her to the door, past another desk where another, almost identical woman was seated, also reading. She looked up and gave Heidi a friendly smile as they passed, and Heidi noticed that she had amber eyes. Lots of these people had amber eyes. She wondered if that meant something. She tried to put it out of her mind – she had other things to think about.

The door opened smoothly, without a single creak or squeak, and Heidi stepped out into a long, curving corridor that spiralled gently upwards and to the left. There were doors along the left-hand side and tall, narrow, stained-glass windows on the right, and she figured they were in one of the towers. The door they had come out of was at the end of the corridor, however, so they must have been at the bottom.

Enne walked briskly up the corridor, her long skirt billowing slightly behind her, without so much as glancing at the guard stationed outside the door they had come from, or at the doors they passed. But Heidi was looking at everything. The floor was polished stone of a deep, almost navy blue, with veins of gold running through it. The walls were the same pale golden stone as the exteriors of the buildings they had walked past. Between each window and door was a tapestry of a forest scene or a painting of some lordly looking Tuatha, so no part of the interior walls was left bare. The doors were of a slightly darker wood than she had seen so far. All arch-shaped like she had seen in churches, with shining plaques on each engraved with names or symbols she couldn't quite make out as she hurried past after the maidservant. The ceiling above them was high, again fashioned in multiple domes, with more of those hovering orbs casting light down upon them, though these ones stayed where they were, one in the centre of each dome. The patterns in the windows were either coloured floral designs or abstract, flowing patterns.

Enne's heels, hidden beneath her skirt, tapped sharply on the polished stone floor. Heidi, barefoot, made no sound as she followed, making her feel small and almost ghostly. Although, of the two of them, Enne looked more ghost-like with her white dress and pale skin. Heidi imagined she looked more like one of the urchins from Oliver Twist in her shabby blue tunic and bare feet. And the floor was cold. She wondered how far along the corridor they would have to go.

As it turned out, they went all the way up the corridor, not stopping until they had climbed up to the very last door, set at the end of the corridor at the top of the tower just as the door to the "guest chambers" was set at the very bottom. This time Heidi did get to read the shiny plaque on the door. It read:

Quintessence Archive
Admittance by Permission of Magister Ceithlenn

'What's a quintessence archive?' Heidi asked, sounding the strange words out carefully.

Enne gave her a slightly surprised look. 'It is the place where the quintessence of the land is stored,' she replied, as if it should be obvious. 'And where the Magister studies and purifies it before she sends it out again.'

'She sends it out?' Heidi asked.

'Yes, to those who require it.' Enne looked away from her and held her palm up to the door, where a small circular glass panel was inserted just below the plaque.

It looked to Heidi like some sort of oversized peephole, but when Enne put her palm before it it glowed with a gentle blue light that then turned green. There was a soft click, and Enne put her hand on the door's round handle and twisted, pushing it open into a strangely illuminated room.

It was strange, because the source of illumination was moving, but much faster than the floating orbs Heidi had seen downstairs, and it was brighter – much brighter. It was a faint blue. The effect was something like a strobe light, with shadows racing around the room faster than her eyes could make them out. It was dizzying and disorienting, and she stumbled blindly forward, her hands going out to grab the arm of the only thing that seemed to stay constant, the white of Enne's dress. Enne seemed either prepared for the influence of the room or not as affected, and she walked forward only a little slower than she had walked in the corridor, bearing Heidi's grasp without comment. After only a few steps she halted and gestured for Heidi to wait in silence. Heidi didn't mind obeying that command at all; she felt like she might be sick. There was a strange, high-pitched whine in here that made her ears hurt and her eyes feel like they were trembling in their sockets.

After a few moments the lights began to slow their dizzying race around the room, and the shadows slowed with them, gradually taking proper, definable form. As they did, the room began to come into focus. Heidi looked around to see the tall, circular room in all its glory - taller than the corridor, the ceiling so high up she had to crane her neck to see it. The ceiling and the walls were made of thick stained glass, with only thin stone columns between them that bent inward at the top to meet in the middle. Unlike the softly coloured glass of the windows she'd seen, these were mostly a deep purplish blue, with strange symbols crafted into them in lines of glittering silver.

All around the edge of the room, beneath the coloured glass dome, ran a low aisle, separated from the main room by only the stone columns, reminding Heidi again of a church or cathedral. With the exception of the door through which they had come, the walls were lined with wooden shelves, designed to curve with the shape of the room. They were crammed with rolled scrolls and string-bound books, crystal globes, numerous vials both empty and full, and other objects that she could not identify. The floor in the aisle was more of the dark blue stone, but in the centre beyond the columns, it changed to a large, singular disc of pale grey marble. Standing on this perfectly smooth stone were three or four large, circular wooden tables, all littered with more scrolls, books, crystals and vials, and one imposing Tuatha. Looking imperious and regal, the figure wore a loose kimono-like garment that matched the colours and patterns in the windows, over a close-fitting grey tunic, trousers and soft grey slippers. Her ivory-white hair fell straight down almost to her ankles in a loose plait, tied in several places with blue ribbon, two loose lengths of it framing her face. Her eyes were bright, burning amber in her softly golden, sharply angular face, and as she turned to look at them they seemed to glow in the light.

But it was not the Tuatha that Heidi's eyes were drawn to, striking as she was; it was the light in the centre of the room that captivated her. Floating above them, in the centre of the dome of stained glass, was a large orb of shimmering pale blue light. It was so large it almost touched the windows. Around it revolved three slender rings of silver with more of the strange symbols engraved into them, reminding Heidi of the rings that floated around Saturn. It gave off a soft, delicate chiming sound, like the sound of dozens of tiny bells ringing. Every now and then it flickered, causing the shadows to leap out and recede like the tide.

Enne gave a low bow. 'Magister Ceithlenn,' she said demurely. 'The first of the children is awake. This is...' She turned to Heidi and gestured for her to step forward.

Heidi did so automatically, trying to gather her thoughts.

'Um ... Heidi, ma'am,' she said, and not sure what else to do, she gave a quick curtsey. 'Heidi Greenford.'

The Magister regarded her coldly for a second, long enough for Heidi to feel a sliver of fear slide across her heart at this intimidating creature. Then the Magister smiled, and in an instant she seemed like a completely different person. Her angular face was suddenly warm and welcoming, and Heidi found herself wondering if she'd ever seen anyone more beautiful.

'Heidi Greenford,' she repeated in a voice like birdsong. 'Welcome! It is so good to meet you properly. Please, come in, come in.' She gestured, and among the clutter Heidi noticed two chairs that she hadn't seen before, placed around the smaller of the three tables. The Magister nodded to Enne, who gave another bow and slipped quietly out of the room.

Heidi made her way to the chairs, careful not to knock anything over, and sat down. She cast her eyes over the strange objects before her – scrolls with more odd symbols, vials that seemed to be filled with more of that flickering blue light, orbs of different coloured crystals, strange contraptions of silver and glass...

The Magister gave a small start and began hurriedly moving the clutter onto the other tables, cramming things in wherever she could. 'My apologies,' she said as she did so. 'I am not a tidy worker. I have so many things to attend to at once, and cleaning is not usually one of them.'

Heidi was somewhat taken aback by this elegant, beautiful creature apologising to her for the mess – what with her sitting there in her scuffed and dirty tunic and bare feet. 'It's okay,' she said shyly.

When the table was clear, the Magister sat down opposite her. 'That's better,' she said, waving her hand, and a crystal decanter and two glasses floated – actually floated – off of one of the shelves and drifted over to the table, landing with a gentle bump. The Magister lifted the decanter and poured out a bright amber liquid into each glass, then pushed one over to her. 'Please,' she said, gesturing to the glass.

Heidi lifted the glass carefully, afraid she would drop it, and took a sip, just to be polite. It tasted of honey and flowers, reminding her somewhat of the drink they'd had in the Firobolga village, but this was lighter and much more refreshing. She took a larger sip, then put the glass back down. 'Th ... that's very nice,' she said.

The Magister beamed. 'I'm glad you like it,' she replied. 'Now, where should we begin? I suppose the formalities. I am called Ceithlenn, Magister of Quintessence Conjuration, Divination and Transmutation, and High Lord of the Shining City. But you may call me Ceithlenn.' Her eyes twinkled with amusement, as if she thought her long title to be ridiculous. 'What may I call you, Heidi Greenford?'

'Heidi is fine,' Heidi responded.

'Heidi,' Ceithlenn nodded. 'As you say. Now, Heidi, I feel compelled to ask what brought you and your companions to our city? It is very unusual that Children of Mil should come to us.'

'Yes,' Heidi said. 'From what I've heard, most of us are brought here first.'

Ceithlenn paused to take a sip from her glass. 'Of course,' she replied smoothly. 'The changes that your poor mortal forms go through are so great. Not to mention the dangers of the world outside our walls; it would be cruel of us to leave you out there alone.'

Now it was Heidi's turn to pause. She hadn't expected an answer like that. Ceithlenn had spoken with an openness that made it hard for her to believe that the Tuatha was lying. 'Well,' she said slowly. 'It has been hard. There were more of us before.'

Ceithlenn's smile faded, replaced by an expression of sympathy so sincere that it brought tears to Heidi's eyes. 'You have lost friends?'

Heidi nodded, swallowing back the lump that was trying to

rise up in her throat. 'Five of us, and some friends we made along the way,' she replied. Her voice cracked as she added, 'It's been horrible!'

With a sweep of her robes, Ceithlenn glided from her chair to Heidi's side, crouching down to gather her in her arms. Unable to help herself, Heidi leaned into the embrace and sobbed, clutching at the soft fabric of the tunic. She felt the Tuatha's long-fingered hand stroking her back and smoothing her hair, murmuring gentle platitudes that made her miss her mother – and even her grandmother – fiercely.

Eventually, the tears stopped, and Ceithlenn released her. Heidi sniffed back the last of her tears and winced at the damp spot on the front of the Magister's tunic. 'I'm so sorry,' she said.

Ceithlenn looked down and smiled. 'No matter,' she replied, and waved her hand, and before Heidi's eyes the damp spot shrank and disappeared. 'Drink some more tea. It will help.'

Obediently, Heidi picked up her glass and took another sip. It was lovely, but she couldn't help but wonder what it was ... and what was in it. As she set the glass back down, Ceithlenn moved back to her chair. 'You must have many questions,' she said gently.

'Hundreds!' Heidi exclaimed, nodding.

'Then ask,' Ceithlenn replied. 'I will answer if I can.'

Heidi eyed her uncertainly. 'What will it cost me?'

Ceithlenn chuckled. 'I have no need to bargain for information, dear child. I divine the Quintessence. I know everything I need to know.'

'Oh ... okay,' Heidi said. 'Well... What's quintessence?'

'I forget how little you have in your world,' Ceithlenn replied sadly. 'It's the essence of all things, the spirit of creation, if you will. If you have the talent and the knowledge to harness it, you can bend reality itself to your will.' She lifted her hand palm up and twitched her fingers, and the decanter rose up from the table and hovered in the air. She turned her hand over and lowered it, and the decanter settled back onto the table.

'Ohhhh,' Heidi sighed, nodding. 'It's magic.'

Ceithlenn frowned. 'Well, *we* don't use such a base word for it ... but yes.'

'Sorry,' Heidi murmured, but the Tuatha gestured for her to go on. 'Why is the quintessence here changing us?'

'It is the nature of things that when in our world, you will change to become of our world,' Ceithlenn replied. 'It is the same for those of us who go to your world. We lose what it is to be fey. Our quintessence fades and we become mundane.'

Heidi wasn't sure what "mundane" meant, but it didn't sound like anything nice. She ignored it and thought about what to ask next. 'So what are we turning into?'

Ceithlenn shrugged. 'There's no way to tell who will become what. It could be any of the fae races – it's unpredictable. I imagine it depends on the individual. But now that it has begun, I can tell you what you're turning into if you wish.'

'Yes please,' Heidi said.

'Hmm, let's see...' Ceithlenn stood up and went to one of the other tables, picked up a sheaf of papers and sifted through them. She picked out one sheet and brought it back to her chair. 'Would you like to know for your friends as well, or just you?'

'All of us, please,' Heidi said quickly.

Ceithlenn nodded. 'Let's see. I don't have their names, so I had to note them by description, forgive me. The pale girl with the red hair is going to become a mermaid.'

Heidi thought of Ricky and Baby being dragged down into the depths of the lake, and suppressed a shudder.

'The small boy with the curly hair will be a faun. It will be up to him which clan he chooses, however.' She looked up at Heidi with a sour smile. 'I would recommend the Firobolga. The Formori are ... difficult.'

Heidi nodded. 'I've heard.' At the Tuatha's questioning look, she added, 'We met the Firobolga.'

'Ah. Good!' Ceithlenn smiled, then looked back at the paper. 'The little one ... a cluricaun of some sort – she will need to change a little more before we can say which.'

'What's a cluricaun?'

'Oh...' Ceithlenn waved her hand vaguely. 'Brownies, leprechauns, redcaps... The smaller labourer types.'

The airy way in which she dismissed Amy's fate made Heidi want to jump up and scream at her. As if a "labourer type" was worth less than any other. She dug her fingernails into her palms to keep herself under control. Ceithlenn didn't seem to notice. She consulted the paper again. 'And ... the dark-skinned boy and yourself...' She looked up and smiled. 'Well, dear girl, the two of you are very fortunate.'

'Why's that?' Heidi asked, but she thought she knew.

'You're going to become Tuatha!' Ceithlenn cried, throwing her arms wide. 'You will be able to join us here, in the Shining City!'

Heidi pressed her lips tightly together. 'Mmmm,' she said. 'That sounds lovely, but we were actually hoping you could help us get home.'

Ceithlenn paused, her arms drooping. 'Excuse me?'

'Home,' Heidi replied. 'To our world.'

Ceithlenn blinked. 'Why in Arcadia would you wish to go back there?' she asked. She seemed honestly shocked.

'It's our home,' Heidi replied. 'Our parents are there. Our friends.'

'You can make new friends here!' Ceithlenn protested.

'And what about our parents? We can't make new ones of those.'

Ceithlenn looked confused. 'Parents? I'm not sure I understand.'

'Our ... our mothers and fathers!' Heidi almost spluttered. How could she not understand?

'Oh!' Ceithlenn laughed. 'I'm sorry. We don't have those here. And you won't need them any more.'

Not need their parents? Heidi was astounded. She still needed her parents; years after their deaths she still felt their absence. She still needed her grandmother, even if she was vaguely aware that she resented having to take her in. The other children clearly still needed their parents. What child wouldn't?

Peter Pan, her mind suggested randomly. Well, perhaps it wasn't so random. She was in Faerieland, after all.

'What do you mean, you don't have parents?' she asked. 'Who is your mother? Your father?'

Ceithlenn sighed. 'My mother and father died an extremely long time ago,' she replied. 'Before we came to this land. In a war.' Her expression lost its warmth, turning cold and hostile. 'Against your kind.' Then the coldness was gone as if it had never been. 'But since we've been here, we've learned that we no longer have to suffer the pangs of childbirth, the whole messy business of mortality. Our lives were long before, but here we are truly immortal. Barring acts of violence, of course.'

Heidi felt a cold shiver creep slowly up her spine. She thought she might know what the Tuatha was going to tell her, but she couldn't help asking the question. 'So if you don't have children, are you just ... dying out?'

Ceithlenn smiled her warm, friendly smile. 'No, dear,' she replied. 'We replenish our numbers from you! You come here, you change, and after a time your memories fade and it is like you have always been here.'

The cold shiver shot up her back and shocked Heidi into jumping to her feet. They would lose their memories? No one had mentioned that! 'That's what the Tithe is for?' she cried. 'So that you won't die out?'

Ceithlenn nodded. 'At first it was only to punish the Milesians,' she replied. 'But when we discovered that the children we claimed changed to be like us, it seemed an excellent solution to our ... ah ... infertility.'

'Well, we would really prefer to go home, if you don't mind,' Heidi said. 'Can you help us get home?'

Ceithlenn paused. 'It is certainly within my power to do so,' she replied.

The shaking was spreading into Heidi's limbs and making her breathless. She did not like that pause, not one bit. She realised her mistake and revised her question. '*Will* you help us get home?'

'Oh, dear child,' Ceithlenn replied, with what sounded like real sorrow in her musical voice. 'I couldn't possibly do that. We need you, you see. Every single one of you! We need you for the war!'

CHAPTER 21

THE PROPHECY

War?!' Heidi cried. 'What war?'

'Our war against the Children of Mil,' Ceithlenn replied. 'Those who used to be your people.'

'They still *are* my people!' Heidi protested.

Ceithlenn smiled indulgently. 'You'll change your mind about that soon enough,' she said. 'When you are more changed.'

'I don't want to *be* more changed!' Heidi protested, starting to pace about the room. 'And I don't want to go to war against anyone! I'm just a little girl!'

'Oh, don't worry,' Ceithlenn replied. 'We still need many more children before we wage the war, and you will be much changed by then. You will be one of us almost fully, and your memories of your old life will be gone. And then - when we have enough numbers - we will cross over to the old world and retake it from those who stole it from us!'

'So *that* is what the Tithe is about?' Heidi could feel her shock giving way to anger, and she ran her hands through her hair as she paced, trying to use up some of that agitation. 'You steal children away from their parents, change them into Tuatha and then take away their memories so they can be soldiers for you in a war against their own people?'

Ceithlenn frowned. 'Not only that,' she said, sounding slightly put out.

'Why do you even want that world any more?' Heidi went on. 'You said yourself that you don't like it! You said it's mundane! And if you go back, you'll have to have babies again, and you just said you're better off not having to do that! And if you're immortal, why do you even need to make more of you? Why don't you just stay here and live forever with your magic and your pretty things and leave us alone?'

'It's not that simple,' Ceithlenn protested. 'The Children of Mil broke their oath to us –'

'So what?!' Heidi was yelling now, but she couldn't seem to stop herself. 'People break their promises all the time! Get over it!'

'We will not!' Abruptly, Ceithlenn rose to her feet, towering over the young girl. Heidi froze in place as the Tuatha's cold, imposing presence suddenly reasserted itself. 'Words have power. The Children of Mil made us a promise. By breaking that promise, they have sealed their own fate as much as our fate is sealed by the Tithe we ourselves set.' She paused, and her expression softened. 'Don't you understand yet? The quintessence seals everything. To break a promise is to curse yourself. To speak too freely is to give of yourself. And to set a tithe or a geas or any kind of curse or decree is to bind yourself to delivering it.'

Abruptly, Heidi's mind flashed back to CeeCee losing her name to Sprickleback – how she had been unable to even so much as speak her own name once he had taken it from her.

Ceithlenn continued, 'If we do not collect our tithe, then we will suffer. The Children of Mil will come and drive us from this home as they did the last one. They will bring their base metals and their pollution and their filth and they will kill the quintessence of this land as surely as they have killed it in that one. They poison their world with *chemicals* and *radiation* and *plastics.*' She spat out each word as if it tasted foul on her tongue. 'They create and spread viruses and drop bombs and kill each other in the thousands.'

'How do you know all this?' Heidi asked.

Ceithlenn pointed to the glowing orb of light above them. 'The quintessence,' she replied. 'Through it, I can see everything that I need to know. I can see your world through the only "magic" left in it – through you.' She pointed at Heidi with one delicate finger. 'Through the children, before it is beaten and drained and poisoned out of you by your elders. And that is why we only take children. Those bereft of quintessence take much longer to succumb to the change, if they survive it at all.'

Heidi felt dizzy and sick. She stumbled back to her chair and sat down. 'Why are you telling me all this?' she gasped.

Ceithlenn's expression filled with remorse, and she crouched down next to the girl, putting an arm around her shoulders. 'Because I want you to understand,' she replied. 'There is nothing you or I could do to change what must be. It is written, in our words and in our prophecy.' She reached out and plucked Heidi's glass from the table, pressing it into her hands. 'Drink.'

Heidi took a sip of the tea. It was sweet and cool in her stomach, and made her feel a little better. 'What prophecy?' she asked.

'One made by the oldest here,' Ceithlenn replied. 'It was made not long after we arrived here. Heed it well, child, and you will see that we cannot change what is to come.'

Ceithlenn sat back, her arm slipping weightlessly away from Heidi's shoulders, and she closed her eyes and spoke from memory.

'The time will come when the Tuatha de Danann
Return to the world which once was their own,

To awaken the usurpers from an enchanted sleep of forgetting.
It will be a time when symbols are sacred,
More real than that they represent,
When the Children of Mil have no minds of their own
And knowledge is stronger than instinct.
They will crave riches over all,
So much so that they destroy the very land in their hunger.'

She opened her eyes and fixed Heidi with her stern gaze. 'Tell me, mortal child, does that not sound familiar to you?'

Heidi lowered her eyes to the glass in her hands. She thought about the way her grandmother complained about how people just believed in what they were told these days, like they couldn't think for themselves. She remembered her history lessons where they talked about the wars being fought, in the past and in the present, over which religion was right despite both preaching for peace. The oil spills and deforestation and fracking that they talked about in geography classes. All the rich and famous people on television, who all the kids wanted to be like when they grew up. She said nothing, but gave a small nod.

Ceithlenn's voice softened. 'I do not know what will happen when we march on your world, young one. I only know that we are bound to do so. Perhaps when we awaken the Children of Mil from their forgetful sleep, we will awaken them to the destruction they are causing, and they will stop. Perhaps we will find a way to coexist in a way we have never tried before, and our quintessence will flourish and grow in the world above like it used to. The prophecy does not say what it means to awaken them. But I hold on to hope.'

'So you're not going to go there and kill them all?' Heidi asked.

Ceithlenn's expression grew stern. 'Not unless they force us to,' she replied

Heidi wanted to think that that would not happen - that the

Tuatha would appear and there could be some kind of peaceful negotiation. But her mind kept drifting back to all the scenes of violence and war she had seen in the history books and on the television in the nightly news. She thought she knew exactly how things would go when an army of otherworldly creatures appeared in their world.

A thought occurred to her then, and she turned to Ceithlenn hopefully. 'Okay, listen,' she said. 'If you send us home, we'll warn them. We'll tell them you're coming, and that they don't have to fight you. We'll tell them you're coming to help! And that there doesn't have to be a war!'

Ceithlenn looked at her sadly. 'Do you really think that if you tell them an army is coming that they will not prepare to fight?' she replied. 'Heidi. You know the hearts of your kinfolk better than that.'

Heidi's heart sank as she looked at the sympathy in the Tuatha's shining amber eyes. 'So you're not going to help us get home?' she asked.

Ceithlenn shook her head. 'I am sorry, dear girl. We need you here. Every one of you.'

At some signal that Heidi did not see, Enne returned and Heidi was taken back to the room at the bottom of the tower. More pleading, begging and crying had not moved the Magister, who had only calmly and sympathetically repeated that she would not send them home. When Heidi returned to the guest chamber, she saw that the other children were now all awake. They looked up at her expectantly, their expressions falling as they noticed her red eyes and tear-stained cheeks.

Enne escorted her back to her bed, then went back to her desk and returned to her reading as if nothing had happened.

The children huddled around as Heidi sat down on the edge of the bed.

Tariq put his hand on her arm. 'What happened?' he asked.

Heidi closed her eyes and sighed. She didn't want to see their faces. 'I spoke to the Magister,' she replied. 'She's the one in charge. She won't send us home.' Even with her eyes closed, she could hear their cries and exhalations of dismay. She could feel their fear and distress. 'I'm really sorry,' she went on, her voice trembling. 'I tried my best.'

Someone wrapped their arms around her and hugged her. Then she felt the mattress behind her sink as someone else joined in the hug. When she opened her eyes, Tim and CeeCee had their arms around her and Tariq still had his hand on her arm. Amy was sitting on the end of the bed, watching them.

They sat like that until the door opened and two new Tuatha walked in. They were both wearing close-fitting, almost modern suits, except the backs of the jackets flared out in long trains that didn't quite touch the floor. One was dressed in pale grey while the other's suit was sea-green. They both had long, straight blonde hair and golden skin – something that Heidi was starting to understand as the norm among these people – but the Tuatha in green had amber eyes. The Tuatha in the grey suit had eyes the same shade of grey as his clothes.

The two approached the children and stopped before them, and the one in grey stepped forward to address them.

'Hello,' he said in a soft, deep voice. 'I am called Iarainn, and this is Eochaid. We are here to examine each of you in order to determine your progression through the change. May we?'

The children looked at them distrustfully. When none of them answered, Iarainn looked at his companion, then cleared his throat uncomfortably. 'We also need to determine your willingness to submit to our treatments,' he added.

'What treatments?' Heidi asked sharply.

Iarainn looked grateful that one of them had spoken. 'To

ease the change,' he replied. 'To speed it along, and make it less ... troublesome for you.'

'What are the treatments?' Tim asked.

'The treatments consist of prolonged exposure to large amounts of quintessence, and the directing of it to the chosen form by the Magister,' Iarainn replied. 'As it appears that you have already begun to change, it will be tailored to the form you are already manifesting. A specialised diet according to your new form will also be provided.'

'The Magister can choose what kids turn into?' Tariq exclaimed.

Iarainn nodded. 'If we find them quickly enough, yes.'

Heidi stood up, her anger from earlier returning in a rush. 'By "find them", do you actually mean if you *kidnap* them quickly enough?' she retorted. 'Because that's what everyone has told us you do.'

There was an awkward silence.

'How the children come to us is not part of our duty,' Iarainn said eventually. 'We just assist with the change.'

'Well, I don't want to change any faster, *thank you*,' Heidi replied, spitting out the last two words like a curse. The two Tuatha flinched satisfyingly as she did so. 'I want to stay myself for as long as I can, and keep my memories for as long as I can. And I *want to go home*!'

The other children were nodding. Iarainn glanced helplessly at Eochaid, who frowned disapprovingly.

'I take it by this little demonstration,' Eochaid said in a much higher, softer voice, 'That you are not going to submit to the treatments?'

Heidi drew herself up to her full height, and looked the strange man in the eyes. 'No,' she said clearly. She turned to look at the children. 'It's up to you what you do,' she told them, 'But I'm not giving in to this. The Magister told me I'm turning into a Tuatha, like them, but I'm going to be human for as long as I can before then.'

Tariq jumped up and stood beside her. 'Damn straight,' he said. 'I'm not submitting either.'

Tim stood up next. 'Me either.'

Then CeeCee. 'Nor me.'

The Tuatha looked down at Amy, who was looking up at them with wide eyes. 'What about you?' Eochaid said.

'She's just a baby,' Heidi said. 'She's not old enough to decide.'

Eochaid gave her an uncomprehending look. 'Who says so? You?'

Heidi looked around. 'Yes,' she replied. 'I'm the oldest, so yes, me.'

Eochaid shrugged. 'Very well,' he said. 'But then she's not old enough to refuse either, and there's no need to leave her locked up down here. She can come with us and make her decision in comfort, when she is old enough.'

Heidi jumped forward as he reached forward to pick Amy up. 'You're not taking her!' she cried.

Eochaid fixed her with an impatient look. 'You'd rather she stayed locked in here with you?' he asked. 'If you do not submit, you will stay here and wait out the rest of the change, as long and uncomfortable as it might be. If you do submit, you come with us and we give you your own rooms, new clothes, we feed you well and we take care of you. We teach you everything you need to know and we make the change as easy as possible for you. Are you going to deny her all that?'

'You could just be saying that to get us to let you take her,' Heidi retorted.

'That would be lying, and we do not lie,' Eochaid replied with an arched eyebrow. 'Unlike your kind. We appreciate the power of words – something we will teach you if you choose to submit. Besides, you have no way of stopping us. If you attack us, you will be subdued.'

He smiled coldly, and in that moment he was much more frightening. All of a sudden he seemed incredibly tall, and his eyes glowed red. 'Though you are welcome to try.'

Heidi felt herself shrinking back despite herself, and from the corner of her eye she could see the others doing the same. None of them tried to stop him as he picked up Amy. She seemed happy to be taken, though she shied away from Eochaid at first, her lip wobbling as if she might cry. But then he smiled at her, and she smiled back and lifted her hands up to touch his long hair.

'If you change your minds,' Eochaid said, 'just let the maid-servants know. Good day.' He and Iarainn swept out of the room, Eochaid carrying Amy in his arms.

Heidi felt something zip past her ear, and she just managed to catch a glimpse of Twist as he darted out of the door after the Tuatha before they closed the door behind them. She started to cry out, but before she could the door thumped gently shut and Twist was gone. She looked around at the others. Tariq shrugged. 'Guess he didn't want to be locked up either,' he said. 'Don't blame him.'

Tim looked up at Heidi, his large eyes swimming with tears. 'What do we do now?' he asked.

Heidi shrugged and looked around. 'I guess we get comfort-able,' she replied. 'We need to keep our eyes open for any chance to escape, and for any way to get Amy back.'

If Enne, sitting at the nearby desk, heard this, she gave no sign of concern.

———

Time passed; how much it was impossible to say. The only means they had of marking the passing hours was by watching the progress of the changes in them. Heidi had told them what Ceithlenn had predicted they would each become, and now they looked for it every day.

Tariq and Heidi had changed a little, their features becoming sharper and more prominent. They had been given mirrors when they asked, and Heidi would check her reflection every day, watching her cheekbones emerge and her childish round-ness fall away. Her clothes felt looser on her too, and her pointed ears were steadily growing longer. Tariq was changing in much the same way, and his hair was growing incredibly fast as well. From short curls that had gathered close to his head he now had long, spiralling curls that brushed his shoulders, and long, pointed ears. She often caught him running his hands along his arms and closely examining his skin. She had asked him why once, and the answer had made her feel cold and uncomfortable - and desperately sad for him - because he had answered her with such sorrow.

'All the Tuatha we've seen are white,' he had said. 'Or close to it, anyway. If I'm turning into one of them, am I gonna turn white too? I don't want to... My Daddy always told me I should be proud of who I am.'

Heidi hadn't known what to say to that, so she had simply hugged him. She was afraid of losing who she was as much as the rest of them, but she had sensed that there was more to it for Tariq; something that she would never be able to fully understand.

Later she'd found Enne and asked her about it. 'We all become pale,' Enne had replied, 'but don't worry, it will take a very long time for one as dark as he. And by then, all his memo-ries of his own life will be gone, and he won't mind.' The answer was supposed to make her feel better, she supposed, but in fact it just made her angry. There was something obscene about how their lives, their identities, were being stripped away from them, and there was nothing they could do to stop it. She'd decided not to repeat what Enne had said to Tariq. She didn't think it would make him feel any better either.

Tim's horns continued to grow, curling out and around his ears, which had also developed pointed ends, though not as pointed as the Tuatha. His blue eyes darkened until they were so black that the pupils could not be told from the irises. His legs grew more hair, which thickened and softened until he had a layer of short fur covering the lower half of his body.

It was CeeCee's changes that could be considered the most drastic, however. The greyish colour on her hands spread, travelling up her arms and lightening to a silvery sheen that covered her entire body. The blue of her eyes faded to nearly white, and her red hair began to lose its curls and develop streaks of white. Her gills grew more pronounced, and sometimes she would wake from a dream, gasping for breath. The webbing between her fingers and toes grew thicker and longer, stretching from the first knuckle of each finger to the next.

During the time it took for these changes to come into effect, the Tuatha brought them food and water and juices and teas, spoke to them kindly and answered their questions. Heidi constantly questioned them about Amy. She was told how well she was doing, and that she was starting to show the rough skin and thick hair that marked her as a brownie. Heidi couldn't help but remember how disparagingly the Magister had spoken of her and she wondered what they would do with her when she had finished changing. She asked if Amy would remain as small as she was now and was told *no, she would likely grow a little and would mature quickly*. She asked if smaller children always turned into smaller faeries and was told *yes, that is normally what happens*. She asked if they could see Amy and was told *no, not unless they decide to submit to the treatment as well*.

They constantly kept their eyes open for ways to escape. But there was always at least one Tuatha in the room with them, and the bars on the windows looked solid and secure and the glass looked thick. There was always a guard outside the door and it was never left open. They would huddle together and talk about trying to overwhelm the guard and whoever came in the next time the door was opened, but Heidi couldn't help thinking back to the way Eochaid had been able to make them all feel so afraid of him with so little effort. It was part of the magic, she suspected, the same way that the maidservants could make them feel at ease, the same way that the Magister had seemed so imposing one minute, and so beautiful and compelling the next.

Every now and then, the maidservants would choose one of them to be taken up to visit the Magister. Heidi was picked on a couple of occasions, and endured Ceithlenn's cheerful questioning and gentle examinations without comment. In fact, she refused to speak a word to her. On the second occasion she had gone in to find the light in the room flashing in the way that it had the first time she had gone up there, and had squinted through the writhing gloom to see the giant ball of light in the centre of the room flickering and flashing madly, with Ceithlenn seemingly pulling strands of it out like caramel, stretching and pulling with her fingers. She seemed to be examining each strand very carefully, her eyes moving as if she were reading something in it, then would release it by letting it slowly snake back through the air into the ball.

The worst thing about their time in the Magister's guest chamber, however, was the very palpable sense that their memories were slowly slipping away from them. Each morning Heidi would wake up and try to recall her parents' names, the name of her grandmother, the name of her boarding school and the friends she had had there. Her friends' names were the first to slip from her mind and she struggled for days trying to recall them, or even to remember what they looked like. Tim woke up weeping at one point, crying that he'd forgotten his father's face. CeeCee would occasionally lapse into recitations in a pretty, lilting language that she said her mother had taught her, but she couldn't remember what it was called. Each time she did, she seemed to be struggling more and more to remember it. And Tariq would spend more and more time looking at his arms and hands, or at his reflection in the mirror, with that sad, lost look on his face.

CHAPTER 22

THE HUNTER

Heidi had discovered that one of the panes of glass in the window above her bed was light enough that she could see through it quite clearly. She had grown a little and was tall enough now to stand on tiptoes on her bed, grab the bars, and pull herself up so that she could look outside.

The view was at street level, so all she really saw was the feet of passing Tuatha, but it was something. She would rest her chin on the narrow windowsill and watch those feet for as long as she could hold herself up. CeeCee was tall enough to do it too, but she tired of it quickly, complaining that her legs felt weak and wobbly.

During one of these feet-watching sessions, she noticed one pair a short distance away stop, and then walk directly toward the window. Curious, she tightened her grip on the bars and tensed her arms, hoping her muscles wouldn't give out before ... before what? The feet stopped in front of the window, and Heidi had a close view of the soft leather slippers and the slender ankles; then the Tuatha crouched, and she was looking at a vaguely familiar face.

A face framed with a mane of bright red hair, the unruly

curls looking a little tidier now, but the milky pale skin and bright green eyes were the same, even if the features of the face were more delicate than they had been. It was the girl from Lagamoora; she had become a Tuatha after all.

The girl looked away from Heidi, then up at the rest of the building. Glancing briefly down again, their eyes met and the girl gave her a short but intense glare. Then she was gone, off to the side where Heidi could not see her. Heidi let her arms drop her and sat down on her bed, pondering. The girl seemed to be trying to communicate something to her with that stare, but what?

Tariq looked at her curiously from where he was sitting on his own bed and opened his mouth as if to ask her what she had seen. But before he could, the door crashed open violently – something that had never happened before. The children all looked around in surprise, then in horror, as a tall, dark shape folded itself through the door and unfurled into the room.

The room was well lit, but the floating orbs closest to the thing seemed to grow dull, casting it in gloomy shadow. The intruder was tall and thin like the Tuatha, but its clothes were inky black, and seemed more like gathered shadows draped across its bones. Its face was grey and gaunt, with a long nose and round, deepset, blazing red eyes, and a fixed grin that displayed sharp, jagged teeth. Lank black hair hung around its face and melded into the darkness of its clothing. Its long ears were crooked and torn, as if it had been in a fight. And in its long-fingered, clawed hands it held a young boy.

The boy hung from its grasp by one arm, his face blank and expressionless, except for the wide, haunted eyes. He had bare feet that appeared to be swollen and hooked into wolf-like claws, and his ears were wide and pointed, coated in short fur the same colour as his chestnut hair. His chest was bare and covered in shallow scratches, and the grey linen trousers he wore were torn and muddy. He neither resisted nor made a sound when the thing that held him tossed him onto one of the beds nearest the door.

The Tuatha sitting at the desk by the door smiled at the creature, although the smile did not come remotely close to reaching her eyes. 'Well done, Jack,' she said evenly. 'I will let the Magister know you found him.'

"Jack" turned to look at her, and even from across the long room, Heidi could see the maidservant flinch back ever so slightly. Then, without a word, it hunched down and disappeared through the door again, pulling it closed behind it with a loud thud.

The maidservant gave a sigh of relief and turned to her colleague at the desk closer to the children. 'I hate having to deal with that thing,' she said, getting up and crossing over to the boy it had brought in.

The other maidservant shrugged as she went over to help her. 'With something like that chasing them, it's a wonder any of them ever run,' she replied. 'Where did the Magister find him, I wonder?'

'I heard he was one of us once,' the first woman said. 'A hunter, way back when the city was still small. But the witches got hold of him and cursed him.'

The children made no attempt to disguise their eavesdropping, and the Tuatha didn't seem to care. They set about inspecting the boy - looking into his eyes, feeling his breath and his heartbeat - and then one went and fetched a bowl of water and a cloth. They cleaned him up and put him in a fresh grey tunic and trousers before they tucked him into the bed and let him be.

Tim sidled over to Heidi. 'Do you think we should go say hello?' he asked.

Heidi nodded. 'When he's awake.'

'What was that thing?'

Heidi shrugged. 'I don't know,' she replied, 'but it chases the children who run.'

Tim shuddered and wrapped his arms around himself. 'So if we...'

'Don't worry,' Heidi interrupted him. 'I'll think of something.'

Tim looked relieved, and went to sit with CeeCee and Tariq on Tariq's bed. Heidi turned away from them, looking back to the new boy, who had curled into a tight ball under his bedsheets. What on Earth was she supposed to think of, she wondered? Why did she have to be the one in charge?

'Because I'm the oldest,' she muttered to herself bitterly. Thoughts of the red-haired girl had faded entirely from her mind.

Some time later the new boy awoke, and he awoke screaming. The maidservants hurried across to him and urged him to drink some water and eat some berries, and gradually he grew calmer. The children watched all this with interest. When the maidservants left him, Heidi looked around to see the other three all staring at her.

'I'll go then, shall I?' she said sourly. The other children nodded eagerly, missing the sarcastic bite to her words. She got up with a sigh and weaved through the empty beds until she came to him. He was sitting up in his bed, still shaking all over, and he looked up anxiously as she approached.

She held up her hands. 'Hi,' she said. 'My name's Heidi. What's yours?'

He glared at her for a moment through narrowed eyes filled with suspicion. Then his shoulders slumped. 'Don't remember,' he replied.

'You don't remember your name?' Heidi exclaimed. 'That's awful!'

'Don't remember a lot,' he added.

'Is that why you ran away?' Heidi asked, lowering her voice.

The boy shot her another suspicious glance. 'Maybe,' he said.

Heidi moved closer. 'It's why I want to,' she whispered. 'I'm forgetting things too.'

The boy nodded. 'That's how it happens,' he said. 'But you'd better not run. The hunter will catch you.'

'Is that who brought you in? The hunter?'

The boy nodded, and gave a shudder so hard he seemed like he might drop the bowl of berries on his lap. 'You don't want him to catch you,' he said fearfully. 'He makes you *see* things...'

He squeezed his eyes closed, and Heidi waited in awkward silence. When he looked up at her again, he looked angry. 'Leave me alone,' he said. 'You'll get me in trouble.'

He looked so fierce, his yellowish eyes boring into her, that she backed away without a word and headed back to the others. When they looked at her questioningly, she shrugged. 'He doesn't want to talk,' she said. 'Maybe one of you can try later on.'

They all tried at various intervals in the time to follow, but the boy was always the same. He was nervous and sad, and then if they asked any questions he would turn sullen and angry and tell them to leave him alone. CeeCee managed to get him to tell her that he wasn't going to try running away again, and that upstairs, as he called it, was nice, but they kept talking about a war. But that was all they could get from the wolf-eared boy.

Some time later – it might have been as long as a few days, for the children all slept at least twice in that time – the door opened again. Two Tuatha walked in, dressed in lighter armour than the gate guards, but wearing ornate helmets and carrying spears. One of them pointed in the direction of the group of children.

'That's them,' they said in a light voice. 'The Magister wants to see them now.'

The maidservant by the door stood up. 'All of them?' she exclaimed, surprised.

The armoured Tuatha nodded. 'That's right. She wants to know about their time in the woods.'

'But the Magister usually only sees the children one at a time...' the maidservant protested.

The other Tuatha stepped forward and lifted his open palm to her. Heidi caught a glimpse of something circular and pale blue glowing there. 'Are you refusing to comply with Her Elite?' he snapped in a voice that, by Tuatha standards, was practically gruff.

The maidservant paled and took a step back. 'Of course not,' she said quickly. 'Please, go ahead.'

The Elite gestured to the children. 'Come on,' he said, 'And be quick about it. The Magister wants to see you right away.'

Reluctantly, the children got up and walked over to them. The first one held the door open while the second, gruffer one walked out in front of them. 'Follow close,' he snapped, 'And don't try anything foolish. Diann here will be right behind you, and she's whip-fast with that spear.'

The children glanced nervously round at Diann, who nodded at them gravely. Heidi met her bright green eyes and was surprised to see her wink at her. She frowned and looked ahead. Green eyes. It was the girl from Goblin Town!

They walked up and around the curving corner of the corridor, then abruptly the guard in front turned left and opened one of the doors. The children hesitated; they'd all been to see the Magister by now and they knew where her room was, and it wasn't here. Behind them, Diann tapped her spear sharply on the stone floor. 'Quickly,' she snapped.

They followed the first guard into what looked like a library, and across to a door on the other side. Heidi cast a greedy glance over the shelves and shelves of books and the comfortable chairs, but all too soon they were out in another corridor which wound up and down just like the other, except that the floor was made of a green marble-like stone. The guard turned left and headed downwards. Before long they came to a large pair of double doors at the corridor's end, flanked by a pair of bored-looking guards in that same light armour. The first guard showed his palm again, and they opened the doors to let them through with a curious glance.

The guards led the children out into the streets of the Shining City. They all turned their faces up to the warm sun gratefully as they walked. The route the guards took them on seemed to wind through much of the city's quieter streets, giving them plenty of time to look around. Heidi saw flowers of impossible colours blooming in front gardens and window boxes, slender trees cultivated into spirals that mimicked the tall towers, and darting little lights here and there that, on closer inspection, looked like glowing pixies. The Tuatha they passed paid these pixies no mind and occasionally shooed them away or swatted at them absently. Most of the Tuatha they passed turned to watch them with open curiosity, and the first guard seemed to quicken his pace each time.

Eventually they reached a large, pale stone wall and followed it along until they reached a small, semicircular drain cut into its base. A thin stream of clear water emerged from beneath the street they stood on and trickled out beyond the wall.

The first guard brought them to a stop and then turned to Diann. 'Here you are,' he said. 'My fee?'

Diann pulled a small velvet pouch from her pocket and handed it to him. 'You'd best make yourself scarce,' she said. 'The word will get back to the Magister before too long.'

The guard nodded. 'Good fortune to you,' he said, and walked briskly off, disappearing around a corner.

Diann crouched down by the drain and examined it. There

was a metal grating across it - a surprisingly dull metal grate compared to everything else they had seen in the city. Diann grabbed two of the bars and, with a pained grunt, yanked it sharply toward her. It came out of the wall with a rasp of metal on stone, and she put it to one side. 'Out,' she said, gesturing for them to go through.

The children looked at Heidi, who nodded, and one by one they filed out, getting down on their hands and knees to crawl through the gap. Thankfully, the water seemed to be fresh. The low tunnel cut straight through the thick stone wall, and after a little over a dozen steps they were emerging out into sunlight again. Diann followed them, pulling the grate through and sliding it back into place behind her. Heidi noticed that when she came out the palms of her hands were an angry red. She saw her staring and rubbed her palms against her thighs.

'Iron,' she said, nodding back toward the grate. 'I suppose it's to deter anyone trying to sneak out. Like us.'

'Er ... sorry,' Tariq said, stepping forward. 'But what's going on?'

Diann grinned and took off her helmet, tossing it carelessly aside, and her mane of thick red curls tumbled down over her shoulders. 'Ask her,' she said, nodding at Heidi.

Heidi grinned at her. 'I met her at the Korrigan's party,' she explained. 'She warned me about staying there, and said she thought she was going to become a Tuatha and be sent to them. I guess you were right about that?'

'About that, yes,' Diann replied, 'But wrong about other things. I'll tell you on the way, but we need to get going before we're spotted outside the walls.'

The children looked around. They were at the top of a gentle slope that rolled down to the edge of the Great Forest, only here the trees were a lot closer than where they'd come into the city.

'Wait,' Heidi protested. 'What about Amy?'

Diann shook her head. 'I can't help her now,' she replied. 'But in truth, she'll be happy enough where she is. She's so little, and the Tuatha love the little ones. She'll be being pampered and adored right now.'

'And changed!' Heidi retorted.

Diann frowned at her. 'She was changing anyway,' she replied. 'Look, maybe we can go back for her at some point. I don't know. But right now I'm here to get you away.'

'I don't want to go back into that forest,' Tim muttered miserably.

'You won't have to,' Diann replied. 'We'll go back the way the Korrigan sent me – through the goblin tunnels. Follow me. And be quick!'

Relieved, the children followed eagerly as the red-haired Tuatha began sprinting through the long grass toward the forest. Just as the trees were looming up before them, she stopped, looked around for a moment and then pointed at a particular tree. 'There,' she said.

As they approached the tree, they saw that nestled in its roots was a circular patch of moss, a little too circular to be natural. Diann dug her fingers into the dirt and pried up the edge of the moss, revealing a carefully disguised wooden door to a steep circular tunnel, with rough steps cut into the soil inside. It looked dark and uninviting, and the children shied away instinctively.

Diann saw and nodded toward the tunnel. 'It's safer than the forest,' she said.

'She's right about that,' a voice said from inside the treeline. 'But you ain't leaving without me, are ya?'

The group spun around to see a small, familiar figure limp out from behind a tree. He grinned and trotted over.

'Nishkyn!' Heidi exclaimed, running to his side. Before he could stop her, she threw her arms around him and hugged him fiercely. 'Oh, I thought we'd never see you again!'

Nishkyn grimaced and pushed her away gently. 'Watch it,' he grumbled. 'I'm all banged up.'

'Why?' Heidi looked him over hurriedly. He had a bite mark on one leg, showing through a hole in his trousers, and one of his eyes looked bruised. 'What happened?'

'Been looking for this tunnel,' Nishkyn replied. 'Been here a while. And like you said, the forest ain't safe. Shall we go?'

Without waiting for an answer, he hopped into the hole and disappeared down the tunnel. Heartened by this, the children followed after him, leaving Diann to close the door behind them.

Once inside, they could see that just a little way down the tunnel it was lit by torches stuck into the walls at regular intervals, burning with an odd yellow light that occasionally flickered blue. The tunnel was tall but narrow, forcing them to walk no more than two abreast. Heidi dropped back, falling in beside Diann. 'How did you know we were there?' she asked.

'I didn't,' Diann replied. 'This one told me.' She pointed to the side of her head. Heidi was about to ask her what she meant when she saw the tiny form of Twist struggle out from beneath her curls. Perching on the fae's shoulder, he gave her a cheeky wave.

'Twist!' Heidi cried, and the other children looked back and grinned when they saw the pixie. 'Did you tell Diann to help us?'

Twist beamed at her and nodded. Heidi put out her hand for him to step on, and when he did she brought him close to her face and gave him a gentle kiss on the top of his tiny head. He looked surprised, then giggled and ran up her arm to sit on her shoulder.

Diann smiled. 'He's the least annoying pixie I've known,' she said. 'Although trying to understand him was a challenge.'

'I didn't even know he could speak,' Heidi exclaimed.

'Of course he can,' Diann replied, 'But pixie speech is usually too quiet and too fast for us to understand. But he managed to make himself clear to me ... eventually.'

'Where did he find you? In the city?'

'Yes. The Korrigan sent me there – like I thought she would.' Diann paused. 'As I said, I was right about that, but I was wrong about other things.'

'What were you wrong about?' Heidi asked.

Diann sighed. 'I was wrong about her intentions,' she replied. 'I thought she just wanted us while we changed, and then abandoned us when she grew bored with us. I thought she sold us to the other races, to be slaves or pets or... Well, I don't really know what I thought. She doesn't do anything like that. She gives us a blessed, happy life while we change, and then when we are changed she explains it all to us. How the Tuatha brought us here with their Tithe... How they want us to bolster their armies... How they stole the magick in this world. And then she tells us that she wants us to fight for her instead. To fight against the Tuatha, and free the magick back into the world. And stop them attacking what used to be our home.' Diann's eyes grew wide and excited. 'She has artifacts from our world; she encourages us to try to remember! And the best part is, she gives us the choice. We don't have to fight if we don't want to. But most of us said that we would.'

'Then why did she send you to the Tuatha?' Heidi asked.

'To spy for her,' Diann replied. 'Which, of course, I can't do now. Maybe no one would recognise me as one of the guards who smuggled you out, but I don't know. A lot of them looked at us as we passed by.'

'It probably wouldn't be a good idea to try and go back,' Heidi agreed. 'For a while.'

'So I'm hoping she'll be happy that I got you out of there, at least,' she went on. 'I don't suppose you would come back with me?'

Heidi sighed. 'Well, it doesn't look like we're going to get home,' she muttered. On her shoulder, Twist patted the edge of her ear consolingly, making small twittering noises, and she suddenly realised that she was close to tears.

Diann was watching her closely, her face twisted into a grimace. She gave a heavy sigh. 'Look,' she said. 'I might have heard about someone else who could help you. But it's not for certain, and I want you to make me a bargain. If I tell you who it is and help you find them, and it doesn't work out for you, you'll come back to the Korrigan.'

Heidi gaped at her. 'Really? You really think you know someone who could help?'

Diann shrugged. 'Like I said, it's not for certain. I heard about her while I was in the city. The Tuatha don't like her very much.'

Heidi's heart, which had taken a huge leap into her throat, started to sink again. 'It's not one of the forest witches, is it?'

Diann gave her a bemused glance. 'Not one of those witches,' she replied cryptically. 'Do we have a bargain?'

'I can't decide that on my own,' Heidi replied. 'You'll have to ask the others too.'

Diann considered this, then nodded. 'That's fair. We'll stop soon for a rest, and I'll ask them then. We've got a way to walk yet.'

They lapsed into a thoughtful silence. Ahead of them, Heidi could hear Nishkyn regaling the boys with a story of how he'd been attacked by a fachan (whatever that was), and had fought it off valiantly. CeeCee seemed to be lost in her own thoughts.

'What happened to the other girl?' Diann asked.

Heidi winced. 'You mean Monifa.' She paused. 'The witches. One of them turned into a wolf and...' She trailed off, her voice shaking.

Diann looked at the ground. 'Oh,' she said softly. 'I see.'

Silence fell again, and soon enough Diann suggested they stop to rest. They all sat down, their backs against the mud walls, facing each other. Nishkyn pulled some dried meat out of his pockets and offered it around, then hunkered down next to Heidi.

'How long were you waiting for us outside the city?' Heidi asked him.

Nishkyn snorted. 'I wasn't waiting for you!' he scoffed. 'I had no idea if I'd ever see you again! Besides, I'd done my job. It just took me a while to find the tunnel, and when I did I couldn't get the blasted door open – it was too heavy. So I hung around, hoping someone would come along and use it.' He grinned at her. 'Just my luck it'd be you lot.'

'Lucky us, I'd say,' Heidi replied, smiling. 'It's really good to have you back, Nishkyn. I was worried the witches would get you.' She put her hand out and took his clawed hand in hers.

Nishkyn seemed about to say something, but his eyes fixed on her hand around his, and his mouth twisted and trembled strangely. Then he pulled his hand away and stuffed some dried meat into his mouth, chewing furiously. Heidi recoiled a little, wondering if she had upset him. She took a bite of the meat herself, but it was terribly salty. She turned it over between her fingers, trying to decide what to say.

Then Nishkyn spoke. 'I was waiting,' he murmured to her quietly, almost as if he was ashamed. 'The door's not that heavy.'

Heidi looked at him. He refused to meet her gaze. 'Oh, Nishkyn,' she said fondly.

'I didn't eat the spriggan, either,' he added. 'Just scared him off.'

'Why would you lie about that?' Heidi exclaimed.

'I don't know!' Nishkyn retorted. 'I'm a bloody goblin. I'm supposed to be... I mean...' He glanced at her, then away again. 'You wouldn't understand, human.'

Heidi smiled. 'You need to act tough around the other goblins,' she said. 'So they don't turn on you. Some humans are like that too, you know.'

Nishkyn gave her a doubtful glance.

'I mean, okay, we don't eat each other,' Heidi admitted, 'but we can be pretty mean.'

'Hmph.' Nishkyn shrugged. 'Alright, maybe you understand a bit,' he said grudgingly. 'But don't tell the others.'

Heidi nodded. 'I won't. And Nishkyn?'

He looked at her. 'What?'

'I'm really, really glad you waited.'

The goblin paused, then shrugged and smiled. 'Yeah yeah, me too,' he muttered.

Diann passed a waterskin around, which after the salty dried meat everyone accepted gratefully. Then she looked at Heidi. 'I have an offer for you,' she said to the group, and reiterated her bargain as she'd explained it to Heidi before.

The children were delighted, and all too willing to agree. 'Besides,' CeeCee added, 'If we can't get home at least we'll see Tyler again!'

'I wonder how big Tyler's tusks are by now,' Tariq added, and they all giggled.

Diann smiled. 'Laugh now,' she said. 'If the Mother was right about what she thinks he's becoming, you won't laugh at him again. Not to his face, anyway.'

'What does she think he's turning into?' Tim asked, scratching at his hairy legs.

Diann lowered her voice dramatically. 'He's going to be a troll,' she replied.

'A troll!' the children echoed in awe, thinking of massive creatures under bridges, or the big fierce monsters in the *Lord of the Rings* movies.

Diann smiled. 'So we all agree?' she asked.

The children all voiced their agreement happily, and Diann nodded. 'Well then, the one I think can help you lives on the Grey Moors, beyond Lagamoora. She's known as the Winter Witch.'

CeeCee's face fell. 'Another witch?' she said doubtfully.

'She's not one of the forest witches,' Diann replied. 'From what I could tell, the Tuatha don't like her because she kept her magick ... and because she visits your world a lot. But they're not scared of her, like they are the other witches. Well, not in the same way. I heard stories about her in Lagamoora, but I didn't hear that she could go between worlds until I was in the Shining City.' She cast Heidi an apologetic glance. 'I would have told you then if I had known.'

Heidi smiled sadly. 'That would have been nice,' she said, thinking of all the trouble it would have saved them. Monifa, Irgoll and Tuan would still have been alive.

'The stories say she's quite kindly, if rather short-tempered,' Diann went on. 'Sometimes she helps folk if they cross her path and don't cause her trouble. But mostly she keeps to herself. I got the impression that she's very powerful, the way they talk about her. Like they know she could hurt them if she wanted to.'

'Doesn't matter how scary she is,' CeeCee said, looking at her webbed, silvery hands. 'She's our last chance to get home.'

The other children nodded solemnly. Diann stood up. 'Then it's settled,' she said. 'Come on – we should get going. I'm sure they'll be looking for you by now.'

A thought occurred to Heidi that made her cold. 'Diann,' she said. 'When we were in the city we saw a ... a thing bring in another child. It was horrible, and...'

Diann's expression sobered. 'You mean Jack,' she replied. 'The hunter.'

'Will they send him after us?' Heidi asked.

Diann nodded. 'Almost certainly.'

They all looked behind them down the tunnel, then ahead. In both directions, it seemed to go on forever.

SCRAPS

EXCERPT FROM A DIARY FOUND IN WALDERSLADE, KENT, UK:

Still dark. Don't remember the last time I saw the sun. Can't have been that long ago, but it feels like forever. Wish we had a clock or a watch down here. Phone's good for nothing now the power's out.

Jen woke up screaming again. Keeps dreaming about the miscarriage, about things taking the baby from her belly. She calmed down faster and managed to get back to sleep though, so there's that. I think it's better this way. Bringing a baby into this? And even if we could keep it alive, there's no reason to think it wouldn't disappear like all the others when the day comes around. Don't even know what day it is today. We wouldn't even know when to expect it. No. Better this way.

Burns on my hands have healed all lumpy. Might be cancer, I don't know. Not a doctor. Bloody ugly, whatever it is. Doesn't matter though. Probably poisoning myself every time I go out looking for food. But we have to eat.

God, I miss the sun. If the clouds ever clear, I think we'll head south. The last news report I saw said that the bombs all hit north of here, so maybe the coast is okay. Don't remember if they said the radius reached that far.

That light over London, though... And the heat and the wind - even here... How quickly the world seemed to fall down.

CHAPTER 23

THE GREY MOORS

The tunnel did not go on forever. It ended after a very long, featureless, dusty trek, coming out into a small building on the edge of the Goblin City.

Nishkyn stuck his head out of the door while they all climbed out, Diann coming out last and manoeuvring the wooden cover back into place. But before she could push the cover entirely across the tunnel's entrance, they heard a long, shrill howl echoing faintly from inside the tunnel.

Diann froze, the cover slipping from her fingers and clattering across the hole. Nishkyn cringed and pushed the door shut hurriedly. The children looked between them fearfully. 'What was that?' Heidi asked. 'Was it...'

Diann met her gaze and nodded. 'The hunter,' she said in a hushed voice. 'We need to hurry.'

Nishkyn opened the door again and peered out, then gestured at them to follow. 'Come with me,' he said, and scurried out into the open. Diann nodded to the children, and they all rushed out in a close line.

Nishkyn led them through the streets, dodging around corners and down alleys with a native sureness. Heidi was completely lost after the first few turns, and Diann didn't seem too certain about where they were either. She kept glancing around at the creatures around them, but they didn't seem to be attracting more than the occasional cursory glance. She supposed they were starting to look more like natives themselves now; they were probably assumed to be more of the Korrigan's changeling children.

Nishkyn stopped at the end of a small alley, where a thick length of rope hung down from an overhead beam of wood. 'Wait here,' he said, and then scrambled nimbly up the rope, gripping with his feet as well as his hands. He disappeared into the eaves of the building, and they could hear him rummaging around. A few minutes later, he yelled down 'Heads up!' and a canvas sack came sailing down into the alley. They ducked out of the way and it hit the dirt with a metallic clunk. Then he was climbing down the rope again, dropping to the ground next to the sack with a grim smile.

'You'll need these,' he said, and started pulling weapons out of the bag. There were two knives as long as his arm, a hand axe, and a hammer with a stone head. He looked at Diann and frowned. 'Where's that spear you had?' he asked.

She shrugged. 'I left it in the city,' she replied.

Nishkyn sighed and rolled his eyes. 'Of course you did,' he muttered, and went back to rummaging in the sack. 'Well, that's all I have.'

Diann picked up the axe and held it away from her, frowning. 'Why do you have all these?' she asked.

Nishkyn shrugged. 'Just in the habit of picking up things that might be useful,' he replied.

'And you thought having lots of weapons would be useful?'

'You lived here,' Nishkyn retorted. 'What do you think?'

Diann considered this, then shrugged and nodded. She passed the axe to Tariq and picked up one of the knives, one that looked to Heidi a lot like a big kitchen knife. 'That's old iron,' she said to Tariq. 'Be careful with it.'

Tariq inspected the axe carefully. 'Why?' he asked. 'I mean, I know it's sharp and stuff...'

Diann smiled. 'I should hope so,' she replied. 'But you're Tuatha now. Iron will burn you.'

Tariq looked at it with fascination. 'Really?' He poked the blade experimentally with one finger. 'I mean, it sort of tingles,' he said, sounding a little disappointed.

'It'll get worse as you change,' Diann replied. 'It did for me.'

Heidi picked up the other knife. It was slightly curved, and looked like something the fauns would use, with a worn leather grip bound with twine. 'Does iron burn goblins too?' she asked Nishkyn.

Nishkyn sneered. 'Nah,' he replied. 'Just itches a bit. We don't have enough magick for it to burn us.' He gave Diann an accusing glare, which she ignored.

CeeCee picked up the hammer and tested its weight in her hand. Tim watched her and looked around. 'What about me?' he asked, drawing himself up to his full height, which was still shorter than CeeCee and Tariq.

Nishkyn regarded him doubtfully, then leaned over and pulled a short dagger from his boot and handed it to him. 'I want this back,' he said.

Tim grinned and took the knife eagerly. It wasn't half as long as the other two, but he held it out as if it was a sword. 'Thank... I mean, sure,' he replied.

Diann tucked the kitchen knife into her belt. 'We need to hurry,' she said. 'The hunter will be in the city soon. He moves fast, and there's nothing in that tunnel to slow him down.'

Nishkyn nodded. 'The moor, right? Follow me.'

He hurried back up the alley and onto the street, and within a few turns he had led them to a small shack crammed into the end of another alley. He pulled a small length of wire from his pocket and in a few seconds he had picked the lock on the door and pushed it open. But instead of opening into a building, it opened out onto a vast stretch of land. Green grass gleamed in the bright sunlight, giving way to silvery grey in the distance.

He ushered them all out, then locked the door behind them. Glancing back as they headed out across the grassland, Heidi could see now that the city was constructed in such a way that the buildings themselves made up its walls, all crowding together at the edges so there were no easy ways in and out except for the entrances at the bridges ... and concealed entrances and exits like the one Nishkyn had brought them through.

'Do you think anyone saw us leave?' she asked.

Nishkyn shrugged. 'Can't promise they didn't,' he replied. 'But if we'd gone by the main roads they definitely would have.'

'Do you think the hunter will find us?'

It was Diann who answered. 'The hunter always finds what he's hunting. We can't lose him. We just have to outrun him.'

Heidi swallowed and gripped her knife tighter. They began trudging across the grassland in silence.

The bright green grass quickly gave way to a coarser, shorter grass of a muted greyish green, which itself gave way to grass that was almost completely grey. Before long the land became dotted with large boulders and scruffs of dark brown, dry-looking briars. The light seemed to dim, and looking up, Heidi realised that a heavy mist had crept in around them – or they'd crept into it – without noticing. The breeze began to feel colder, but at the speed at which they were trekking through the grassland, it was quite welcome.

The ground began to get softer underfoot, and here and there mud sucked at their feet. CeeCee stumbled and complained as she lost first one boot, and then the other, to the mud. Tariq and Tim laughed and teased her. Tariq lifted one foot and wiggled his toes at her. 'Feels goooooood,' he cried. 'Get it in between dem toes!'

'Gross,' CeeCee grumbled, but she was smiling.

Before long, they began to see small patches of sunken, waterlogged ground, shining silver in the fog-filtered sunlight. As they wound their way through the muddy pools, Heidi realised that they'd heard absolutely no animals or birds here. She looked around, but even though the mist was light and she could see for a fair distance, everything was still and silent.

'Do you know where we're going?' she asked Diann. 'Where to find the witch?'

Diann shook her head. 'We just have to look for her,' she replied.

'And what are we looking for?'

Diann gave her an uncertain glance. 'Cold,' she replied.

Heidi wanted to ask more, but before she could, Tariq grabbed her arm. 'You hear that?' he asked.

Heidi and Diann halted, and the others stopped with them. They listened, but could hear nothing other than their own breathing. Tariq lifted a finger, his eyes narrowed in concentration. 'Wait,' he said.

They all waited. Then Tariq looked up. 'There!'

They all heard it that time; a distant, sorrowful wailing. In the mist, it was difficult to tell what direction it was coming from; it seemed to surround and envelop them. It was beautiful and heartbreaking - a raw, feminine howl that seemed to dip and lilt in a strange, primal melody - and Heidi felt herself sagging under a sudden blanket of despair that seemed to settle across her mind. She could see the others begin to droop and draw in, and knew that they were feeling it too. Then, after the despair, came a slow, mounting dread that made her want to turn and run back Lagamoora, to the Shining City, to anywhere but here.

'Wh-what is that?' she asked Diann.

Diann shook her head, her green eyes wide and terrified. 'I don't know.'

Nishkyn spoke up. 'It's a banshee,' he said in a low mutter.

'I've never seen one, but I've heard them now and then. I've been told they sing to frighten people away, but no one I've spoken to seems to know what happens if you get close to one.'

'I vote we don't get close,' Tariq piped up in a tremulous voice.

Diann nodded. 'Press on,' she said. 'Stay close, and if any of you see anything, speak up.'

They clustered closer together and carried on trudging through the boggy grass. The large rocks became more frequent, and Nishkyn started hopping from one to the other, keeping clear of the mud. The children copied him in silence. Heidi couldn't help thinking that they looked quite jolly, jumping from rock to rock, and it felt strange to not be laughing and joking around, like Tariq had with the mud. But she didn't feel like laughing. That singing was robbing them of any joy they might have.

Diann carried on walking through the mud, and from slightly above her Heidi noticed that she wasn't sinking in as far as they had; she was practically walking on the surface, as if she were weightless. She wondered if that was another Tuatha thing.

She was startled out of her thoughts by Tariq softly calling out: 'Over there!'

They all looked up to see him pointing into the mist off to one side. Following his finger, Heidi could make out a slowly moving silhouette in the mist. It looked like a tall, thin woman, with long hair flowing out behind her as if caught in a strong wind, even though the breeze was quite gentle. Her limbs were thinner even than Diann's, and were held out slightly at her sides as if buoyed up. She appeared to be floating above the ground, her garments ragged and streaming out in a similar way to her hair. Then, she realised that her first impression of a strong wind was wrong – this figure looked like it was submerged underwater. She squinted, trying to see more detail, but in the mist she couldn't make out more than a grey shape. It seemed to look in their direction, the dim light picking out a pair of pearlescent white eyes. As those eyes travelled over them, Heidi found her feet grinding to a halt on the rock she was on, refusing to take another step, and she had to fight with every ounce of her being not to turn and run. In front of her, Tim whimpered and backed up into CeeCee, who jumped as if she had been grabbed and half-turned, as if to run, before she caught herself and stopped. Nishkyn had hunkered down as if he were trying to hide, and Tariq and Diann were standing as still as statues, their hands gripped tightly around their weapons.

Then the figure looked away, and that grip of terror loosened. Diann took a deep breath and pointed away from the figure. 'This way,' she whispered, her voice carrying in the still air.

The children all nodded and followed after her. The mournful wailing still seemed to be coming from all around them, and they kept their eyes out in case another ghostly figure emerged from the mist ahead of them. They didn't, though Tariq mumbled about thinking he saw another one further off to the other side; he really did seem to have very sharp eyes.

After what seemed like an eternity, the singing, which never seemed to get any further away, faltered and died. They all breathed a sigh of relief in unison, and the tension around them lifted.

Tim stumbled and sat down on a rock. 'I need a break,' he said. 'My feet hurt.'

Diann looked around and nodded, and they all sat down, finding dry spots on rocks or raised patches of grass. Tim immediately started rubbing the balls of his feet, and CeeCee started trying to rub the mud off of hers. After a few minutes she looked around, then got up and went over to a pool of water, and sat down next to it, trying to wash the mud away. Eventually, she gave up and just sat with her feet submerged in the water, a small smile on her face.

Tariq looked around at the group. 'Do we have any food?' he asked.

They all looked at Nishkyn, who patted his pockets and came away with a few scraps of dried meat. 'That's the last of it,' he said, handing it round.

Diann refused it, and so did Tim, who was frowning and still rubbing his feet. CeeCee and Tariq took some, and Heidi, seeing that there was hardly any left, shook her head. 'You keep it,' she said to Nishkyn. 'I'm not hungry.'

Nishkyn shrugged and stuffed the remainder into his mouth. Twist popped out of her hair with a scowl, and hopped across to CeeCee's shoulder, where he started begging for scraps. CeeCee obligingly fed him small bits of the dried meat.

'Guys,' Tim said. 'My feet really hurt. And they feel weird.'

Heidi and Diann got up and went to sit with him so they could see. The balls of his feet looked red and sore, the skin across them looking stretched and thin. 'Oh Tim,' Heidi said reproachfully. 'Why didn't you say anything before?'

Tim shrugged. 'There was the banshee,' he replied. 'I didn't want to slow us down.'

'Maybe it's from jumping on the rocks,' Diann suggested.

Tim shook his head. 'It hurt before then, just not as bad. I just thought it was all the walking.'

Heidi reached out with one finger and gently touched the sore skin. She had expected it to feel swollen, like a blister, but it felt strangely hard underneath. She took her finger away, and Tim immediately started rubbing it again. She was about to suggest that he not do that, when beneath his fingers the skin abruptly split open. She and Tim yelled in surprise and disgust as a small amount of clear fluid leaked out, revealing something hard and greyish-black beneath.

At their yell, the others crowded round. 'Oh, gross!' Tariq cried.

Tim looked almost hysterical. 'What is it, what is it?' he

wailed, holding his hands up to his chest as if he was afraid to touch it. 'Get it out!'

Diann leaned close and inspected it carefully. 'We can't get it out,' she replied, sounding oddly calm compared to the rest of them. 'It's your hoof.'

Tim gaped at her. 'What?!'

'Your hoof,' Diann replied. 'You're still changing, remember. You're growing your hooves.'

'I don't want hooves!' Tim cried, tears starting to leak from his eyes. 'I want feet!'

Diann shrugged. 'Too bad,' she said. 'You're getting hooves.'

Heidi gave her a disapproving glare and pulled Tim into a hug, letting him sob into her shoulder. 'Don't worry, Tim,' she said gently. 'Just think, once they're grown, you'll be running all over the place faster than any of us, I bet.'

Tim looked up at her. 'You think?'

Tariq piped up. 'And you'll never have to go shoe shopping again!'

Tim giggled at that, and relaxed a little. Heidi let him go, and before long he and Tariq were poking at his feet experimentally, Tim every now and then letting out a yelp of pain.

CeeCee was sitting on a rock, studying her own feet. 'The Magister said I'm changing into a mermaid,' she said. 'When do you think my legs will … you know…'

Diann shrugged again. 'I've no idea. Mermaids aren't actually all that common, as I understand it – they need large bodies of water, and there aren't that many here.'

CeeCee thought about this and her face paled. 'Am I going to have to go into the lake under the hill?' she exclaimed. 'With those horrible things that took Ricky and Baby?'

Nobody answered her. Heidi repressed a shudder at the thought that some day, CeeCee would *be* one of those things. She examined her friend quietly and noticed how silvery her skin was, and how much of her hair was now white, and less curly.

Then, she looked at her own hands and wondered if it was her imagination that her fingers seemed so much longer and thinner than they had been.

'Diann,' she said. 'How come you're not like the other Tuatha?'

Diann smiled. 'You mean how come I'm not a total snob?' The children laughed at that, and her smile widened for a second before it faded. 'Because Old Mother Korrigan encourages us to remember our old lives. We forget eventually, of course - the magick makes us - but while we still remember, we remember what we lost, and that the Tuatha took it from us.' She paused, thinking. 'I suppose eventually when I do forget, I might end up like them, but for now I still hate them. And Mother says that makes me a perfect spy.'

'Is she really going to fight the Tuatha?' Tariq asked.

Diann nodded. 'If she can get enough of us on her side. At the moment it's more like ... what do you call it...' She paused and looked round at the others, but they only looked at her blankly. She sighed. 'She sends the children out once they've changed to tell others about what she's doing, to try to get them to agree to help. You know, like...'

'Recruiting,' CeeCee said. 'She's sending you out to recruit more people - faeries, I mean - to your cause. So they're on your side.'

'Right,' Diann agreed. 'Eventually, she says we might get all the other races on our side, and if we do we'll be able to stand up to the Tuatha. Then, we'll all get our magick back and the Tuatha won't be able to steal any more children away.'

'But we still couldn't go home,' Heidi said.

Diann looked at her sadly and shook her head. 'Once we're changed, how could we?' she replied. 'What do you think would happen? We'd be put in a zoo.'

'Or a science lab,' Tim said glumly. Then he brightened. 'So when I'm changed, I'll get to go to the fauns and tell them to join the fight so they can come out of the hills and have magick again?'

Diann nodded. 'Exactly.'

'Hey, wait a minute,' Heidi interrupted. 'Don't you still want to go home?'

The other children looked at her doubtfully. Tariq spoke up. 'I do,' he said. 'But... Heidi, me and you might be okay, but CeeCee's silver, and Tim's got horns.'

'And hooves,' Tim added, waving his split foot.

'But we might change back,' Heidi argued.

'Maybe,' Tariq agreed, but he didn't look convinced.

Nishkyn looked around at them all, his expression strangely angry. 'The Winter Witch will probably know,' he put in, shooting a glare at Diann.

Diann looked confused, but nodded. 'That's right,' she said. 'She's very old. If anyone knows, it will be her.'

'Sounds like what they said about the Tuatha,' Tim grumbled, poking at his feet.

Heidi had had enough. 'Stop poking that or it'll get infected,' she snapped at Tim. 'That's enough resting, let's get going. There's a hunter after us, remember. Diann, where are we going?'

'I told you,' Diann replied. 'I don't know. We have to find her.'

'Right,' Heidi said irritably. '"Look for cold." That's so helpful, Diann, *thank you*.' She got up and walked off, roughly in the direction they had been going, not waiting for the others to follow her.

The conversation had frightened her. Didn't they want to go home any more? Did they really want to stay here, in this dangerous, terrifying world?

She struggled to remember her old home and the boarding school. The details were indistinct in her mind, hard to catch, like tiny fish slipping through her fingers. She had to admit, it was hard to miss what you couldn't remember. But she still remembered enough. She remembered lessons, and grown-ups making her feel safe. She remembered cartoons, and pizza, and her bedroom at home with all her cuddly toys. She remembered being scolded by her grandmother. She remembered the day the police had told her her parents wouldn't be coming home. She remembered the news on tv, so full of violence and sadness. She remembered crying herself to sleep at night, feeling like no one really wanted her. She remembered...

She stopped herself, dismayed at how her thoughts had turned sour. What was that? Was it more of the magic of this place? As well as making her forget, was it poisoning what memories she had left? She let out a frustrated cry and sank down on a nearby rock, pressing her clenched fists into her eyes to keep back tears. This was hopeless – what was the point?

Somewhere nearby she heard a soft, stealthy sound, the gentle ripple of something moving through water. She looked around hurriedly, but could see nothing. Nearby was a large waterlogged section of grass, with more boulders behind it, disappearing into the mist. She could distantly hear the others shouting for her, but couldn't see them in the fog. She got to her feet, vaguely startled that she had managed to get so far away from them without noticing. That had been careless of her. In this mist, she could easily get –

'Lossssssssst,' a low, sibilant rumble said from behind her. She whirled round, but could still see nothing. Only the water, the rocks, the grey grass... Except - had that dark shape in the water been there before?

She fixed her gaze on it, and as she watched, the dark shape broke the surface of the water and rose up, revealing a head covered in matted dark grey fur, dripping with foul muddy water. A beak-like snout protruded from the fur, and above it two bulbous, milky eyes stared blindly in her direction. The beak opened and that voice came again. *'Lossssssssssst,'* it repeated in its low rumble.

Heidi stared at it in disbelief and alarm, not sure if she should run, and as she looked into those dead, milky eyes she realised she did feel lost – terribly lost, and alone, and hopeless, and so tired. She found herself sinking back down onto the rock again, suddenly weary to the point where she didn't think her legs would hold her up.

The thing inched closer in the water, and she wondered how it fit in the shallow puddle when its head was as big as hers. It lifted a long, furry arm out of the water, a hand-like paw extending to her as if inviting her to take its hand. She saw thick pads on its palm like a dog.

'Sleeeeeeeeeeeeeep,' it rumbled.

Heidi felt her eyelids droop, and without really noticing she slipped onto her side and slid off of the rock into the muddy, sodden grass. The water, hardly even an inch deep, soaked into her tunic and trousers, cold and dank-smelling. That thick-padded paw reached out and she felt long, clawed fingers wrap around her ankle. A dim note of alarm sounded in the back of her mind. She struggled to stay awake, but weariness weighed on her like a heavy blanket. She felt herself sliding slowly over the waterlogged ground, dragged by her ankle deeper into the pool of water.

'HEIDI!' someone yelled, and it startled her into wakefulness. She blinked and realised that she was being slowly dragged down *into* the mud by this thing, her lower legs already submerged, and she shrieked and kicked out instinctively. It flinched back, not letting go of her ankle. Its huge eyes narrowed and it let out a gut-trembling growl. The water splashed out onto the grass as it rose up on four legs, revealing a body like a long-furred dog. With one strong tug it yanked her closer, towering above her in a mass of dripping, stinking fur.

Before the muddy water splashed into her face and eyes,

Heidi saw the figures of her friends bounding toward her over the rocks and puddles, calling her name. Nishkyn pointed and yelled 'Bunyip!', his eyes wide and frightened. Diann had her knife in her hand as she raced forward. Then Heidi was splashing and flailing in the grey, muddy murk as strong, furred hands wrestled with her thrashing limbs, hot weight bearing down on her, trying to sink her into the mud. A wave of cold washed over her, icy coldness that made her breathless, and she wondered for a moment if she was dying.

'*Sleeeeeeeeeeeeeep,*' that voice rumbled again, and despite herself she could feel her consciousness trying to slip away. She kicked harder, trying to stay awake.

Then another voice rang out, seemingly in her mind as well as in her ears: '*That's enough of this ruckus!*'

The thing's grip around her loosened, and her head popped up out of the water. She drew in a gasping breath, flailing wildly, trying to drag herself out onto solid land. The creature's claws dug cruelly into her shoulders, holding her down. She glanced up to see that her companions had stopped at the water's edge, and were standing, staring past the thing that held her, their eyes wide, their breath clouding in the frosty air.

Oh God, what now? She thought miserably, and turned her head to look.

An old woman, clad in loose grey robes, stood on a rock on the other side of the pool of water, a gnarled staff clutched in one hand. She was hunched over, but that did nothing to detract from how tall she was, or from the angry gleam in her icy blue eyes. Long grey-white hair fell in tangles around her shoulders and her grey-white face was a mass of deep wrinkles. She was surrounded in a faint white glow as her clothes, hair and skin all glimmered with a delicate layer of frost, and the air around her whirled in eddies of wind so icy they swirled visibly, like smoke. Her mouth twisted in disapproval as she shouted again in a voice Heidi seemed to think as well as hear:

'I said that's enough!'

The creature's grip on Heidi loosened a little more, and she struggled free. The creature stared balefully at the woman. She stepped forward, knocking the base of her staff on the rock. 'Don't you turn that stare on me, bunyip, or I'll freeze ye into the mud where ye stand and let ye starve! Now git!'

She bashed the rock again, and Heidi saw bolts of ice like lightning shooting out from the base of the staff, crackling across the stone. The bunyip glowered and slowly sank down into the muddy water, its baleful eyes staying on the woman until it disappeared.

The woman paused, then turned her gaze to Heidi. She felt her legs pop free of the sucking mud, which suddenly felt much more solid underneath her. She shivered under the old woman's icy glare. It was freezing!

'Are ... are you the Winter Witch?' Heidi asked hesitantly.

'What the bloody iron do you think?' the old woman replied. 'And what the bloody iron are ye doing, making such a racket? You think I live out here for the scenery? Piss off, the lot of ye, or the next bunyip that catches you can keep ye!'

The rest of the group seemed stunned to silence by this outburst. The other children looked cowed as if they'd been scolded by a teacher, and Diann and Nishkyn just stood, their mouths agape. Heidi struggled to her feet, trying to ignore how shaky her legs felt, and stood facing the woman.

'I'm very sorry for the noise,' she said, 'But we came here to find you. We need your help.'

The old woman's expression softened ... slightly. 'Do ye now?' she muttered, her free hand rising to stroke her chin. 'And what exactly do a bunch of changeling brats want from me?'

Heidi looked back at the others, who still seemed too awed to speak. Once again it seemed it was up to her. She took a deep breath. 'We were hoping you could help us get back home,' she said.

The old woman looked at her thoughtfully. 'I see,' she replied slowly. The wintry aura around her seemed to lessen as the anger in her eyes ebbed away. The chill in the air grew less biting and the frost flurries faded. 'Alright,' she said, turning away. 'Follow me.'

Heidi's heart leaped. 'You'll help us?' she cried.

The woman looked back sharply. 'I haven't decided yet,' she replied. 'But it is within my power to do so, and I sense there's a story to be told here, and I want to hear it. So come on, I've a camp not far away that'll be a sight more comfortable than sitting in this here puddle with a bunyip lurking beneath our feet.' She gestured with her staff. 'Bring yer friends.'

Heidi looked back at the others. They seemed to shake themselves, and hurried forward to follow the old woman who, as they gathered in her wake, turned once more and said, 'Oh, and if ye don't mind, leave off with that Winter Witch nonsense. It makes me sound akin to those three lunatics in the woods.'

'Two,' Nishkyn corrected her from the back of the group.

She caught this and her eyes gleamed. 'Oho, I was right about that story,' she chuckled. 'This'll be good. Hurry up, and I'll make some tea.'

The camp was indeed not far - only a few minutes' walk - and there was a campfire burning merrily when they arrived, with rocks placed around it in a close circle and a wicker basket off to one side. The children were all shivering in the frigid air by the time they arrived at the camp. The old woman gestured for them to sit, then nudged Diann with the tip of her staff. Diann flinched and bit her lip like she'd been touched with a piece of ice. 'That there basket is full of blankets. Pass them round, would ye? You'll need them around me.'

Diann nodded and did as she was told. The blankets were made of thick grey wool, and once the frost had been shaken off them they were very warm. The children wrapped themselves up in the blankets and sat close to the fire. Meanwhile, the old woman busied herself with some of the objects that were placed near the fire. She poured water from a clay bottle into a copper kettle, which immediately frosted over at her touch, then hung it over the fire from a tripod made of thick wooden poles and a metal chain. The flames from the fire seemed to shy away from her hands as she did so, but leaped up eagerly to warm the kettle once she took her hands away.

'What may we call you, old one?' Diann asked as she wrapped herself up in a blanket. Much like with the forest witch, there seemed to be just the right amount of blankets, and just the right amount of stones to sit on. Heidi noticed this and swallowed the sour panic that threatened to rise in her throat. This woman was their last chance.

'Well, not that, for one,' the old woman replied with a small smile. 'I know I'm old, no need to remind me. You can call me Cailleach, for that is my name. One of them, anyways.'

The children tested the word on their tongues. It was a little awkward. Cailleach listened to them, her smile twisting with amusement. 'I didn't bring you here to listen to ye mangle my name,' she said. 'I want to hear this story, the one that tells why there's only two witches instead of three.'

The children all looked to Heidi, and she fought the urge to roll her eyes. 'I don't really know where to start,' she said.

'I find the beginning's usually a good place,' Cailleach said, spooning herbs into the kettle.

Heidi felt as if she were being gently mocked by a teacher at school. Strangely, it seemed to calm her, and she continued with a little more confidence. 'Alright. For me, it started when I was in bed at my boarding school...'

Heidi told the tale, from beginning to end, pausing only occasionally to confirm a detail with one of the others. Cailleach listened intently, nodding lots and interrupting only once or twice for clarification. When the kettle began to whistle, she took it off the fire and served hot, fragrant tea in little clay cups to them all. The tea was flowery and delicious, and its warmth seemed to linger pleasantly in Heidi's chest and stomach for a long time.

When she reached the part where they had left Lagamoora to venture out onto the moors, Cailleach stopped her. 'I know the rest from here,' she said. 'You upset the banshees and got tangled up with a bunyip, and disturbed my peace and quiet.'

'Sorry,' Heidi said automatically.

Cailleach shook her head. 'No need,' she replied. 'That was a fine story. And ye killed one of the witches, you say? Impressive. Shame about the two fauns, though. The Firobolga are good folk, if a little fierce sometimes.' She looked at Nishkyn. 'You don't strike me as the normal goblin type, though.'

Nishkyn squirmed uncomfortably. 'I made a bargain,' he said defensively.

'No,' Cailleach replied. 'Your bargain ended the moment these children passed into the Shining City. You could have been long gone by the time they got out. Yet you weren't.' She peered at him carefully. 'Shun you for being so small, did they?' Nishkyn looked up, startled, and she nodded. 'Thought so. Seems to have done you good though, being shot of yer own kin. Maybe the meanness isn't in yer blood after all. Very interesting.' She looked at CeeCee, then down at her hands, where Twist was leaning into her cup, scooping up handfuls of tea. 'And that one. Not just a pest. And you, Tuatha...' She looked at Diann. 'Yes. Very interesting indeed.'

'What do you mean?' Diann asked.

Cailleach smiled. 'The thing about magick,' she said, 'Is it's ruled by words and ideas. If you know how to do it, your words and ideas shape magick into forms. If you don't, but there's enough of it about, ye do it without meaning to. This world is made of magick, and even if the Tuatha have leeched away most of the ambient magick, that doesn't change what it's made of. It's why you children all change into different things. And it's probably why the different races here all act in very particular ways.'

The children looked confused. 'I don't understand,' Heidi said, speaking for all of them.

Cailleach nodded. 'Look at it like this. The Tuatha have all the power here, yes?' They all nodded, like students eagerly learning from a teacher. 'Well, the Tuatha say that goblins are selfish little savages who only care about themselves. So they are. The Tuatha say the Firobolga are primal savages, and the Formori are worse – feral. So they are. The Tuatha say the witches in the forest are dangerous and evil. So they are. The Tuatha say that the Tuatha are the superior race, the ones best at controlling the magick. So they are. The Tuatha say the children who come here change. So they do. Do ye see?'

Slowly, the children all nodded. Cailleach went on, 'But you children arrive here, escape them, and go roaming through the lands freely, without them telling you how it all should be. And suddenly, the folk you meet aren't all behaving like the Tuatha say they should any more. It's interesting. Very interesting.'

'What does it mean?' Diann asked.

Cailleach shook her head. 'I don't know,' she replied. 'Not yet. But I'll be thinking on it, that's for sure.'

'What do the Tuatha say about you?' Tariq asked.

Cailleach shot him a stern look. 'As little as possible, if they know what's good for 'em,' she replied.

Diann grinned. 'That's about right,' she replied. 'They say you're powerful, and you're trouble.'

Cailleach cackled. 'For them, I probably am – they can't box me in with their shiny words.'

Heidi looked down at her tea, afraid to look at the old woman as she asked. 'So ... will you help us get home?'

Cailleach looked at her very carefully for a moment. Then her gaze fell to the other children. 'I will,' she said at last. 'If ye really want to go. I warn you though, time passes differently here than it does there. You may not like what you go back to.'

'I don't care,' Heidi said immediately. 'I just want to go home.'

Cailleach looked at her carefully again. 'Well, you have come all this way,' she conceded. 'Alright. Finish yer tea. Then we'll get going.'

Heidi noticed Diann look up unhappily and thought she saw a look pass between her and the old woman, but she couldn't be sure what kind of look it was. At that moment she didn't really care. They were going home! She drank the rest of her tea hurriedly and stood up. The other children did the same, Tim limping as he got to his feet.

Cailleach sighed and put her cup down beside the fire. 'In such a hurry,' she said sadly, shaking her head. 'So be it. Come to me, children.' She stood up and moved a few feet away from the fire, picking up her staff in one hand.

The children gathered around her. Heidi looked around at them all, smiling excitedly. Tariq looked back with the same excited smile; CeeCee looked nervous and unsure; Tim just looked pained. Cailleach opened her arms to them. 'Come in good and close,' she said. 'You'll need to be touching me to pass through with me.'

Heidi stepped in and took hold of the old woman's robes. The frost on the fabric crunched under her fingers, then quickly spread across them and up her arm, chilling her to the bone. She shivered.

'Sorry about that,' Cailleach said. 'Can't be helped. Won't hurt ye none, though.'

Heidi forced a smile. 'It's okay,' she said through chattering teeth.

Tariq stepped forward next, making a little 'Hoo!' sound as he touched Cailleach's robes. Then Tim stepped in, squeezing between Heidi and Tariq. CeeCee was last. She hesitated. 'Will we change back?' she asked. 'If we go home?'

Cailleach nodded. 'You will,' she replied. 'In time.'

CeeCee gave a small smile, and stepped into the old woman's arms. She closed her icy arms around the four children, and closed her eyes. Then the world around them rippled and blurred, and the light in the sky went out.

CHAPTER 24

A WORLD FALLEN DOWN

The light returned, but only dimly. Looking around, they saw above them a nighttime sky choked with dirty grey-green clouds. The smell of dust and smoke surrounded them, and gritty ground crunched beneath their bare feet.

Cailleach opened her arms, and the children looked around. Through the ripples, they saw a world completely unlike the one they had left. They stood at the top of a low hill, among abandoned and ruined buildings, looking down upon what had once been a city. It was now a huge crater, surrounded by destruction.

'What happened?' Heidi cried. Her voice sounded strange to her; it vibrated, as if she were standing on a shaking surface.

Tim's voice sounded the same. 'A bomb,' he said glumly. 'Like in the wars. They taught us about them in school.' Hushed, he added, 'It looks like a video game...'

It didn't look real. There was no sign of life anywhere – no birds, no animals, no people. The only thing that moved was the dust as a strong wind blew it about.

'Where are we?' Heidi asked.

Cailleach shrugged. 'The place you began your story,' she replied. 'It seemed fitting.'

Heidi gaped. 'This is *London*?'

Cailleach didn't reply.

Heidi looked around again. There was no sign of any landmark that identified the place as London, not one. Just rubble and dust and scorched, dry earth. Tears started to well in her eyes, and she let them fall. 'What did they do?!' she cried.

CeeCee spoke up. 'Do you think outside of London...?'

'It depends on the type of bomb,' Tim replied. 'If it was a nuclear bomb, then there would be fallout. It would spread out and poison everything.'

'I can tell you that the air *is* poisoned,' Cailleach said. 'I can feel it. In my connection to the earth. They've poisoned the air, the ground, the water... Everything. For miles and miles.' She looked down at their questioning faces and smiled. 'I'm much more than I appear to be, young ones.'

'Why is the air all wavy?' Tariq asked. 'And why do we sound funny?'

'We're not yet in the same place as this world,' Cailleach replied. 'Given the poison in everything, I thought it best to keep us a little separate. Until you've made your decision, at least.'

Heidi turned and glared at her. 'You knew about this?' she cried angrily. 'And you didn't warn us?'

'Would you have believed me?' Cailleach replied smoothly. 'Yes, I knew. I've been here and back a few times since all this mess happened.' She gestured with her free hand. 'You had to see, child. I saw it in your eyes after you told me yer tale. For what it's worth, I'm sorry for you. No one should have to see all they knew destroyed.'

Something in her tone struck Heidi's heart. She sounded like she knew how it felt. Her sudden anger faded, and she looked back out over the ruined city. 'Are there any people left alive?' she asked.

Cailleach nodded. 'Go look for them, if you like,' she said. 'But don't touch anyone, and on no account eat or drink anything. If you do it'll pull you all the way into this world and you'll be stuck, whether you want to stay or not.'

Heidi looked back at her. 'You're giving us the choice?'

'What kind of monster do ye think I am, to abandon children to a world like this?' Cailleach laughed. 'Of course I am. You have tonight. Look around. Think on it. Meet me back here at dawn. Only mind what I said, now. If you get yourself pulled back all the way, I won't be able to find you again. You'll be stuck here, and all the time you've missed will catch up with you, and all the magick you picked up will be leeched away. I think it's only been some years - but for ones so young, that's a big change to go through all at once.'

'Years?' Heidi exclaimed. 'It feels like we've only been gone for a few weeks!'

'Looks like we've been gone a lifetime,' Tariq said glumly, gazing out across the ruined city.

Cailleach nodded. 'I told you, time's different over there.'

'Is that how we'll change back?' CeeCee asked. 'All at once when we step back into the world, like Thomas the Rhymer in the fairytale?'

'It varies,' Cailleach said vaguely. 'But that's it, more or less.' She sighed and stepped back. 'Now, I must be off. I have things to do. I'll meet you here at dawn.'

CeeCee frowned. 'What do you have to do?'

Cailleach smiled at them, and suddenly they could plainly see the agelessness of this creature that appeared on the surface to be a wisened old woman. 'I have to bring the winter,' she replied.

She banged her staff on the floor and suddenly she was gone, leaving only a quickly melting flower of frost on the ground where she had once stood.

The children milled around aimlessly for a moment, uncertain what to do next. From CeeCee's hair, Twist emerged, looked around curiously, and then stuck his tongue out, blew a very loud raspberry for one so small, and disappeared again. CeeCee let out a giggle that sounded on the verge of hysteria.

Heidi picked out what seemed to be the remains of a street - a thin line of clear, cracked tarmac amongst the rubble - and started walking away from the massive crater. The other children fell in behind her, walking single file. The gritty surface beneath their feet felt almost faint, as if they were walking on a thin cushion of air, and that gentle ripple in the air went on all around them, a constant distortion. Heidi thought that it would give her a headache if she had to look at it for too long. All around them, the ruins were silent, except for a cool wind that turned sharp and biting in between the shelter of crumbled buildings.

A short distance down the road, they came across a huddled figure curled up to one side of the road. Remembering Cailleach's warning, Heidi crept forward to investigate it, careful not to touch anything. She didn't have to touch the figure to see that it was dead; it was perfectly still, with greyish skin and a few sickly looking flies crawling around on its face. It had once been a man, but the raw, oozing burns and strange swellings made it look almost inhuman. And these weren't even what had killed him; Heidi could plainly see the raw, red wound - no longer bleeding - across his neck. Someone had cut his throat.

She shuddered and moved away. 'Don't look,' she told the others, but of course they all did. Tim made some strangled sounds that might have been gagging, but the distortion around them made it sound like a strange kind of gargling. The others came away looking sick and tired. Without a word, they moved on.

The next person they saw was some time later. A haggard looking woman in rags was searching around in what was left of a supermarket, stuffing the few intact cans that she could find into a worn backpack. Heidi thought at first that she must be old, because of the way she stooped, but as they got closer she realised that this woman was relatively young – maybe in her twenties? Her hair was a dirty blonde colour and her skin, though filthy and riddled with lumps and sores, was not wrinkled. The children exchanged wary looks, and then nodded at each other. Cautiously, they approached the woman.

'Excuse me?' Heidi called, when they were close enough.

The woman jumped, dropping a can she had been inspecting, and looked around wildly. Her bloodshot blue eyes fixed on Heidi, and on the children behind her, and she gave a horrified shriek. Before the children could say another word, she turned and fled. They watched her go, bewildered.

'What did we do?' Tariq muttered.

'We probably look pretty weird,' CeeCee said glumly, looking at her silvery hands.

'She can talk,' Tariq scoffed. 'You see the lumps on her face?'

Heidi glanced around, and in the blackened remains of a freezer unit she caught sight of their reflection. She didn't see the long-eared red-head, the fine-boned boy with dark skin, the small curly-haired boy with horns, or the silver skinned girl. She saw four indistinct shadowy figures with bright eyes. Figures that looked very much like those dark creatures who had stolen into her boarding school that night in June, and snatched her and her classmates away.

'Look,' she said, pointing. 'That's why she ran.'

The other children looked, and murmured in surprise. 'We look like the ones who took us,' Tim said wonderingly.

'It must be because we're not in the world properly,' CeeCee added. 'You know, like Cailleach said.'

'No one's going to talk to us if we look like that,' Tariq sighed.

Heidi uttered a bitter laugh. 'There isn't anyone to talk to!' she cried. 'Look at it! It's all ruined!' She swept her arms around her, gesturing at their surroundings. 'Everything we've been through, and this is what we get to come back to!'

'If everywhere's like this,' Tariq added, 'our families are probably dead.' He winced. 'Sorry, Heidi.'

Heidi looked around again. He was right. Her grandmother, her teachers - everyone she'd known - had all been in London. They were almost certainly all dead. The realisation hit her like a punch to her gut, and she dropped down onto the dusty ground and burst into tears. The others gathered around her. 'I'm sorry,' Tariq repeated. 'I didn't mean it! You never know... Maybe they're alright?'

Heidi shook her head. 'They're gone,' she sobbed. 'They're all gone.'

'Maybe not everywhere's like this,' Tim said slowly. 'They probably didn't bomb Cornwall. That's where I'm from.'

'Or Ireland, maybe,' CeeCee added hopefully.

Tariq let out a long sigh. 'Well, I'm from Essex,' he said. 'And that's just outside London, so it's probably all radiated and they're probably all mutants by now.' He paused, then added almost guiltily, 'I don't really remember them all that well anyway.'

The others murmured in agreement. Heidi looked up and sniffed. 'It's just... I didn't realise it until you said it,' she said. 'I don't really remember anyone except my grandma. I remember that my parents died a long time before, but I don't really remember what they were like.' Her lips trembled at this, and she started to cry again, this time more softly.

Tariq hugged her tightly. 'Hey,' he said gently. 'Maybe ... maybe we should think about what Diann and Cailleach said. You know? We've got a choice. We don't have to stay here.'

CeeCee crouched down and put her arms around both of them. 'I don't think I'd do too well here anyway,' she said. 'I'm turning into a fish.'

They all laughed. Tim wandered over shyly and took Heidi's hand. She squeezed it affectionately. 'We could stay together,' he suggested. 'Go back and stay with Nishkyn and Diann and Twist?'

'We'll be rebel Tuatha, like Diann,' Tariq added with relish in his voice. 'We'll be like the badasses in *Star Wars*, fighting the evil Empire! I bet we'll even get glowing swords!'

Heidi giggled. 'That's stupid,' she said. 'We'll be more like spies, like...' She paused, trying to remember some movie she had seen or book she had read, but the memories eluded her. 'Like, um... I can't think of anything.'

Tariq shrugged. 'Whatever,' he said. 'We can help take down the bad guys, and then we'll be heroes!'

'Better than growing up to get a job and get married and have babies,' CeeCee said solemnly.

'Better than being bullied,' Tim added.

'Better than all this,' Tariq finished, nodding at the devastation around them.

Heidi let out a long, heavy sigh and looked around. The sky was dark and clouded with diseased-looking smog. The ground was gritty and broken, and the air tasted dry and dusty and full of smoke and ... something else, unpleasant and ... *wrong* that she couldn't define. She tried to remember her parents clearly, and failed. She tried to remember her grandmother, and only found a lingering resentment. She tried to remember what she had hoped for, what she had dreamed of, and came up with nothing. She had an uneasy feeling that these things weren't there because they had been stolen, rather than because she had never had them... But at this moment it was all the same.

'Alright,' she said at last. 'Let's go back and find Cailleach.'

When they got back to the point where they had been brought over, they found the old woman sitting primly on the corner of a section of broken wall, waiting for them. Her staff was laid horizontally across her knees. She saw them approaching and stood up. 'Well?' she said. 'What's it to be?'

The children all looked at each other. Heidi opened her

mouth to reply, but Tariq was the one who spoke. 'We'll come back with you,' he said.

Cailleach smiled. 'I don't blame you,' she replied. 'And I think your friends back there will be pleased to see you again.' She opened her arms. 'Come along, then. No sense dallying in this awful place.'

The children stepped forward into her icy embrace once more, the shock of the cold stealing their breath for a moment. Cailleach lifted her staff and struck the ground, and the light faded from the world once more.

Diann and Nishkyn were still sitting around the fire when they returned, looking at each other gloomily. As Cailleach unfolded her arms and released the children, they both jumped up, Nishkyn grinning from ear to ear and Diann wearing a relieved smile. The children rushed forward and they embraced each other. Twist hopped out of CeeCee's hair and scrambled over to the fire, avoiding the crush.

'You came back,' Nishkyn exclaimed happily. 'I thought I was never gonna see you again!'

'What happened?' Diann asked.

Heidi shook her head sadly. 'It's awful,' she replied. 'Everything's ruined there ... everything's gone.'

Diann's smile faded. 'What do you mean?'

'Why don't I put the kettle back on, and we'll tell you about it over some more tea?' Cailleach suggested.

The group wandered back over to the fire and took their seats. As Cailleach lifted the kettle over the fire, a long, shrill shriek echoed through the mists around them. The children jumped and looked around anxiously, and they saw that the colour had drained from Diann's face. Nishkyn was shrinking down on his seat.

'What was that?' Tariq asked.

Diann's reply was hushed. 'The hunter,' she whispered. 'He's found us.'

Almost as if she had summoned him with her words, a tall, thin, black shape appeared in the mist, striding toward them with long, exaggerated steps. As it grew closer, they saw the gaunt, grey face and piercing eyes of the figure they had seen in the Shining City ... only this time it was looking directly at them.

Diann drew her knife and stood to face it. The others did the same, though Heidi could see Diann trembling violently, and she was pretty sure she was doing the same. Those burning eyes filled her with icy dread, and all she wanted to do was curl into a ball and wait for it to be over.

The iciness she was feeling spread throughout her body, until her fingers felt numb and useless. Then she realised that the ground around her was growing icy too, and that the mist was coalescing into frosty spirals in the air. She glanced around at Cailleach and saw the old woman standing upright, her staff held defiantly in one hand as she strode around the group to stand between the children and the hunter. As she moved, her hair and robes swirled out as a frigid gale tore across the moor, and the little campfire snuffed out.

The hunter stopped and regarded the smaller figure, his head cocked in what seemed to be curiosity, his wicked grin never faltering.

'*Out of my way, hag,*' he hissed through jagged teeth, his lips not moving. '*I am here to collect my prey.*'

'Like piss, you are,' Cailleach spat. 'These ones are under my protection. You can go and tell that to your Shining Queen.'

'*Mmmmmmagisssterrrrr,*' the Hunter rasped.

'I don't care two farts for what she calls herself now,' the Cailleach retorted. 'You're not taking anyone with you this time.'

The hunter snarled through his rictus grin and stepped forward. The Cailleach didn't flinch. The icy gale grew stronger, ripping past her, pushing and buffeting against the hunter's tall, spindly form and pushing him backwards. Heidi could see his black garments turning grey and stiff with frost. He staggered, and his grin finally began to wane. He took a few small steps closer, then gave a low, shrill whine that grated in their ears and made their teeth ache. Then, with one last look at the children, he retreated. As he did so, the wind dropped.

'Tell your pretty mistress that these ones do not belong to her,' Cailleach said firmly.

The hunter gave a grating roar. '*I ALWAYS CATCH MY PREY!*'

'Well, you're not catching them now!' Cailleach roared back. 'Now leave, and take my message with you, for it's all you're taking from this place!'

The creature's roar dwindled until it became a sullen rumble. He peered around the old woman at the children again, who were huddled together, their weapons forgotten. His mouth was a wide, leering gash in his face. '*I always catch my prey,*' he repeated, then slowly turned and limped away, his garments cracking and creaking from the frost on them. With a few long strides, the mist swallowed him up, and he was gone.

Cailleach relaxed, and the freezing air around them began to warm up a little. Turning back, she plodded back to the fire and picked up the kettle again. 'Sorry about that,' she said. 'Once we've had our tea, we'd best get you safely back to the Korrigan. That one won't give up, you know. Not 'til he's got you.' She paused, and looked at them. 'That is what you're doing now, isn't it? Going back to the Korrigan?'

The children exchanged glances, and nodded. 'That's what we agreed,' Heidi replied, smiling at Diann.

Cailleach gave a satisfied nod. 'Good. You're better off away from those bloody Tuatha. No offence, dear,' she added to Diann.

Diann paused, then smiled. 'I'm not a Tuatha,' she replied. 'I'm a changeling.' She looked at the children. 'Like you.'

'Changeling,' Heidi said, trying the word out on her tongue. She liked it – the truth of it seemed to fit, somehow. 'Is that what we are?'

'Well, you're not Children of Mil anymore,' Nishkyn put in. 'Not really.'

'And you're not solely children of the Tithe,' Cailleach added. 'Changeling's a good name for what you are, though... At least until your changing's done.'

Heidi sighed wearily. 'I feel like we've already changed so much,' she said.

'Well, that's the funny thing about changing,' Cailleach replied. 'It tends to just keep on going. Even when you think you can't possibly change any more. You've plenty more ahead of you, I'm afraid, my dears – what with the hunter after you, the Tuatha wanting you, and the Korrigan taking you in. But you know what?' She smiled warmly. 'I've got a good feeling about you lot. And I'd wager there's plenty more changes to come - and not just for you.'

The kettle began to whistle thinly, and the old woman plucked it off of the fire. 'But that's enough of this nonsense for now. Gather around the fire, dears, and pass me your cups. Let's have some tea.'

ACKNOWLEDGMENTS

I have been writing stories since I was a child, and there are many many stories under my belt that have been left unfinished or just left, not quite ready to put out there to others. *Children of the Tithe* is not the first book I felt brave enough to put out into the world, but it is the first one where someone else saw the potential in it.

If I am lucky, it will be the first of many, because I have no plans to stop writing any time soon! Getting my stories published has been a dream of mine since I was first asked what I wanted to be when I grew up, and I have plenty more dreaming left in me yet.

There are so many people I should thank, and I hope I don't forget any of them. Working backwards, let me first thank the lovely people at SmashBear Publishing, first for giving my creepy faery story a chance, and then for giving me such a great team of editors to help tweak and twist the story until it was ready to hit the pages.

Thank you to Kristian Brown and Jack Greenway who had the misfortune of living with me during the process and were nothing but supportive, helpful and excited for me.

Thank you to Ellie Nye, aka The Paint Dipped Pixie, for mentioning that they knew a publisher while they were tattooing me, and giving me the contact details.

Thank you to Kestrel and Bat and the Goblin Writers' Circle for keeping me motivated!

Thank you to Shelby Scott of the *Scare You To Sleep* podcast for giving me the confidence I needed to go full length!

Thank you to all the excellent authors who inspire me every day, most notably the fantastic Stephen King and the sublime Anne Rice (RIP).

Thank you to all the people I've ever larped with or played D&D with, for instilling in me a deep love of fantasy.

Thank you (going back a bit here) to my Creative Writing teacher at school, who told me that horror fiction wasn't worth writing and I should write straight fiction instead – which only made me more determined to write what I love!

Thank you to my Nana Joy, for always being so proud of me.

And last but absolutely not least, thank you to my mother, Mary, the "M" in my pen name, who is always my first test reader and always gives me feedback and encouragement and is already my biggest fan.

Now, on to the next one....

About the Author

Tracey M Carvill lives in Rochester, UK (where Charles Dickens was born). She lives with her black cat Siouxsie and her biggest fan, Jack. She can often be found wandering Rochester High Street looking for ghosts or charity shop bargains, and never misses the Sweeps Festival. Occasionally she goes into the forest and pretends to be a fairytale creature.

Thank you for supporting
SmashBear Publishing and our
authors.

For more information about our
authors, upcoming releases and
what we publish, you can check out
our website

www.smashbearpublishing.com

Or find us on:

Printed in Great Britain
by Amazon